THE LIES
THEY TOLD

Books by Ellen Marie Wiseman

THE PLUM TREE

WHAT SHE LEFT BEHIND

COAL RIVER

THE LIFE SHE WAS GIVEN

THE ORPHAN COLLECTOR

THE LOST GIRLS OF WILLOWBROOK

THE LIES THEY TOLD

Published by Kensington Publishing Corp.

THE LIES THEY TOLD

ELLEN MARIE WISEMAN

kensingtonbooks.com

This book is a work of fiction. Names, characters, businesses, organizations, places, events, and incidents either are the product of the author's imagination or are used fictitiously. Any resemblance to actual persons, living or dead, events, or locales is entirely coincidental.

To the extent that the image or images on the cover of this book depict a person or persons, such person or persons are merely models, and are not intended to portray any character or characters featured in the book.

KENSINGTON BOOKS are published by

Kensington Publishing Corp.
900 Third Ave.
New York, NY 10022

Copyright © 2025 by Ellen Marie Wiseman

All rights reserved. No part of this book may be reproduced in any form or by any means without the prior written consent of the Publisher, excepting brief quotes used in reviews.

Without limiting the author's and publisher's exclusive rights, any unauthorized use of this publication to train generative artificial intelligence (AI) technologies is expressly prohibited.

All Kensington titles, imprints, and distributed lines are available at special quantity discounts for bulk purchases for sales promotion, premiums, fundraising, educational, or institutional use. Special book excerpts or customized printings can also be created to fit specific needs. For details, write or phone the office of the Kensington Special Sales Manager: Attn. Special Sales Department. Kensington Publishing Corp., 900 Third Ave., New York, NY 10022. Phone: 1-800-221-2647.

KENSINGTON and the K with book logo Reg. US Pat. & TM Off.

ISBN: 978-1-4967-4150-9
First Kensington Trade Edition: August 2025

ISBN: 978-1-4967-4151-6 (ebook)

10 9 8 7 6 5 4 3 2 1

Printed in the United States of America

The authorized representative in the EU for product safety and compliance is eucomply OU, Parnu mnt 139b-14, Apt 123
Tallinn, Berlin 11317, hello@eucompliancepartner.com

For my littlest darlings, Owen Benjamin and Elena Catherine—what miraculous wonders and precious treasures you are

ACKNOWLEDGMENTS

When I wrote my first novel, THE PLUM TREE, I never dreamed I'd write a second one, let alone six more (soon to be seven). I also had no idea it would be the beginning of the most difficult, wildest, extraordinary, unbelievable journey of my life. If you had told me back then, or even five years ago, that I would become a New York Times Bestselling author, I would have said you were out of your mind. To say I can't wrap my head around that is the understatement of the century. With all that being said, there *is* one thing I know for sure—I owe my success to my readers and everyone who has buoyed and believed in me along the way. And so, to that end, I'm happy to once again thank all the marvelous people who make my writing career possible.

Thank you to Kate Benson for sending me the historical articles and booklets about eugenics in America. It's one thing to read about the horrors of that awful crusade; it's quite another to hold the unsettling evidence in your hands. I'm truly appreciative of your generosity. Thank you to Buddy Woodward for the invaluable articles about the removal of the Blue Ridge Mountain people from their homes to form Shenandoah National Park. Your insights provided interesting layers to this story. And once again, I'm grateful to Elayne Morgan for helping me make this manuscript shine.

Thank you to the bloggers, podcast hosts, reviewers, booksellers, librarians, and book clubs who've read and spread the word about my books, along with a ton of appreciation to everyone who invited me to talk about my work, either virtually or in person. Of course, I can never express enough gratitude to the booksellers and librarians who took the time to read and endorse my novels. I'm looking at you, Pamela Klinger-Horn, Kerry Clemm, Linda Bond, Annie Philbrick, Marianne Colton, Rosemary Smith, Sarah L. Johnson, Christie Johnston, Paul Lane, Mia D'Alessandro, and Cyndi Larsen. Your generosity and kind words mean more than you know.

Thank you again to Bill Reilly, Mindy Reilly, Emil Christmann, and Megan Irland, owners of the River's End Bookstore in Oswego, NY, for taking preorders and everything else you've done for me over the past twelve years. Extra thanks and big hugs go out to Rebecca Kinnie, owner of The Little Book Store in Clayton, NY, for selling books at my events, taking preorders, spreading the word about my work, and everything else you do for me. You all rock!

Thank you to Suzanne Leopold of Suzy Approved Book Tours for the phenomenal job you do getting ARCs out to bloggers and keeping me updated on posts, reviews, and bestseller lists. I'm also sending another special shout-out and thanks to my online friends and readers who happily talk about my stories and make social media a more pleasant place to be—Susan Peterson, Nita Joy Haddad, Martin Moore, Jenny Collins Belk, Kayleigh Wilkes, Barbara Khan, Andrea Preskind Katz, Jill Drew, Lauren Blank Margolin, Melissa Amster, Linda Levack Zagon, Tonni Callan, Denise Birt, Jackie Shepard, Renee Weise Weingarten, and Vivian Peyton. If I've forgotten to mention you by name here, please forgive me and know that I sincerely appreciate every one of you.

To all of my loyal readers, I can never thank you enough for your continued support and always giving my books a chance. You have no idea how much your reassurance means when I feel like I'll never find my way out of a crappy manuscript. Thank you for believing in me, especially when I lose faith in myself, and for all your delightful reviews. To the people in and around my community, thank you for your enduring enthusiasm and encouragement. Seeing your smiling faces at my book launches has been one of the highlights of being an author! A special thanks to Patti Hughes and everyone at the Lyme Free Library for always being ready to celebrate my new releases. It means the world to me.

Thank you to my friends and family for loving and supporting me while I continue to navigate this unpredictable, exhilarating, demanding profession. And thank you to my mentor William Kowalski for your patient guidance all those years ago. Your voice is still in my head during the writing of every novel. As always, I'm indebted to my trusted agent, Michael Carr, for giving me a chance at that lovely café in Vermont. It seems like ages ago but I'll never forget it. A thousand thanks to my fantastic editor John Scognamiglio for saying yes to my first manuscript, for your steadfast confidence in me, and for your unending patience as I slowly find my way to the end of my stories. To everyone at Kensington, there truly are no words to tell you how grateful and lucky I am to be part of your wonderful family: Steven Zacharius, Adam Zacharius, Jackie Dinas, Lynn Cully, Alex Nicholson, Lauren Jernigan, Kristin McLaughlin, Carly Sommerstein, and everyone else who works so hard behind the scenes, with added appreciation to Kristine Mills for designing my gorgeous covers. And I know I could never navigate the crazy promotional aspect of this career without Vida Engstrand by my side. All of you have changed my life in ways you can't begin to imagine.

To my mother, Sigrid, thank you for always being there for me no matter what, even while you deal with your own sorrow and hardship. You inspire me every day to stay strong and be a better person. To my husband Bill, my best friend and partner, thank you for walking every step of this crazy, indescribable journey with me, and for being the best grampa ever to our darling grandchildren. Seeing how much you love them makes me love you even more. Thank you to my incredible children, Benjamin, Jessica, Shanae, and Andrew for making me laugh, for keeping me humble, and for forgiving me when I get your names mixed up because I have too much going on inside my head. And last but certainly not least, thank you to my six cherished grandchildren, Rylee, Harper, Lincoln, Liam, Owen, and Elena for filling my heart with so much joy. How can I ever explain how much I adore you? It's impossible. Just know that you are my world and not a day goes by that I don't celebrate the magnificent gift of being your gramma.

Oh, why are you men so foolish—
You breeders who breed our men
Let the fools, the weaklings and crazy
Keep breeding and breeding again?
The criminal, deformed, and the misfit,
Dependent, diseased, and the rest—
As we breed the human family
The worst is as good as the best.
Go to the house of some farmer,
Look through his barns and sheds,
Look at his horses and cattle,
Even his hogs are thoroughbreds;
Then look at his stamp on his children,
Low-browed with the monkey jaw,
Ape-handed, and silly, and foolish—
Bred true to Mendel's law.
Go to some homes in the village,
Look at the garden beds,
The cabbage, the lettuce and turnips,
Even the beets are thoroughbreds;
Then look at the many children
With hands like the monkey's paw,
Bowlegged, flat-headed, and foolish—
Bred true to Mendel's law.
This is the law of Mendel,
And often he makes it plain,
Defectives will breed defectives
And the insane breed insane.
Oh, why do we allow these people
To breed back to the monkey's nest,

To increase our country's burdens
When we should only breed the best?

Oh, you wise men take up the burden,
And make this your loudest creed,
Sterilize the misfits promptly—
All not fit to breed!
Then our race will be strengthened and bettered,
And our men and our women be blest,
Not apish, repulsive and foolish,
For the best will breed the best.

Joseph S. DeJarnette,
Director of Western State Hospital and American eugenicist

"... one can hardly escape the conviction that the intelligence of the average 'third class' immigrant is low, perhaps of moron grade." —Dr. Henry Goddard, American psychologist, eugenicist, and founder of intelligence testing program on Ellis Island

Eugenics: from the Greek words meaning "well" and "born"

"No one—not even the town's oldest living residents—remembers the summer when teams of researchers came to administer intelligence tests and ask about people's genealogy, taking notes and saying little. No one knew their medical records were being read, their family histories documented, their children, spouses, and grandparents screened for perceived hereditary 'defects' including pauperism, 'immorality,' and 'feeblemindedness.' No one knew the town was already considered 'a network of degeneracy'—its people 'socially unfit'—by the followers of a popular pseudoscience called eugenics, a movement that sought to identify people with 'inferior' traits as a first step toward purifying the gene pool. The testing was to be done 'quietly and without the residents knowing what is going on or what it is all about,' read a directive of the time. [... This study] was part of a campaign to promote sterilization, segregation, selective breeding, and immigration restrictions—a campaign with leadership and widespread support among academics from Harvard and other top New England colleges and universities." —"The Master Race," by Welling Savo, *Boston Magazine* https://www.bostonmagazine.com/2006/05/15/the-master-race/

"The biggest problem was the influx of emigrants ... unwanted human debris ... from abroad, degrading good pioneer stock through intermarriage ..." —Leon Whitney, *The Case for Sterilization* (1934)

"We cannot have too much immigration of the right kind, and we should have none of the wrong kind." —President Theodore Roosevelt (1905)

"A word as to the feebleminded. Not only are they likely to become a public charge on the community, but they are also quite likely to join the ranks of the criminal classes. In addition, they may have feebleminded descendants. Now is the time to take greater precautions to differentiate between the good and the bad immigrants... this will be possible only when parasites who come here with no purpose of becoming productive forces shall be held back and they shall not fill up our congested cities. Many children under five come here, and it is probably correct to say that nothing short of an inquiry into their heredity will enable the government to determine whether or not they will grow up feebleminded." —William Williams, Immigration Commissioner, Ellis Island

"This book is my Bible." —Adolf Hitler in a fan letter to Madison Grant, American supremacist eugenicist and author of *The Passing of the Great Race*

CHAPTER 1

Ellis Island
May 31, 1928

A sick, nervous sweat rolled down Magdalena Conti's neck when she saw what the soldiers were doing. If she'd known the dangers awaiting her here on the other side of the Atlantic, she would have stayed home and taken her chances. Now she was trapped, surrounded by the heart-wrenching cries of terrified mothers, shrieking children, shouting men, and weeping women echoing inside the cavernous building. The harsh noises bounced off the arched ceilings and surged through the locked gates and iron bars like a rolling storm. As if the pandemonium of thousands of desperate people crammed together in the enormous, boiling space wasn't bad enough, the rank odors of sweat and fear hung in the air like an invisible haze, trunks and luggage scraped across the wooden floor, feet shuffled and stirred up dust, and voices murmured and shouted in what seemed like a hundred different languages, adding to the chaos in Magdalena's anxious mind.

How was it possible that just a few hours earlier she'd

longed to get off the ship, couldn't wait to leave the foul confines of steerage and set foot on the shining shores of America? Maybe the rumors were true—maybe Ellis Island really was the island of tears. Maybe the Americans still detained "alien enemies" like they had during the Great War, or maybe they'd reverted to hanging pirates, criminals, and anyone else deemed a threat. Maybe the soldiers were taking immigrants out back and shooting them. Right now, anything seemed possible.

Up ahead, a stern-looking soldier behind a high desk questioned her fellow steerage passengers before sending them on for further examination. Another soldier pulled a frail-looking woman with a cane from a young boy's side and hauled her away. A second soldier grabbed a man with one arm and an old woman trying to catch her breath and disappeared with them down a dim hallway. Two more soldiers removed an entire family from the line, ignoring the parents' frantic pleas and nervous questions. Sometimes a soldier would pry a toddler from their mother's arms, taking the child in one direction while the parents were dragged in another, all of them reaching for each other, screaming and fighting desperately not to be separated. Husbands and wives were yanked apart too, confused and struggling to break free. Quite often the soldiers wrote letters on the immigrants' coats with white chalk—*C, H, X, N, P, L, S*—before sending them away.

No one knew what the letters meant.

No one knew where the men, women, and children were being taken, or why.

Trying to contain her panic, Magdalena looked down at her two-year-old daughter, Ella, strapped to her chest in a red shawl, and placed a protective hand over her knitted cap. Already small for her age, partially thanks to malnourishment stealing the milk from her mother's breasts soon after she was born, Ella gazed up at her with tired, anxious eyes, her thin face betraying the nearly constant hunger she'd suffered during the first difficult years of her life. Doing her best to give her daughter a reassuring smile, Magdalena hummed a lullaby, her voice shaking. If the soldiers tried to take Ella away, they'd have to break Magdalena's arms to do it.

She'd heard the tragic stories that made their way across the ocean about grieving mothers who lost their babies to contagious diseases while being quarantined on Ellis Island, of husbands and wives who lost spouses the same way. She'd heard about fathers who had finally saved enough money to have their families join them in America, only to lose children on the way, to mourn babies they'd never seen. But she had no idea families could be *intentionally* torn apart, that babies could be ripped from their mother's arms.

Obviously, she'd made a terrible mistake.

But what choice did she have?

The country she loved as a little girl no longer existed. Germany had not yet recovered from the aftermath of war, with so many men drafted and killed, so many civilians starved, so much land plundered. The men who survived were left stranded, jobless, hungry, and bitter, and the economy was still suffering the effects of out-of-control inflation. For years now, she and her family had survived on half a cup of milk a day between them, and the majority of their meals consisted of potatoes and turnips. She'd tried talking her mother into moving out of the city into the country, where they could have a garden and chickens, but they had no means to buy a house or land, and Mutti knew nothing about gardening or raising poultry anyway.

In America, opportunities were endless; one could easily move from poverty to riches. And that was why she'd gotten on the ship. Because she would do anything to make sure her daughter never went hungry again. But the terrifying possibility of being separated from Ella had never entered her mind. Now, that fear erased everything.

With every passing minute, the temperature inside the building seemed to rise faster and faster. On top of feeling like she was roasting, Magdalena's feet and legs ached, and Ella seemed to grow heavier and heavier. Trying not to hyperventilate, she hooked one hand through her brother's arm for support, and to remind herself that she was not alone.

Enzo looked down at her with a faint smile, exhaustion and dread shining in his brown eyes. Despite the fact that his stomach, like all of theirs, had twisted with hunger more times than they cared to remember, at fourteen, he was already taller than her and Mutti, and his quiet, stoic presence always made Magdalena feel protected. Even with their wooden trunk resting on one broad shoulder, he stood straight as a tree, as if the battered chest filled with their meager belongings weighed nothing.

Mutti used to make her feel safe too, but she had aged greatly in the three years since typhoid took Vater, and her shoulders slumped under the burdens she carried. Magdalena was reluctant to add to her load by leaning on her for comfort, especially after putting her through the shame of having a seventeen-year-old unwed daughter turn up pregnant. Oh, how some of the neighbors had talked behind their backs during the long wait to be approved to go to America! And how foolish Magdalena had been, believing the British officer's promise to take her home to meet his family and get married. He even said she could send money back to Mutti after the wedding.

She should have known Officer Jonathan Dankworth was too good to be true when he came to her rescue after the wheel of her hand wagon fell off in the village square, clattered along the cobblestones, and landed near his boot. She had feared a scolding but unlike the other British soldiers who still treated German citizens like the enemy, he had politely offered to help, looking genuinely concerned. Or so she thought. After his attempt to fix the wheel failed, he insisted on carrying the wagon—and the load of sewing inside—back to her apartment, despite the fact that she lived twenty blocks away. By the time they reached her building, he had charmed her into meeting him near the river that evening, where he would be waiting on a park bench with wine, imported cheese, and British shortbread. At first, she agreed to his invitation because her stomach growled at the mention of cheese and shortbread, and it had been forever since she'd tasted wine, but as they sat for hours in the moonlight next to the river, his easy smile, intelligence, and willingness to see her as an equal, along with his silver-blue eyes and chiseled jaw, ultimately won her over in the end. Over the next three months, he professed his love to her, provided her family with extra provisions, and promised to rescue her from the devastating poverty of post-war Germany. By the time she realized she was expecting his child, he was already gone—back to his wife and children, his fellow comrades said.

It had taken weeks for her heartache to turn to anger, and finally to gratitude that she was rid of a man who'd turned out to be a liar and a cheat. At least he'd taught her more English than she'd learned in eight years of school. And of course she'd always be thankful for Ella, her very reason for living. It helped knowing that he was the one losing out; he would never see his daughter's dimpled smile or fall in love with her toes and tiny fingers. He would never hear her laugh or have even one memory of her. All the wondrous joys of being Ella's parent belonged wholly to Magdalena, and he could never take that away from her.

She glanced at Mutti's gray, pallid face, the dread in her chestnut eyes making Magdalena's already exhausted legs tremble. For the first time in the fourteen days since leaving home, Mutti looked more than tired and sick. She looked scared.

"Are you feeling all right, Mutti?" Magdalena said.

"I am fine, Lena," Mutti said, the familiar nickname another comforting reminder that Lena and Ella were not on their own. "*Bitte,* do not worry about me." She put a loving hand on Ella's small head. "Just hold tight to our *kleine Engel,* little angel."

Lena nodded, her chin quivering. Protecting her child was more important than anything in the world, but she worried about Mutti too. They'd already been waiting for hours, first on the ship, then on the barges, and now in line. Yes, it was getting close to their turn, but now that they could see what all the commotion was about, Mutti was looking worse by the minute. On the ship she'd been too seasick to do anything but sleep and take sips of cool water, only coming around once they were anchored in New York Harbor. Lena and Enzo had been sick too, especially during the two-day storm that had rolled the ship like a toy, making it rock and crack. But not nearly as sick as Mutti, who'd been unable to even lift her head during the worst of it.

Lena had wiped the sweat from Mutti's face, held her up while she vomited, and worried constantly that they might lose her—a possibility that had never occurred to her when they set out. But after an old man in the same bunkroom passed away, the terrifying thought took hold like poison in her mind. At one point the weather was so bad the steerage doors were locked and tied shut to keep the passengers from going up on deck and being swept overboard, and Lena thought for sure they were all going to die. But luckily, the storm ended quickly and Ella had been fine, other than being uneasy and hungry. Again.

Now, Lena looked around at the weary, fearful passengers in the other lines—at the unshaven men carrying trunks on their heads or shoulders, at the women wearing embroidered skirts and babushkas, carrying or holding the hands of small children. Many were whispering desperate prayers, and all their faces were gaunt with hunger. So many helpless and hopeful souls, crowded and anxious, their clothes reeking of steerage and seasickness. Who knew what they had suffered before stepping on board the ship—what losses, atrocities, or other hardships they'd lived through before deciding to come to the United States? And now, on top of everything, they had to worry about being torn from the people they loved most. As if that weren't difficult and confusing enough, for some infuriating reason the first- and second-class passengers had been allowed to disembark straight into Manhattan, while the steerage passengers were taken from the ship, put on barges, and sent over to the Ellis Island inspection station, where they were being lined up and judged like cattle.

Before turning forward again, Lena caught the haunted gaze of a pregnant woman in another line, a curly-haired toddler bound to her chest in a tattered gray scarf. The young mother's feverish, bloodshot eyes reflected everything Lena felt, every hope and untethered fear, every impossible dream, every possible nightmare. Lena scanned the people around the woman for another family member, a husband or mother, but she appeared to be alone. Hopefully she was meeting someone in America, someone who would look out for her and her children. Remembering the con men she'd been warned about—who targeted immigrant women traveling alone by offering rooms in boardinghouses and jobs in "good Christian homes," when in reality they'd end up putting them to work as unpaid servants, or worse, forcing them to sell themselves for money—Lena felt compelled to invite the young mother to stand with her and her family. Then the woman peered at Ella with narrowed eyes and Lena looked away, suddenly worried that the stranger could tell she had no husband . . . and that she had come to America under false pretenses.

Of course, that was ridiculous. No one could possibly know that the man who had agreed to hire Mutti and Enzo had no idea she and Ella were also coming. No one else in the world knew the truth. She felt the slight weight of the leather pouch on the cord around her neck, hidden beneath her peasant dress, two blouses, a knitted sweater, and her wool coat, all of which she'd been wearing since they left Bremerhaven. Mutti wore a similar pouch beneath her clothes, a dumpling-sized sack holding the other half of what little money they had after selling everything they owned to buy Lena's ticket. They'd been warned to bring enough cash to prove they wouldn't end up begging in the streets, but she had no idea if a few dozen *Rentenmarks* would be enough—the new German money had only been in circulation a few years. Before that, two billion *Papiermarks* were barely enough to buy a loaf of bread, and people had burned the old money in their woodstoves to keep warm. Now there was no telling what the new Mark was worth in the United States. Hopefully what they had in their pouches would be sufficient, because other than the clothes on their backs, the individual satchels they each carried, a few pots and pans, Mutti's sewing basket, a hand-sewn quilt, and other sentimental possessions in the ancient wooden trunk, the money was all they had.

Just then, the line moved forward, jolting her out of her thoughts. Soon they would be in front of the stern-looking soldier behind the high desk. Up ahead, a couple with a young girl stepped up to him. The soldier took one look at the child and motioned another soldier over. The mother grabbed her daughter by the shoulders and frantically shook her head.

"*No, per favore!*" she cried, backing away. "No!"

Her husband stepped in front of the soldier, his arms out, ready to protect his family. "*Il bambina resta con noi,*" he said, his voice hard.

"*Il bambino e malato,*" the soldier said, stumbling over the Italian words. "*Ha bisogno di cure mediche. Capisci?*" And then, in English, "She is ill. She has measles. We will treat her in the hospital but you must pay for her care or she will be sent back home. Do you understand?"

The husband's face crumpled in misery and he nodded. He turned back to his wife, spoke soft words to her, then stepped aside. With watery eyes, the woman knelt down, stroked the girl's cheek, and whispered in her ear. The child cried out and threw her arms around her mother, who hugged her for a moment, then stood and led her over to the soldier. When the soldier took her by the wrist and led her away, the little girl shrieked, struggling to get free.

"*Voglio andare con mia mama!*" she cried.

"No," the soldier said. "You must come with me."

"*Va tutto bene,*" the mother called out. "*Ci rivedremo presto amore mio.*" Then she fell into her husband's arms, weeping. Within seconds, another soldier appeared and led the parents in the other direction, the mother burying her face in her hands.

"What's wrong with her?" Enzo asked.

Mutti, who understood Italian better than her children, thanks to having married a man from that country, explained. "They said she is sick and needs medical attention. I think I saw a rash on her face."

The exchange reminded Lena that, although Mutti knew Italian and German, she knew very little English. And Enzo knew even less. Now that they were in America, she needed to teach them more.

Determined to appear strong and healthy despite the fact that she'd just spent endless days and nights in the bowels of a rat-infested ship taking care of her daughter, mother, and brother, with little food, less sleep, and thousands of sick and reeking steerage passengers, she let go of Enzo's arm, stood up straighter, and rubbed the moisture and grit from her eyes, which felt swollen from exhaustion and foul air. She pushed loose locks of her grimy hair away from her face, hoping that, despite her petite frame, she looked older than nineteen. Now more than ever she had to look capable and strong, even while terrified. Ella needed her. Mutti and Enzo did too.

She took off her brother's cap, wiped his sweaty bangs off his forehead, put his cap back on, then smoothed his coat and straightened Mutti's collar. After everything they'd been through and everything they'd lost, they had to stay together. They just *had* to. Then she had another thought, and a chill ran through her. What if they were all denied entry? What if they were deported for some strange reason? They had nothing to go home to now—no home, no jobs, no money.

She could barely believe they'd done it, sold what few items they owned and come all this way. She'd never forget walking out the door of their cramped apartment for the last time, looking back over the worn threshold into the place she'd always called home, trying to remind herself that nothing had been the same since Vater died anyway. Not her mother, her brother, or herself. Sometimes she wondered if Mutti wanted to leave Germany to run away from her heartache.

Except moving across the ocean wouldn't mend Mutti's broken heart or bury her misery. She and Lena and Enzo would carry the wretched grief, the horrible, heavy agony of losing Vater, in their hearts forever, no matter where they went. Between sorrow, starvation, and the pain of being deserted by Ella's father, Lena thought she was more than ready to start over someplace new. But now, being inside Ellis Island where dreams were being shattered and families were being ripped apart, she longed desperately for the tiny kitchen with the woodstove and handmade table, the even tinier bedroom she'd shared with Ella, the cobblestone streets and the sound of cathedral bells outside her window.

For what seemed like the thousandth time, she struggled to push away the hollow ache of homesickness. There was no sense in wanting something she couldn't have. The decision had been made to come to America and that was that. Not to mention it had taken months for Mutti's and Enzo's numbers to come in so the man who agreed to hire them could buy tickets.

Things will be better in America, Mutti had said. *We will have steady work and you will no longer need to spend your days picking up coal by the train tracks or searching through garbage for food. We will never again be hungry and poor.*

She wanted to believe her mother's words, but right now it seemed impossible. And what if their American benefactor refused to take her and Ella in?

Before she knew what was happening, it was their turn. She stepped up to the soldier standing behind the high desk, nerves crackling under her skin. Between the badge, the black leather straps across the chest of his uniform, and his grizzled face, the soldier looked even more intimidating up close. His badge read: IMMIGRATION OFFICER.

"Name, number, and nationality," he barked without looking up from his clipboard.

"Magdalena Sofia Russo Conti," Lena said. "Number 527. German Italian." She put a hand on Ella. "And this is my daughter, Ella Gianni Conti. Number 526. German. This is my mother, Katrina Pauline Conti, Number 528, German, and my brother, Enzo Nikolas Conti. Number 529. German Italian."

The officer looked up then, scowling and studying her through small, round spectacles. "Are your mother and brother unable to speak?"

"*Nein*," she said. "I mean, *ja*. Yes." Cringing inside, she berated herself for speaking incorrectly. "I am sorry. I was thinking it would be better for me to answer for them. They are still learning English and—"

He held out his hand. "Inspection cards and papers."

Digging her papers out of her coat pocket, Lena translated for Mutti and Enzo. They held out their cards and papers.

"You were born in Italy?" the officer said, eyeing Lena.

"Yes. We moved to Germany when I was one year of age."

"Are you Jewish?"

"No," she said.

"Male or female?" the officer said.

Lena raised her eyebrows. "Me?"

The officer nodded.

"Female," she said.

"Occupation?"

"My mother and I took in laundry and sewing. In America we hope to—"

"Where is the child's father?"

For a second, she thought about telling the truth, that Ella's father had abandoned them, but being honest about the situation might be too big a risk. And Ella's father might as well be dead anyway. "He is deceased."

"And you were not married." It was not a question.

She swallowed. How did he know? Then she remembered; she still had her mother's last name. "He died before the wedding."

With a disapproving scowl, he scribbled something down on a piece of paper, then looked at her again.

"Can you read and write?"

"Yes." She gritted her teeth. Why were they being asked so many questions? They had already been screened numerous times, before leaving Germany and again at a checkpoint before getting off the ship to take the barge to Ellis Island. Inspectors had boarded the ship on rope ladders to look for signs of smallpox, yellow fever, cholera, plague, and leprosy. And once the ship passed inspection, more officers came aboard to ask additional questions before they docked.

"Last residence?"

"Beckingen, Germany."

"Final destination?"

"Virginia."

"What city?"

She turned to her mother. "Where are we going? What is the city?"

Mutti cleared her throat and in broken English said, "Old Rag Mountain."

The officer wrote down the name and regarded Lena again. "Do you have a sponsor?"

Lena frowned, confused by the English word.

He sighed. "Is a friend or relative meeting you here?"

She nodded. "Yes. A cousin to my mother."

"What is this person's name and where does he live?"

"His name is Mr. Silas Wolfe. He lives in Virginia in . . ." She glanced at Mutti again, unsure, then she remembered. "Old Rag Mountain."

"Have you been to the United States before?"

She shook her head. "No."

"Have you ever been in prison or a hospital or institution for the care and treatment of the insane?"

She only understood the words *hospital* and *prison* but answered anyway. "No."

"Have you come here because of any offer, solicitation, promise or agreement, expressed or implied, to perform labor in the United States?"

"I am not sure what you are asking me," she said.

"Have you been offered or promised a job or work in this country?"

"Yes," she said. "My brother will work for Mr. Wolfe, and my mother and I will take care of his house and children."

"Where is his wife?"

"She is dead," she said.

"Are you a polygamist?"

She frowned again.

"A two-timer," he said. "An adulteress, a person who breaks the laws of marriage."

She knew what breaking the law meant. "No."

"Are you an anarchist?"

"I'm sorry?" she said, raising her brows.

"Are you a troublemaker? A person who doesn't follow rules?"

"No."

"Did you pay for your own passage, or was it paid for by any other person or by any corporation, society, municipality or government, and if so, by whom?"

"Mr. Silas Wolfe paid for my mother and brother," she said. "We paid for my ticket."

"Are you in possession of at least twenty-five dollars?"

"We have thirty-four German Marks."

"Between all of you?"

"Yes," she said.

The officer scoffed. "You do realize that is less than ten U.S. dollars."

A coil of fear twisted in her gut. Would they be turned away because they didn't have enough money? She nodded, unsure of what else to say.

"Your sponsor will need to report to the Board of Inquiry to sign papers proving he has work for you," the officer said. "Do you understand?"

Another flash of panic ignited inside her chest. How was Mr. Wolfe going to prove he had work for her when he had no idea she was coming?

"Do you understand?" the officer said again. "No one is allowed entry who might become a public charge. We will not allow you to become a burden to the United States."

She nodded.

When he'd finished interrogating her, he questioned Enzo. She translated.

"I thought you said he could speak English," the officer said.

"Only a little," she said. "But he is learning more."

Enzo shrugged at some questions and looked baffled by others. She did her best to explain everything. In some instances, she answered for him.

"How many feet does a cat have?" the officer said.

She translated.

"That's a stupid question," Enzo said to her in German.

"Just answer it," she said.

Irritation pinched the officer's features. "Is he feebleminded?"

"I do not understand what you—" she said.

"Is he an idiot? A moron? Insane?"

She was unsure what the words meant, but could tell by the man's tone that they were not good. "No," she said, "He worked delivering telegrams in Germany and—"

"Four," Enzo said in English, holding up four fingers and glaring at the officer.

"He will need to be questioned further by the Board of Inquiry," the officer said. He came around the desk and marked Enzo's coat with a chalk *X*. "Make sure he doesn't wipe it off."

"Why?" Lena said. "What does it mean?"

"It means he needs to be more thoroughly examined," the officer said. "The only way to keep America pure is by checking immigrants for poor stock."

She shook her head. "I'm sorry, I am still not understanding."

"I don't have time to explain. There are others waiting." He studied Mutti. "Is your mother unwell?"

"No," Lena said. "She was ill on the ship but she is better now."

The officer looked doubtful. "What was wrong with her?"

"The waves made her very sick," she said.

In addition to the same questions the officer asked Lena and Enzo, he asked Mutti how long she was married, if she had other children, if she had any differences with her husband, and if they got along all right. Lena hated the pained look on her mother's face when she translated the ridiculous inquiries. Why did her relationship with Vater matter? Her poor father was dead and buried three thousand miles away, cold and alone in the graveyard next to the stone church where Lena and Enzo were baptized as children.

Finally, the officer gave them each a stringed tag stating their name, ship, manifest number, and destination. "Display these landing tags on your clothes where we can see them," he said.

In English and nine other languages, the back of the card read: *When landing at New York this card is to be attached to the coat or dress of the passenger in a prominent position.*

Lena tied a tag to Ella's jacket button and her own, while Mutti and Enzo tied the tags to each other.

"Move along to the doctor behind me," the officer said.

Lena glanced at the soldier behind him, then looked at him again, perplexed. "I see no doctors," she said.

"Those men are military surgeons," he said. "Doctors. Now move along. They will tell you what to do next."

For the first time, she noticed the men behind him were wearing different uniforms. After she explained everything to Mutti and Enzo, the three of them moved past the desk toward the first doctor. When they were about ten feet away from the doctor, he held up a hand to make them stop. Then he pointed at Lena and Ella.

"You first," he said. "Put the child down and make her walk."

Trembling, Lena unwrapped Ella from the shawl with Mutti's help and put her on the floor, the weight of her warm little body on her chest suddenly gone, like a terrible hollowness inside her heart. What if one of the soldiers grabbed Ella and carried her away?

Ella reached up for Lena, crying, "Mama! Mama!"

"Come forward," the doctor said, motioning Lena toward him. "She will follow you."

"It's all right," Lena said to Ella. "Don't cry. Come with me and I will pick you up again."

Glancing over her shoulder to make sure Ella followed, Lena

walked toward the doctor, her arms and legs vibrating. Ella toddled after her, wailing.

The doctor studied them while they walked, looking them up and down with critical eyes. When Lena reached him, he told her to hold out her hands, palms up. "Do you have any deformities? Crooked fingers or an artificial limb?"

She shook her head.

He gave her hands a quick glance, then told her to turn them over. "Have you been in the company of anyone with cholera, plague, smallpox, leprosy, or typhus?"

Some of the words were unfamiliar, but she understood the term *typhus*. "No," she said.

Ella pulled on the hem of Lena's coat, her face red and wet. "Up, Mama. Up."

"Loosen your collar, please," the doctor said.

Lena opened her coat, unbuttoned her sweater and two blouses partway, then unhooked the collar of her peasant dress.

The doctor felt underneath her jaw, then told her to look down as he examined her scalp. When he was finished, he said, "Pick up the child." After examining Ella, he sent them on to the next doctor, who held what looked like a buttonhook.

"You must stand very still while I examine your eyes," the second doctor said, resting a hand on Lena's cheek.

The smell of disinfectant filled her nostrils as he pinched her eyelid between his thumb and forefinger, put the edge of the buttonhook beneath her lid, and turned her eyelid inside out. It was all she could do not to cry out in pain. It felt like he was ripping it off. After examining both of her eyes, he wiped his fingers on a towel draped over his shoulder, then grabbed a piece of chalk and marked her coat with chalk — *TC*.

"What does this mean?" she said, touching the letters.

"Leave it alone," the doctor said in a stern voice. "You may have trachoma, so you need to pass another inspection before we decide whether to treat you or send you home."

"But I have nothing wrong with me," she said. "I am strong and healthy."

"It's possible you have a problem with your eyes," he said. "It's a serious disease that can cause you to become blind."

Lena's stomach turned over. She understood what the word *blind* meant. But her eyes felt fine. She was just exhausted and had been either crying or on the verge of tears for the past two weeks. It was no wonder her eyes looked bloodshot and her lids felt swollen.

"Now your daughter," the doctor said.

Lena picked up Ella.

"Hold her still," the doctor said. "Keep her hands down."

Reluctantly, Lena pinned Ella's arms to her sides and the doctor examined her lids with the buttonhook. Ella screeched in terror and pain, struggling to get free, and Lena did her best not to cry. As soon as the examination was over, she loosened her grip and kissed Ella's forehead.

"Shhh," she said. "It's done. You're all right."

Then, to Lena's horror, the doctor pointed to the left.

A soldier took her by the arm and started to lead her away. She dug in her heels. "Where are you taking me?" she said. "I have to stay with my family!" She looked back at Mutti and Enzo, who watched helplessly. When the second doctor motioned Mutti forward, she did as she was told, petrified eyes locked on Lena.

Terror rushed like fire through Lena's chest. She was being separated from her family, and Mutti and Enzo were getting farther and farther away. She couldn't remember letting go of Enzo's arm, scolded herself for not clinging to them as long as she could. Before she knew what was happening, she and Ella were being whisked down a long hall to a wide room filled with other women, some with babies and children. Everyone looked as scared as she felt, all with different letters—*H, G, L, P, B, X*— on their coats and jackets. The room was cold and bare, with white walls and glass-fronted cabinets. Two inspectors sat with clipboards and pens behind long tables, while several doctors stood in front of them, watching as more women and children filed in, crying and asking questions in different languages. Lena searched the crowd for Mutti, praying she would appear, but she was nowhere to be seen. After the door was closed, one of the doctors read from a piece of paper.

"All passengers are liable to be rejected who, upon examination, are found to be lunatic, idiot, deaf, dumb, blind, maimed, or infirm, or above the age of sixty years, or a widow with a child or children, or any woman without a husband with a child or children, or any person unable to take care of himself or herself without becoming a public charge, or who from any attending circumstances are likely to become a public charge, or who from sickness or disease, existing at the time of departure, are likely soon to become a public charge. Sick persons or widows with children cannot be taken, nor lame persons, unless full security be given for the bonds to be entered into by the steamer to the United States Government, that the parties will not become chargeable to the State."

Lena had difficulty understanding everything he said, but she understood enough to intensify the snarl of fear growing inside her. She had a child and no husband. And Mutti was a widow with children.

If they were going to be deported, she needed to get back to her family, to make sure they were together when it happened. Holding Ella tightly in her arms, she looked around desperately for an escape but saw none. And where would she run, anyway? The immigrant officer had already said Enzo needed to be examined further, and for all she knew, Mutti had been taken somewhere else too. How would they ever find each other?

Taking slow, deep breaths, Lena struggled to calm down as the doctors moved around the cold room inspecting the women and children one by one, examining the skin near their open collars, using a metal caliper to methodically measure their heads, noses, and ears. They shared their findings with the men at the tables, who wrote the information down.

A nurse entered the room to examine the scalp of a pregnant woman with the letters *SC* chalked on her lapel. The nurse made the woman sit on a stool so she could part her hair section by section. Another doctor made an old woman with the letter *L* on her sweater walk back and forth across the room, despite the fact that the woman was clearly limping and in pain. After one of the doctors examined the eyes of a young girl with the same letters Lena had on her jacket, he shook his head at the mother, who had two more young children at her side.

"She has trachoma," the doctor said to the mother. "She cannot enter."

When an interpreter translated from English to German, the mother wailed and sobbed, pleading with the doctor.

"What am I to do?" she cried in German. "We have traveled all this way to be with my husband. We have not seen him in two years. He has a new home for us now. You must let her enter."

"I'm sorry," the doctor said. "But you and the rest of your children must return home with the diseased one."

When the interpreter translated, the mother fainted and fell to the floor. The nurse ran over, put smelling salts beneath her nose, then helped her up and out the door, the children weeping behind her.

Lena clenched her jaw, anger and fear swirling in her stomach. How could they deport a mother and her children when the father was already in America? How could they separate entire families again and again and again? It was barbaric and beyond cruel. She gazed at Ella's face, fighting back tears. If anyone tried to separate them, she would die before she let it happen. When she looked up again, a bearded doctor was coming toward her. He glanced at the letter on her coat, then peered into her eyes. She held her breath. What would she do if the doctor said she could not enter the country? Would they deport Mutti and Enzo too? No, she would insist they stay in America without her. She would not ruin Mutti's and Enzo's chances for a better life. But what would she do about Ella?

"Put the child down," the doctor said.

Lena did as he said, trying to look brave and strong.

"Mamaaaaaa," Ella shrieked.

The doctor put a stethoscope to Lena's chest, looked in her nose and ears, then examined her eyes with the buttonhook a second time. She swallowed her cries of pain until he was finished, then finally exhaled and picked up Ella, her heart thundering in her chest.

"Do you speak English?" the doctor said.

"*Ja.* I mean, yes."

"Do your eyes hurt or itch?"

"No."

"Does the light bother them?"

"No," she said. "I am only tired. And I've been crying."

"I agree with you," the doctor said. "I believe your eyes are just irritated. And your daughter seems fine as well." He turned to one of the men at the table. "No signs of trachoma."

Lena nearly collapsed with relief.

After everyone had been examined, the doctors stepped back and looked at the women.

"Remove your outerwear and open your blouses," one of them said.

Lena tensed. Had she heard correctly? Were they to bare their breasts in front of these men?

When the translators repeated the instructions in different languages, gasps echoed throughout the room and shocked expressions filled the women's faces. Like Lena, most of them had probably not exposed their chests to anyone since they were children, when they were bathed or had their clothes changed by mothers and older sisters. Even husbands and lovers likely only saw glimpses of their bare breasts underneath bedcovers or inside darkened bedrooms.

"Why must we do this?" Lena said in a loud voice.

The other women looked at her with wide eyes, their cheeks blotchy with shame and dread.

"Because you want to become American citizens," the bearded doctor said. "And to do that, you must pass our examinations."

Another doctor glared at Lena, daring her to contradict him. "If you'd rather not do as you're told, we can sign your deportation papers here and now."

Lena dropped her gaze, praying it would be the last of the examinations. Reluctantly, she put Ella down again, slipped her cloth satchel from her back, took off her coat, and wadded them both on the floor between her feet. She unbuttoned her sweater all the way and the two cotton blouses she wore underneath, then undid the hooks on the front of her dress, grateful she was wearing a brassiere and that she could keep her dress on, unlike some of the other women who wore garments that needed to be taken off over their heads.

While the women stood exposed and shaking, the doctors went around the room, searching for signs of disease by examining the skin on their chests. Thankfully, the bearded doctor was the one who examined Lena. When he was finished, he said, "You seem to be healthy."

Before Lena could ask what would happen next or when she'd see her family again, he told her to get dressed, then moved on to the next woman. After redoing her buttons and clasps, and returning her satchel to her back, she lifted Ella onto her hip, hugging her close and kissing her cheeks. Ella leaned into Lena's neck, her breath hitching as she struggled to stop crying.

One by one, Lena and the other women who passed the examinations were led out of the room and lined up in the hall.

When the last woman exited the room, two officers led them farther down the hallway, their heels clicking along the stone floor. No one knew where they were being taken or why. Some women cried quietly while others murmured anxious words and prayers in different languages.

Every several yards, more hallways turned off the first, like a giant maze. At the end of the hall, the officers led the women left into a corridor the size of an ocean liner. On one side of the massive space, floor-to-ceiling cages lined the wall, each cage large enough to house three train engines side by side. To Lena's horror, men, women, and children filled every cage, sitting on benches, pacing, praying. Children cried and men pleaded with the soldiers walking by, begging to be let out, asking questions no one answered.

A new fear tightened Lena's chest. Were she and the other women going to be locked in a cage? Why? And for how long? Scanning every face, searching for familiar features, checking every group of young boys to see if her brother was among them, she called out for Mutti and Enzo. But her family was nowhere to be seen. Farther down the hall, they turned and approached a man in a tailored suit, who was talking to another immigration officer. When the men saw the group of women coming, they stepped aside but kept up their conversation.

"Admitting mentally defective immigrants into the United States strikes at the very roots of the nation's existence," the man in the suit said. "We must protect our country against this spreading poison. Especially the Jews, who are highly inbred and amoral, and we know their defects are almost entirely due to heredity. Every effort must be made to pick out those who look even remotely feebleminded or mentally backward. And the children need to be examined more closely. We should also refuse to land any of the unclean Italians and Russian Hebrews. We have enough dirt, misery, crime, and death of our own without permitting more to be pushed on us."

"But Commissioner Williams," the officer said, "we can't depend on a single test or procedure that results in automatically grinding out a diagnosis. A poor farmer who has been living in a hut can hardly be expected to name all the things he sees here, because he has never seen or heard of them before. Many of these immigrants come from poor countries. They have left their relatives and friends, undergone a long voyage, and suffered many hardships. They've come here to start new lives. Certainly their behaviors have been shaped by all of those circumstances."

"Perhaps, but that is not our doing or our problem to fix. We also need to be concerned about the diseases those filthy people bring into our country. The Asians carry tuberculosis, and the Spanish spread smallpox and yellow fever. And as you know, most of the Jews have cholera."

Lena had trouble understanding everything the men were saying, but the meaning seemed clear. The immigration officer understood that everyone's backgrounds were different, while the man in the suit thought he could measure someone's intelligence by their appearance, and that most immigrants were dirty and diseased. Could he be the reason for all the questions and examinations? The reason children were being ripped from their mother's arms? The reason people were being kept in cages? She wanted to scream at him, wanted to tell him he would surely go to hell for treating his fellow human beings without a shred of decency or compassion. But she was nothing to him, just another filthy immigrant. He would not care what she said. And she had to think of Ella. Getting in trouble would not help their situation. Still, she slowed, tempted to tell him what she thought, until one of the guards shouted at her to keep moving.

Farther along the corridor, a door opened and a man in a white outfit came out into the hall, pushing a little girl strapped to a wheeled bed, followed by a woman wearing a babushka and embroidered dress, a handkerchief pressed to her lips. The little girl cried hysterically, calling for her mother and struggling to break free. The man in white turned the bed toward the end of the hall and pushed it through a door below a sign in block letters that read: TO HOSPITAL. The woman followed, her shoulders convulsing.

Without warning, one of the inspectors pulled Lena out of line and put her in an office-sized room, closing the door behind her. Miniature flags from different countries and photos of men in suits filled the back wall. Two immigration officers looked up at her from behind a long desk, one with pitted cheeks, the other with a bottle-brush mustache. Anxiety quickened her breathing. Was she in trouble? Did they have bad news? The officer with pitted cheeks instructed her to take a seat. She did as she was told, trembling hands holding Ella on her lap. The officer with the mustache gazed at her, his face devoid of emotion.

"Can you speak English or shall I call on the interpreter?" he said in a flat voice.

She nodded. "I . . . I speak English."

He glanced down at a clipboard, then addressed her again. "What is your name and number?"

"Magdalena Sofia Russo Conti. Number 527."

"And this is your child?"

"Yes."

"What is your native language?"

"German."

He made several check marks on the paper, while the officer with the pitted cheeks looked through a stack of cards, then handed one to him. "Do you know any other languages?" he said.

"A little Italian," she said.

"Can you read and write in your native language?"

"Yes."

The mustached officer handed her the card. "Read this to yourself please."

In German, the card read: After you have read this card please pick up the pencil, which is on the table before you, and hand it to the immigration officer. This demonstrates your ability to read.

She put the card down, picked up the pencil, and handed it to him.

"Very good," the mustached officer said. He made another check mark on his paper, then placed a crude, wooden rectangle in front of her, along with wooden cutouts of stars, circles, squares, and triangles. "Now, complete this puzzle."

Ella reached for the puzzle and Lena held her back, pinning her small arms beneath one hand. With her free hand, Lena quickly put the pieces in place, wondering if they thought she was a child. Ella could have completed it just as fast, if she'd let her.

"What is two, plus three, plus five?" the pitted-cheeked officer said.

She closed her eyes, desperate to remember the English numbers. Math was never her strong suit. She counted on her fingers by pressing them one by one on her leg. Once, twice, and a third time to make sure.

"Miss Conti," the mustached officer said, "do you understand the question?"

She opened her eyes. "Ten," she said, praying she was right.

He nodded. "Now, tell me, is it better to sweep a dirty staircase from the top to the bottom or the bottom to the top?"

She frowned. What kind of trick question was that? Would Mutti and Enzo be asked these questions too? They would get the sweeping question right, but Enzo was even worse with numbers than she was. And his coat had already been marked with an *X* because the first immigration officer they talked to thought he was . . . What had he called him? Feebleminded?

Despite her nerves, she started to get irritated. She and her family were good people. And Enzo might not be the smartest fourteen-year-old, but he was kind and funny and a hard worker. They were not criminals or troublemakers or idiots. And they were definitely not poison, like the man in the hall said. "I did not come all this way to sweep stairs."

To her surprise, the mustached officer cracked a smile. Then he caught himself and grew serious again. "What is your answer, please?" he said.

"Top to bottom," she said.

He made another check mark on his paper.

"If you had three horses, two cows, and five sheep, how many animals would you have?"

"If I were as rich as that, I would not have come to America," she said.

This time the mustached officer laughed out loud. Then the pitted-cheeked officer gave him a stern look and he pulled himself together. "Perhaps that's true," he said. "But I need you to answer. Three horses, two cows, and five sheep make how many animals?"

"Ten," she said. "And the two of you and the two of us makes four."

Irritation lined the pitted-cheeked officer's forehead. "This is not a game, Miss Conti. Your very future depends on your answers to our questions." His voice was hard. "Do these words mean the same or opposite? Wet and dry."

Before she could reply, the door opened and another officer leaned into the room.

"Picking up for Hoffman Island," he said.

Suddenly the officers stood and took several steps back, fear written on their faces. Lena gaped at them. Why were they suddenly afraid of her?

"She's free to go," the mustached officer said.

"Come with me," the officer in the doorway said, opening the door all the way and stepping back.

She stood. "What is wrong?" she said. "Where are you taking us?"

"To the delousing plant," the officer said.

Chapter 2

Leaning against the railing of the slow-moving barge crowded with confused and frightened women and children, Lena held a sleeping Ella against her chest and squinted at the barge behind them as it pulled away from Ellis Island, praying to catch sight of Mutti and Enzo. For one elated moment, she thought she saw an older woman and a tall boy who might have been her mother and brother, but they were too far away to make out any facial features. Regardless, she told herself it was them and they would be reunited when they reached Hoffman Island. She had to believe it. Otherwise, how would she ever find them again?

Earlier, while searching the barge she was on for Mutti and Enzo, she'd asked the other German-speaking women on board if they'd seen an older woman with a tall, dark-haired boy, and if they knew what a delousing plant was or why they were being taken there. They all shook their heads, except for a pale young woman wearing a high-collared blouse and shiny leather shoes. Between her clothes and her styled hair, she looked too rich to have traveled in steerage.

"Delousing means to get rid of *Läuse*, lice," the pale woman said.

"But I have no lice," a nearby woman said. "And neither do my children."

Several others chimed in.

"We don't either."

"That's right."

"If we have lice, we got it on the ship."

"They're worried about typhus," the pale woman said. "They need to be certain all lice are eliminated." Her voice was clear and calm, her dialect High German, unlike the southern dialect Lena and her family spoke.

"*Danke* for explaining it to us," Lena said. "Do you know how they will do it?"

Everyone stared at the pale woman, anxiously awaiting her answer.

She shook her head. "I'm sorry, but I don't know for sure. They could use powder or Zyklon B."

One of the other women gasped. "But Zyklon was banned after the war."

The pale woman shrugged. "You asked questions, I answered. Now please, leave me be. I lost my son on the ship, and my husband was placed in the hospital on Ellis Island. I do not wish to speak any longer."

"*Ach, Gott,*" Lena said. "I'm very sorry for your loss."

The other women also offered their condolences, but the pale woman only grew silent and stared out to sea. Everyone else glanced at each other with shared sympathy, then turned inward again, preoccupied by their own troubles and worries.

Now, Lena lowered her gaze to the waves lapping against the hull of the barge, unable to believe they were on the water again. Hopefully it would be a short trip and Mutti's seasickness would not return. Then again, if the inspectors and doctors were worried about typhus, getting seasick would be the least of their concerns. Had they come all this way just to lose their lives to disease? No. She refused to think that way. She had to believe that delousing was only a precaution, and some day they would look back on all of this like a bad dream.

Gazing across the harbor at the tangle of Manhattan skyscrapers, a strange sensation came over her—a confusing, nauseating mixture of homesickness and jealousy that made her envy the people who already lived and worked in the city, who had regular routines and felt at home among the sidewalks and buildings, who slept in familiar beds and looked out familiar windows. What she wouldn't give to feel that sense of home again, to experience the comfort of the everyday mundane, to walk the worn cobblestone streets and alleys that led to well-known people and places—the grocery market, the gothic cathedral in the village square, her best friend Ingrid's house—to know where she belonged. Life in Germany had certainly been difficult, but now she felt lost and adrift, any sense of normality shattered and thrown to the winds.

As the barge traveled past Lady Liberty, a burning lump formed in her throat. How was it possible that, only hours earlier, the sight of the grand statue had filled her with so much hope? And now, seeing the symbolic figure and the American flag fluttering beside it, her heart ached with sadness and fear. It seemed that "give me your tired, your poor" meant only those who were not really tired or poor. That if you were in need of help, if you were judged to be ignorant or ill, the gates that led to freedom were closed to you.

Turning away from the railing, she scanned the crowded boat for a place to sit. She needed to rest, and Ella was getting heavier by the second. But every bench was taken, every seat filled with women and young girls, their faces creased with similar lines of distress and exhaustion. Seeing no open spot, Lena removed her satchel, sat down on the musty barge floor, and leaned against the cold steel wall, indifferent to the dirt and grease soiling her coat and dress. With one arm around her satchel and Ella still asleep on her chest, she closed her eyes and tried to doze, but the constant pounding of the powerful engine vibrated the entire boat, thudding in time with her throbbing pulse and making every thought more intense and urgent, every heartbeat like a bomb ready to explode.

Along with everything, her stomach cramped with hunger. What she wouldn't give for a slice of the rye bread and liverwurst Mutti had packed for the voyage to America. Unfortunately, that extra food had only lasted a few days, even with Mutti unable to eat, and the only nourishment they'd had on the ship was meager rations of lukewarm soup, stringy beef, and herrings. Remembering the nauseating smell of the fish, she wondered if she'd ever see liverwurst again. But right now, she'd settle for the herring.

When the barge finally slowed a short time later, the women craned their necks to see where they were stopping. Lena struggled to her feet, trying not to wake Ella, and looked toward the bow of the boat. Up ahead, waves broke along the rocky edge of a small island covered by a massive two-story building with several wings and a dozen chimneys. Doorways and arched windows lined the structure, some sealed off by bricks marked with giant, white *X*'s. Two smokestacks rose high above a metal water tower, one square and one round.

It looked like a prison. Or a hospital.

The words she heard back on Ellis Island echoed inside her head. *We should refuse to land any of the unclean* . . .

Maybe it wasn't lice the Americans were getting rid of on Hoffman Island; maybe it was people. Maybe they were going to be locked up forever, or worse. No. She needed to stop having such horrible thoughts. The Americans were trying to stop the spread of a dangerous disease—nothing less, nothing more. If anything, she should be thankful they were being so careful. Except it was becoming more and more difficult to feel gratitude, especially while feeling so unwelcome.

Once the barge docked, uniformed guards instructed the women and children to disembark, while more guards checked identification cards and wrote passenger numbers on baggage.

"After your luggage has been marked with your manifest number," a guard shouted, "leave it on the wharf. From there it will be transferred to the fumigation chambers where it will be exposed to the vacuum cyanide process for the destruction of any contained vermin. Your baggage will not be opened, and the exposure will be complete in less than one-and-one-half hours. During that time, you will be sent to the delousing chambers where you will be supplied with more bags for your valuables and other clothing."

Gaping at each other in confusion, the women and children voiced fearful questions in a cacophony of different languages. Fumigation chambers? Vacuum cyanide process? Vermin? What did those words mean? Lena scanned the crowd for the pale young woman, hoping she could help, but she was nowhere to be seen and the guards had ordered everyone to stay in line. She glanced over her shoulder to see if the other barge had landed yet, praying Mutti and Enzo were on board, but it was still too far away to tell.

When all the baggage had been marked and left on the wharf, the guards moved the passengers into a nearby section of the brick building, herding them into a wide, cement hallway. At the end of the hallway, military doctors wearing masks handed out burlap bags outside a set of heavy double doors while translators shouted in English and other languages, "All apparel is to be removed and placed inside your bag. While you are inside the chambers, your clothes will be passed through a chute into the fumigation room where they will also be exposed to the cyanide process."

Shocked and horrified, the women looked at each other with wide, frantic eyes, asking more questions no one had the answers to and shaking their heads. Were they expected to strip naked in front of these men? In front of everyone? *This can't be happening,* Lena thought. Even Ella's father had never seen her fully undressed. And what about the children? What about poor little Ella? Was she to be stripped naked too?

"Loosen your hair so it can be thoroughly cleaned," the translators said.

A stocky redhead vehemently refused to cooperate, then turned and started out of the building. Two guards grabbed her by the arms and shoved her back in line.

"Do as you're told!" a doctor shouted. "Or you'll be placed in quarantine indefinitely!"

Confused and frightened, the women took off their headscarves and hats and babushkas, loosened braids and buns and removed combs from their hair. Lena did the same, undoing her single braid with one hand and letting her long hair fall free down her back. Mothers undressed their children and babies and told them everything would be all right, their worried faces betraying their words. Older children started to cry while others looked around with anxious eyes. When they were done with the children, the women unfastened their outerwear and untied their bodices, unbuttoned their blouses, and stepped out of their underclothes, their faces flushed red with embarrassment. Many whimpered and started to weep while the doctors marked cloth bags with their numbers, and guards gathered their shoes and belts and satchels.

"Your leather goods will be treated with gasoline and oil," the translators announced. "These treatments will kill the lice and nits that spread disease."

While Ella cried at her feet, Lena took off her worn leather shoes along with the homemade belt that held the skirt over her dress and handed them to a doctor. She took off her coat and the multiple layers she wore underneath, along with her money pouch, her brassiere, cotton camisole, and underwear. Fully naked now, she undressed Ella, gently removing her coat and sweater, the two dresses she wore underneath, her knitted tights and little shoes, and finally, her saturated diaper. Exhausted and starving and cold, Ella wailed until her nose ran, her breath hitching in her bony chest.

"Hush, *mein Engel*," Lena said. "I'm right here. Everything will be all right." Even as she said the words, she wondered if she believed them. But that was what mothers did, wasn't it? Comforted their children until the very last second, until there was no denying everything was most definitely not going to be all right?

After wrapping her money pouch inside her undergarments and stuffing their clothes inside the burlap bag, she handed everything to a doctor who marked the bag with her number and told her it would be returned to her later. Then she picked Ella up again, held her thin little body against her bare breasts, and tried to make her warm, her teeth chattering from nerves and humiliation.

When everyone was undressed, they all stood there, hundreds of them, naked and shivering from fear and cold, like something out of a nightmare, with wide eyes and trembling chins. Young women, old women, fat women, skinny women, little boys and little girls all stood together, wondering what was going to happen next. Then the military doctors herded them into a cement room with no windows. Multiple nozzles protruded from the ceiling and metal drains lined the floor. Some women held on to one another and sobbed, their forlorn cries echoing in the hollow room. Some stood silently while others prayed or wept.

Lena wanted the women to be quiet, to stop scaring the children and making a terrible situation worse. At the same time, she couldn't be surprised that some of them were close to hysterics. After spending endless days in the bowels of a ship that had seemed, at times, about to capsize and disappear beneath the waves, followed by the unwelcoming dealings and intense interrogations on Ellis Island, it was easy for these desperate women to imagine that they were somehow being disposed of, especially when they were being treated like animals led to slaughter.

Lena closed her eyes and held Ella's head tucked under her chin, covering her small nose and mouth with her hands and hair. Other women held babies and small children too, their eyes locked on the nozzles in the ceiling. After the doctors had ushered the last woman into the cold, damp room, they shut and locked the doors. Shaking, the women gaped at each other and waited. Metal screeched. Pipes banged. Then the showers came on. One woman screamed. Others clawed their way toward the doors.

The liquid coming out of the nozzles smelled of chemicals, like a mixture of gasoline and lye soap. It burned Lena's eyes and nostrils and made her cough. She hung her head, doing her best to protect Ella's face, and waited for it to be over. Ella cried hysterically, as did numerous other children and women. After a few minutes, the smell disappeared and plain water washed over them. Sighs of relief and faint laughter filled the room. Lena rinsed Ella's skin off with the cool water, first wiping her face and eyes and mouth. Then the doors opened and, one by one, they were ordered out. Lena stood on her tiptoes trying to see where they were headed, but wet heads and pale shoulders blocked her view. Finally, she got closer to the exit, where two nurses stopped each woman to spray something in their hair. Why did they need to be covered with more chemicals? More than anything, Lena wanted to dry Ella off, to get her dressed again before she caught cold, but there was nothing to be gained by disobeying. When it was Lena's turn, a nurse instructed her to put Ella down and lift her arms. Still wet and shaking, Lena did as she was told and raised her hands while Ella shivered and howled on the ground. The nurse drenched Lena's armpits with a volatile-smelling mixture that stung her skin and reeked of either kerosene or turpentine.

"Spread your legs," the nurse said.

"Excuse me?" Lena said.

"I need to spray your pubic area," the nurse said. "To kill the nits."

Mortified, Lena did as she was asked, her face burning with embarrassment.

After the nurse finished spraying the mixture between Lena's thighs, she said, "I need to treat your hair too. Unless you want us to cut it off like we do the men's."

Lena shook her head, her teeth chattering. Her chocolate-brown hair was the dirtiest it had ever been, but when it was clean and curled using strips of rags, it was the one thing she liked about her appearance. Other than that, her nose was too big, her brows too thick, her lips too fat. And these people had taken enough from her—her privacy, her dignity, her hope, maybe even her mother and brother. She would not let them take her hair. "No, do not cut it."

"Then you need to turn around," the nurse said.

While Ella continued sobbing on the ground, Lena closed her eyes and waited for the application to be over, trying not to flinch when the nurse pulled her hair apart in clumps and the oily mixture hit her scalp.

"The child's hair too," the nurse said.

Lena picked up Ella and covered her face with one hand while the nurse sprayed her downy blond hair with the rank mixture. Ella squirmed and wailed, trying to get away, and Lena hated every bit of it. Luckily it was over in a matter of seconds. When they were done being treated, Lena held Ella close, rubbing her skin to warm her up, and followed the other women into the next room, where their numbered bags of clothes waited, returned from the fumigation room. After finding her bag, she tore it open and pulled out their clothes, anxious to get dressed and leave this place behind. She knelt beside Ella and started to put an undershirt over her head, then recoiled. The clothes reeked of disinfectant. Trying to air them out, she waved them around, but the smell remained. And poor Ella's lips were turning blue. Moving quickly, she pulled the clothes over Ella's damp skin, then got herself dressed, wrapped Ella inside the red shawl, and tied her to her chest.

At the other end of the room, nurses and translators shouted instructions in different languages. "After you've gathered your belongings, go outside and return to the boat. It will take you back to Ellis Island."

Lena found her shoes and belt inside her leather goods bag, put them on, and made her way over to the nurses and translators, zigzagging through the half-dressed mob of women and children, stepping around shoes and dodging wayward arms and coat sleeves. When she heard a nurse speaking German, she approached her and said, "Where are the people from the other boat? I am looking for my mother and brother."

"Everyone on the second barge has been put in quarantine," the nurse said.

Lena's throat grew hot and tight. "How long will they be there?"

Earlier, she'd convinced herself that Mutti and Enzo were on the other boat, but now she prayed she was wrong. Surely the doctors on Ellis Island had realized Mutti was recovering from the rough voyage. Surely they recognized that she and Enzo were healthy and strong.

"Until they're no longer contagious," the nurse said. "Could be weeks or months, even years if they can't be released or deported. If they survive."

Chapter 3

Back inside the turreted brick building on Ellis Island, Lena stood in line again, her exhausted daughter strapped to her chest, her oiled hair dripping down her back, the fumigated satchel hanging from her wrist like a lifeless animal. Unfortunately, the ocean breeze had done little to evict the delousing stench from their clothes while they were on the barge, but at least she was wearing only one layer beneath her coat now instead of four. And she'd been able to wipe most of the oil out of Ella's fine hair before it dripped into her eyes. Hopefully, none of their clothes had been ruined and she'd be able to wash everything as soon as they arrived at their destination. Not that they owned many garments—her satchel held the blouses and knitted sweater she'd worn earlier, an extra dress, a sleeping gown, undergarments, a hand-embroidered skirt from her late grandmother, and Ella's clothes, of course—but the last thing she wanted was to have to spend money on material for new outfits.

Craning her neck, she looked around for Mutti or Enzo, hoping against hope that they had not been quarantined on Hoffman Island but were waiting somewhere here instead. Fewer immigrants crowded the inspection stations than before, but her mother and brother were nowhere to be seen. Up ahead, immigration officers processed those coming in from the delousing plant, the foul-smelling, shell-shocked group of women and children who looked like they'd been soaked in oil. When it was finally her turn, Lena had to repeat her and Ella's names and numbers for what seemed like the hundredth time. The officer behind the desk took their cards, studied them for a moment, then found their names on a manifest and checked them off.

"I came from the ship with my mother and brother but I cannot find them now," she said. "Can you help me, please?"

"Their names?" the inspector said.

"Katrina Pauline Conti, number 528. And Enzo Nikolas Conti, number 529."

The officer ran a finger down the list, then shook his head. "I'm sorry," he said. "But they're both being deported."

For a second, she couldn't move. She couldn't breathe. What he said wasn't true. It couldn't be. Maybe she had misunderstood. "I am sorry," she said. "Did you say they are being deported?"

"Yes. They will be detained here on the island until they can be sent back to Germany on the next ship."

She opened her mouth to speak but no words came out. He had to be wrong. He just had to be. Then her voice finally came, shaking with anger, hoarse with fear. "But why? There is no reason to send them back."

"Enzo Conti, number 529, has been deemed feebleminded. Therefore, he has been denied entry into the U.S."

She shook her head and her mind raced, trying to remember what feebleminded meant. The officer who'd marked Enzo's coat with an *X* said it meant idiot and moron, but those words were unclear too. "I do not know what *feebleminded* is."

"According to this report," the officer said, "Enzo Conti is slow, dim-witted. He is lacking in his mental capacity and would end up being a delinquent or a criminal due to the fact that he is not smart enough to be a productive member of our society."

She shook her head again. More big words. But she understood *slow* and *not smart enough* and *criminal.* "That is not true! There is nothing wrong with him, and he is not a criminal!"

"I'm sorry," the officer said. "We cannot allow anyone into the country if they fail our inspections. The only way to preserve the purity of Americans is to limit the influx of people endowed with inferior blood."

"But my brother is still young," she said. "A child!" She was close to shouting. "He is only now learning English. He cannot know the answers to all your questions!"

"Yes, he is too young to be sent back alone, so your mother must accompany him."

"*Nein*," she said. "*Nein*! You have made a mistake. Enzo is healthy and strong. He did nothing wrong." She leaned over his desk, trying to see the manifest. "Please. Check again. Perhaps you are looking at the wrong names."

The officer let the pages fall closed, an irritated look on his face. "I can assure you I checked the right names."

"But you cannot send my family back," she cried. "They have nothing in Germany. No jobs, no house, no money!"

"Would you rather we commit your brother to our Psychopathic Pavilion?"

Her breath grew shallow and fast. She had no idea what he was talking about, but it did not sound good. "I do not know what that is."

"It's a hospital for the idiots, the insane, and the epileptics. If your brother is put in there, he'll never get out. People like him can't be helped."

The room seemed to spin around her. "But I told you, there is nothing wrong with him!"

The officer shrugged. "It's not my decision. I'm not a doctor and I don't make the rules."

Tears welled in her eyes. "Then you must send me back to Germany too. My daughter and I cannot stay in America alone. We won't." Even as she said the words, a nauseating awareness churned in her stomach. If they went back to Germany, Ella would go hungry. And she had come all this way to make sure that never happened again. Her own fears and desires no longer mattered.

"Do you have enough money for a return ticket?" the officer said.

She shook her head.

"Then I'm afraid it will be impossible for you to go back until you do. The shipping company is responsible for sending defective people in the first place, so they will only pay for immigrants who are deliberately being deported. You have a sponsor here, correct? Someone promising you a job?"

She swallowed the panic rising in her throat and looked down at Ella. If she told the truth—that the jobs being offered were meant for Mutti and Enzo and the sponsor had no idea she was coming—the officer would likely deport her. And Ella would be the one who suffered. She had no choice. She had to stay. "Yes, I will have work."

"Then you've already been approved to enter the country," the officer said. He leaned forward and pointed down a hallway to his left. "Make your way over to the currency exchange. After that, your sponsor should be waiting for you at the kissing post, the area between the two giant pillars at the end of the great hall. He'll need to sign papers before you're legally allowed to enter the country." He stamped her card and handed it back to her. "Welcome to America." Then he looked over her shoulder at the woman behind her. "Next."

Lena refused to move. "I want to see my family first."

He shot her an exasperated look. "Move along or I'll send you *and* your brother to the Psychopathic Pavilion."

"Please," she said. "You have a mother, yes? Maybe a brother too? Please. Tell me where they are. I only wish to say goodbye."

The officer stared at her for what seemed like forever, then sighed noisily and gestured to the right. "The detention rooms are that way. Stop at the clerk's office and tell them who you're looking for. But it won't do you any good. You can't change the rules."

"Thank you," she said, and hurried in the direction he pointed. She couldn't let Mutti and Enzo be sent back. Somehow she had to stop it from happening, had to prove to the American inspectors that they would be good, productive citizens.

When she reached the clerk's office, a blank-faced man glanced up from his desk, clearly unmoved by her frantic pleas for help. After rifling through a stack of papers, he made a phone call, stumbling over Mutti's and Enzo's names, then told her to continue down the hall, take a right, and follow the corridor all the way to the end. Praying she was not too late, she ran the entire way, her arms around Ella as she bounced against her chest.

At the end of the corridor, a wall of heavy mesh with a padlocked door covered a wide entrance into a dim space. It was another cage. Lena grabbed the mesh door, hooking her fingers through the openings, and peered into a vast, sparse room. An assortment of immigrants, men and women, young adults and children, sat on wooden bunk beds and low cots, sleeping, playing cards, or talking. Some paced the floor while others were still and silent, a lost look on their faces. She gave the cage door a hard shake, desperate to rip it open.

"Mutti?" she cried. "Enzo? Are you in there?"

No answer.

Then she saw her mother lying on a bunk, Enzo sitting on the cot beside it with his head in his hands.

"Enzo!" she shouted. "Mutti! I'm over here!"

Finally, Enzo saw her. He shook Mutti's shoulder and stood.

At first, her mother sat up and looked around, weary and confused. Then she got to her feet and hurried over to the cage door with Enzo.

Mutti grabbed the mesh, lacing her fingers through Lena's. "Oh, *mein Liebchen*," she cried. "Are you all right? Where have you been? What did they do to you?"

"I'm fine," Lena said. "But they told me they're sending you back to Germany!"

Mutti nodded, her eyes growing glassy. "*Ja*, I'm afraid that is true. I'm so sorry."

"It's not your fault," Lena said. "And Enzo has nothing wrong with him. It's not right, what they are doing!"

Enzo's face darkened with remorse. "They gave me a strange test but the translator was no good. I didn't understand what they wanted me to do."

Mutti put a comforting hand on his shoulder. "It's not your fault either. Lena is right. There is nothing wrong with you. Unfortunately, they are not wrong about me."

"What do you mean, they're not wrong about you?" Lena said. "They said you only had to go back because Enzo is too young to go alone."

"*Ja*," Mutti said. "That is true. But they also said I am not strong enough to work and I will become a burden to this country."

"They don't know what they're talking about," Lena said. And then, for the first time, she noticed the chalk *H* on Mutti's jacket, the white mark smeared like powder across the wool. A new flicker of fear quickened her already frantic breathing. "But . . . but you're fine. You had a difficult time on the ship, that's all. They can't send you back because you were seasick."

Mutti dropped her sorrow-filled gaze and shook her head. "*Nein, mein Liebling*," she said. "I didn't tell you because I didn't want you to worry. And I was hoping they wouldn't notice. I thought they would let us through."

Lena's eyes flooded. "You didn't tell us what? That you knew something was wrong?"

Mutti nodded. "A woman knows when her age is catching up to her. I've felt some discomfort here." She rested a heavy hand on her chest. "And some weakness. My heart is broken from missing your father."

Enzo put an arm around her. "You have been worrying too much," he said. "And taking care of us instead of yourself."

Tears spilled down Lena's cheeks. She knew that excruciating misery, that raw, hollow space inside her that only her father could fill. "But Mutti," she said, "grieving Vater doesn't mean you're sick. You'll get better with rest and food and the proper care. And Enzo is not feebleminded or whatever ridiculous name they called him. You need to stay in America. Both of you. You deserve to be here!"

"There is nothing we can do now," Mutti said. "We must do as they say or they will lock your brother away."

"Then Ella and I will go too," Lena said. "We can't stay here without you. We won't." But even as she said the words, she knew she couldn't leave. Ella came first.

Mutti shook her head, her mind made up. "*Nein,* you must stay. You have been accepted into this new world. You cannot throw away the opportunity to give our sweet Ella a better life."

Although Lena was relieved Mutti knew she had to stay and had not begged her to go back with them, it did nothing to ease her fear and anguish. "But Silas Wolfe doesn't know Ella and I are coming," she said. "What if he turns us away?"

"If he tries to do that," Mutti said, "you remind him that you are family. You tell him that you and Ella will take up less room and eat less food than your brother and I. You tell him you will work twice as hard as he thinks you can, and that he cannot turn you away or he will deal with me and your brother when we return." Despite the grief and worry in her eyes,

Mutti's voice was calm and firm, as if she were telling Lena how to roll out noodles or knead bread dough. "You must go to Virginia and start over with your daughter. Enzo and I will return to Germany. We will find jobs and save enough money to come back. We will try again as soon as we can."

"*Ja*," Enzo said. "And I will practice my English. Then we will join you in Virginia. If we already have family in America, it will make it easier for us to be accepted when we return. I know it will be hard, Lena, but it will help us more if you stay."

Lena wiped her face and nodded, trying to look strong. Enzo was right. Staying in America would benefit him and Mutti more than going back to Germany with them. And she could make more money working for Silas Wolfe than she could back home—*if* he took her in. But even if he refused, somehow, some way, she would find a way to give Ella a better life and help her family return. "I will send money," she said. "Enough to buy second-class tickets so you don't have to go through Ellis Island again."

Mutti dug her money pouch out from under her blouse, yanked on the string to break it, and started pushing it through the door. "Take this," she said. "You might need it."

Lena put her hand against the mesh to stop the pouch from coming through. "*Nein*, take mine." She untied the pouch from around her neck. "You will need it more than we will."

Mutti shook her head. "Keep it," she said. "For Ella."

"*Bitte*," Lena said. She looked at Enzo with pleading eyes. "You have to take both halves of the money. It will be all you have for a while."

"*Nein*," Enzo said. "Mutti is right. You need to keep half for Ella. I will find work as soon as I can."

With her eyes filling again, Lena retied the pouch around her neck. "Promise me you will write as soon as you can. I need to know where you are and that you're safe."

Mutti nodded, a raw wave of grief crumpling her features. "*Auf wiedersehen, mein Liebe* Lena and Ella."

Lena undid her shawl to let Ella down, then knelt beside her, gently holding her thin shoulders. "Say *auf wiedersehen* to *dein Onkel* Enzo and *Liebe* Oma," she said, her voice breaking.

Mutti got down on her knees, eye level with Ella, and mustered a shaky smile. "*Auf wiedersehen,* Ella."

Still sleepy, Ella lifted her tiny hand and moved her fingers in a half-hearted wave. "*Auf wiedersehen,*" she said in a soft, baby-doll voice. It was her first attempt at saying the words.

Lena kissed her cheek. "Good job, *mein süsses Mädchen*. My sweet girl," she said. "*Dein Onkel* and Oma love you so much. They're going to miss you."

"Don't forget me, Ella," Enzo said, sniffing.

"Please take care of each other," Lena said. "And come back as soon as you can."

Mutti got to her feet and held a wrinkled handkerchief under her nose. "Tell Silas Wolfe to take good care of you. If he doesn't, he will answer to me."

Lena picked up Ella and propped her on one hip, helpless to stop her tears. "I will." She put a hand on the mesh and Mutti did the same, pressing their palms together. Enzo put his hand over Mutti's, his long fingers touching Lena's.

"This isn't fair," Lena cried.

"Life isn't fair," Mutti said. "You learned that a long time ago. Now go. Start a new life in America with our precious Ella and make us proud. We will see you again soon."

"Do you promise?" Lena said.

Mutti nodded, her chin trembling. But she did not say the words.

Chapter 4

With her stomach in knots, Lena carried Ella through the teeming crowds, past the registry room to the currency exchange where hordes of immigrants milled about, buying train tickets and trading their foreign money for U.S. dollars. After exchanging what little money she had and returning it to the pouch around her neck, she headed toward what the officer had called the kissing post and the giant pillars he had mentioned, where Silas Wolfe would be waiting. She held her chin up and walked fast, pretending to know exactly what she was doing despite being terrified, heartbroken, trembling, confused, and starving, all at the same time. If one of the immigration officers stopped her to ask why she was alone, he'd surely think she was ill or insane. Then they'd send her to the Ellis Island hospital. Or worse, the Psychopathic Pavilion.

Before reaching the kissing post, she came to a row of vendors selling food and drinks, the handwritten menus above their counters in multiple languages. Red apples and golden pears overflowed in wicker baskets next to deep barrels of emerald-colored pickles and jars of hard-boiled eggs. The aroma of fried onions, boiled potatoes, and fresh bread made her stomach ache with hunger. She hadn't seen so much food in one place since before the war, even in the German stores.

Whispering a quiet thanks to Mutti for making her keep half the money, she took a bill from her pouch and stepped up to one of the vendors. A basket of pale-colored rolls sat on the counter next to a jar of eggs, a bin of pears, bottles filled with water, and chunks of cheese beneath a glass cloche. How she wished she could buy two of everything, but she needed to be careful with her money in case Silas Wolfe turned them away.

"I would like one roll and one piece of cheese, please," she said to the man behind the counter. "And one water."

"That'll be twelve cents," the man said.

She handed him the bill, hoping it would be enough. After handing her back a handful of coins, he put the roll and cheese in a paper bag and gave it to her, along with the water, and smiled the first genuine smile she'd seen since arriving on Ellis Island.

"Good luck," he said.

"Thank you," she said, doing her best to return his smile. It felt strange beneath her swollen eyes.

To her surprise, he picked up a pear and held it out to her. "For the little one," he said.

She hesitated, unsure. Did he want her to pay for the pear, or was he offering it for free?

"Please," he said. "Take it. She looks hungry."

A lump swelled in her throat, his kind gesture opening a tiny crack in her frightened, protective shell. Maybe they would be welcome here after all. Maybe there were more people in America like this man, and she and Ella would be all right. She had no idea what to do except thank him again and take the pear. Satisfied, he turned to the next customer.

Buoyed by the man's compassion, Lena found a less crowded spot on the other side of the vast room, opened the water bottle, and gave Ella a drink. After taking a few sips for herself, she set the bottle on the floor next to her feet and gave Ella the piece of cheese. Ella took a bite and grinned up at her mother, her eyes filled with so much gratitude it nearly broke Lena's heart.

"Is it good?" Lena said, smiling.

Ella nodded, chewing and content.

The roll was soft and white, not dark and chewy like the bread at home, but it smelled delicious. Lena tore off a piece and fed it to Ella, who opened her mouth like a little bird, then took a bite herself. Maybe it was because she'd been eating stringy beef and herrings for so long, or maybe it was because she was starving, but the roll was the best thing she'd tasted in a long time. In between Ella's bites of cheese, Lena fed her the pear, more of the roll, and gave her drinks of water. When Ella was full and the food was gone, she folded the paper bag and put it in her coat pocket.

Suddenly, a grizzled man in a black jacket approached. "Do you need work?" he asked.

Lena shook her head and put a protective arm around Ella, hoping he would go away.

"I have job openings in many places of employment," he said. "I can help you take care of your little girl."

"I have work," she said.

Without warning, he grabbed her hand and pressed a piece of paper into her palm, making her jump. "If you change your mind, come find me at the address on this pamphlet."

She dropped the pamphlet and hurried into the crowd, glancing over her shoulder to make sure he wasn't following her. Thankfully, he was nowhere to be seen. She slowed, relieved and hoping she'd lost him. Then she realized she'd left the water bottle behind and it was still half full. But if she went back for it, the man might think she was looking for him. And she needed to find Silas Wolfe. At least she and Ella had gotten enough nourishment to last a few more hours.

A nun emerged from the crowd of immigrants and pressed toward her.

"Are you alone, my child?" the nun said.

Lena nodded and kept moving.

The nun walked beside her, her black skirts rustling like curtains. "If you are in need of help," she said, "come to Our Lady of Grace in Hoboken." She held out a sheet of paper with the church's name and address.

Lena hesitated, then took the paper and stuffed it in her coat pocket, just in case. "Thank you," she said. "But I do not need help."

The nun slowed. "May God be with you, my child," she said before being swallowed up by the masses.

Finally, Lena reached the kissing post, where friends and family waited at the far end of the great hall, scanning the new arrivals for familiar faces, their eyes filled with nervous excitement. Some held posters with names: *Massimo Salvatore. Jacob Allen. Elijah Spielman.* Others stood on their tiptoes, raising their chins to look above heads and shoulders, anxious for the first glance of long-awaited relatives and friends. Elated shouts, happy greetings, and what seemed like a hundred different languages echoed off the high walls, the sense of joy and relief in the air so unlike the rest of Ellis Island.

A woman with two young children rushed past Lena and ran into the arms of a handsome man, sobbing with joy while the children watched with apprehension, as if their mother were hugging a stranger. Beside them, a barrel-chested man greeted a younger man with a tense nod, trying not to cry, then clapped him on the back and pulled him into his arms. A stick-thin woman wailed when she saw her husband, then collapsed into his waiting embrace. Men walked up to other men, shook hands in introduction, then proceeded toward the exit. When a young girl jumped into her father's arms, grief and loneliness squeezed Lena's heart. Everyone seemed to be finding the people they were looking for, all of them happy and excited to be in this new country. Everyone except her.

Mutti and Enzo were supposed to be with her, on the verge of starting a new life in America. They were supposed to be together when they met Silas Wolfe for the first time so Mutti could kindly ask him to take her and Ella in as well and convince him they would not be a burden. Instead, she was on her own, alone with a young child in an unfamiliar country, their entire future dependent on one person. Maybe she should have kept the pamphlet from the grizzled man in the black jacket, just in case.

Slowing as she neared the waiting Americans, she scanned the crowd, wondering which stranger would determine the next direction of her life, berating herself for not asking Mutti if she knew what Silas Wolfe looked like. For all she knew, he could have been the man in the fisherman's cap and overalls; the short man with the bowlegs who looked ready for a fight; the overweight man with the scraggly brown beard. Whoever Silas turned out to be, she prayed he was kind. But surely a man who helped distant relatives come to the U.S. had to be nice, didn't he? Unless he was a con man, like the man who pressed the pamphlet into her hand probably had been. Unless his job offers were a lie, and he was looking for free labor—or worse. Either way, whether he turned out to be merciful or a fraud, there was no telling what he'd do when he learned Enzo and Mutti were being deported. If he declined to sign the papers for Lena, she and Ella would be forced to find another way into the country, with very little money, no prospects, and no way home.

Of course, everything depended on her being able to find him. And him showing up. What if he'd changed his mind?

No. She was letting her imagination run away with her. Mutti said he would be there. He would take her in, and Lena would make him happy about the decision. She had no idea if she could do the job he had waiting for Enzo, but she could try.

And she would cook, clean, and take care of his children as well as Mutti would have. Then she realized she had no idea how many children he had. Four? Six? Ten?

Just then, a deep voice boomed over the mayhem.

"Conti?"

She searched the crowd for the source.

"Any y'all got the last name Conti?"

She stood on her tiptoes to see better.

"Conti?" the voice bellowed again.

Finally, she saw him—a man in a black hat and a coal-colored jacket standing head and shoulders above the crowd, his long beard the shade of dirty water. He called out again, his face stern, his forehead furrowed. It was hard to tell if he was concerned or angry.

She gathered her courage and made her way through the other immigrants, zigzagging between women and men and children. With her heart in her throat, she stepped out of the crowd and moved toward Silas Wolfe, the empty space between the Americans and hopeful newcomers like a great divide between the old world and the new, the air filled with judgment and nervous expectation. When she reached the other side, she stopped and raised her hand to get Silas Wolfe's attention. He saw her and moved in her direction, pushing his way through the multitude.

She glanced down at Ella, trying to breathe normally. "Here he comes," she whispered. "Be a good girl now."

When Silas Wolfe reached her, she took a step back. Up close, he was like a giant, the shoulders of his coal-colored jacket stretched to the seams, his trousers pulled tight across his thighs. Mutti said he was in his thirties, but he seemed older. Behind the dishwater beard, his straight nose and light blue eyes hinted at a man whose handsome features had been hardened by suffering. He looked poor, too—nothing like the rich, glamorous American she'd imagined.

"Y'all Conti?" he said. Gruffness edged his voice.

"*Ja,*" she said. "I mean, yes."

"Y'all speak English?"

She nodded. "Yes."

To her surprise, his way of talking sounded strange compared to the immigration officers. Maybe different parts of America spoke in different dialects, like the people in northern and southern Germany. Hopefully she would understand everything he said. Of course, that was the least of her worries.

"This ain't right," he said.

"What is not right?"

"I'm here to fetch Katrina and Enzo Conti. Y'all ain't them."

She forced a weak smile. "My name is Magdalena. My mother, Katrina, calls me Lena."

Annoyed, he looked behind her, scanning the crowd. "Where in tarnation is your mother?"

"She is not here."

His eyes drilled holes in her. "What y'all mean, she's not here? I sent her a ticket. Her boy too. You steal 'em?"

Of all possible reactions, she had not expected to be called a thief. Mutti always said you could tell a person was lying if they glanced away while talking, so Lena fixed her eyes on his, hoping she looked confident and trustworthy, though she was shaking inside. "No. I had my own ticket."

"Then where's your mother?"

Grief and panic blocked her throat. Not only did it break her heart to say the words, but she had no idea what he'd do when he heard them. "She and my brother, Enzo, are being sent back to Germany."

He scowled. "They do something wrong?"

She shook her head, feeling dizzier by the second. "No, they did not do anything wrong. They said Enzo is fee... feebleminded and my mother is ill. But it's not true." Her voice caught and she hesitated, trying not to cry again. She could not let him see her weakness. "They are both strong and healthy. And they will return to America as soon as they are able."

Anger flashed behind his eyes. "Who sent them back?"

"I am not sure. A doctor, I think."

"You get his name?"

"*Nein.* I mean, no. There is more than one."

"How come they ain't sending y'all back?"

"I am healthy. And I am a hard worker. You will see."

He glowered at her again. "I didn't spend all that money for a filthy, skinny girl with a hungry young'un. I paid for a man to do real work and a grown woman to look after my house and kids, not two more mouths to feed."

"I can do the work," she said. "And we will not make any problems. I will make a promise to you."

"Y'all ain't capable of patching a barn roof or working in a sawmill," he said.

"If that is what you need, I will try."

He let out a frustrated sigh, then glanced down at Ella. "Where's her daddy at?"

"He is dead."

"She born on the wrong side of the blanket?"

Lena furrowed her brow, confused.

"Outta wedlock," he said. "Did y'all have a wedding or not?"

At first, she lowered her eyes, her face growing warm. Then she gazed up at him again, refusing to let him see any fault in her. He had no way of learning the truth anyway. "He died before we were to get married."

He stared at her for what seemed like forever, thinking. She held her breath. Was he going to refuse to take her in because she'd had a child without being married? Then, without warning, he pushed past her toward the swarm of immigrants, plowing forward like a charging bull. Everyone stepped out of his way, parting to let him pass.

Lena stood rooted to the floor, unable to think or speak. He was abandoning her. He was leaving her and Ella to fend for themselves. Terror gripped her. Where would they go? What would they do? How would she feed Ella? Maybe she should go back and look for the nun. No, she would not give up that easily. Before she lost sight of Silas Wolfe, she rushed after him through the crowd, determined to make him give her a chance. To her surprise and relief, he stopped to look back at her, waiting for her to catch up.

A tiny spark of hope ignited inside her. Maybe he was going to take her and Ella in after all. Or maybe he could stop Mutti and Enzo from being deported. She followed him to the line at the registry office where he waited with his hands fisted, anger emanating from him like heat from a woodstove. Eyes down, heart skipping in her chest, she stood silently beside him, patting Ella's back to keep her quiet. Lena had hoped he would be kind, but Silas Wolfe seemed like a man to be feared.

Mutti probably thought her family would be safe as long as they were together, and if Silas turned out to be a bad person, at least they would already be in the United States and could start over without him. She'd had no idea Lena and Ella would be facing him alone. And how could she have? Then Lena had another thought and fear roiled in her stomach again. Maybe Silas was furious enough to send her back to Germany. Maybe he was going to refuse to sign her papers and demand she be deported.

She looked up at him, trying to decide if she should keep quiet or speak up. Sheer exhaustion made it hard to think clearly. But if he was sending her back, she had to ask for one small favor. Finally she tapped him on the arm. "Excuse me, Mr. Wolfe?"

He looked down at her.

"Will you please ask the men to put me on the same ship as my mother and brother so we do not have to search for each other in Germany?"

He wrinkled his brow. "Y'all *want* to be deported?"

Heat rose in her cheeks. "I thought you were going to send us back."

He grunted and gave her a disapproving look. "I reckon that would be dadgum stupid of me. I still need someone to cook and clean and help look after my young'uns. You can do them things, can't you?"

She nodded, relief washing over her. For the first time since she had set foot on American soil, the vise grip of tension inside her eased. "Thank you," she said. "I promise to work very hard."

"Damn right you will, 'cause I ain't no charity. And the first thing you're gonna do is get rid of them clothes and warsh up. You smell like something a bear left behind."

"They put . . ." She tried to think of the word for chemicals, but it escaped her. "They sprayed us to get rid of lice."

He shook his head in disgust. "Lord almighty. I'm starting to think I warn't right in the head when I agreed to this."

She opened her mouth to tell him again he wouldn't be sorry but decided against it. If she annoyed him, he might change his mind about letting her stay. While they waited in line, she stole glances up at him, studying the broken veins on his cheeks and the puffiness beneath his eyes. His plank-thick hands were rough and raw, his knuckles stained and worn. Like her father, he had the look of a man who had worked hard all his life. Unfortunately, he did not seem to have her father's gentle heart.

When it was finally their turn, he stepped up to the station and slammed his fist on the counter. "Y'all wanna tell me why two of my kin's being sent back to Germany?"

The young clerk gave him a stern look but seemed unfazed by his outburst. He'd apparently seen all manner of behaviors at his post. "Name?" he said in a bored voice.

"Mine or theirs?" Silas boomed.

"Theirs," the clerk said.

Silas turned to Lena. "Tell him."

She did as she was asked.

"And you are?" the clerk said.

"Magdalena Conti, Katrina Conti's daughter."

"And you arrived with your mother and brother today?"

"Yes. We were on the SS *Hermannsburg*."

"What reason was given for their denied entry?" the clerk said.

"They said my brother is feebleminded and my mother is ill. But that is not true. They are healthy and able to work."

The clerk turned his attention to Silas. "Well, there you have it," he said. "Now you know why they're being deported."

Silas practically growled at him. "Listen here, you little whippersnapper, don't be sitting on no high horse with me." He jabbed a finger in Lena's direction. "She says her family's right as rain, so there ain't no need to not let 'em in!"

The clerk shrugged. "Sorry, but I don't make the rules. And I'm inclined to believe the immigration inspectors' opinions over this young woman's."

"Then how 'bout letting me talk to somebody who does make the rules," Silas snarled.

Behind the clerk, two uniformed guards came forward, observing Silas.

"I suggest you calm down, sir," the clerk said, "or the gentlemen behind me will detain you until you do."

"I ain't calming down," Silas said. "I paid for two goldurn tickets 'cause I need work from them people. So I reckon I got some say in what happens here."

One of the guards moved closer to the counter. "You have no say whatsoever concerning who is or is not allowed into the United States of America," he said in a threatening tone. "Now if you have no further business here, I suggest you move along."

"What about my damn money?" Silas said. "Y'all need to give me a refund if my kin's gonna be sent home."

The clerk chuckled under his breath. "That's impossible," he said.

Silas pounded his fist on the counter again. "What y'all mean, 'impossible'? I want my money back!"

"Sir," the guard said, "you need to step away from the counter and be on your way or—"

"Or what?" Silas barked. "Y'all gonna throw me in jail? You're all the same, you low-down government types and your bureaucrat bullshit. You're nothing but a bunch of no-good thieves, taking whatever the hell y'all want even when it ain't yours! And now you're telling me you can take my hard-earned money and I don't get nothing in return? Who in damnation do you think you *are*?"

The guard moved around the counter, ready to apprehend Silas.

Lena stepped between them. "Wait!" she said. "He needs to sign my papers." She dug out her inspection card, put it on the counter, and looked up at Silas. He was red-faced and breathing hard. "Please. We have nowhere else to go."

Silas locked eyes with the guard as if trying to decide whether or not to do battle. Then, finally, his breathing slowed. He swore under his breath and nodded.

The guard gave him a warning glare. "I suggest you sign what you need to sign, then move along before I change my mind about arresting you."

The clerk examined Lena's card and rifled through a stack of papers until he found the one with her name on it—a single sheet that would admit her and Ella into America. Then he pushed it across the counter and offered Silas a pen.

Chapter 5

After a short ferry ride from Ellis Island to Hoboken, New Jersey, Lena walked fast to keep up with Silas on the way to the train station, her coat over one arm, Ella still strapped to her chest. When oncoming pedestrians saw Silas approaching, they stepped aside to give him room, making it easy for Lena to follow in his wake. Still, despite her nerves and exhaustion, she wanted him to slow down so she could take in the bustling town, the trolleys, motorcars, and horse-drawn buggies that packed the noisy, muddy streets, and the people of all sizes and shapes who filled the sidewalks. Everything was so different here—the tall wooden buildings and colorful vehicles; the women in slim, silky skirts and delicate pointed heels; the men in fitted suits and straw hats; the honking horns; the smells of exhaust and cement. Back home, the buildings were made of stucco or stone; people walked everywhere or drove horse-drawn wagons and sputtering motorbikes; the air smelled of baking bread and frying sausage; the women wore aprons and peasant dresses; and the men saved their suits for Sunday church.

When she saw bright-colored signs on buildings and fences

and telephone poles, she tried to sound out the words, eager to learn anything about America that might be useful in the future. One sign advertised a brown liquid in a glass bottle with the strange word Coca-Cola written on the side. Another pictured a red-and-white can that read Campbell's Pea Soup. And a black-and-white sign showed a woman making coffee below the words Morning Sip Coffee.

With every new picture of food, her stomach cramped with hunger. The half a roll she'd eaten earlier was not nearly enough to sustain her. And surely Ella was getting hungry again too. After Silas's encounter with the guard at the registry office, he'd purchased two boxes from a vendor whose sign read BOXED LUNCH. Lena had no idea what was inside the boxes or if one of them was meant for her and Ella, but she hoped she'd find out soon because, along with everything else, the lack of food made her weak and shaky.

After briefly slowing to study a sign featuring irons and fans and teakettles, she realized Silas had disappeared along the crowded sidewalk. A rush of panic shot through her. How had she managed to lose track of the biggest man she'd ever seen? Then, to her relief, she spotted him half a block away and hurried to catch up, trying to avoid bumping into anyone along the way. The last thing she needed was to get lost in a strange city. And, she reminded herself, now that she lived in America, there would be plenty of time to see and learn about everything. Keeping up with Silas was essential at the moment, no matter how interesting the new world might be.

Then they turned a corner and a sign with a flashing light made her pause. She silently sounded out the words, unsure what they all meant.

AMERICAN EUGENICS SOCIETY
Some people are born to be a burden on the rest.
This light flashes every 15 seconds. Every 15 seconds,

> $100 of your money goes for the care of someone with bad heredity, such as the insane, feebleminded, criminals, and others.

Next to that, another sign read:

> UNFIT HUMAN TRAITS:
> Feeblemindedness, criminality, insanity, alcoholism, and many other defects run in families and are inherited in exactly the same way as color in guinea pigs. If all marriages were eugenic, we could breed out most of this unfitness in three generations.

There was that word again: *feebleminded*. Before she could make sense of what she was reading, Silas called to her from the sidewalk in front of the station, pulling her attention away from the strange signs.

"You fixing to make the train or stand there gawking all day?" he shouted. "There ain't another one till morning!"

She walked faster. Waiting another night to reach her destination was not something she wanted to experience. Ella needed to be fed, bathed, and put to bed. And Lena couldn't wait to get out of her rank clothes, take a bath, and get some rest herself. Like Mutti always said, everything looked better after a good night's sleep.

Mutti.

Fresh tears filled Lena's eyes. Mutti was supposed to be with her and Ella, and Enzo too, marveling at all the different sights and sounds. Instead, they were locked up like criminals inside the inspection station on Ellis Island, waiting to be put on the next ship home. It was beyond unfair. And who knew how long it would be before they saw each other again? Six months? A year? Two years?

No. Not that long. They would all be together again soon.

Surely it would only be a few months before she saved enough money to buy their tickets. By then, Enzo would have learned enough English to pass the immigration tests, and Mutti would be healthy again. And certainly Silas would agree to send for them a second time, especially if there was no need for him to pay their way. Then they'd easily be accepted into America, because Lena and Ella were already there. She had to believe it. Otherwise, the thought of Ella growing up without her uncle to play games with, or her Oma to teach her how to make perfect plum tortes, sauerbraten, and Christmas stars out of yellow straw, was too much to bear. Missing her father was hard enough.

Pushing the worrisome thoughts from her mind, she caught up to Silas and followed him into the train station, where hundreds of passengers filled wooden benches or waited in line at the ticket window, holding the hands of young children and carrying luggage and boxes and bags. Luckily, Silas had purchased their tickets on Ellis Island so they were able to skip the lines. As she followed him across the room, people stared up at him, amazed by his size, then studied her with curious eyes. Some of them glared at her with disgust, as if she polluted the very air they breathed.

She glanced down at her handmade dress and high leather shoes. They were out of style and smelled bad, but at least they looked fairly clean. Had people been staring at her out on the sidewalks too? Maybe she'd been too distracted by the advertisements to notice. Or maybe, now that she was inside, everyone could smell the chemicals from the delousing plant. Then she remembered the oil, smeared and tangled in her hair. It had to look dreadful. Shame and anger burned her face. Hopefully, someday she'd have fashionable clothes and the latest hairstyle, but there was nothing she could do about it now. And these people had no idea what she and Ella had been through; otherwise, they might have shown compassion instead of scorn.

Then again, except for the kind vendor who had given Ella a pear, Lena had not experienced a lot of kindness in America so far.

Thankfully they were getting close to the exit leading out to the platform, where she hoped to avoid more prying eyes. Silas, who seemed equally anxious to get out of the station, ducked his head, hurried through one side of the double door, and kept going. She rushed forward to catch the door before it closed all the way, but a man in a suit stepped in front of her and she stopped short.

"Why don't you go back where you came from!" he said. "We don't need the likes of you bringing your filthy blood into our country!" Then he spat at her feet.

She took a step back, her heart thumping hard against her ribs. Was that why everyone was staring at her? Because they could tell she was an immigrant? She wrapped protective arms around Ella and looked over the man's shoulder, searching the platform for Silas. He was nowhere to be seen. Suddenly someone yanked hard on her satchel, trying to pull it off her back. She spun around, ready for a struggle. A boy in short pants and suspenders sneered up at her.

"Dirty immigrant," he said. "Dirty, smelly immigrant." Then he laughed and ran away.

She turned to face the man again, gearing up to go around him. To her surprise, Silas was behind him, bent over and holding the door open, his mouth next to the man's ear.

"Y'all need to be on your way," Silas said.

The man smirked and turned to face him, ready for a confrontation. But when his gaze landed on Silas's broad chest and traveled up to his head, his eyes went wide and he hurried away.

Silas regarded Lena. "The train's waiting."

Before she could thank him, he turned and headed toward the tracks. She followed on shaking legs, trying not to think about what might have happened if he had not come back for her. Was this how it was going to be? Would everyone tell her to go back to where she had come from? If only she could.

Out on the platform, the sooty smell of burning coal and hot iron filled the air, and a massive black engine chugged on the tracks, smoke billowing out of its stack in gray waves. Porters carried luggage, couples kissed, and families said goodbye. Men holding their hats on their heads hurried toward the train, and women in fancy clothes stepped carefully onto the passenger cars. Silas waited by one of the cars for Lena, then lumbered up the steps and ducked through the narrow door. Before they could find a seat, a whistle shrieked, the train lurched forward, and the car began crawling along the tracks. The other passengers stared up at them as they made their way down the aisle, a hundred pairs of eyes scrutinizing, judging, gaping. Lena avoided their gazes, afraid someone would yell or spit at her again.

When they finally found two seats together, Silas let her in first to sit next to the window. She slid in, sat down, and put her satchel on the floor, relieved to be off her feet. Then she unwrapped Ella from the shawl. Ella squirmed and stretched, happy to be free of her binding. Silas took off his jacket and sat down, his shoulders and arms spilling over the armrests.

He looked as miserable as Lena felt. Clearly, he was angry about Mutti and Enzo being deported, but there was something else bothering him that she couldn't quite put her finger on. He seemed almost as uncomfortable as she did. But that made no sense. His great-grandparents had moved from Germany to America years ago, and he had been born here. Of course, she'd heard rumors about the anti-German sentiment pervading the United States since the war, but he was a natural-born citizen, an American. Surely that made all the difference. Maybe he was embarrassed to be seen with her and Ella. Maybe he didn't want anyone thinking he was an immigrant too. Then she had another thought. Maybe his immense size made him uncomfortable, especially in the narrow passenger car.

With the train fully underway, she moved Ella to one side of her lap and leaned toward the window to give him more room. In the enclosed space, the stench of chemicals seeping out of their clothes and hair was stronger than ever. Desperate for relief, she stood, placed Ella on the seat, and pulled open the train window. Then she lifted Ella up to the fresh air and took deep, cleansing breaths. The outside smelled of burning coal, but it was better than the noxious fumes inside the car.

"Y'all ain't sickly, are you?" Silas said. "I got no use for somebody who can't work."

She shook her head, hoping he wouldn't notice the sheen of sweat on her forehead. "No," she said, "we only need some air." After taking a few more deep breaths, she pushed the window closed, leaving it open just a crack, and sat down again. "How long will we be on the train?"

"I reckon about seven hours," he said. "Then another hour or so up the road a piece to get to Wolfe Holler."

She groaned inside. How were she and Ella supposed to sit in their filthy clothes in this cramped space for seven hours? It felt nearly as awful as steerage. And if she didn't eat something soon, she'd either get sick or pass out.

As if reading her mind, Silas handed her one of the boxes he'd purchased on Ellis Island. She nearly cried with relief. Whatever was inside, she and Ella would eat it and be thankful. Before she could untie the string around the box, Silas pulled two bottles of brown liquid out of his jacket pocket and handed one to her. Like the bottles on the advertisement outside the train station, the side read Coca-Cola.

"Thank you," she said, and tried to open it. The top was too tight.

He took the bottle, pulled off the cap, and handed it back to her. Then he opened his and took a long drink.

She took a small sip. It was sweet and strange and bubbly. And she liked it. A lot. She let Ella have a sip. At first, Ella puckered her lips and wrinkled her nose, but then she swallowed and wanted more.

Silas opened his box and unwrapped two pieces of pale bread filled with something that looked like sliced meat. He pointed at hers. "Y'all got the same. It's a ham and pickle sandwich. Might want to save half for later."

She opened her box and picked up the food. The bread was soft and white like the roll they'd eaten earlier, and the meat was thin and pink. Whatever it was, it smelled delicious. She broke off a small piece and fed it to Ella, then took a bite for herself. It tasted even better than the roll.

"Is it good, *mein Schätzelein*?" she said to Ella.

Ella nodded and opened her little mouth for more.

When they'd eaten half the sandwich, with most of it going to Ella, Lena rewrapped the other half and put it in the box for later. After sharing a little more Coca-Cola with Ella, she leaned back in her seat, sighing in relief. She felt better already. Hopefully Ella did too.

While Ella drifted off to sleep on her lap, Lena tried to imagine what their future might be like: the house they'd be living in, the people they'd meet, the opportunities that might come their way. She wanted to be strong for her little girl, which meant looking to the future instead of dwelling on her pain and heartache, instead of grieving her father and wishing Mutti and Enzo were there too. She needed to reach deep inside for the hope she had felt the day they left Germany, and the confidence that they would find a better life. At the same time, her mind felt fragmented, filled with the disjointed, jolting images of the day—the families being torn apart, the exhaustive physical inspections and intelligence tests, the horrible delousing plant, the man spitting at her feet, the little boy calling her a dirty immigrant. Then she had another thought, and darkness clouded her mind again. What if the Americans in Silas's town told her to go back to where she came from? What if they called her and Ella names and never accepted them? Yes, Silas's family had been accepted as immigrants, but that had been before the war, before Germany had pledged its support to Austria-Hungary in their fight against the Allies, before everyone blamed Germany for the conflict.

Maybe she should say they were full-blooded Italian and she'd lived in her father's tiny village most of her life until moving to Germany a few months ago. After all, she *had* been born in Italy, and her last name *was* Italian. The illusion could work, as long as no one tried having a conversation with her in that language or picked up on her heavy German accent.

She glanced at Silas. How she wanted to ask him about his home, what it was like, if the people living there were nice. But he was leaning back in his seat, his forehead pinched like he was still in a foul mood. It would have to wait. She would find out soon enough. And there was nothing she could do to change anything anyway.

Reminding herself to stay calm, she watched the strange-looking city lumber past the passenger car window. Tall buildings and busy streets filled the view, then wooden warehouses gave way to slanted sheds with makeshift roofs made of tattered blankets and worn rugs. To her shock and confusion, people in ripped jackets, dirty shoes, and shabby hats stood gathered around open fires, cooking and talking. Others went in and out of the ramshackle sheds while children in filthy clothes played nearby. Something cold and hard pressed against her chest. Why did the people near the tracks look like the poverty-stricken Germans she'd seen living in streets and alleyways? Was the American dream a lie?

Eventually, the city gave way to small towns, open fields, rolling mountains, and green forests, every mile revealing more of the countryside. She craned her neck to look at lakes and rivers and bridges, at huge red barns surrounded by crops and herds of cows and horses and sheep. Everything looked so different here, so big and far apart. In Germany, some farms were located within village limits, their barns and manure pits nestled between houses and other buildings. And the farmers' pastures and fields, as little as they were, were on the outskirts of town. She'd heard about the wide-open spaces in America, but she had no idea the land would be so vast.

Over the next few hours, she fell into a mind-numbing pattern of staring out the window alternating with fitful dozing, then waking with a start when Ella stirred or someone coughed, her heart hammering until she realized she was on a train in America, not in the filthy bowels of a ship filled with sick and frightened immigrants. Relief washed over her, followed by a hollow draft of grief when she remembered Mutti and Enzo were not with her. Trying to remind herself how lucky she and Ella were to be there, she told herself she was paving the way for her mother and brother to come to America too, and that she and Ella would be the first of her immediate family to settle in the land of the free. Someday, her grandchildren and great-grandchildren would look back and be grateful for her courage. And Enzo's grandchildren too. She wanted to believe those things with all her heart. At the same time, she wished more than anything in the world that she were headed home with Mutti and Enzo.

As the miles passed, Silas dozed off and on too, his head back and his mouth open, snoring. Whenever he got up and walked to stretch his legs, she did the same, letting Ella toddle down the aisle in front of her. They spoke little to each other, despite the fact that she had so many questions about where they were going and what life in America was really like. The only thing she could do was wait and see—and pray she would find at least one friend in her new country.

After what felt like a hundred years, the train finally reached

Virginia. When Silas ate the other half of his sandwich, Lena and Ella ate theirs too. Several hours later, when the train crossed a high trestle over a raging river, it started to pour outside, the trees and telephone poles like smudges of green and brown blurring past the streaked windows. In the distance, mountains sloped down toward the riverbed as far as the eye could see. Then the train slowed and a stone station came into view. A sign on the platform read: HARRISONBURG, VA.

"This here's where we get off," Silas said.

Nerves prickled across Lena's skin. In the next few minutes, she would have to stand up and get off the train. That was it. There was no reason to think beyond that. No reason to wonder and worry about what would happen next, because she was powerless to change it. While she rewrapped Ella inside the shawl, laughter and conversation droned in her ears along with the clacking of the iron wheels and the pounding of the engine. When the train slowed and jerked to a stop, letting out a blast of steam, the other passengers stood and gathered their belongings, eager to exit after the long journey. Silas remained seated during the chaos and Lena did the same, pointing at different things out the window and trying to act excited for Ella's sake. Men in waistcoats and straw hats, children in summer whites, and women in traveling dresses crowded the platform. What would they do when they saw her and Ella, an immigrant and her baby with smelly peasant dresses and oily hair? Then she realized that because of the rain, everyone looked wet and miserable. Maybe no one would notice them. She could only hope.

When the majority of the passengers had disembarked, Silas stood and put on his jacket. Lena did the same, then gathered her satchel and followed him off the train. The outside air felt hot and moist, like stepping into a steaming bath. Even the drizzle felt warm. Several passengers eyed her and Silas briefly, then moved out of their way and hurried toward the station, anxious to get out of the rain. Other passengers waved and called out to waiting friends and relatives.

On the other side of the train depot, horses, wagons, and noisy motorcars filled a muddy road, and rain-soaked pedestrians and bicyclists hurried along a plank sidewalk. Silas made his way toward a grassy area filled with farm trucks and motorbikes, bicycles and tractors, wagons and horse-drawn buggies. Blinking against the rain and trying to keep up, she followed him into the parking area, wondering which vehicle was his. To her surprise, he stopped beside a black truck with rusty fenders and a pile of wet straw in the beat-up bed, which was partially enclosed with wooden slats. He opened the passenger door and told her to get in. She had to admit she'd imagined him owning a shiny motorcar like the ones she'd seen in New Jersey, but at least it was better than a horse and wagon. Not that she wanted to ride in a fancy automobile, but it made her wonder about his home. Hopefully it was nicer than the ramshackle sheds she'd seen on the side of the railroad tracks. Taking off her wet satchel, she grabbed the truck door and started to heave herself up, one hand beneath Ella. Silas tapped her arm and pointed to a metal step. She put her foot on it and climbed in. Grateful to be out of the rain, she wiped Ella's face and pushed her own damp hair away from her forehead and cheeks, the runny, watered-down oil like grease on her skin. Now that their clothes were wet, the chemical smell was nearly overwhelming. She felt like a drowned rat covered in rancid lard.

After turning the crank on the front of the truck to start it, Silas opened the driver's side door, took off his hat, tossed it on the bench seat, and climbed inside. His knees pressed against the dashboard, his chest was mere inches from the steering wheel, and he sat with his back hunched and his head forward. He wiped the rain from his face with one wide hand, then wrestled the stick shift into reverse. The truck lurched backward, making Lena jump. Oblivious, he wrenched the stick shift again and pushed the gas. The truck lurched forward, almost hitting the back of a nearby wagon, then swung around toward the exit. Lena hugged Ella to her chest and held on for dear life.

After steering the truck out of the lot, Silas drove along the muddy road, weaving around puddle-filled ruts, honking at slow horses, and swerving to miss wayward children. While he drove, he cranked a lever next to the steering wheel, which made a blade wipe away the rain from the front window.

As they traveled through the town, Lena wondered what Enzo and Mutti would have thought about everything she was seeing. Then she realized she and Enzo would have been riding in the straw-filled back while Mutti sat where she was sitting now. Grief and homesickness washed over her again. Were they still locked in that cage, or had they already boarded a ship? How long would it be before they wrote to say they were safe and sound back in Germany? Would Mutti be all right on the trip? Sorrow constricted inside her chest. But as the buildings grew farther and farther apart and they made their way out of town, past clapboard houses and cabins set back in the woods, little by little, determination overpowered her anguish. Someday soon, Mutti and Enzo would be going down this same road, seeing the same things she was seeing, on their way to their new home in America. She would make it happen; she was sure of it. And no one would stop her.

By the time they reached the farthest outskirts of town, the rain had quit and Silas stopped cranking the window blade. The truck lumbered over a rutted road and headed toward mountains covered with evergreens, maple, and oak trees. The road bent left, came to a spur leading to the right, then went down to a ford across a gravel river bottom. Silas gunned the engine and the truck lunged across the stony stream, then climbed a narrow dirt road toward a sloping field across from high cliffs. In the distance, a locomotive crawled behind a crew of men laying railroad tracks, and cattle and other livestock grazed on stony foothills.

Higher up the mountain, they drove next to steep, rocky drop-offs, along craggy gravel roads, and through black woods set so close that the light within looked green. A horse-drawn wagon of fresh cut logs headed downhill past them, the wagon drivers waving hello. In some places, especially when it felt like they were driving straight up a cliff, Lena held Ella tight, certain they were going to flip over backward. Ella, on the other hand, giggled when the truck hit the biggest bumps, tossing them around in their seats.

Every few miles or so, they passed houses and barns and sheds, grouped two or three together like tiny, haphazard towns. Children in worn clothing played barefoot in front yards or ran to the edge of the road to wave. Women in aprons and old-fashioned dresses hung clothes on lines or pulled buckets of water from dug wells. Old men and old women smoked pipes and pumped butter churns on front porches, watching them drive by with wizened eyes. To Lena's disbelief, some of the houses looked like animal sheds with broken windows and patchwork roofs. And a lot of the people looked tired and poor, resembling the people beside the railroad tracks.

Apprehension vibrated inside her, making her feel drained and sick. If Silas lived in a wooden shed and had no money, everything she and her family had gone through was for nothing—selling everything they owned, the harrowing journey across the ocean, being separated from each other. Granted, most of the children she'd seen looked happy and well fed, but where were their shoes? And why were all the houses and barns made of logs or weathered wood, not stucco and stone like back home? Did Silas live in these mountains or were they on their way to another town?

She leaned back in the seat and let her shoulders drop, trying to keep her imagination from running away with her. Surely a man who could afford two ocean liner tickets and pay someone to take care of his children had money and lived in a sturdy, well-tended house. *His children.* Between missing her family and the numerous new sights and sounds, she'd forgotten about the children. Hopefully they were well behaved and would not tell her and Ella to go back where they came from.

Farther up the mountain, Silas steered the truck across a wooden bridge with a multitiered waterfall on one side and a fast-running stream on the other. Praying they'd reach his village soon, Lena grew hopeful that the end of the journey was near when they passed a white church on one side of a narrow river, and what looked like a group of houses and barns on the other. When she saw a building with the words POST OFFICE above the door, she took note of where it was located. She had no idea how long a letter took to travel across the ocean, but if the post office was close to Silas's house, she could check the mail every day. And as soon as she heard from Mutti, she would write back, hopefully with a little money tucked inside the envelope. But then the post office and all signs of civilization disappeared and they drove into wilderness again. And the higher up the mountain they went, the narrower and rockier the roads grew.

Just when it seemed like they'd never stop, Silas wrenched the stick shift into low and turned onto a dirt road running between thick rows of spruce trees. Less than a minute later, the trees fell away on one side, revealing a panoramic view of mountain ridges stretching for miles in all directions, like the blue humps of a thousand sleeping giants. In the hills and valleys below, rooftops and chimneys dotted the landscape, huddled here and there between trees and winding footpaths.

Up ahead, tucked within the mountains, a hand-hewn cabin with a massive rock chimney and a front porch on stilts sat on a grassy slope edged by soaring pines, mountain laurel, oak, walnut, and white birch trees. Off to one side of the weather-bleached house, brown chickens roamed beneath a grape arbor and a cluster of apple trees. A hog pen and chicken coop sat beside a wide timber barn, where two mules and a trio of brown cows grazed inside a split-rail fence. On the other side of the house, three clapboard sheds surrounded a fenced garden, and a rocky stream rushed down the grassy slope, ran beneath a small shack, and came out the other side.

Lena breathed a sigh of relief. Silas's home was simpler and more remote than she had expected—if she was being honest, it looked nothing like the mansion she'd pictured—but it looked spacious and sturdy, with a roof made of tin, not blankets or rugs. And obviously he knew how to grow food and raise chickens, which seemed like a good sign.

Silas turned off the narrow road, took a dirt drive up to the middle of the slope, and parked the truck. With some effort, he extracted himself from behind the steering wheel, then went around front and opened the passenger door. Lena put an arm around Ella, grabbed her satchel, and got out. After being in crowded spaces for so long—first steerage, then Ellis Island and the delousing plant, the ferry and the train—the wide-open sky and endless mountains felt like breathing for the first time. In a strange yet familiar way, the view reminded her of the hills surrounding her hometown. And the air was filled with the smell of pine, like it always was on those high, winding trails she used to hike. Waves of homesickness tightened her throat again.

"We need to get inside," Silas said, startling her. "I got chores waiting."

She blinked back the moisture in her eyes and turned toward him, but he was already heading up the slope toward the cabin.

"At least our new home is beautiful," she whispered to Ella, who squirmed in the shawl and whined to get down. "Shhhh, I'll let you down soon." She kissed Ella's forehead and followed Silas toward the house.

A hand-carved sign beneath the eaves spelled out WOLFE HOLLOW FARM. Under the porch, neatly stacked firewood filled the area, along with a half dozen wooden barrels. Shovels, rakes, and rusty saws hung on part of the rock foundation, and bright patches of black-eyed Susans ran along both sides of the porch steps. Now that they were closer, Lena noticed shifting stones in the foundation, crooked patches on the roof, and strips of gray wood nailed here and there over the outer walls of the house, which looked like they were made of wood and dried mud. Maybe Silas's home was not as sturdy as she thought—not that she could change anything now. At least it was not a shed. And besides, she was determined to make the best of things no matter what.

Suddenly the front door banged open and two children ran out to look over the porch railing. In worn overalls and bare feet, the boy was tall and lanky, with dark blond hair cropped close to his head. The girl wore a faded blue dress with a ragged hem that fell just above her dirty knees, her scrawny legs and bare feet pale as bone. Tattered strips of yellow cloth held the ends of her white-blond braids. They looked to be around nine or ten years old.

"Daddy!" the children shouted. "You're back!" They hurried down the porch steps and ran across the grass toward their father.

Silas put a hand on the girl's shoulder, drew her in for a quick hug, and patted the boy's head. Lena moved closer, trying to look friendly and praying Ella would stop fussing. She had no idea what had happened to the children's mother, but she recognized the grief and suffering in their eyes. And it had to be difficult having a stranger show up to take care of you, especially a stranger with oily hair and foul-smelling clothes.

The boy saw her first. When he stopped short and his smile faltered, Lena's heart dropped. She was unwelcome here too. Then, to her relief, he smiled again, a warm, genuine smile that lit up his blue eyes. Silas and the girl turned to face her, but unlike the boy, the girl frowned and moved closer to her father, studying Lena suspiciously. They were beautiful children, but something she couldn't place troubled their features. Surely losing their mother had forced them to grow up too fast, as the cruelty of the world often did, but what she sensed in them seemed like something else. Or maybe her own insecurities had risen closer to the surface.

"This here's Miss Conti," Silas said. "She'll be looking after y'all."

"You didn't tell us there was a baby," the girl said.

"Didn't know," Silas said.

"I thought she was your older cousin," the boy said. "She ain't old."

"They's been a change a plans," Silas said.

"Where's the other one?" the girl said. "The boy?"

"Couldn't come," Silas said.

"Why not?" the boy said.

"Y'all ain't got no need to know that," Silas said. "What matters is we got somebody to help out around here." He directed his attention to Lena. "The one with all the questions is Jack Henry, and the one hiding here by me is our . . . my oldest, Bonnie."

If Lena were to judge the ages of the children by height, she would have sworn the boy was older. "Hello," she said, trying to sound pleasant. "It is very nice to meet you." She put a loving hand on Ella. "This is my daughter, Ella."

"Y'all talk funny," Bonnie said. "And you look like something the cat drug in."

"Mind your manners," Silas said, his voice stern. "Your kin came to these hills from Germany and this here girl did too. I ain't gonna tell you again to respect your elders."

"Yes, sir," Bonnie said, hanging her head.

"It is all right," Lena said. "I am sure I sound strange to them."

Silas frowned. "No, it ain't all right. I expect my children to be mannerly. And if you're gonna work for me, I expect y'all to follow the rules of my house."

Lena lowered her gaze. She needed to remember she was

there to take care of the house and children, to work hard and make enough money to send for Mutti and Enzo. "I'm sorry."

To her relief, Silas turned his attention to Jack Henry. "Y'all run into any hitches while I was gone?"

"No, sir," Jack Henry said. "I kept the animals fed and the cows milked. Bonnie took care of the house and gathered the eggs every morning."

"Anyone come nosing around?"

Jack Henry nodded. "The sheriff did, just like you said he would."

Silas's face went dark. "Did y'all hide like I told you?"

"'Course we did, Daddy," Bonnie said, looking up with eager-to-please eyes. "We heard his motorcar coming up the drive so we hid before he even made it to the porch."

Alarm quickened in Lena's chest. If memory served her right, the word *sheriff* meant someone who worked with *die polizei*. Why on earth were the children being told to hide from the police?

"He didn't see y'all running to the shed?" Silas said.

Jack Henry glanced at Bonnie, suddenly nervous.

"No, sir," Bonnie said.

"What are y'all not telling me?" Silas said.

"Nothing," Jack Henry said.

"Hogwash," Silas said. "I know fibbing when I see it. 'Fess up."

"We didn't hide in the shed," Bonnie said. "We hid in the 'tater hole."

Jack Henry shot her a panicked look.

She shrugged and mouthed, *Sorry.*

"Why in the damn hell did you do that?" Silas said.

"Sheriff Dixon was getting close to the house and . . ." Jack Henry said. He put his hands in his pockets and looked at the ground.

"And what?" Silas said.

"I reckoned meeting him at the door with a rifle would scare him off," Jack Henry said.

Anger hardened Silas's features. "Damn it all! How many times I got to tell you, guns ain't gonna do nothing but bring more trouble. We got guns to put food on the table, not for fighting and killing!"

"Yes, sir," Jack Henry said, scuffing his foot in the dirt.

Silas grabbed his chin and lifted his face, forcing him to look up. "You reckon you can shoot a man? 'Cause it ain't nothing like shooting a possum."

Jack Henry shook his head, the bottom half of his face squished inside his father's massive hand.

"You kill somebody, they'll throw your ass in jail," Silas said. "You kill *the sheriff* and they'll lynch you first and ask questions later, understand?"

Jack Henry nodded. "I remembered what you said about guns, 'cept I did it in a fever and it was too late by then. That's why we had to get in the 'tater hole."

Silas let go of his chin, sighing heavily. "I reckon what's done is done. But y'all got lucky this time. You do that again, I'll get the hickory switch, you hear?"

Jack Henry nodded a second time. Bonnie nodded too, glancing at her brother with a sympathetic frown.

"How long was Sheriff Dixon lurking around?" Silas said.

"We ain't sure," Bonnie said. "We stayed hiding for a good long time, until we reckoned for sure he'd be gone."

"Anybody else come around?" Silas said. "Any folks you ain't seen before?"

Bonnie and Jack Henry shook their heads.

Silas rubbed a hand over his forehead as if rearranging his thoughts. "Good," he said, more to himself than anyone else. "That's good."

While Bonnie and Jack Henry's shoulders relaxed, unease gnawed at Lena's insides. She started to ask why the children had to hide but stopped. Annoying Silas a second time before she had even set foot in his house was probably a bad idea. And there was nothing she could do about it anyway. Somehow, some way she'd find the answers, but for now she needed to keep quiet. Not to mention she and Ella were desperate for a bath and a good night's rest.

"I need to get out of these good clothes so I can check the barn," Silas said. "Bonnie, stoke the stove for hot water." He jerked a thumb at Lena and Ella. "These two are in need of a good scrubbing."

Despite the stench not being her fault, embarrassment warmed Lena's cheeks. She didn't want the children to think she and Ella always smelled. At the same time, she was relieved she wouldn't have to ask about taking a bath. "Our hair and all of our clothing were sprayed," she said. "I will need to wash it all."

Silas let out another loud sigh, then addressed Bonnie again. "Give her one of your mother's dresses. And you know where the baby clothes are. Then put their clothes in the warsher and fetch 'em some vittles."

"Yes, sir," Bonnie said.

Silas gave Lena a quick, hesitant nod, then trudged toward the cabin, went up the porch steps, and disappeared inside. Lena and the children followed. She had no idea what a *warsher* and *vittles* were, but she figured she'd find out eventually. Closer to the house, the warm, yeasty smell of baking bread drifted out the open windows, making her stomach twist with hunger again. Up on the porch, two rocking chairs sat beside a butter churn and a wooden table filled with enamel bowls, tin kitchenware, and purple pansies in ceramic pots. A multitiered ring of hanging silver spoons swayed in the breeze, tinkling softly in the quiet afternoon. While Bonnie entered the house, Jack Henry stopped near the door next to an enamel pot filled with water. Using a long-handled ladle, he took a drink, then dipped the ladle in again and offered it to Lena.

"This here's the best mountain water y'all'll ever taste," Jack Henry said.

Despite her thirst, Lena hesitated. In Germany, water was

for thinning fruit juice and making tea and coffee, not drinking. And it certainly was not kept on the porch or consumed with a shared utensil. But if she wanted to fit in, how could she say no? She took the ladle and put it to her lips. The water was cool and soothing, like a balm to her parched throat. She gave Ella a sip too, then handed the ladle back to Jack Henry.

"You are right," she said with a smile. "It is very good. Thank you."

With a proud grin, Henry returned the ladle to the pot, then went into the house. Before following him inside, Lena removed her shoes and placed them next to the door, hoping fresh air would help rid them of the delousing stench. Then she paused briefly on the threshold, took a deep breath, and entered her new home.

A narrow, rough-hewn staircase with a simple railing divided the first floor of the cabin in half, with a kitchen on one side and a living room on the other. A wooden table, four cane-bottom chairs, and a bench were centered in the middle of the simple cooking area, where a red water pump had been mounted on a sink, a cast-iron woodstove dominated the back wall, and a painted cabinet filled with baskets and mismatched dishware sat kitty-corner near the front window. A worn sofa sat in the living room opposite two rocking chairs and a sewing machine on a pine table. A pair of long-barreled rifles hung above a massive cobblestone fireplace.

Unlike the rough exterior of the cabin, the inside felt cozy and inviting, with wide plank floors, braided rugs, lace curtains, kerosene lanterns, and black-and-white portraits on the gray slat walls. A shelf clock along with blue and green vases adorned the fireplace mantel, and ceramic jugs and crocks had been artfully arranged near the hearth. Granted, the rugs and furniture were threadbare and worn, and the vases and jugs looked quite old, but the way everything was set up made for a welcoming home.

While Bonnie opened the stove and threw wood inside, Jack

Henry carried a white enamel kettle over to the sink, placed it beneath the red pump, and began filling it with water. Lena left her satchel near the door, took Ella out of the shawl, and carried her into the kitchen. A bowl of apples sat on the table next to a cast-iron skillet filled with something yellow that looked like a torte. Lena's stomach growled long and loud.

"You have a lovely home," she said, hoping no one had heard the rumble.

"Thank you kindly, ma'am," Jack Henry said.

"Please, call me Lena."

Over at the woodstove, Bonnie slammed the door, and then trudged over to the sink, her lips pressed together in a thin, hard line. Lena wondered if she'd said something wrong when suddenly Ella leaned forward in her arms, reaching for the apples on the table. Lena pulled her back.

"*Nein*," she whispered. "They do not belong to us."

Ella started to cry.

"Ain't no never mind," Jack Henry said. "Your young'un can help herself. We got plenty."

"Are you certain?" Lena said.

"'Course I am," Jack Henry said.

Lena started to thank him, but Bonnie came over and snatched the bowl of apples off the table.

"I'm fixing to make a pie with these," she said. "So you can leave them be."

Jack Henry stopped pumping water into the kettle and scowled at her. "When did you ever fix a pie?"

"I'm fixing on learning," Bonnie said. "I just ain't done it yet."

"Quit being ugly," Jack Henry said. "You ain't gonna miss one apple."

Bonnie put the bowl of apples next to the sink. "If they're hungry they can eat corn bread."

Jack Henry shook his head, disgusted, then took two glasses

out of the cupboard and set them on the table. "Grab yourself a seat," he said to Lena.

Despite her empty stomach, Lena would have liked to bathe and change before eating, but Ella was hungry now. She pulled out a chair and sat down, Ella still crying on her lap. While Bonnie crossed her arms and watched, Jack Henry cut a thick square of the yellow torte, which Lena supposed was the corn bread, and offered it to them. Lena took it and held it to Ella's mouth. It was still warm. Jack Henry grabbed a milk jug from the counter and filled the glasses. Ella took a bite of the corn bread, then, with eager fingers, tried to take the whole piece out of Lena's hands.

"Ain't you gonna put it in her glass?" Jack Henry said. "She'll like it better that way."

"In the milk?" Lena said.

Bonnie rolled her eyes, grabbed a spoon from a drawer, and came over to the table. She cut another piece of corn bread, broke it up into one of the milk-filled glasses, then set it and the spoon in front of Lena.

"That's how y'all eat corn bread," she said. "With sweet milk."

Jack Henry nodded in agreement. "That's right," he said. "Give it a try."

Assuming they knew best, Lena spooned a piece of corn bread from the glass and tasted it. The warm bread and cool milk made for an interesting but delicious mix, almost like the *stollen* and hot cocoa her mother used to make on Christmas. She smiled and nodded at Jack Henry and Bonnie, then fed some of the milky corn bread to Ella, who gobbled it up.

"Thank you," Lena said. "It is delicious."

While Lena and Ella finished eating the corn bread, Bonnie checked the fire in the woodstove and Jack Henry filled another kettle with water, lifted it from the sink, and hauled it over to the burner, grimacing with the effort. Lena thought about asking why they had to hide from *die polizei,* but it was too soon. After putting the kettle on the woodstove, Jack Henry turned to look at her.

"This time a year we mostly warsh up outside in the crick," he said. "You scared of critters?"

"'Warsh up'?" Lena said. The strange word felt odd in her mouth. Silas had said the same thing to her back on Ellis Island and she thought she had an idea what it meant, but she hadn't asked him to clarify. And what were the other words Jack Henry just used?

Jack Henry looked at her like she should have understood what he was saying. "You know," he said. "When you scrub the dirt off to get clean? Like when you warsh your dishes and warsh your clothes?"

"Oh," Lena said. She was right; *warsh* meant *wash.* And when Silas said to put the clothes in the warsher, he meant the tub to wash clothes in. "I understand now. But what is a critter?"

"Critters are snakes and frogs and fish," Jack Henry said. "You scared of them?"

"No. My brother and I sometimes played with frogs when I was a young girl. Why do you want to know if I am afraid of them?"

"I reckoned that was why we had to heat up water so you could warsh inside," Jack Henry said. "Guess not."

Relieved that Silas had not made her and Ella bathe outside in the cold water, she wondered if he was more thoughtful than he seemed. Or maybe he didn't want a naked woman in his yard. Either way, she could hardly wait to get clean.

"How come we gotta let you wear our momma's clothes?" Bonnie said. "Ain't y'all got nothing to wear except that filthy dress?"

"Dagnabit, Bonnie," Jack Henry said. "What's gotten into you?"

"It is all right," Lena said. She looked at Bonnie, hoping to find the right words to explain. "Our dirty clothes make me unhappy too. When we left home our clothes were clean, but many things happened on the way here. They sprayed us with . . . with something that smelled bad. It was done to make sure we did not get ill and spread sickness. But as soon as our clothes are clean, we can wear them again. Will you show me where to wash them?"

Bonnie made an irritated face. "I reckon I ain't got a choice," she said. She started out of the kitchen, heading toward a narrow hallway behind the stairs. "The warsher's out back."

Lena got up from the table, put Ella on her hip, grabbed her satchel, and hurried after Bonnie. At the end of the hall, they went through a screen door onto a narrow porch, then followed it around one side of the house to a weathered shed filled with crates of odds and ends, and shelves lined with empty canning jars. In the center of the shed, a short, wooden vat with a hinged cover sat on thick wooden supports, like a wine barrel with legs. On one side of the barrel, an oversized iron wheel was held in place by a strange apparatus in the center. On the other side, a wood box with a metal crank housed what looked like two horizontal rolling pins.

"This here's the warsher," Bonnie said, pointing at the vat.

It looked nothing like the tubs Lena and Mutti used to scrub their clothes in back home. "How does it work?" she said.

Bonnie's brows shot up. "You ain't never seen a warsher before?"

"No."

"How come?"

Lena shrugged. "We did not have money for one. My mother and I washed our clothes in a tub and squeezed the water out by hand. We took our baths in the tub too."

Bonnie gaped at her like she was the oddest person she'd ever met. "Well, I reckon that's about the dumbest thing I ever heard," she said. "This here warsher works when you chunk your clothes inside, add the soap, and turn the wheel."

"The clothes will get clean on their own?" Lena widened her eyes more than necessary, hoping Bonnie would appreciate her reaction. She had to make friends with this girl. More importantly, she needed to earn her trust.

Bonnie nodded. "As long as you keep turning this wheel. And after they're rinsed, you crank the clothes through the wringers so they ain't sopping wet when you hang them out to dry."

"'The wringers'?"

Bonnie pointed at the two horizontal rolling pins.

Lena shook her head in exaggerated disbelief. "This is the most wonderful thing I have seen." She turned to Ella, bouncing her on her hip. "Is it not wonderful, *mein Schatz*?"

Ella smiled and let out a happy, little squeal. It was amazing what a full belly could do.

To Lena's surprise, Bonnie gazed at Ella with soft eyes, a small, proud smile flickering across her face. A tiny crack seemed to have opened up in her tough exterior.

"And the corn cake was wonderful too," Lena said. "You made it, yes? Did your mother teach you how to cook?"

Bonnie pulled her eyes away from Ella, her gentle look replaced by impatience. Lena had said too much, tried too hard, spoke too soon.

"It's corn bread, not corn *cake*," Bonnie said. "And 'course I made it. Ain't nobody else doing the cooking round here."

"*Corn bread*," Lena said, berating herself for bringing up Bonnie's mother so soon. "Is that the right way to say it?" She bounced Ella on her hip again. "Can you say corn bread, Ella?"

"O bed," Ella said in a baby-doll voice.

Another small smile flickered across Bonnie's lips, but she glanced at the floor to hide it. Clearly she was charmed by Ella.

"Will you help me teach Ella English?" Lena said. "You will be much better at it than me."

Bonnie's face softened a second time and she nodded, almost, but not quite, pleased again.

"You will need to teach me many other things too," Lena said. "Like how to make the delicious corn bread."

Bonnie scoffed. "Warshing clothes and making corn bread ain't hard."

"Not for you," Lena said. "But I have never done those things."

"You ain't never cooked?"

"A little," Lena said. "But I do not know what people in this country like to eat, or how to make it. I will need someone smart like you to teach me everything about America."

For the first time, Bonnie looked directly at Lena, her eyes wide with wonder, as if Lena had said cats could fly. It was as if no one had ever paid her a compliment before. Lena waited to see what she was going to say, but then the spell was broken and Bonnie looked away again.

"Did I say another word wrong?" Lena said. "I hope you will help me with my English too."

Bonnie shook her head. "No, it's just . . . ain't nobody ever called me smart before."

Lena opened her mouth in surprise. "I do not believe that," she said. "I can tell you are very smart."

Bonnie let out a quick, quiet laugh, as if she had no idea how to respond to praise. Lena could have sworn she was blushing. Then, in the next instant, her face turned serious again.

"By the way," Bonnie said. "Y'all need to be careful with this here warsher. Don't ever get your fingers caught in the mangler."

"'The mangler'?"

Bonnie put her hand on top of the wringer box. "Yeah. I learnt that lesson the hard way."

Lena gasped, truly horrified by the prospect of someone's hands going between the two rollers.

"Didn't break no bones," Bonnie said. "But I'm here to tell

you, it smart like the dickens. Momma had to put my hand in the crick to stop the swelling."

"*Ach, der lieber,*" Lena said. "I am sorry you were hurt. But thank you for telling me. You have taught me many important things already."

"Well, I'm worn slap out from doing all the work around this place myself," Bonnie said. Then her eyes went misty and she slowly turned the crank on the mangler, her mind elsewhere. For the first time since Lena had met her, she seemed sad and vulnerable, as if the memory of her mother taking care of her injured hand had pulled her into the past.

Again, Lena thought about asking why she and Jack Henry had to hide from the police. But before she could decide whether or not to say something, Silas shouted from inside the house.

"Bonnie! What in the devil are y'all doing out there?"

Bonnie startled, snapping back to reality. "Coming, Daddy!" she shouted. Then, to Lena, "Leave your clothes here. After you get cleaned up, we'll put the dress you're wearing in the warsher too."

Lena opened her satchel and started to pull out her clothes.

"Not now," Bonnie said. "Just chunk everything in here till later."

When Lena looked around for a place to put the satchel, Bonnie grabbed it and threw it on the floor. "Come on," she hissed. "Daddy ain't one for waiting."

Back inside, Jack Henry was putting more logs in the woodstove and three kettles of water simmered on the fire, filling the air with steam. Having changed out of his good clothes into patched overalls, buckskin gloves, and work boots, Silas carried a wooden tub into the kitchen and set it near the stove, shirtless except for the bib of his overalls. Corded muscle lined his massive arms and shoulders like the flanks of a workhorse, and the heavy-looking tub seemed to weigh nothing in his hands. It was hard to imagine him being afraid of the sheriff, let alone anyone else.

"Bonnie," he said, "get upstairs and fetch Lena and the young-'un something to wear, then go on out to the garden while they get cleaned up. Jack Henry, you come out to the barn with me."

"Yes, sir," the children said at the same time. Bonnie hurried across the room and padded up the stairs, quiet as a cat in her bare feet. Jack Henry poured the kettles of hot water into the tub, then stood still and silent, like a soldier awaiting orders.

Silas addressed Lena. "There's soap on the table and towels on the chair. When you're done warshing up, your room is upstairs, second on the left. Y'all can rest tonight, but tomorrow, you work."

"Yes, sir," Lena said.

Chapter 6

After Silas and Jack Henry went out to the barn, Bonnie came down from upstairs with a pained expression, crossed the kitchen, and tossed a blue housedress, a set of undergarments, and a yellow, toddler-size jumper over the back of a chair.

"Thank you for the clothes," Lena said. "I promise I will be careful with them."

"Thank Daddy, not me," Bonnie said.

Before Lena could respond, Bonnie trudged down the back hall and went outside, slamming the screen door behind her.

Lena sighed. It was easy to understand why Bonnie was upset about lending her late mother's clothes to a stranger, but what little progress Lena thought they'd made seemed to have vanished. Luckily, there was always tomorrow. And the day after that. And the day after that. Surely, by the time Mutti and Enzo arrived, Lena and Bonnie would be friends. *If* Lena ended up staying that long. Not that Wolfe Hollow Farm was lacking or the children unbearable, but something unsettling was going on there, something that might force her to leave. Of course, she had no idea where she would go or how she would get there—the nearest town might as well be a thousand miles away—but if the reason Silas made Bonnie and Jack Henry hide from the sheriff posed the slightest danger to Ella, it would be impossible to stay.

Leaving would make it difficult to save money for Mutti and Enzo, and it would be even harder to find a place to live and a job, but she had to keep Ella safe no matter what. If only her family were there now, they could leave together and start over someplace new. But that was not the case. She had to figure this out on her own. If nothing else, she still had the paper from the nun; but how much help could a church really be? And for how long? Hopefully, there was a good explanation for Silas's precautions, but at the moment she couldn't think of any that made sense. And she was too exhausted to think about what might happen tomorrow, let alone in the future. Right now, she needed to get herself and Ella cleaned up so they could rest. There was no reason to think beyond that.

After giving Ella a bath and dressing her in the yellow jumper, which hung on her tiny frame like a flour sack, Lena found a tin bowl and a wooden spoon for her to play with, then got in the water and scrubbed herself clean. Washing the oil out of her hair took longer than she had hoped, and she worried the entire time that Silas and Jack Henry would come back inside to find her naked in the middle of the kitchen, but luckily, they were gone long enough for her to dry off and slip into Silas's dead wife's clothes. She was surprised by how well they fit. After weaving her wet hair into one long braid, she hung the towels on the back of the kitchen chairs and took Ella upstairs to find their room. Now that she was clean and fed, Ella was getting sleepy.

Upstairs, three doors—one on the right, two on the left—lined a narrow corridor with black and white portraits on the walls. Barefoot and shivering, Lena gave the photos only a cursory look. She needed to put Ella to bed and go back downstairs to wash their dirty clothes. Then she noticed a photograph of a young man with a neatly trimmed beard beside a beautiful young woman with high cheekbones and long blond hair, he in a dark suit and she in a white lace dress. Stopping to examine the wedding portrait of Silas and his new bride, both trying to look properly serious despite the slight smirks on their faces, his grin showing in his eyes, hers in the upturned corners of her delicate lips, she could see that Bonnie and Jack Henry had their mother's fair coloring and gentle smile. But Bonnie favored her mother's dainty physique while it seemed Jack Henry would eventually inherit his father's immense height and build. Lena tried to reconcile the handsome young groom with the ill-tempered mountain man whose own children seemed to fear him, but could not make the connection. Other than losing his wife—which was certainly horrible enough—what else had made Silas so miserable? Then she had another thought and she trembled. Maybe he was responsible for his wife's death. Maybe the sheriff came to the house looking to put him in jail. Maybe that was why he told his children to hide when he was gone, so the police would think they'd all left.

No. That made no sense. Her weary mind was running away with her. Between the laundry on the line, the garden, the chickens, and the mules, the house was clearly occupied. And if Silas was worried about being arrested, he would have gone into hiding instead of parking his truck in the front yard for the whole world to see. Whatever his reason was for ordering Bonnie and Jack Henry to hide, it had to lie somewhere else. And even though Lena could not fathom what that reason might be, she knew one thing for sure: Silas had lost his wife because life was unfair, like Papa dying was unfair, like Ella's father deserting her was unfair, like Mutti and Enzo being deported was unfair.

Just as a flood of painful memories nearly carried Lena away, Ella reached up and touched her face, grinning and sleepy-eyed. "Mama," she said.

Lena hugged her tighter, kissing her cheeks and forehead.

"Oh, *mein Engel,* my angel," she whispered. "*Danke Gott,* I still have you."

She wiped her eyes, pushed away the painful thoughts, and went to the last door on the left. Inside the narrow, low-roofed room, a wrought iron bed covered with a patchwork blanket sat against one wall, and a wooden washstand stood next to an ancient-looking dresser. A white nightdress sat folded on the bed, along with a toddler-size nightgown for Ella. Lena smiled. Maybe Bonnie liked her after all. After changing Ella into the nightdress, Lena went to the open window, where a warm breeze fluttered through thin curtains embroidered with yellow daisies.

Outside, the sun was dropping in the dusky sky, swathing the clouds in blue and pink, and Jack Henry was leading three brown cows down a rocky hill, the bells around their necks clanging as they made their way through the trees and brush. Closer to the house, Bonnie yanked weeds from the garden filled with tomato plants, beans, onions, and other vegetables, and tossed them into a rusty bucket. Bearing right from the garden, a worn footpath led to three wooden sheds, one with red roses trailing up one side. Was that the shed where the children hid, or was it the one with the low, crooked roof? Would she and Ella be expected to hide there too? And what would happen if the sheriff found them?

Again, she reminded herself not to worry about something that hadn't happened yet. Her daughter needed to sleep. And maybe she should rest for a few minutes before going back downstairs where she had to pretend to be someone she wasn't— a confident, eager woman happy to be there, ready and willing to take on her new roles as housekeeper and caregiver. Because in truth, she was a scared, exhausted, and confused young immigrant who wanted her mother, probably as much as Bonnie and Jack Henry wanted theirs.

Chapter 7

Lena woke with a start, immediately reaching for Ella to make sure she was there. When she felt her daughter beside her, curled up and warm inside a soft nightgown, she relaxed, but only a little. She sat up and looked around the dim room. Was it dusk or dawn? Day or night? Were they home in bed or on a ship in the middle of the ocean? Then she remembered. They were in America. High in the mountains of Virginia. And she was wearing a dead woman's dress. How long had she been asleep? An hour? Two hours? All night? She only meant to take a short nap. Trying not to disturb Ella, she slid off the straw mattress and went over to the window. Outside, the rising sun was turning the cloudless sky a light, hazy orange, and a thick mist surrounded the distant peaks like a white sea surrounding blue islands. She pushed stray hairs back from her face and smoothed the front of the dress. Hopefully, no one would notice she'd slept in it all night. Looking for her shoes, she started to panic. Had she lost them inside the delousing plant? On the ferry or the train? Then she remembered. She'd left them on the porch to air out. For now, she would have to go barefoot like the children.

After watching Ella for a moment to make sure she was still asleep, she tiptoed out of the room and quietly closed the door behind her. The smell of fresh coffee and fried eggs wafted up from downstairs, making her stomach growl. She hurried along the hall and down the steps, hoping she wasn't the last one out of bed. In the kitchen, Silas sat alone at the table, eating a plate of eggs and fried potatoes. When he looked up, he started to smile. Then he quickly lowered his eyes and picked up his coffee cup, a strange, strangled look on his face. At first, she thought his breakfast had gotten stuck in his throat. Then she remembered what she was wearing. Seeing another woman in his late wife's dress had to be a shock.

"Good morning," she said. "Would you like me to get the children from their beds?"

He shook his head. "They'll be down directly."

She clasped her hands together, pressing her fingertips into her knuckles hard enough to hurt. What should she say? What should she do? Wash the cast-iron pan on the stove, pour a cup of coffee and sit down at the table, leave him alone, ask why his children had to hide from the *polizei*? No. That question should probably wait. At least for part of the day. "Do you know where to find the soap for washing clothes?"

"Bonnie warshed your clothes last night," he said without looking up. "They're out on the line."

Heat rose in her cheeks. "Oh," she said. "I am sorry. I laid down with Ella to make sure she was sleeping but I—"

"Ain't no need to explain," he said. "Y'all had a long trip. But from here on out it'll do you good to remember you're here to look after my young'uns, not the other way around." He picked up his plate and stood, pushing his chair back with a loud scrape.

"*Ja*. I mean, yes. I was very tired and—"

"Y'all can start by fixing their morning vittles," he said, putting his dishes in the sink. "Bonnie can help clean up the kitchen and show you what else needs doing. When Jack

Henry is done eating, he needs to get out to the barn so I can run to the sawmill. I'll be back late morning." Then he turned, grabbed his black hat off a nail in the wall, and started out of the kitchen.

Alarm crackled through her. He was already leaving her alone with the children? What if the sheriff came? What was she supposed to do? She had to stop him. She had too many unanswered questions. And if he was going to the sawmill, the question she was afraid to ask could no longer wait. She clenched her hands into fists and steeled herself. "Please, wait," she said, louder than she intended.

He came to a halt and turned, his eyebrows raised.

"I have come very far to care for your home and children, is this right?"

"Your mother was supposed to be fixing vittles and looking after the house and young'uns, not you."

"Yes. I wish very much that she was here. And I will do the work. But I need to know what is to happen when you are not here and the *polizei* come."

A dark shadow crossed over his face. He understood what she wanted to know. "I got chores waiting," he said, his voice hard. "Bonnie knows what to do."

"But why do—"

"I ain't explaining right now." He started toward the back hall again.

"Do the children know why they are to hide?"

He kept walking.

"Am I to hide too?"

He spun around to face her again, his face sour. "Yes. But I ain't got time to talk about it, understand? We done?"

She wrinkled her brow, confused.

"Y'all got more questions or can I get to work?"

She twisted her fingers together. He was losing patience with her, but there were certain things she had to know. "*Ja*, I mean, yes. One more question, please. My mother and brother have little money and no home in Germany. When I know where they are staying, I would like to send them my . . . my . . ." She groaned inwardly. Why was it suddenly so hard to remember the right words? Was it because Silas was the size of an ox? Because anger simmered from his body like steam from a kettle? Because he held her and Ella's future in his hands? Very likely, it was all of those things, but she had to be strong, despite feeling anything but. "I would like to send my mother money from my work and I—"

"Your work?"

"Yes. The work I will be doing for you."

He gaped at her with a strange mixture of fury and disbelief. "Y'all think you're getting paid?"

Paid. Pay. Yes. That was the word. She nodded, relieved he understood. Then she realized what he had said. *Y'all think you're getting paid?* And his temples were pulsing in and out.

"Let me see if I got this right," he said. "I take y'all in when it ain't what I agreed to. I give you vittles, clothes, and a sturdy roof over your head, and you think I ought to be giving you money too? Y'all got any idea how much I paid for your mother and brother's tickets? And all I got out of the deal was you and a baby to feed?" His tone was glacial.

The floor swayed beneath her, the first twinges of panic making her lightheaded. She nearly had to grab the table to keep from falling over. Yes, she'd been under the impression she'd be paid for her work. Mutti had thought so too. And along with helping on the farm, Enzo was going to work at a sawmill with Silas. They'd all believed they'd have real jobs in America, with paychecks and a chance to build a new life. Of course, Lena was beyond grateful that Silas had taken her and Ella in, but if he had no intention of paying her, she was trapped. Starting over on her own or choosing to live someplace else was out of the question. Even worse, she could not send money to

Mutti and Enzo for food or rent. She could not send them money for tickets to America. Silas might not have pressed a pamphlet into her hand on Ellis Island, promising work that was actually slave labor, but this was the same thing. And there was nothing she could do about it. Tears flooded her eyes. She tried to think of something to say but could not speak.

"Bring up money again," Silas growled, "and I'll slap your eyeballs into one, understand? Now make yourself useful before I take you back down the mountain and leave you there."

Before she could respond, he shoved his hat on his head, stomped down the hall, and went outside, letting the back door slam. She clasped a hand over her stomach, certain she was going to be sick. If Mutti and Enzo could not make enough money for tickets, she might never see them again. She pulled out a chair and sat down, her face in her hands, her shoulders convulsing. She wanted to scream and yell, wanted to break or throw something. But that would change nothing. After a few minutes of letting herself cry, when she thought she could stand without falling, she got up and looked around the kitchen, her vision blurry. She would work as hard as possible. She would do more than necessary and become indispensable. And then, however long it took, she would convince Silas to send for Mutti and Enzo again.

A clutch of brown eggs sat in a blue ceramic bowl next to the sink, along with a crock of butter and a jug of milk. A cast-iron pan and a coffeepot like the one they had at home sat on the woodstove. At least no one would have to tell her how to use those things. She grabbed a dishtowel to protect her hand and opened the stove door to check the fire—it was roaring. After melting some butter in the frying pan, she cracked six eggs, one by one, into the sizzling skillet. While the eggs fried, she took plates from a shelf, put them on the table, and found a drawer of silverware.

Just then, voices floated down the stairs. The children were awake. She wiped her cheeks and turned to face them, resolute. She would become important to Bonnie and Jack Henry too.

In overalls and tie-up boots, Jack Henry came down first, followed by Bonnie, who was barefoot in a thin cotton dress. Bonnie hesitated at the bottom step, eyeing Lena with a cross look before coming into the kitchen.

"Good morning," Lena said, trying to sound cheerful. She took a metal spatula from a drawer and checked the eggs.

"Morning," Jack Henry said.

Bonnie came over to the stove and looked in the frying pan. "We like our eggs over easy," she said. "And crispy around the edges." Then she went to a counter drawer and pulled out a loaf of homemade bread.

"I'm sorry," Lena said, "but I do not know what 'over easy' means."

Bonnie rolled her eyes, came back to the stove, and took the spatula from Lena. "It means cooking them until they start getting crispy, then turning them over without breaking the yolk. Real quick like, only until the yolk starts cooking." She flipped the eggs over one by one, then handed the spatula back to Lena. "Take them out in a second or two, starting with the first one I flipped."

While Jack Henry got a knife and started cutting the bread, Bonnie set glasses and coffee mugs on the table. Then she buttered the bread slices and Jack Henry placed them one by one on the plates. Working together like a well-oiled machine, they poured milk into cloudy glasses, filled the mugs with black coffee, then pulled out their chairs and sat down. Careful not to break the yolks, Lena served the eggs, two on each plate, then put the skillet back on the stove and returned to the table.

"Thank you for the bedclothes, Bonnie," she said.

Bonnie took a bite of bread and stared at her plate, silent and stewing.

Lena tried again. "They fit us well."

Bonnie stabbed her eggs with her fork. It was as if she'd gone deaf. Lena took a deep, quiet breath and pulled out a chair. She had no idea if it was normal for Bonnie to be moody in the morning or if it was only a result of Lena's presence. Of course, the fact that Lena was wearing one of Bonnie's late mother's dresses certainly didn't help. At least for a moment, Lena could take comfort in a hot breakfast on her plate. Taking a sip of coffee, she savored the rich, dark liquid. The last time she'd had coffee—not chicory—was at a café with Ella's father, back when she believed her life was about to change for the better. It felt like a thousand years ago. And now, here she was again, on the other side of hoping things would improve, wondering what was going to happen next and how she would get through it. She picked up her fork and turned to Jack Henry.

"Where do you get the . . . the . . ." Unable to remember the right word, she let out a small, impatient huff. "Where do you get the post?"

He frowned.

"The post," she said. "The . . . the letters."

"The mail?"

She nodded. Yes. The *mail*. That was the word she'd been searching for. She'd seen a post office on the way here, but it seemed like a hundred miles back down the mountain and after all the twists and turns on the drive up, she'd never find it. Even if she remembered where it was, it would take forever to walk there and back. Hopefully the Wolfe family sent and received their letters somewhere closer. "My mother is going to send a letter when she and my brother have returned to Germany."

"The mail wagon stops once a week," Jack Henry said. "So long as the roads ain't warshed out."

Ach, Gott. Now she had to worry about the roads being closed too? But at least there was no need to walk halfway down the mountain for the mail. And right now, she needed to be grateful for the little things. "I would like to write back when I receive her letter. Do you have writing paper and, and—" What was the word for the folded paper you mail a letter in?

"Bonnie can get you all that," Jack Henry said. "Envelopes too. Right, Bonnie?"

Bonnie grunted.

Lena let out a quiet, relieved sigh. At least she knew how she would keep in touch with her family. Just then, Ella's cries floated down the stairs. Lena stood and started across the kitchen, worried Ella might fall off the bed before she reached her. To her surprise, Bonnie jumped up and hurried past her.

"I'll fetch her," Bonnie said.

"You do not want to finish your food?" Lena said.

"I will," Bonnie said, already bounding up the stairs.

Lena started to follow her, unsure what Ella would do when someone she barely knew came into the unfamiliar room. But then she stopped to listen at the bottom step, ready to go up if Ella sounded scared. When the bedroom door opened, Ella's cries got louder.

"Morning, baby doll," Bonnie said in a high, singsong voice.

Ella quieted, but only a little.

"Oh, don't cry," Bonnie said sweetly. "It's all right. Y'all don't gotta be scared. I ain't gonna hurt you." And then, "There we go. Come on. Now, let's go see your momma."

When they came out of the room into the hall, Ella was still fussing. And then, to Lena's surprise, Bonnie started to sing.

> My Bonnie lies over the ocean,
> My Bonnie lies over the sea.
> My Bonnie lies over the ocean,
> Oh, bring back my Bonnie to me.
>
> Bring back, bring back,
> Oh, bring back my Bonnie to me, to me.
> Bring back, bring back,
> Oh, bring back my Bonnie to me.

A smile played across Lena's lips. Bonnie had a clear, mellow voice with the charming touch of her mountain accent. If Lena hadn't known better, she would have sworn it was the mature voice of a young woman, not a little girl. When Bonnie came to the top of the staircase, grinning with Ella in her arms, she pointed down at Lena.

"See?" she said. "There's your momma, right there waiting for y'all."

Lena waved up at her daughter, who was staring up at Bonnie with wonder-filled eyes, her mouth hanging open as if she'd never heard a person sing before.

Bonnie carried Ella down the steps, continuing the song, and took her over to the kitchen table.

> Oh, blow ye winds over the ocean,
> Oh, blow ye winds over the sea.
> Oh, blow ye winds over the ocean,
> And bring back my Bonnie to me.

Bonnie set Ella in the chair and said to Jack Henry, "I reckon we should get the high chair down from the attic. And the crib too."

Jack Henry nodded but kept his focus on his food, dipping his bread in his egg yolks and eating fast.

Grateful for Bonnie's improved mood, Lena sat next to her daughter. Clearly, Bonnie had a soft spot for Ella, and she was good with her too. Along with the food, and learning where the Wolfe family got their mail, there was that to be thankful for too.

"Thank you for getting her," Lena said. "I think she loves your singing." She poured half a cup of milk and gave it to Ella, who grabbed it with both hands and took a long drink, wet drips running down her chin. "I do too. Your voice is beautiful."

Bonnie gave her a small, appreciative smile and sat down on the other side of Ella, moving her chair closer to hers. Then, like an old mother hen, she wiped Ella's chin and handed her little hunks of buttered bread to eat, careful not to make them too big. But when Lena slid one of her eggs onto Ella's plate, Bonnie grabbed the plate, bread pieces and all, and took it over to the stove. Ella started to wail.

"What are you doing?" Lena said.

"Her egg needs to be hard-cooked or she'll be a goldarn mess," Bonnie said.

Lena wanted to say she'd wash Ella's hands afterward, but despite her frustration that Bonnie had taken Ella's plate away, she bit her tongue and tried to get Ella to eat another piece of bread. "Shhh," she said. "It will be all right. Bonnie will give the egg back soon."

After Bonnie finished cooking the egg, she blew on it to cool it down, cut it into small pieces, and gave it back to Ella, who immediately stopped crying.

"We have not had eggs in some time," Lena said.

Jack Henry shot her a puzzled look, one cheek filled with food. "How come?"

"We had very little food in Germany," Lena said. "And where we lived, you could not have chickens or a garden. I have said to Bonnie, I am here to take care of you, but I will need help to learn about America."

Bonnie let out a quick, scornful laugh. "We don't need no taking care of. We been doing fine on our own. We just need a few extra hands around here." She was not going to make things easy on Lena.

Lena ate the rest of her egg and bread, wondering what she had to do to prove she only wanted to be friends. "I hope to do most of the work soon, so you and Jack Henry can play games and read books."

Jack Henry chuckled. "She can't read."

Bonnie pounded her fist on the table, startling Ella. "Shut your pie hole, you big lunk. I can too read!"

Ella started to cry and Jack Henry scowled at Bonnie. "How the devil would you know if you can read?" he said. "We ain't been to school in nearly two years."

"I said shut up!" Bonnie shouted. "I know how to read 'cause I read Momma's books every night!"

Lena lifted Ella onto her lap to comfort her and addressed Bonnie. "Please do not yell," she said. "You are scaring her."

With that, Bonnie's shoulders dropped and she looked at Ella, her face filled with a blend of anger and regret. "Sorry, baby doll, but my brother can be a dad-gum jackass sometimes. If his brains was made of leather, he wouldn't have enough to saddle a June bug."

Jack Henry's face fell. He got to his feet, took his empty plate over to the sink, and trudged across the kitchen into the back hall. "I'm telling Daddy you cussed," he hollered over his shoulder.

"Go ahead," Bonnie yelled after him. "See if I give a good god damn!"

Still on Lena's lap, Ella quieted and stared at Bonnie, no doubt wondering how the singing lamb had so quickly turned into a roaring lion. Lena helped her finish eating while Bonnie moped and pushed her food around on her plate, her elbow propped on the table, her chin resting on her hand.

"Sometimes I would fight with my brother too," Lena said. "Mutti got very mad when I called him a *Scheisskopf*. I think in English it means shithead."

Although she tried not to, Bonnie smirked.

It was the reaction Lena was hoping for. "Do you think your father will understand if I say bad words in German?"

Bonnie shrugged one shoulder. "I don't reckon. But he says cussin's not ladylike."

"Then maybe I should teach you a little German," Lena said, winking.

Bonnie nodded, a grin growing on her face.

"It can be our . . ." Lena said. "What is the word for something you do not tell?"

"Secret?"

"*Ja,* it can be our secret."

Finally, Bonnie smiled and sat up straight, her eyes shining with mischief.

Relieved to have made more progress, no matter how small or fleeting, Lena drank the rest of her coffee. She was reluctant to take advantage of the moment but there was no other way to get the answers she needed. "Would it be all right if I ask you about some things I do not understand?"

"I reckon."

"Why does your father tell you and Jack Henry to hide when the police come?"

"Daddy says Sheriff Dixon is a bad man."

Out of all the different reasons Lena had imagined, it was not one she expected. A shiver ran through her. Maybe Silas had good reason to hide his children. "Why is he bad? What did he do?"

Bonnie shrugged "I ain't sure. Daddy ain't said."

Lena groaned inside. She needed to find out the truth so she could stop imagining the worst. "Why do you and Jack Henry no longer go to school?"

Bonnie took a drink of milk and wiped her mouth on the back of her hand. "After Momma died, we had to stay home to help Daddy with the house and the farm."

Lena berated herself for asking the question. Of course that was why. She wanted to ask what had happened to her mother, but Bonnie was finally starting to open up a little and she didn't want to upset her again. "Do you wish to go to school?"

Bonnie nodded. "I sure do, but Jack Henry don't care nothing for learning. The only thing he liked about school was Daddy letting us ride Ole Sal there and back."

"Ole Sal?"

"Our gray mule. He takes real good care of us too. Knows the way home, even in a snowstorm. We got two mules, Ole Sal and Buttercup. But Buttercup's biscuit ain't cooked all the way in the middle, if you know what I mean."

Lena shook her head.

"She ain't very smart."

"I have not heard that before," Lena said. "But you and your family say a lot of things I have not heard before."

Bonnie laughed. "I reckon that's true."

Ella grew restless on Lena's lap. Lena let her down to toddle around the kitchen, keeping an eye on her while she explored. "You have read the books belonging to your mother?"

"Only one so far. There's lots of big words so it takes me a while."

"Many English words are hard for me too, but perhaps we can figure them out together."

Bonnie shrugged. "Maybe. But I keep them under my bed 'cause seeing them makes Daddy sad."

"Does it make you sad?"

"Sometimes, but Momma loved reading and singing more than sugar candy, so reading her books makes me feel close to her."

"I am sure it makes her happy when you read them too."

Bonnie gazed at Lena, curiosity shining in her eyes. "Y'all think she can see me doing that?"

Lena nodded. "Your mother will always be with you."

"That's what Daddy said," Bonnie said. "When he used to talk about her."

"He does not talk about her any longer?"

Bonnie shook her head, her chin starting to tremble. "No. And I want him to talk about her so I don't forget her."

The familiar ache of sorrow tightened Lena's chest. She was sixteen when her father died and had a thousand memories of him. But Bonnie was so young when she lost her mother. Sure, Lena had experienced and witnessed her fair share of suffering and loss during the war—an uncle killed in battle, a cousin dead from the Spanish flu, schoolmates who lost parents and grandparents—but losing a parent was different. It was no wonder Bonnie worried about forgetting her mother, especially if Silas did nothing to keep her memory alive. Suddenly Lena was reminded of her own mother and the fact that she had no idea when, or if, she would see her again. And Enzo too. Tears stung her eyes. She wanted to hug Bonnie, to tell her she understood, but that would do nothing to help. And Bonnie might not welcome a hug anyway.

"If you would like to talk about your mother," Lena said, "I will listen."

Bonnie wiped her cheek with a rough hand, angry with herself for crying. "Maybe later. We got chores first."

Lena put a gentle hand on Bonnie's arm, saddened that she was so worried about getting her chores done. "Then we can talk and work at the same time. But only if you would like to. And when we are finished with the kitchen, maybe you can show me Ole Sal and Buttercup before you teach me all the things that need to be done. Because the sooner I can do the work here, the sooner you can return to school."

"I don't reckon Daddy's letting us go to school just yet," Bonnie said.

"Why not?"

Bonnie shrugged, then got up to start clearing the table. Lena stood to help. Bonnie took the glasses over to the sink, gave Ella measuring cups and wooden spoons to play with, then threw more logs on the fire to heat water for the dishes, and put the eggshells and coffee grounds in a chipped enamel bowl. While Lena finished picking up the dirty dishes from the table and straightening the counter, she kept quiet, waiting to see if Bonnie wanted to talk about her mother, but Bonnie worked in silence.

After the silverware and plates were washed and put away, and the cast-iron pan had been scrubbed and left on the woodstove to dry, Lena lifted Ella onto her hip and followed Bonnie into a closet-size room just off the kitchen.

"This here's the pantry," Bonnie said.

Every shelf and available space was filled with dry goods and cooking utensils—a bin of flour and sacks of dried beans, rolling pins and a meat grinder, coffee and a box of matches, a jug of vinegar and a ceramic crock. Lena had never seen so much food in one place, or so many tools to prepare it.

"Daddy picks up sugar and salt down the mountain and we grow our own herbs," Bonnie said, pointing at the bouquets that hung upside down from the ceiling. "We get the cornmeal and buckwheat from Mr. Early's gristmill over on Weakley Stream. That's over yonder in the next holler."

"What is buckwheat?"

"It's the flour we use to fix pancakes with sorghum molasses, which we get from Dewey Fray over in Walnut Holler. We get regular flour from Homer Ring over on Pond Ridge Gap. And we get honey and maple syrup from Lydia and Roy Stanton over on Old Pigbump Road."

Lena shook her head. How would she ever keep everything straight? "Perhaps you can write this down for me. I will never remember."

"I reckon I could, but I ain't going nowhere anytime soon, so I can help until you get the hang of it."

Near the back wall of the pantry, Bonnie opened a handcrafted cubby to reveal milky white plates with matching saucers and cups, all rimmed with yellow roses. "This here's the china set Momma ordered from the Sears and Roebuck catalog. Momma only used it on Christmas and birthdays but Daddy ain't letting us use it now on account of it costing thirteen dollars."

"It's beautiful," Lena said.

"Momma said it's mine when I get hitched and have my own family," Bonnie said. "But I don't think Daddy's gonna remember." She closed the cubby door and started out of the pantry. "Come on, we got lots to do yet."

In the back hall, she bent over, grabbed a heavy ring in the floor, and yanked open a trapdoor. "This here's the 'tater hole." She leaned the heavy door against the wall and started down a set of steep, wooden stairs.

Holding on to Ella for dear life and taking the steps one at a time, Lena followed Bonnie into the dark pit. Thankfully, at the bottom step, Bonnie pulled a string on a single bulb, illuminating a hand-dug basement with rough-sawn joists overhead and rocks lining the walls. The smell of dirt and damp wood filled the air, along with the sweet cider scent of stored apples. Straw-lined bins of potatoes and turnips sat against one wall, and rows of canning jars filled with fruits and vegetables—yellow, purple, white, green, red—lined makeshift shelves along the others. Lena shook her head in amazement. When it came to food, at least, it seemed the American dream was true after all.

And then, despite her astonishment, a wave of unease hit her and she was pulled back in time to the endless nights spent hiding in the cellar beneath their apartment, cramped together in the near dark with the other residents while bombs exploded overhead, everyone exhausted and terrified that they would be next, burned to death or buried alive beneath mountains of rubble. The air left her lungs and for a second, she couldn't breathe.

She squeezed her eyes shut and pushed the image away. The war was in the past, and she needed to look forward. Then she imagined Bonnie and Jack Henry hiding in the basement, silent and afraid, waiting to see if the sheriff would find them, and the trapped feeling returned with a vengeance. Life was supposed to be different in America; children were supposed to be happy and carefree, not hiding in fear. Bonnie and Jack Henry might not have to worry about bombs falling on their house, but fear was fear no matter the cause.

"You fixing to have a spell?" Bonnie said.

Lena shook her head, reminding herself to breathe. She had no idea what a *spell* was, but she heard the concern in Bonnie's voice. "I do not like to think of you and your brother hiding down here."

"This ain't nothing," Bonnie said. "Wait till you lay eyes on the hidey-hole under the shed."

Lena swallowed. She thought the children had to hide *in* the shed, not under it. "Why?" she said, not at all sure she wanted to hear the answer.

"It ain't too big, that's all. But we ain't got time to fret about that right now. I need to tell you what we got down here in the 'tater hole."

Lena nodded and did her best to pay attention while Bonnie pointed at the various canning jars.

"You got your corn relish, pickled beets, pickled onions, cherries, rhubarb, green tomatoes, strawberry preserves, and apple jelly," Bonnie said. "Over here you got pickled eggs, green beans, ham hocks, peas, and sauerkraut. And this summer we'll have a mess of garden vegetables to put up."

"You did all of this?" Lena said.

"Daddy and Jack Henry helped some," Bonnie said. "But this ain't nothing. Pretty soon we'll have watercress, poke greens, dandelion greens, mushrooms, blackberries, and raspberries too. And after we let the hogs loose to fatten up on acorns this fall, we'll be putting up pork too. 'Course that's a full day's work, after gathering the vats, the lard press, the sausage grinder, and the other equipment." She pointed at several burlap bags in the corner. "We also got hazelnuts, hickory nuts, and walnuts."

Lena's head was spinning. How was it possible for one family to have so much food? "I have not heard of some things you are telling me."

Bonnie looked at her like she had two heads. "Y'all ain't never heard of mushrooms and hazelnuts?"

"*Ja,*" Lena said. "I know mushrooms and hazelnuts. They grow wild in Germany. But I do not know the other things you said. You have a lot to teach me, remember?"

Bonnie grinned. "Well, I reckon we got time."

After quick lessons on how to gather eggs and feed chickens, Bonnie took Lena over to the barn to meet Ole Sal and Buttercup, then showed her around the rest of the property, barefoot and carrying Ella on her hip as if she'd raised a hundred babies. Ella giggled in delight at everything Bonnie pointed out, and even paid attention when she tried to teach her the English names for things—mule, flower, chicken, grass, sky. As they followed a path toward the sheds, Bonnie broke into song again and Ella smiled so hard she drooled, her downy hair blowing in the warm breeze. If Lena hadn't known any better, she would have thought they were sisters, bonded together in easy familiarity since the day Ella was born. Maybe it was a sign of good things to come. She hoped so, anyway.

When they reached a small shack sitting over the mountain stream, Bonnie handed Ella to Lena, opened the door, and led them inside. Crystal clear water ran under a square opening in the middle of the floor, and stone crocks, glass jars, and wooden barrels sat like rocks in the gurgling flow.

"This here's the springhouse," Bonnie said. "It's where we keep the butter, sweet milk, salt pickles, fresh chicken and pork, and anything else we need to stay cold." She lifted a jar out of the water, pulled off the lid, and held it out to Lena. "Wanna try a sip? It's my favorite."

"What is it?"

"Wild cherry bitters. Sure to cure what ails you."

Lena took the can, carefully tried the liquid inside, and made a disgusted face. It tasted like dirt and burnt wood mixed with stale water. She handed the jar back to Bonnie and wiped her mouth, her lips puckering. "That is horrible!"

Bonnie laughed. "Jack Henry don't care none for it neither. Daddy likes it, but only with a shot of white mule."

"White mule?"

"Moonshine."

"What is moonshine?" Lena said.

Bonnie gaped at her. "Y'all ain't never heard of moonshine?"

Lena shook her head.

"Dang, I reckon I do gotta lot to teach you, don't I? Moonshine is whiskey made a corn mash, apples, or peaches. Lotsa folks make it and drink it up here, and lotsa folks sell it too, even though they ain't supposed to."

"Does your father make it?"

Bonnie shook her head. "Nah. He said we got enough trouble without worrying about being thrown in jail for making moonshine."

"Is that why he does not like the sheriff?"

"It ain't the only reason." She returned the jar of bitters to the water.

"Do you know the other reasons?"

"I ain't sure."

Suddenly, somehow, Lena had the feeling Bonnie knew exactly why Silas felt the way he did about the sheriff, but Lena didn't want to push for answers right now. They were getting along so well, and Lena was already overwhelmed with all the new things she was seeing and learning. "Do you really like the cherry drink or were you playing a . . . What is the word? A trick?"

Bonnie laughed. "Sorry about that, but at least it weren't sweet nanny tea."

Lena laughed too. Ella looked up at her and grinned, no doubt surprised to hear her mother sounding happy. "And what is sweet nanny tea?" Lena said.

"I ain't certain," Bonnie said. "The adults won't say. But the fixins come from sheep. After wrapping the fixins in a cloth and boiling it on the stove, they burn it. So, I think it has to be something pretty awful. The adults say they'll give it to us if we get sick, but it tastes so gosh darn terrible nobody ever complains about feeling bad."

Lena laughed again. "That is like the medicine my mother used to give me and my brother. It tasted like dead fish. I wish she could be here to taste your cherry drink and see all of the food you have grown and saved. She would be surprised."

And just like that, Bonnie's smile disappeared. "Did your momma pass too?" she said in a quiet voice.

"*Nein*," Lena said. "I mean, no. She was to come here with me and Ella to help your father, but the men at Ellis Island said she and my brother must return to Germany. I do not know if they are still waiting to get on a ship or if they are on their way home."

"Why'd they make them go back?"

"They said my brother was feebleminded so he was not allowed to stay. And they said my mother had to go with him because he was too young to go alone. They said she was sick too, but it is not true. They made a mistake. A terrible mistake. Mutti is fine and Enzo only needs to learn more English. He is not feebleminded." Her throat worked against her tears, but she refused to cry. Bonnie had enough sorrow in her life without burdening her with more.

"What does 'feebleminded' mean?" Bonnie said. "I ain't ever heard of it."

"They said it means slow or . . . or . . . dim-witted. They said my brother was not smart enough to stay in America. That he would not be able to get a job or make money."

A troubled look darkened Bonnie's features. She knelt down to rearrange the jars in the stream, hiding her face.

"What is it?" Lena said. "What is wrong?" She waited a moment, but Bonnie said nothing. "Are you thinking of your mother?"

Bonnie straightened and shook her head. "No," she said. "It ain't got nothing to do with my momma. It's just . . . it's just . . . that's what they say about us too. Me and Jack Henry. And Daddy, even. They say we're slow and ignorant, that we're fee . . . feebleminded."

Lena frowned. "Who says that?"

"I ain't sure. Some important folk. I heard Daddy talking about it with Mr. Corbin."

Lena couldn't believe what she was hearing. What made "important folk" think they could judge what others could and could not do? Bonnie was smarter and more capable than some adults Lena knew back home. And neither Jack Henry nor Silas seemed slow or stupid. Then she had another thought and her blood ran cold. Maybe the sheriff wanted to take Silas's children for the same reasons the doctors on Ellis Island had threatened to imprison Enzo if he stayed in the United States. But it made no sense. The Wolfes were American citizens. They couldn't be pulled apart and locked up for no reason, could they? Whatever the answer was, Bonnie surely didn't know or understand it. Lena would have to ask Silas.

"The people who said that about you and your family do not know what they are talking about," she said. "You are very smart. Look at all the things you have been showing me and teaching me. And I still do not understand all the things you are saying."

Bonnie shrugged half-heartedly, apparently resigned to the fact that there was nothing she could do about the opinion of others. Then she held out her arms for Ella again, smiling, and Ella reached for her, delighted to be carried again by her new friend.

After the springhouse, Bonnie showed Lena the hand-dug well and the woodshed, where cords of firewood were stacked to the ceiling. Next, they entered a low-roofed shed containing garden and hand tools, shelves and bins filled with strange machinery, and rusty chains hanging on the back wall. After making her way around an old tractor, Bonnie gave Ella back to Lena, then moved a wheelbarrow full of rocks off a worn, dirty rug, pushed the rug to one side, grabbed an iron ring in the floor, and pulled open a trapdoor. Steep primitive steps led down into darkness.

"This is where you and Jack Henry go when the police come?" Lena said in a hushed voice.

Still holding the door, Bonnie nodded, her face suddenly pale.

"I still do not understand," Lena said. "*Why* must you hide?"

"I already told you," Bonnie whispered. "'Cause we ain't smart."

Chapter 8

By noon, Bonnie and Lena had hung three loads of laundry on the line, shucked a bowlful of sweet peas on the front porch, and patched three pair of trousers. Thankfully, Ella toddled after them without complaint, entertaining herself with wooden spoons and pots in the house, dirt and grass outside, and chasing the chickens in the yard. After picking green beans in the garden, Lena washed Ella's face and hands in the kitchen sink while Bonnie put a kettle of water on the woodstove and threw in the beans.

"We're gonna need more milk for the cathead biscuits," Bonnie said. "I'll run out to the springhouse to fetch it. Daddy and Jack Henry will be wanting vittles soon."

"Cathead biscuits?" Lena said.

"Yup, they're called that on account a being the size of a cat's head."

Lena shook her head, marveled by the many strange things she'd learned already, wondering how she'd ever remember everything. She dried Ella's hands and carried her over to the window to watch Bonnie, who was running down the path toward the springhouse as if being chased, dirt flying up from her bare heels. Anyone else would have seen a young girl having fun, playing a game or hurrying into the woods to pick berries. But Lena imagined Bonnie running to the low-roofed shed, to hide in the dark hole with Jack Henry.

She gently kissed Ella's hands and face, desperate for the innocent, clean smell and feel of her baby-soft skin. "Why is Bonnie such a fast runner?" she said, thinking out loud. "Why does she need to hide?"

"H . . . hide," Ella said, her little tongue slipping between her tiny teeth.

After having beans and cathead biscuits with milk gravy for the midday meal, which Lena learned was called supper, Jack Henry and Bonnie brought a white iron crib down from the attic, dusted it off, and put it in Lena and Ella's bedroom. They also brought down a wicker baby carriage, several of Bonnie's old baby dresses and bonnets, a set of wooden blocks, a rattle shaped like a stork, and a rag doll with yellow yarn hair. While Lena covered the crib mattress with a soft blanket, Bonnie played with Ella on the floor.

"This here's Poppy," she said, holding the rag doll out for Ella. "My momma made her for me when I was little like you, but you can have her. She's yours now."

Ella took the rag doll and hugged it under her chin, beaming and rocking back and forth. Lena picked Ella up, careful not to let her drop Poppy, and kissed her cheek.

"It is time for a little sleep," she said, and laid Ella in the crib. Ella fussed, rolled over, and stood, the rag doll forgotten.

Bonnie got up from the floor and stood by the crib. "You reckon it'll help if I sing to her like my momma used to sing to me?"

"You can try," Lena said. She laid Ella back down, tucked

Poppy under her arm, and rubbed gentle fingers along the side of her face. Ella started to fuss and sit up, refusing to cooperate, but when Bonnie started to sing, she grew still and gazed up at her with sleepy eyes.

> Lullaby and good night, thy mother's delight
> With lilies bedecked, 'neath baby's sweet bed
> May thou sleep, may thou rest, may thy slumber be blest.
> May thou sleep, may thou rest, may thy slumber be blest.
> Lullaby and good night, thy mother's delight
> Bright angels around, my darling shall guard.
> They will guide thee from harm, thou art safe in my arms.
> They will guide thee from harm, thou art safe in my arms.

By the time Bonnie had finished the song, Ella was sound asleep and Lena was nearly in tears. Mutti used to sing the same lullaby to her and Enzo when they were little—in German, of course, but Lena had recognized the melody immediately. And Bonnie sang it so beautifully it would have touched anyone who heard it. After tiptoeing out of the bedroom and quietly closing the door behind them, she and Bonnie went downstairs, where Bonnie was going to teach her how to brew sassafras tea and make a salve from a plant called mouse's ear for healing insect bites and fever blisters.

"Where did you learn to sing like that?" Lena said as they went down the steps.

"Momma said I got it from her," Bonnie said. "And I'm here to tell you she was the best dang singer in these here hollers. Ask anybody and they'll tell you the same. She and Daddy used to sing together all the time, but he won't no more."

Lena had a hard time envisioning Silas breaking out in song, but then she remembered the portrait of the handsome young groom looking so full of life and mischief, and she could see his past potential. Sadly, it seemed Bonnie and Jack Henry had lost both parents when their mother died.

Back in the kitchen, Bonnie dropped handfuls of mouse's ears—bluish-gray leaves with rounded edges—in a kettle of boiling water while Lena cut up sassafras roots for tea.

"I am sure your father misses your mother very much," Lena said.

"'Course he does," Bonnie said. "Except he forgets he ain't the only one." She banged the wooden spoon on the edge of the kettle with more force than necessary, then went over to the sink.

Lena's heart sank further. Bonnie was wise beyond her years in more ways than one, and in ways no child should have to be. "You do not need to tell me if you do not want to," she said. "But I have been wondering how you lost your mother."

Keeping her back to Lena, Bonnie took a deep breath and held it, her shoulders high and tight. Then she exhaled, slowly. "She died giving birth two years, three months, and five days ago. The baby girl was born dead."

Lena sucked in a quick breath. "*Ach, Gott.* I am very sorry."

"Daddy and Granny Creed tried to save them both, but there warn't nothing they coulda done. People could hear Momma hollering from a mile away, she suffered so. Before she passed, she called me and Jack Henry to the bedside and told us to be good so we could meet her in heaven. Then she told Daddy to take care of us and see that we was brought up right. 'Cept I'm the one been taking care of everybody."

"That must have been very hard for you and your brother. When my father died, I did not think I would ever stop crying."

Bonnie turned from the sink, the dark shadows of grief haunting her eyes. "What happened to him?"

"He had a very bad disease. The doctors could not save him."

"I reckon y'all get how much I miss my momma then," Bonnie said.

"I do," Lena said. "And missing someone you love is the worst feeling in the world."

"It sure is. I'd rather get run over by a log wagon pulled by ten mules. At least then I'd feel better after a while."

Lena had no argument for that. Heartbreak was the wound that never healed. "I know I have said this before," she said. "But I am here to help with the work, and also to listen if you want to talk. About anything."

Bonnie nodded, then pulled an enamel colander from underneath the sink and set it on the counter. "After the mouse ear's done boiling, we gotta drain the liquid back in the kettle and add hog lard and a bottle of turpentine. Then we need to mix it good, let it cool, and put it in tins."

Apparently, she was done talking about her mother and wanted to get back to work, which Lena understood. Talking about the past did nothing to change it. But Bonnie had lost her mother and a baby sister at the same time. It was too much for someone so young to deal with alone. And as far as Lena could tell, Silas had failed at making sure his children were being comforted. She could only imagine the days after the funeral: Bonnie running around the house, waiting on her father and brother, making sure they had food and anything else they needed. Had she even let herself cry? Lena wanted Bonnie to keep talking, but at least she'd opened up a little bit, which was enough for now.

"While the mouse's ears are cooking," Bonnie said, "we can start supper."

Lena could hardly believe they had to make more food. She was still full from the cathead biscuits and milk gravy they'd had earlier. "I thought we already had supper."

"The evening vittles is called supper too," Bonnie said. She reached into a burlap sack hanging on the wall and pulled out an onion. "But I ain't decided if we should make mustard salad and cheese grits, or black-eyed peas and fried fatback."

"Do you have the . . . ?" Lena couldn't recall the right word; it was on the tip of her tongue. "The . . . the way to make the different foods. I cannot remember what it is called. The words that tell you what to do."

"The recipes?" Bonnie said.

"*Ja.* Yes. The recipes."

"I got some. Momma wrote a few down, but there warn't no need to write down the basics, like making beans and corn bread."

"Will you write them down for me?"

"I reckon so."

Seeing Bonnie work so efficiently reminded Lena of Mutti, who was happiest making a meal for her family when she had enough ingredients. How she would have loved to be here, cooking in this cozy kitchen with so many food choices at hand. Thinking of her mother, Lena remembered the other thing she wanted to ask Bonnie. "Jack Henry said you have paper for writing letters?"

Bonnie nodded and pulled an oversized cleaver out of a drawer. "I got lots of writing paper leftover from when the schoolteacher set us up with pen pals. Mine lived in Washington, D.C. Her name was Caroline." She took the cleaver over to the counter and cut the onion in half with one quick swipe, the thick metal hitting the wood with a heavy clunk. "But when I told her 'bout how one of our roosters run bleeding all over the yard after I chopped its head off, I ain't never heard from her again. I don't think she cottoned to that story."

"'Cottoned to'?" Lena said.

"She didn't like it."

Picturing a bloody rooster running around the yard, Lena couldn't blame Caroline for not wanting to read about it. Hopefully, Bonnie would be around when they had to prepare chicken for supper.

Just then, Jack Henry came into the kitchen, grinning proudly and holding up a skinned, headless animal by the tail. It looked like a giant rat.

Lena drew in a sharp breath and took a step back.

"Ain't you never seen a possum before?" Jack Henry said. "I trapped it and already sold the skin."

Lena shook her head, her hand over her stomach.

Bonnie picked up the skinless carcass, inspected its insides, and took it over to the sink to rinse out the stomach cavity. "Good timing, Jack Henry," she said. "I was just wondering what to fix for supper." She put a second kettle on the woodstove, threw the possum inside, and looked at Lena. "Y'all ain't never made possum stew before?"

"No," Lena said. "We had very little meat at home. And nothing that looked like a . . . a possum. When we did have meat, Mutti always cooked it a certain way so it would not go to waste."

"Do y'all know how to cook squirrel?" Bonnie said.

Lena shook her head.

"How about raccoon or muskrat?" Jack Henry said.

Lena shook her head again.

Bonnie gaped at her, bewildered. "Groundhog? Quail? Trout?"

"No," Lena said. "I do not know what those things are. Do you eat meat every day?"

"'Course we do," Jack Henry said. "Me and Daddy are the best hunters around these parts."

Bonnie rolled her eyes.

"I seen that," Jack Henry said.

Bonnie ignored him and addressed Lena. "Fetch the salt out of the pantry and I'll teach you how to make the best possum stew you'll ever eat."

"We catch buckets of fish over at Rust Creek too," Jack Henry said. "And if I get a deer in the fall, we got venison all winter. Ain't that right, Bonnie?"

"Sure," Bonnie said. "Whatever you say, Jack Henry."

Jack Henry's face flushed with anger. "Well, maybe I'll just fish that possum right out of that darn kettle and you can tell Daddy where it went!"

When Lena started toward the pantry to get the salt, she nearly ran into Silas coming in from the back hall. The smell of sawdust, metal, and sweat wafted into the kitchen with him, filling the air like a storm.

"Tell me where what went?" he said.

"Nothing, Daddy," Bonnie said. "Jack Henry was just bragging on being the best hunter in these here mountains."

"Was not!" Jack Henry said.

"Were too!" Bonnie said. "And you know darn well I can hunt and fish just as good as you and Daddy. Who got those two grouse the other day after you missed them, huh? I did."

"I warn't shooting at those!" Jack Henry shouted. "I was aiming at the groundhog y'all didn't even see!"

"Stop your goldurn hollering!" Silas said, his voice hard. He grabbed the back of a kitchen chair with both hands, his knuckles turning white. "I won't have this bickering in my house. We got enough troubles without you two going at each other like a coupla feral hogs!"

Bonnie and Jack Henry fell silent and Lena disappeared into the pantry, grateful for the escape. When she returned to the kitchen, Silas was still there, a silent tension hanging in the room. She took the salt over to Bonnie, who stood quietly at the stove stirring the kettles.

"What else do you need me to do?" Lena said quietly.

Bonnie pointed at the onion on the counter. "Y'all can slice that up and add it to the possum stew."

Lena did as she said.

"Where's the young'un?" Silas said.

Lena glanced over his shoulder to make sure he was speaking

to her. He was looking directly at her. "She is sleeping upstairs," she said.

"Jack Henry," Silas said, "get out to the crick and warsh up for supper."

"Yes, sir," Jack Henry said. He turned on his heels, went down the hall, and out the back door.

"Bonnie," Silas said, "after y'all finish putting the stew on, get on out there with Jack Henry. I need to talk to Lena. I'll fetch you when we're done."

Heat prickled along Lena's neck and chest. Had she done something wrong or did he have news of Mutti and Enzo? Would she be buoyed by the news or collapsing in a heap on the floor?

After Bonnie added pepper and other spices to the kettle, she wiped her hands on a dish towel and went outside with Jack Henry. Lena put the onion in with the possum and turned to face Silas, her nerves on edge.

His face was serious, his eyebrows knitted. "Take a seat."

Lena pulled out a chair and sat, her hands clasped together in her lap to keep them from shaking. Silas remained behind the other chair, still gripping the wooden back like he wanted to break it in two. It was hard to tell if he was uncomfortable or angry.

"I'll be working at the sawmill over on Corbin Holler tomorrow," he said. "And from here on out, I'll be there two days a week, more if I can get another shift. There'll be times when I deliver a load of wood down the mountain and I'll be gone overnight. That means you'll be here with the young'uns alone."

Lena nodded.

"Jack Henry can take care of the farm chores tomorrow, but you and Bonnie need to get cornmeal from the gristmill over on Weakley Stream. Normally I'd go and take the young'uns with me, but y'all need to do it from here on out. Bonnie'll show you how to get there. She's not to go by herself, no matter how many times she tells you she'll be fine. Stay on the trails on the way there and the way back."

"Yes, sir," Lena said.

"And Bonnie and Jack Henry know what to do if Sheriff Dixon or his deputy come nosing around. It'd be best if y'all make yourself scarce too. I don't need nobody asking questions if somebody finds you and your young'un here . . ." He trailed off, as if his words had led his mind elsewhere.

"Bonnie said the sheriff is a bad man. Is that why we must hide?"

"It ain't just Sheriff Dixon and his deputy you need to worry about. You need to go to the shed if anybody Bonnie and Jack Henry don't know comes around."

"But if you will not tell me why, how am I supposed to—"

He picked up the chair and slammed it on the floor, his face contorted with rage. "Y'all think you need to know my reasons for protecting my children? You only got a need to do what I tell you to do. And I don't cotton to you asking so many damn questions!"

She pressed her lips together and waited for him to calm down. If he wanted to yell at her, fine, but she still wanted answers. "If Bonnie and Jack Henry are in danger, is my Ella in danger too?"

His jaw worked in and out, like he was fighting the urge to strangle her. Maybe he wanted to hit her with the hickory switch he'd threatened his children with, not that she knew what one was. Finally, he spoke. "They ain't got no reason to take you or your girl away."

"Does the sheriff want to take Bonnie and Jack Henry away? Is it because someone said they are feebleminded?"

To her surprise, a look of pain flickered across his face.

Then, as quickly as it came, it disappeared and his anger returned. "That ain't the entire reason. And I ain't got time to explain the rest. I got too many chores to do before supper. I'll send the young'uns back in to help you finish fixing it."

She started to respond, but he turned, walked down the back hall, and left the house.

Chapter 9

With Ella riding piggyback, Bonnie led the way through the woods toward the gristmill, following a worn footpath that wound around oak and maple trees, climbed up rocky trails, and squeezed between cliffs and boulders. Lena had offered to wrap Ella in her shawl several times, but Bonnie insisted on carrying her, promising to hand her off if she got too tired. Besides, Bonnie reasoned, one of them had to carry the sack of cornmeal on the way home, and she figured Lena might as well give it a try. The problem was, even without a sack of cornmeal in her arms, Lena could hardly keep up, so she was secretly relieved Bonnie wanted to carry Ella.

Earlier that morning when they left the house, she had been looking forward to the walk, eager to stretch her legs and breathe in the pine-scented air like she used to back home. Granted, it had been some time since she hiked the hills surrounding her hometown—surely it was before she'd given birth to Ella—but she thought the journey to the mill would be easy. She was wrong. It didn't help that Bonnie was wearing shoes now, which made her as fast and surefooted as a mountain goat. And somehow, even carrying Ella, she was singing at the top of her lungs, not once sounding winded.

By the time they reached a patch of level land, Lena was panting and sticky with sweat, wondering how she would manage to carry a bag of cornmeal home. When she stopped to catch her breath, Bonnie slowed to look back at her.

"Come on," she said. "I want to show you something over yonder. But you gotta promise not to tell anyone, all right?"

Lena would have laughed if she had the strength. She had no one to tell. She nodded and rested her hands on her hips, still trying to collect herself. While Bonnie made her way back to where she stood, Lena was grateful for the respite.

"You gotta promise," Bonnie said.

"I promise," Lena said.

After they started walking again, they came to a field of wildflowers, the petals of blue and yellow, purple and red, white and pink swaying in the breeze like splattered paint. Bonnie picked a tiny bouquet of purple and pink blossoms and gave them to Ella.

"It is beautiful here," Lena said. "Is this what you wished to show me?"

Bonnie shook her head. "No. I ain't the only one who knows about this field. Momma showed it to me forever ago. And this is where Granny Creed gets some of her fixins, like bergamot, bee balm, pink rose, foxglove, cone flower, coreopsis, meadow rue, bluebell, bloodroot, butterfly weed, and some others I ain't remembering right now."

"I cannot believe you remember the names of *that* many," Lena said. "And who is Granny Creed? You have said her name to me before."

"We fetch Granny Creed if we get sick or hurt. She learnt healing from her great-grandfather, who learnt from the Cherokee. 'Course, everybody knows to use powdered sulfur on insect bites and that thinking of Willie Cook gets rid of hiccups.

We know willow bark tea helps aches and pains, catnip tea fixes a colicky young'un, cocklebur can help snake bites, and, depending on if you cut it up or down, slippery elm fixes stomach troubles, but Granny Creed does everything from birthing babies to prescribing medicines to fixing broken legs and bleeding innards."

Lena shook her head in wonder. Her family had their own natural remedies, like warm milk with honey for coughs and salt-water gargles for sore throats, but she had never heard of the treatments Bonnie mentioned.

"I'll tell y'all something else," Bonnie said, smirking. "You better hope you don't get the arthritis when you're old, 'cause Granny Creed's cure for that is melted worms and moonshine." She laughed, and then, to Lena's dismay, she started to run across the field, Ella giggling on her back.

Lena groaned and ran to catch up. At the edge of the wildflowers, Bonnie ducked under a low-hanging branch and disappeared. Lena went after her, then followed her along a narrow, overgrown path through gangly trees and thick brush. When they came to a circular clearing, Bonnie let Ella down, took her by the hand, and led her over to a circle of trees, where old cans, pieces of tin, brown bottles, and rusty buckets hung by strings from low branches. Bonnie let go of Ella's hand, picked up two sticks, and began singing a simple song while drumming on the cans and bottles and buckets. Ella giggled in delight and rocked side to side, dancing in time with the rhythm. Lena smiled and put a hand over her heart, amazed and enchanted by both the magical place and Bonnie's remarkable talent. Bonnie picked up another stick and handed it to Ella, who tentatively hit a low-hanging bucket. Then she whacked it harder, her face filled with glee. Lena found a stick and joined Bonnie, matching her tempo with a one-two beat. After a minute, they lost their rhythm and started to laugh.

"What is this place?" Lena said.

"Jack Henry and me made it a couple summers ago, back when Daddy used to let us wander alone. Don't say nothing, but every now and then we sneak out here to add more to it. Maybe we can come back more often now, on account of y'all being here and all."

Lena beamed at Bonnie, touched by her willingness to share something so special, grateful she trusted her not to tell. "I love it. Thank you for showing me."

"Don't forget it's a secret. We ain't looking for it to get ruined."

"I promise not to tell."

After letting Ella play and drum for a few more minutes, Bonnie squatted down to let her climb on her back again. "Hop on up, baby doll. This horse is fixing to leave."

To Lena's amazement, Ella immediately dropped the stick and toddled toward Bonnie, grinning. It was as if they'd developed their own secret language.

Nearby, a bird called loud and quick, and another answered.

Before Ella reached her, Bonnie did a sudden somersault in the thick grass, then knelt for Ella again. Ella stopped and stared at her with wide eyes, delighted yet surprised.

"Sorry, baby doll," Bonnie said. "But when y'all hear a whippoorwill calling, you turn a somersault so your back don't ache no more that year."

"Does your back hurt?" Lena said.

Bonnie smiled. "No, I just like doing somersaults. But Granny Creed swears it works." After Ella climbed on her back again, she stood, her arms hooked beneath Ella's thin legs. "The other thing she told me is when you hear the big old owl in the mountains holler, hear it late in the evening, you might just as well prepare for snow. And that's the truth 'cause I seen it happen."

Again, Lena thought about how much she had to learn, and how ridiculous it was that anyone could think Bonnie was feebleminded. If anything, she was a sage old soul, a wise woman reincarnated as a child, baptized by and deep-rooted in the secrets of these ancient mountains. Surely, she could teach a thing or two to those blind to her intelligence.

With Bonnie in the lead, they left the clearing and climbed another slight hill, then came to a steep, grassy embankment leading up to a dirt road.

"The mill's around the bend just a piece," Bonnie said. "Less than a mile up this here road." She put Ella down to let her walk, then pointed toward a narrower road cutting off to the left. "Used to be a store down yonder in Walnut Holler, but that was before the railway came through. Now we got to drive all the way down to Swift Run Gap to get supplies."

"Where is the school?" Lena said.

"Y'all passed it on your way up to Wolfe Holler," Bonnie said. "The church across from the post office is the school during the week. It ain't got no outhouse though. The boys go downhill and the girls go uphill. And I'm here to tell you that ain't no fun when the winter wind sweeps across the ridge. I sure don't miss that part a learning."

Lena remembered seeing a church across from the post office. It seemed like a hundred miles back down the mountain. "You rode a mule that far to school?"

Bonnie nodded. "Sure did. Left shortly after sunup and got home with plenty of time for fixing supper. And like I said, we loved riding Ole Sal. In the winter we got right cold sometimes, but Ole Sal could move pretty fast when he wanted to. And when the weather was good, there warn't nothing nicer than plodding along dirt roads, just singing or listening to the birds in the trees and the bees buzzing in the long grass."

Bonnie's reminiscing was interrupted by the approaching thud of horses' hooves and the crunch of wagon wheels coming around the bend up ahead. Before Lena knew what was happening, Bonnie grabbed Ella and headed into the woods.

"Come on!" she hissed.

Startled and confused, Lena followed her into the trees, pushing aside branches and bushes. Several yards from the road, they crouched behind a lichen-covered boulder, Ella standing between them. Lena took Ella's hands to keep her still.

Bonnie put a finger to her lips. "Shhh," she said to Ella.

"Who is it?" Lena whispered.

Bonnie shrugged, the worry line between her eyes growing deeper. When the wagon grew closer, she peeked around the boulder, moving as slow and quiet as a hunting cat. Then, to Lena's shock, she suddenly stood and stepped out from behind the boulder.

"Hey, Virgil!" she called out. "I ain't seen you in a coon's age." She headed toward the road. "How y'all doing?"

Lena straightened, picked up Ella, and followed Bonnie out of the woods. Apparently, it wasn't the sheriff, and hopefully Bonnie knew it was all right to talk to whoever was in the wagon. Didn't she?

Out on the road, the horse and wagon came to a stop, stirring up thin clouds of dust. Stacks of wooden crates in the back of the wagon shifted slightly and glass clinked against glass. Turning in the driver's seat, Virgil took a corncob pipe out of his mouth and peered at them through round glasses.

"What the devil are y'all doing over there in them woods?" he said.

"I weren't sure who was coming round the bend," Bonnie said. "We're heading to the mill."

"Better safe than sorry, I reckon," Virgil said. "But y'all know Sheriff Dixon don't drive no wagon. He's got himself a paddy wagon now. Where's Jack Henry?"

"He's back home doing the farming on account of Daddy working at the sawmill."

"He getting more hours these days?" Virgil said.

"Trying to," Bonnie said.

Virgil eyed Lena and Ella. "And who are these two pretty gals?"

"This here's Lena and Ella," Bonnie said. "Lena's gonna be helping around the house from here on out."

"Glad to hear it," Virgil said. "It's about time your daddy got some help instead of making you young'uns take care a things." He gave Lena a quick nod. "Pleased to make your acquaintance, Miss Lena. Welcome to Old Rag. Me and Silas used to roam these hollers together when we was young whippersnappers, looking for trouble, o'course. Fought overseas together too."

"It is nice to meet you," Lena said.

"Now, I know y'all ain't asking for advice," he said. "But be sure and listen to Silas and don't be foolhardy while you're here. These creeks and hollers are beautiful and most of the mountain folk are decent people, but just like the wilderness can turn on you without warning, so can some individuals. And some who ain't from around here too, if you know what I'm getting at." He regarded Bonnie again. "Widow Spinney is on the bridge again, so mind the young'un."

"Thanks for the warning," Bonnie said. "We'll take the creek instead."

"Good thinking," Virgil said. "I'd turn around and take you across myself but I got to get this load of moonshine delivered." He looked at Lena again. "In case no one ain't told you yet, Silas Wolfe might come off as a hard ass, but he's a decent and honest man. For a long patch, some of the churchgoers and even some of his own relatives were down on him 'cause he drank liquor and ran around with women. But I ain't never once seen Silas Wolfe drunk. And after he got married, he settled down and done good ever since. I just wanna say, for the record, he's a hardworking, respectable family man."

Surprised by Virgil's concern, Lena smiled and nodded to

show her appreciation for the information. As suspected, Silas was more complicated than he appeared.

Encouraged by her reaction, Virgil continued. "I'd put money on him being the strongest man that ever lived in the Blue Ridge too. Me and my brother was working on Hog Back Road one day when Silas went by carrying a bag of groceries in one hand, a sack of buckwheat slung over one shoulder, and a can of coal oil in the other hand. He stopped and talked to us for a good hour without putting any of that down, and that sack a buckwheat by itself had to weigh a good fifty pounds. Another time I saw him pick up a wooden barrel, one of them big ones they used to keep sody pop in, you know? He picked up that barrel and carried it right up the mountain without running outta breath. Did the same thing during the war, he did. Carried two injured men at a time back to get patched up. He ain't ever gonna admit it, but he's a war hero. The thing you need to know is, losing his wife broke him and he ain't been the same since. Between that and losing four young'uns, he ain't got a fair shake. And now he's hell-bent on making everyone around him pay. 'Cept for his cousin Teensy McDaniel, most of his family is dead or moved out of these mountains, so Bonnie and Jack Henry is all he's got. I guess what I'm saying is, don't take his anger personal-like. Tragedy turns some people softer and some people harder. And Silas Wolfe is hard as stone."

Lena had no idea what to say. She'd seen what war could do to people. And losing a spouse had to be incredibly difficult. But losing a child, let alone four, would surely crush anyone's soul. If she lost Ella she would surely die. While it helped to know why Silas was miserable and her sympathy for him grew, it was no excuse for the way he treated Jack Henry and Bonnie. Yes, he wanted to protect them from the sheriff, but he needed to show them love and compassion too. Then she noticed Bonnie wiping her cheeks.

"What is wrong? Are you all right?"

Bonnie nodded. "I'm right as rain," she said, blinking back the rest of her tears. Then she looked up at Virgil, steadfastness and determination returning to her eyes. Either she'd inherited a different kind of strength from her father or she'd learned how to be strong on her own. The poor girl had lost her mother and, according to Virgil, several siblings too, yet she found joy and beauty in simple things, like singing and making music with old bottles and pieces of tin. Not to mention how much she loved children, which was obvious in the way she'd immediately taken to Ella despite her grief and suffering. A sense of shame suddenly overcame Lena. Yes, she missed Mutti and Enzo, but at least they were alive.

"Stop by sometime, will y'all?" Bonnie said. "It'd make Daddy mighty happy."

Virgil looked doubtful. "I ain't sure about that. Your daddy wouldn't even let me on the porch last time I came calling."

"I know," Bonnie said. "But I wish you'd keep trying."

Virgil's shoulders dropped. "I reckon you're right. I ought to try again. In the meantime, I gotta get moving. I'm meeting the Nicholsons over at Slaughter Pen Branch and I wanna get back home before dark."

"Sure thing," Bonnie said. "See you around, Virgil."

"I reckon you will," Virgil said. "Nice meeting you, Miss Lena." Then he picked up the wagon reins and drove off.

Lena and Bonnie started walking again, Ella toddling along between them. Suddenly a squirrel scurried across the road in front of them, scampered up a tree, and chattered at them from a high branch. Ella stopped to look up at it, giggling. Lena and Bonnie slowed, waiting for her to catch up.

"Would your father be upset that you were talking to Virgil?" Lena said.

"I reckon, but Virgil is like family and Daddy's just being stubborn. He's fit to be tied on account of Virgil selling moonshine."

"Fit to be tied?"

"Means he's mad. Daddy thinks Virgil's gonna have Sheriff Dixon sniffing around more than he already is. That's why he wants him to stay away from us."

"I asked your father about the sheriff, but he did not say much."

"'Course not. Daddy don't say much of anything anymore, unless he's mad."

"Yes," Lena said. "I have noticed that."

They walked in silence for a minute or two, each lost in their own thoughts while Ella kicked pebbles and picked up leaves.

"May I ask you about some of the other things Virgil said?" Lena said.

Bonnie shrugged.

"If you do not want to talk about it, we do not have to. I only want to understand, to help if I can. Virgil said your parents have lost other children?"

Bonnie nodded, her eyes fixed on the road. "Georgie and Matilda Grace got the smallpox, and Jeramiah drowned in the bee-gum spring when he was two. You already know about the last one being born dead. But Daddy never gave her a name on account of he says she killed Momma."

"*Ach, Gott.* I am so sorry. You and your family have had too much sadness. But you know it was not the baby's fault that your mother died, right?"

Bonnie shrugged again. "I reckon it don't matter now." She stopped near a rocky outcropping where the road started to turn around a wooded hill. "Up ahead is Sugar Gulch Bridge. Virgil said the Widow Spinney is on it again so we gotta cut into the woods and cross the creek bed."

"Who is the Widow Spinney?"

"All I know for sure is she's nuttier than a squirrel turd. Been walking back and forth on that bridge for years now, sobbing with a baby in her arms. 'Cept her husband and baby are dead and she ain't carrying nothing but a bundle of old blankets. Some folk say her husband left her and she threw the baby over the bridge to spite him. Other folks say her husband got killed in the war and the baby died of starvation 'cause she was so torn up she forgot to feed it." She picked up Ella. "The thing is, every time she sees a baby, she starts screaming it's hers."

Lena shivered and wrapped her arms around herself. What a ghastly story. And she had enough to worry about without a crazy woman trying to take her daughter. Before she could say anything, Bonnie turned and cut into the dark woods. Lena followed, trying to keep up as they made their way through low, scratchy brush, towering pines, and thick oaks. Suddenly, a long, low moan drifted through the trees. Lena froze. Bonnie kept going, unfazed.

"What was that?" Lena whispered.

"The Widow Spinney," Bonnie said. "Come on, we need to hurry."

Further into the forest, they scrambled down a steep, rocky embankment toward the edge of a creek, where a wooden bridge soared above their heads. The widow's cries floated out over the wood railing, wheeling and echoing through the gulley like the howl of a tortured animal. Goose bumps prickled on Lena's skin. She recognized that horrible, wretched scream of grief. She'd heard it as a little girl when the neighborhood women learned their husbands and sons had been killed in the war. And again, from her own mother's throat when Vater died. But she'd never heard it go on and on and on and on. At the bottom of the embankment, she looked up at the bridge. A dark figure moved across the spaces between the planks, then stopped and peered over the railing.

"Keep moving," Bonnie said, hurrying toward the creek's stony bank. She moved Ella from her hip to her back, hooking her arms under Ella's legs. "She nearly caught me and Jeramiah once."

Lena looked out over the low, swift water, and toward the boiling rapids downstream. "Give Ella to me," she said.

"Better let me carry her," Bonnie said. "Getting to the other side can be a mite tricky if you don't know the way."

Then she started across the creek, stepping from rock to rock as agile as a tightrope walker despite carrying a toddler on her back. Lena summoned her courage and followed her along the slippery stones, her arms out for balance. Then she glanced up at the bridge again. The Widow Spinney was staring down at them, her eyes black as night, her skin white as bone, her long, gray hair hanging over the railing like tangled ropes. Lena's foot slipped and she almost fell, her shoe filling with cold water. Then she caught herself and crossed the creek as if she'd done it a hundred times, moving as fast as she could without falling.

CHAPTER 10

The weathered gristmill stood on rough-hewn stilts over a narrow creek, its wooden waterwheel turning in the swift current created by a rocky waterfall. A split-rail fence ran along the millpond before climbing a grassy slope toward a crooked-roofed cabin, a pig shed with a broken window, and a squat woodshed flanked by apple trees. Two horse-drawn carts sat at the edge of the road and three women gathered near the mill talking to a stick-thin man with frizzy white hair. In the area between the house and the mill, a group of girls played tag and jump rope while several boys took turns hitting a ball with a stick. Happy shouts and laughter filled the air. Lena slowed and picked up Ella, her nerves mounting.

"Do you know all of these people?" she asked Bonnie.

"Sure do," Bonnie said. "They ain't too many folks we don't know around these parts. Come on, they ain't gonna bite."

Lena hoped Bonnie was right. It was bad enough worrying about being accepted here; now, thanks to Silas, she had a new fear of strangers.

The frizzy-haired man lifted his chin as they approached and the women looked over their shoulders to see who was coming. One turned and waved at Bonnie, her thin arms and quick movements like those of a bird.

"Well, hey there, Bonnie," the birdlike woman said. "It's been a spell since I seen you here without your daddy."

"Hey, Nellie," Bonnie said. "Daddy's working at the sawmill today."

The other two women turned and smiled too, one with a face as wrinkled and tan as a hazelnut, the other with the wavy hair and pretty face of a movie star.

When the wrinkled-faced woman saw Ella in Lena's arms, her eyes lit up. "Oh, my word," she said. "Who is this little cherub?"

"This here's Ella," Bonnie said. "And her momma, Lena. They're staying with us at the farm."

"Is that right?" Nellie said.

"Yep," Bonnie said. "Came all the way here from Germany, they did." She addressed Lena. "This here's Nellie McCauley, Betty Lee Blanchard, and Sandy Craig. Nellie lives over on the Ridgeline. Betty Lee and Sandy come from over by Sugar Hollow near the north fork of Moorman's River. And Mr. Early owns this here mill."

"It is nice to meet you," Lena said.

"Good to meet y'all too," Sandy said.

The others nodded.

"Your husband come to the States too?" Betty Lee said.

Despite knowing the question would come up eventually, Lena cringed inside. Who knew how these women would react to her daughter being born out of wedlock? What did Silas call it—"on the wrong side of the blanket"? She'd had enough judgment about her lack of a husband back in Germany; she had no desire for it here. And, like she'd said to herself a hundred times, Ella's father might as well be dead anyway. "No," she said. "The man I was to marry passed away before the wedding." Hopefully, the excuse would draw more sympathy than scrutiny.

"Gracious me, that's just awful," Sandy said.

"You poor thing," Betty Lee said.

"I'm so sorry," Nellie said.

"Thank you," Lena said, relieved. Dropping her gaze just long enough to look properly distressed, she hoped no one would ask how he died.

"So, how'd y'all end up living here in the Blue Ridge?" Nellie said.

"Y'all one of them mail-order brides?" Mr. Early said. "Seeing if you and Silas will take to each other?"

Nellie gave him a scolding look. "Mr. Early," she said. "Even if that were true, I reckon it ain't none of our business now, is it?"

"She's Daddy's kin," Bonnie said. "A distant cousin. They didn't have nothing back home so Daddy said they could come stay with us and help out."

"Well, ain't that something?" Sandy said. "Guess Silas Wolfe has a heart in him after all."

"Be nice now," Nellie said.

"She's just got a knot in her tail 'cause Silas ain't looked her way," Betty Lee said.

Sandy gave Betty Lee a sour look. "Did y'all know you go to hell for lying just as quick as you do for stealing?"

"All right, gals," Mr. Early said. "Let's not scare Miss Lena off." He looked at Lena with apologetic eyes. "Sorry for saying something out a turn. I meant no disrespect."

Lena nodded, giving him a weak smile. She had no idea what a mail-order bride was anyway.

Mr. Early addressed the other women. "Now tell me what y'all need and let's get back to business."

"I need fifty pounds of cornmeal," Nellie said.

"We need the same," Bonnie said.

"We're fetching buckwheat and cornmeal," Sandy said, indicating herself and Betty Lee. "Fifty pounds each."

"Cornmeal might take a spell," Mr. Early said. "I ain't bagged it up yet."

"That ain't a problem," Nellie said. "We all got some catching up to do anyway. Ain't that right, ladies?"

The other women nodded.

Bonnie tugged on Lena's sleeve and pointed at the children playing in the yard. "I'm gonna jump rope with Ruby Ann and Jessomay."

"Would your father agree?" Lena said.

Bonnie nodded, her eyes eager. "Daddy always lets me and Jack Henry run loose while he catches up with Mr. Early." For the first time since Lena arrived, Bonnie sounded and acted her age.

"All right," Lena said. "I will try to get Ella to sleep while we wait for the cornmeal."

Bonnie grinned and ran toward the other children, her blond hair flying. After finding a soft spot in the grass to sit down, Lena wrapped Ella inside her shawl and leaned against the mill wall, gently rocking her side to side and humming a German lullaby. Between the long walk to get there and the rhythmic whoosh of the waterwheel vibrating like the beat of a giant heart on the other side of the building, Ella was asleep within seconds. While the women gossiped and paid Mr. Early—Nellie with cash, Betty Lee and Sandy with eggs and vegetables—Lena listened.

"Y'all know Beulah Mae's youngest had his leg cut off in a bush hog last week," Sandy said. "Bobby Roy, I think it is. You don't remember? Well, you know Granny was a Sawyer and her sister, Flora, she was the one just eaten up with cancer, she married Emmet's oldest boy, Luke. Beulah Mae married Dale's second cousin Hollis. You remember Hollis, he used to come every Thanksgiving."

"Was he the tall, skinny one with moles or the stubby one with the black-rimmed fingernails?" Betty Lee said.

"The tall, skinny one," Sandy said.

"That was Bobby Roy's brother?"

"I think so but I ain't for sure."

"That George Pollock came around again," Nellie said. "I made the young'uns come inside as soon as I seen him."

"That man's crazier than a runover dog," Sandy said. "Up there in his fancy resort, strutting around in a cowboy suit, playing with rattlesnakes and throwing drunken dress-up shindigs for his rich friends."

"Was Sheriff Dixon with him?" Betty Lee asked.

"Not that I seen," Nellie said.

"Y'all wouldn't have seen him," Sandy said. "'Cause he's lower than a snake's belly in a wagon rut."

Lena stopped humming and stilled, hoping the women would say more about the sheriff. Apparently, Silas wasn't the only one who didn't trust him, which eased her mind a little. But who was George Pollock? And why would Nellie make her children come inside when he came around?

"Did y'all hear Sheriff Dixon and his deputy took the Corbin boy the other day?" Betty Lee said. "Told his momma he was taking him to be evaluated."

A chill crawled up Lena's spine. The sheriff had actually taken a child? And after Enzo had been *evaluated* on Ellis Island, the doctors had threatened to lock him up for the rest of his life. Maybe Bonnie was right. Maybe Silas wanted her and Jack Henry to hide because someone had called them feebleminded. But why would the sheriff want to lock them up? And why would he do that to American citizens, especially children? Did he think Bonnie and Jack Henry would be unable to get a job? Did he think they would become criminals who could not contribute to society? It made no sense.

"Evaluated?" Sandy said. "What for? And by who?"

"I ain't sure," Betty Lee said. "Gertie Corbin was so shook up she didn't think to ask."

Before the women could say more, the bang and sputter of an approaching vehicle drew their attention to the road. A dust-covered automobile came over the crest of the hill, a brown cloud of dirt rising behind it, then motored toward the mill and came to a hard stop in the grass. Bonnie and the other children stopped playing and looked up to see who was coming. Mr. Early came out of the mill, puzzlement worrying his brow. A man in a black hat and fitted jacket got out of the driver's side, then opened the back door and pulled out a brown rucksack.

"Who in tarnation is that?" Sandy said.

"Darned if I know," Mr. Early said. "I ain't seen that particular person round here before."

"Looks like a city slicker to me," Nellie said.

When the passenger side door opened, a heavyset woman with round glasses climbed out, hooked a purse over her elbow, and went around to the man. She said something to him, gesturing toward the mill.

"That there looks like Miss Sizer," Betty Lee said.

"Who?" Mr. Early said.

"Miss Miriam Sizer," Betty Lee said. "That new teacher over at the summer school."

"What's she doing way up here?" Nellie said. "My Jacob went to that school for a few days and if you ask me, that woman is a mite too nosy for my taste."

"What makes you say that?" Sandy said.

"I say that 'cause she spent more time asking questions than teaching," Nellie said. "She asked my boy about my husband and what he does for money. How many sisters and brothers he has, what kind of food we eat, that kind of thing. Tell me what teacher has a need to know all that?"

"I heard she taught the class how to sing 'America'," Betty Lee said.

"What for?" Sandy said.

Betty Lee shrugged.

The man left the car and started toward them. The woman followed. Halfway to the mill, the man reached into his rucksack and pulled out a black, hand-size box with what looked like silver dials.

"Is that a camera?" Sandy said.

"Sure looks like it," Mr. Early said.

The man raised the camera and pointed it at the mill.

"He taking pictures of us?" Sandy said.

"I reckon he is," Mr. Early said.

Lena pushed herself up from the grass, careful not to wake Ella, and motioned for Bonnie to come back. Bonnie, who had been watching the newcomers with suspicion, was already headed in her direction. When she reached Lena, they stayed next to the mill, several yards behind the others.

The man lowered his camera and started toward them. He was young and slender, with a confident walk. The woman, middle-aged and stubborn-mouthed with a double chin, followed a few feet behind, carefully stepping around rocks and uneven ground.

Betty Lee hurried to gather up her toddler, who was playing in a muddy puddle near the millpond fence. Then she yelled at a little girl building a twig house beneath an oak tree, "Mary Frances, y'all get over here with Momma right now!" The little girl dropped the twigs in her hand and did as she was told. Betty Lee met her halfway, grabbed her by the arm, and led her back to the safety of her friends.

"Do you know that man and woman?" Lena whispered to Bonnie.

Bonnie shook her head.

One of the older boys ran up to the strangers, happy and excited. "Will y'all take my picture?"

Another boy followed. "Mine too!"

The man nodded and kept walking. "Sure thing, boys."

When he and Miss Sizer reached the group, she spoke first.

"Good morning, ladies," she said. She gave Mr. Early a curt nod. "Sir. As some of you may know, I'm Miss Miriam Sizer, the temporary summer schoolteacher at Old Rag. I also do research for the psychologist, Mandel Sherman, and the science writer, Thomas Henry. I'd like to introduce you to Mr. Rothstein, who has been commissioned by the Historical Section of the Resettlement Administration to take photographs up here in the Blue Ridge. He just spent a week in a cabin near the Corbin family, but he'd like to get a few more photographs before he leaves."

"What's the reason behind all this picture-taking?" Mr. Early said.

"Why, it's for posterity's sake, of course," Miss Sizer said. "And Mr. Rothstein is a fine photographer."

Mr. Rothstein grinned as if embarrassed. "It's true I'm getting paid to take photographs, but I'm also hoping to put together a book about these mountains and the people who live here." He regarded Mr. Early. "Are you the owner of this fine mill?"

"I am," Mr. Early said.

"Well, it's just beautiful," Mr. Rothstein said. "One of the finest I've ever seen. A little weather-beaten, but in my opinion that just adds to the charm. It would make a perfect cover for my book."

"Thank you kindly," Mr. Early said. "Been in my family for six generations now."

"Is that right?" Mr. Rothstein said. "What an amazing legacy." He addressed the women. "Would you mind having your pictures taken today?"

"Y'all want photographs of *us*?" Nellie said.

"And your children, if that's all right," Mr. Rothstein said.

"Well, I don't know," Nellie said, looking worriedly at the other women.

Betty Lee shook her head.

Sandy shrugged, unsure.

"Maybe we should leave," Lena whispered to Bonnie.

"But we ain't got the cornmeal yet, and I'm plumb out," Bonnie whispered back. "And Daddy ain't gonna know nothing about this unless you tell him."

Lena sighed. Bonnie had a point. There was no reason to tell Silas about these strangers showing up. The mill was not his house.

Mr. Early hooked his thumbs through his suspenders. "Y'all mean to tell me you came all the way up in these here hollers to take pictures of us folk?"

"Yes, sir," Mr. Rothstein said. "But to be honest, I didn't realize how far up some of you lived, otherwise I would have hired a horse and wagon. These steep roads have been a little rough on my car." He turned to take in the view. "But I can see why you love it up here."

Miss Sizer grimaced like she'd swallowed something rotten. "I warned you these primitive roads weren't made for modern vehicles. These people are backward and ignorant. They don't know a thing about being civilized and do not possess the ambition to make things better for themselves." Then, as if suddenly realizing what she'd said, she stopped talking, her face filled with a mixture of embarrassment and disgust. "I'll wait in the car," she said, then turned on her heel and waddled back to the vehicle, her purse swinging like a pendulum from her arm.

Mr. Rothstein chuckled. "Some people just don't recognize old-fashioned charm when they see it," he said, as if being amused and friendly would excuse Miss Sizer's behavior.

"And some people ain't worth a pot to piss in," Mr. Early said.

"I'm sorry," Mr. Rothstein said. "Miss Sizer is sore at me more than anything else. All the driving and traveling can be dusty and hot, and I'm afraid I've done a poor job of making sure she's comfortable."

The women and Mr. Early glanced at each other, deciding whether to accept his apology or tell him to be on his way.

Sandy chewed on her lip, then said to Mr. Rothstein, "Will a whole lot of people be seeing your pictures?"

"Of course," Mr. Rothstein said. "Some of them will even be in newspapers all over the country."

Sandy's eyes lit up with excitement. "Well, I'll be jiggered," she said. "Where do you want us to stand?"

Lena glanced at Bonnie, a ripple of unease spreading through her. If only they could get their cornmeal and go home.

With a satisfied grin, Mr. Rothstein did a quick study of the surrounding area. "How about over there near that woodshed?"

"Can I be in the picture too?" Mary Frances said, stepping forward.

Betty Lee pulled her back. "Shush, child."

"That's up to your mother," Mr. Rothstein said. "But I sure would like to take a picture of a pretty little girl like you." He nodded at the toddler in Betty Lee's arms. "Your cute little brother too. You've got a beautiful family, ma'am. If I were a betting man, I'd put money on you all winning the Fitter Family Contest over at the state fair, easy as pie."

With that, Betty Lee blushed and gazed down at her daughter and son with a proud smile. "Well, I reckon a couple a pictures can't hurt."

"Mountain folk ain't allowed to enter that contest," Sandy said.

Nellie elbowed Sandy, irritated. "That ain't no never mind. He was just saying something nice about her and her young'uns."

Ignoring the exchange, Betty Lee used her apron to start wiping the mud off her toddler's hands and face.

"Oh, don't worry about that," Mr. Rothstein said. "Little ones like to play in the dirt and everyone knows it. Why don't you let . . ." He looked down at Betty Lee's little girl. "What's your name again, darling?"

"Mary Frances," she said.

Mr. Rothstein smiled up Betty Lee again. "Why don't you let Mary Frances hold the boy while I take pictures of the adults. After that, I'll photograph the children."

"All right," Betty Lee said, and handed the muddy toddler to Mary Frances.

Mr. Rothstein addressed the others. "Would you all mind being in the photographs too? It will only take a few minutes of your time. And don't tell anyone I said so, but you're the most comely group I've run into so far. It would be an honor and a privilege to have you featured in my work."

Mr. Early chuckled. "You're quite the charmer, ain't you?"

Waiting for the women to answer, Mr. Rothstein pretended not to hear what he said. But Lena had to agree with Mr. Early. Maybe it was because of what she'd gone through with Ella's father, but she had a hard time trusting anyone who was overly friendly and complimentary to strangers.

Sandy put a playful hand on Nellie's arm. "Come on, it'll be fun."

"I reckon it don't matter if I do or I don't," Nellie said.

Sandy clapped her hands together in delight and glanced back at Lena. "Y'all coming?"

Lena shook her head. "No, thank you."

"Come along, Mr. Early," Mr. Rothstein said. "I want the owner of this fine mill in the photograph too. Everyone, please gather under the apple trees in front of the woodshed."

Chattering and giggling, the group moved toward the trees, Betty Lee untying her apron and starting to take it off, Sandy running her fingers through her hair.

"Please don't worry about your aprons or your hair, ladies," Mr. Rothstein said. "You're already pretty as can be and I want to capture you in your normal, everyday life in these beautiful mountains. My book will be about what living up here is really like."

Next to the mill, Lena laid Ella down on the grass, still inside the shawl, then sat down beside her to watch. Bonnie sat down too. When everyone had gathered beneath the apple trees, Mr. Rothstein told Sandy to pick up a burlap bag lying in the crotch of a tree and hold it like she was picking apples. Then he instructed Mr. Early to lean against the woodshed with his hands in his pockets.

"That's it," he said. "Move to the front a little more. What's your name again? Sandy? All right Sandy, yes, that's perfect." He glanced back at Lena. "Are you sure you and your children wouldn't like to be in the pictures, ma'am?"

Lena shook her head again.

Mr. Rothstein shrugged. "Suit yourself," he said, then turned back to his subjects. "Everyone ready?"

The women smiled and nodded.

"I reckon," said Mr. Early. "'Cept I don't get why you want me looking lazy as a pet coon."

"Please don't smile, ladies," Mr. Rothstein said. "I want this to look natural, like I just happened across you on this fine morning while you were doing chores and visiting."

The women tried to follow his directions by looking more solemn, but Sandy couldn't stop smirking.

"Picture something sad," Mr. Rothstein said. "Something that almost makes you want to cry."

Sandy did what he said, the smile falling from her face.

"That's it," he said. "By golly, I swear you could be an actress."

Encouraged, Sandy took on a more serious look, frowning and furrowing her brow.

"Perfect," Mr. Rothstein said.

The other women imitated Sandy, moping and sulking and brooding. They looked like they were going to a funeral.

After taking a few photos, Mr. Rothstein instructed Sandy and four of the children to stand on the front porch of Mr. Early's cabin, including Mary Frances and her muddy-faced brother.

"Would you mind taking off your shoes?" Mr. Rothstein

said. "I want everyone to think these photographs were taken in the height of summer."

The children and Sandy removed their shoes and tossed them in the grass beside the cabin. Mary Frances was already barefoot, as was her brother.

"Y'all want me to hold the baby?" Sandy said.

"No," Mr. Rothstein said. "I want Mary Frances to keep holding him. But if you could stand near the stairs and stare off into the distance like you're waiting for someone, that would be wonderful."

" 'Course I can," Sandy said. She skipped up the steps and took her place at the top.

"Now wipe your hands on your apron," Mr. Rothstein said. "Like you just finished washing dishes."

Taking his instructions seriously, Sandy leaned against the rail post with her apron in her hands and gazed out over the mountains with a forlorn look. A few steps behind her, near the front door, Mary Frances held her muddy-faced brother.

"Now look up at Sandy, Mary Frances," Mr. Rothstein said. "Like you're sad and waiting for her to help with the baby." Then he said to one of the boys, "Sit on the edge of the porch and hang your head." And to another boy, "Put your hands in the pockets of your overalls and look mad, like your momma just scolded you." The boys did as he asked.

Lena glanced at Bonnie to see if she was confused too, but her face was hard to read. She'd seen portraits of miserable-looking people before, most of them taken years ago, back when everyone was afraid of looking drunk or insane due to the fact that cameras took so long to capture images. But times had changed. Cameras were faster now and it was acceptable to smile when having your picture taken. The expressions Mr. Rothstein was asking for were the gloomiest Lena had ever seen. Granted, she'd only met a few people since arriving in Wolfe Hollow, but none had acted as miserable as Sandy and the others looked now. Except Silas, of course.

When Mr. Rothstein finished taking the pictures on the porch, he told the children to stand next to the pig shed, where cracked boards hung from the roof and crumpled rags filled the panes of a broken window. One boy started to put his shoes back on but Mr. Rothstein said to leave them off.

Bonnie tapped Lena on the arm. "I want to be in a photograph."

Lena shook her head. "I do not think that is a good idea. What would your father say?"

"Daddy ain't got a need to know. He won't never see the pictures."

"But he would not like it if you talk to that man. You don't know him."

"I ain't planning on talking to him," Bonnie said. "I just want to be in a picture with the others. Their mothers don't care none about the photographer being a stranger. Mr. Early don't care neither and he's Tad and Garth's grandpappy." She pointed at two boys around Jack Henry's age. "I ain't never had my picture taken before."

Lena let out a sigh. In the grand scheme of things, being photographed with the other children was such a small thing. And Bonnie was right; no one else seemed overly concerned about the photographer being a stranger.

Bonnie got up and wiped the grass off her dress. "Momma would let me."

"All right," Lena said. "But we cannot tell your—" Before she finished speaking, Bonnie had run off to join the others.

Despite her concern about Bonnie being in the pictures, Lena couldn't help smiling when Bonnie laughed with the other children after Mr. Rothstein told them to smear mud on their cheeks. Lena couldn't imagine why he wanted them to be so dirty, but it was good to see Bonnie happy and acting like a child.

After taking a few more shots of the children next to the pig shed, Mr. Rothstein told everyone to stand next to the mill, on the side with a broken window and missing rocks in the foundation. While he got ready to take more photographs, the women gathered their children. Then the sudden sounds of an approaching wagon filled the air; hooves thudding, wheels creaking, chains clanking. Everyone stopped to see who was coming and Mr. Rothstein turned toward the road. Four massive draft horses, their sides and underbellies slick with sweat, hauled an oversize wagon piled high with logs down the hill. Two men sat on the high driver's bench, one holding the leather reins, the other a head taller and a foot wider than the first. Lena's stomach tightened.

It was Silas.

Lena scrambled up from the grass, scanning the children for Bonnie. At first, Bonnie was nowhere to be seen, but then there she was, in the center of the group, barefoot and muddy-faced, ready to pose for another picture. Lena scooped Ella off the ground, shawl and all, and started toward her. If they hurried, maybe they could hide behind the mill before Silas saw them.

"Bonnie!" Lena shouted. "Come here!"

But it was too late. Silas had already seen them.

He grabbed the reins from the wagon driver and yanked the horses to a stop next to Mr. Rothstein's vehicle, nearly toppling the load of logs. The driver cursed at him and yanked the reins out of his hands, gaping at him like he'd lost his mind. Silas jumped down from the high bench and marched toward the mill, his hands in fists.

Bonnie ran over to Lena, her face pale with worry. Ella stirred in Lena's arms, starting to wake. When Mr. Rothstein saw Silas marching toward them, he took a step back, but not far enough. Silas jabbed a finger in his chest.

"Who the hell are you and what in the hell is going on here?"

"I . . . I'm Arthur Rothstein, photographer. I'm not looking for trouble. I'm just taking a few pictures." He offered his hand.

Ignoring his outstretched hand, Silas glowered down at him. "Y'all need to get the hell out of here before I wallop you so hard it'll kill your relatives."

Startled by the shouting, Ella woke up and started to cry. Lena shushed her, bouncing her gently up and down. Trying to help despite her own fears, Bonnie patted Ella's back while keeping an eye on her father. Thankfully, Ella settled quickly, then blinked and looked around with sleepy eyes.

"Now listen here, Silas," Mr. Early said. "This young man ain't doing nothing wrong. He took a likin' to my mill and asked to take pictures of it for his book, that's all. And we all agreed to letting him take our portraits too. There ain't no harm in it."

Over by the road, Miriam Sizer got out of the car and waddled up the path toward them, alarm pinching her face.

"I ain't agreed to letting him take pictures of *my* young'un!" Silas said. He gave Lena a stern look, then turned his attention back to Mr. Early. "What if he's in cahoots with that crook George Pollock?" He addressed the other women. "You seen him, Sandy and Nellie, I know you have, parading them slick-faced men around up here in their fancy coats and black riding boots, pointing at us like we was a bunch of animals in a zoo."

Nellie and Sandy nodded sheepishly and dropped their eyes.

"What if this man's up here taking pictures for those government types Pollock's working with?" Silas said.

Miriam came up behind him, trying to catch her breath. "Who are you and what in the world do you think you're doing?"

Nostrils flaring, Silas turned to face her. "Y'all don't got a need to know who I am or what I'm doing. Just take your man here and get."

Miriam gasped. "I beg your pardon, but I will not tolerate you speaking to me in that tone. I have not done one single thing to deserve such blatant disrespect and neither has Mr. Rothstein."

Silas's eyes flashed hot. "I know you city folk despise us. Y'all think we're all inbred white trash, that we're ignorant and poor and you can take what's ours 'cause you're better than us. But you ain't nothing but a pack of crooks!"

Miriam's mouth fell open. "How dare you accuse me of such things! Why, I've done nothing but try to improve the lives of the children in these godforsaken hills."

Nellie stepped forward, critical eyes on Miriam Sizer. "Is that why you asked my Jacob how his daddy makes a living and what we eat for supper? You planning on handing out cash and vittles?"

Flustered, Miriam opened her mouth to speak but no words came out.

"Everyone please, just calm down," Mr. Rothstein said. "Miss Sizer only brought me here so I could try to capture life up in these mountains, to show what it's really like to live and work here."

"Horseshit," Silas said. He pointed at the children. "My girl don't ever parade around with dirt on her face like that."

"They were playing in the puddles," Mr. Rothstein said.

"I weren't," Mary Frances said.

"He done told me to rub mud on my face," one of Mr. Early's grandsons said.

"Me too," his brother said. "Told us to take our shoes off too."

"You were already barefoot," Mr. Rothstein said. "My only instructions were where to stand so I could take a photograph."

"That ain't true," Nellie said.

"You're fibbing!" Mary Frances shouted.

The other children and women nodded in agreement.

Silas eyed Mr. Early. "He lying?"

Mr. Early nodded.

Silas took another step toward the photographer, his chin jutting out. "I reckon y'all need to be on your way, Mr. Rothstein. You ain't got no business here. And if I catch wind of you being up here in these hollers again, you're gonna wish you was never born. Got that?" He scowled at Miriam. "Now the two of you get and don't come back!"

Miriam harrumphed, then turned on her heel and headed back toward the vehicle. Without a word, Mr. Rothstein put his camera back in its case and followed her, head down. Silas regarded Bonnie and Lena, his face hard.

"What'd I tell you about talking to people you ain't met before?"

"I was just being in a picture," Bonnie said. "I warn't talking to him."

"Don't sass me, young lady," Silas said. "You know damn well what I'm getting at."

Dropping her eyes, Bonnie scuffed her foot in the grass.

Silas heaved a frustrated sigh, then looked toward the mountains as if searching for answers about what to do next, his jaw working in and out. After a long, tense minute, he dropped his shoulders and scowled at Bonnie and Lena again. "I'll deal with you two when I get home." Then he turned and trudged back to the wagon.

With a sick feeling in the pit of her stomach, Lena watched him climb onto the high driver's bench without looking back. Then the wagon disappeared down the road.

Nellie put a hand on Bonnie's shoulder. "You all right, sugar?"

Bonnie nodded.

Betty Lee looked panic-stricken. "Do y'all reckon Silas is right?" she said. "What if that photographer is in cahoots with George Pollock?"

"What if he is?" Sandy said. "What's he gonna do with a bunch of photographs?"

"I ain't sure," Betty Lee said. "But Miss Sizer said he was just over at the Corbin place."

"So?" Sandy said.

"Sheriff Dixon just took one of their boys," Betty Lee said.

Sandy's eyes went wide and Mr. Early stomped his foot on the ground, his face filled with anger.

"Dagnabit!" he said. "I shoulda known better. I shoulda kicked his hide off my property the minute he stepped foot on it. I hope y'all can forgive me, ladies."

Nellie looked annoyed and confused. "Y'all ain't making no sense," she said. "That photographer spending time at the Corbins' place ain't got nothing to do with Sheriff Dixon. It don't amount to a hill a beans."

Her words seemed to calm Betty Lee and Sandy, but only a little. Sandy twisted her fingers together, looking at Betty Lee like she was about to cry. Betty Lee picked up her toddler, took Mary Frances's hand, and regarded Mr. Early with a serious look.

"How about that buckwheat and cornmeal?' she said. "We need to get home."

"Ah, yes," Mr. Early said, raising a finger as though he just remembered. "Coming right up." He nodded, still flustered, then turned and went into the mill.

Listening to the exchange, Lena wondered if she should tell the women about Enzo and her suspicions about why Silas wanted his children to hide, and why the sheriff took the Corbin boy. But she had to be sure. She needed to ask Silas about Pollock and the "government types" he mentioned. And frightening everyone further was probably a bad idea. Plus, they might not listen to her anyway; they had just met her, after all. While she patted Ella's back and tried to decide what to do, Bonnie moved closer, almost but not quite leaning against her.

"It will be all right," Lena said, doubting her own words.

"Daddy didn't used to get mad like that," Bonnie said. "But ever since Momma died, he gets mad as spit. I don't like it."

Lena had to admit she was relieved Bonnie was so worried about her father being angry that she hadn't yet made the possible connection between the Corbin boy being taken and being photographed by Mr. Rothstein—or maybe her innocent young mind could not comprehend something so horrible. Lena could barely work it out in her own head.

"Try not to worry," she said. "I will tell your father it was my idea that you join the other children in the pictures." And then, slowly and with some trepidation, she put an arm around Bonnie, pulling her closer. To her surprise, Bonnie leaned hard against her and took Ella's hand, finally receptive to the comfort Lena so desperately wanted to give.

After Mr. Early came out of the mill and loaded the buckwheat and cornmeal on the wagons, Betty Lee, Sandy, and Nellie gathered their children and headed home. When Mr. Early came out with the last sack of cornmeal, Bonnie took it with both hands and heaved it over her shoulder, grunting with the effort, then started toward the road. Lena followed with Ella snuggled quietly in her arms.

"I thought you wanted me to carry that," she said.

"No," Bonnie said. "I done caused you enough trouble today."

Chapter 11

After Lena and Bonnie finished setting the table for supper, Silas tromped into the kitchen through the back door, his beard and hair peppered with sawdust. Lena was hoping his rage had lessened over the past several hours, but furrows of anger still lined his brow, and his mouth was set in a thin, hard line. She put the last plate on the table and turned toward the stove, checking the slices of pork that sizzled in a cast-iron pan.

"I hope y'all are hungry, Daddy," Bonnie said. "We made your favorite, pork chops and fried apples."

"Where's Jack Henry?" Silas said.

"He ain't come in from the barn yet," Bonnie said. "Want me to fetch him?"

"No," Silas said. "Take the young'un upstairs until I call you back down. I need to have a discussion with Lena."

"Yes, sir," Bonnie said. She picked up Ella, hurried out of the kitchen, and went up the steps.

Lena turned from the stove to face him, struggling to look calmer than she felt. "It is my fault," she said. "The other women allowed the man to take photographs of their children so I told Bonnie—"

"If I ever catch you letting some stranger around my young-'uns again, you'll be out of here faster than a pig ruts a 'tater, understand?"

She nodded, then took a deep breath and gathered her courage. "I understand you are worried. And it does not help that you have lost your wife and other children, but—"

"What happened to me ain't none of your damn business!"

"But it did not just happen to you," she said. "It happened to Bonnie and Jack Henry too." She could hear the quiver in her voice.

He locked furious eyes on her.

For a panicked second, she thought he was going to hit her or throw her out. She kept talking anyway. "Bonnie said she and Jack Henry must hide because someone said they are feebleminded. But you and I know that is not true. She is one of the smartest girls I have ever known. And Jack Henry is sweet and kind and clever. Bonnie acts like she is strong, when inside she is afraid and sad. And Jack Henry is trying hard to be a man like you, but he is only a little boy. I know this is not for me to say, but they only want to be loved. They do not want to be treated like a . . . a problem."

He glared at her for what felt like forever, his eyes burning with fury and something that looked like anguish. And then, like a switch, his shoulders dropped and he looked away, exhaustion and grief weighing him down. "I know my young'uns ain't ignorant. But they're saying they are."

"*Who* is saying that?" She shook her head in frustration. "I do not understand. Is this what they do in America? They said my brother was feebleminded too. They said they would lock him up if—"

"The state wants my land," he said. Dread filled his voice and he would not meet her gaze. "They're planning on turning these hollers into a park so the city folk can come on the weekends and stomp around in the trees. They want the Wilderness, the McDaniel lands, Browns' Camp, the Bardeens' and Corbins' property, the Shifflet farm, Sydney Allan's house, and half of Jones, Chapman, and Fork Mountains. That's over five thousand acres in this area alone." Finally, he looked at her, his face angry again. "So you know what them bastards been doing? They been sending scientific folk up here to ask questions and study us. Now they're saying we're a bunch of backward, inbred, uneducated hillbillies living in squalor, and removing us from these mountains would be doing us a favor."

Lena's mouth went dry. She'd seen people driven out of their houses during the war, but this was America. Things like that weren't supposed to happen here. And Bonnie and Jack Henry had already lost so much. They couldn't lose their home too. Not to mention, she and Ella had no place else to go. "How is this possible?"

He let out a weary, cynical laugh. "It's possible 'cause they're a pack of heartless crooks. You got something the government wants, they have the right to take it whether you agree to it or not. If y'all don't believe me, ask the Indians how they feel about it." He pulled out a chair and sat down hard, a man with the weight of the world on his shoulders. "John Nicholson over on Pigbump Road has fifteen children and a cabin on two acres. You know what they offered him for his house and land? Two dollars. *Two dollars*! I got twelve acres but they ain't offering me a nickel for it on account of my kin never filed a deed with the county courthouse. Ain't no never mind that we been on this mountain since the eighteen hundreds and the whole damn holler is named after us. My great-grandpappy always said they didn't need no papers when a handshake and a man's word would do. But now the state's saying I'm a squatter and they ain't gotta pay me a red cent. They can just take everything I own."

For the first time ever, he sounded vulnerable and scared, which frightened Lena more than anything. And nothing she could say would help either of them. She'd experienced firsthand how callous a government could be toward innocent citizens, and now it seemed she would face it again. "I am sorry they are doing this to you and your family," she said. "But why do they want to take your children?"

He shrugged. "Damn if I know. I reckon they're trying to beat us down, or they want less folks to force off the mountain. Either that or they think we're so ignorant and poor, we'd be grateful to have less mouths to feed."

She could hardly believe what she was hearing. No wonder Silas was so angry. No wonder he told his children to hide. But why would the government say the children were feebleminded? So it wouldn't sound like they were being stolen?

"Someone at the mill said the sheriff took a boy the other day," she said.

Silas nodded. "The Corbin boy, Herbert. They took Shady Bale's son too, on account of him being a little slow. Said he was retarded. Then they took Cory Beck's daughter, who was born missing an arm. And they since raided others too. Grabbed six brothers from the Jenkins clan, shoved them into their vehicles, and disappeared down the road. Roy Jenkins tried to stop them, and they dang near lynched him."

Lena felt ill. She pulled out a chair and sat down too, her legs suddenly weak. Thinking about Bonnie and Jack Henry being taken was horrible enough, but ever since she'd stepped foot in this country, she'd been worried about losing Ella. And now that danger was more real than ever. To think she had come here to give her daughter a better life. She would've laughed if she hadn't been so scared. "Do you know where they took the children? The women at the mill said the Corbin boy was to be evaluated."

"Ain't nobody can say for sure yet. Shady Bale and Cory Beck went down the mountain looking for help but the police refused. Said they was a bunch of dumb hillbillies. Folks been writing letters and getting nowhere. All I know for sure is my kin is buried on this land. In the city, you get old and die, you're forgotten in a week. Up in these here mountains, some of the people in the graveyards been dead long before I was born, but I feel as if I know them. People I heard talked about all my life. And my wife and other young'uns are buried here too. So if anybody wants to take my land, they're gonna have to kill me first. And if they take Bonnie and Jack Henry, I might as well be dead anyway."

Lena knew exactly what he meant. If anyone took Ella, she might as well be dead too. Just thinking about her being stolen was almost more than she could bear.

How was it possible for the mountain families to live like this, with the constant fear of the government taking their homes and children? And why hadn't they fought back? Then she remembered how helpless her family and other German citizens had felt during the war, and how people had been taken then too. She also remembered the day she'd arrived, how Jack Henry had wanted to scare away the sheriff with a rifle, and how Silas said it would only bring more trouble. He was right, of course, but how could she sit back and do nothing if they came for her child?

Chapter 12

Early the next morning, on Lena's third full day at the Wolfe Farm, the rising sun slowly dissolved a low layer of clouds surrounding the mountains, gradually revealing the bluish-green peaks and deep valleys. Birds chirped and sang in the trees, flitting like black arrows across the powder blue sky, and the flowers and vegetable garden glistened with dew. Lena sat in a cane-back chair on the front porch, pumping the dasher of a butter churn while Ella played at her feet. In the rocking chair next to her, Bonnie patched overalls and shirts, occasionally looking up at Jack Henry, who was repairing fences near the barn.

Now more than ever, especially after her conversation with Silas, Lena was on high alert, repeatedly scanning the dirt road and driveway for vehicles or wagons, ready to grab Ella and run to the shed with Bonnie and Jack Henry. The haunted remnants of nightmares inside her head did not help—waking up to find Ella's crib empty, the Widow Spinney disappearing into the forest with Ella wrapped inside a moldy blanket, Lena searching and screaming and getting lost in the dark.

Lena stood and went over to the water barrel, struggling to push the terrible images away. She filled the ladle and took a long drink, grateful for the cool water on her dry throat. When she returned to the butter churn, Ella lifted her hand to show her something.

"Mama, see," Ella said.

Lena bent over to get a closer look. "What is it, *mein Liebling*?"

Ella giggled and straightened one small finger. A black-and-red ladybug crawled along her knuckle, then made its way up to the tiny tip of her fingernail. Ella laughed again and Lena beamed, grateful for her daughter's innocence and shining eyes, praying she would stay that way as long as possible. She reached out to caress Ella's soft cheek, but the thud of hooves made her bolt upright. Bonnie snapped to attention too, looking up from the overalls on her lap. Two dusty brown horses pulled an enclosed black-and-white carriage up the road toward the drive. But instead of sitting on a bench in front of the carriage, the driver sat inside, making it hard to see who it was.

Thankfully, Bonnie relaxed immediately. "It ain't nothing, just the mail wagon," she said, draping the overalls over the arm of the rocking chair. She got up and went to the steps.

Lena breathed a sigh of relief and smiled at Ella again to let her know everything was all right. Then a swirl of butterflies flickered in her stomach. Maybe the mail wagon was bringing a letter from Mutti. Maybe she would finally learn her family was safe back in Germany. No. That was impossible. It was much too soon to hear from them, even though it felt like they'd been apart forever. Hopefully Mutti and Enzo had gotten out of that awful cage at Ellis Island and were on their way home, but they would not be there for quite some time. Picturing them on another ship, cramped together in the rank rooms of steerage, Lena's stomach tightened with more heartache and worry. Hopefully Mutti was not seasick again, and when they arrived in Germany, she and Enzo would easily find a place to live. With any luck, a letter would arrive from them soon afterward, to put Lena's mind at ease about *that* at least. Of course, writing back meant telling Mutti about Silas not paying her, and that sending money for tickets was no longer a possibility. But first Lena would explain that she and Ella had a sturdy roof over their heads, warm beds to sleep in, and plenty of food. And obviously, she'd leave out the part about the need to hide when the police came. The last thing she wanted to do was make Mutti worry.

When Bonnie started down the hill to meet the mail wagon, Lena got up and called after her, suddenly anxious again. "Are you certain it is the mail?"

"Of course," Bonnie called over her shoulder. "It says so right on the dang vehicle."

She was right. Now that the carriage was closer, Lena could make out the words on the side: U.S. MAIL. Still, she fought the urge to run after Bonnie, to catch her by the arm and say they needed to run and hide. Because what if Bonnie was wrong? What if someone other than the postman was inside? Picking up Ella just in case, she watched the wagon come to a stop at the bottom of the grassy slope. When the driver secured the reins and got out, she held her breath. He reached inside the carriage and handed Bonnie several envelopes. Only after he climbed back in and closed the door did she exhale. And when he turned the wagon to drive away, she set Ella back on the porch floor and returned to the butter churn.

Bonnie ran up the steps. "Sorry, ain't nothing for y'all yet. Just a letter for Daddy from the State of Virginia and an advertisement from the Frank E. Davis Fish Company. Can you imagine getting a mess of dead codfish and lobster in the mail?"

Remembering the herring she'd eaten on the ship, Lena made a face and shook her head.

Bonnie laughed. "Me neither. Sounds plumb crazy if y'all ask me."

Later that afternoon, while Ella played with wooden blocks on the kitchen floor, Bonnie taught Lena how to cook pinto beans and cornmeal.

"The secret to good cornmeal is getting the grease hot before you chunk the batter in the skillet," Bonnie said. "Then you put the whole thing in the woodstove."

After pushing the corn bread in to bake, Bonnie took a kettle of pinto beans that had been soaking overnight and set it on a burner.

"Y'all gotta make sure there's enough water covering the beans or they'll turn dark and won't be good," Bonnie said. "You can use drippings for the seasoning, but ain't nothing works better than a good ham hock." She gave the beans a good stir with a wooden spoon. "These should be ready right about the time Daddy gets home." Then she pulled a cabbage from a sack under the sink and handed it to Lena. "Fry this up in a hunk of bacon grease while I fetch more milk from the springhouse. Daddy always gets a hankering for extra sweet milk with his corn bread."

After Bonnie left the kitchen, Lena cut the cabbage, carefully slicing it thin like she'd been taught. Just as she was about to put a cast-iron skillet on the stove, Bonnie flew back in from outside, wide-eyed and breathless. Lena almost dropped the skillet.

"What is it?" she said. "What's wrong?" She put the skillet on the counter.

"There's a woman," Bonnie said, gasping for air. "In the barn. Talking to Jack Henry."

"The woman from the bridge?"

Bonnie shook her head. "No. I ain't never laid eyes on her before."

Lena picked up Ella and started toward the back hall, panic buzzing like a hornet in her head.

Bonnie followed. "I hightailed it out of there as soon as I

seen her. Jack Henry must'a left the main door open. He looked scared as all get-out."

Outside, Lena ran on the path toward the barn with Ella on her hip, yelling as loud as she could in the hopes it would scare the woman away. "We are coming, Jack Henry!"

Bonnie yelled too. "Get away from my brother, you egg-sucking dawg!"

When they were halfway to the barn, fat raindrops started to fall and the wind picked up, rustling the leaves on the trees. Blinking against the sudden storm, Lena and Bonnie hurried along the footpath, their aprons and hair flying. Ella bounced up and down in her mother's arms, laughing as if it were a game.

"Ain't no wonder we didn't hear her coming," Bonnie shouted above the wind. "She stopped down yonder." She pointed at a boxy red vehicle with dirt-covered wheels, nearly out of sight on the road.

Lena ran faster. When they reached the barn, Bonnie yanked open a side door and they rushed inside. The woman had cornered Jack Henry next to the ladder leading up to the haymow.

"Can I help you?" Lena shouted, trying to sound intimidating.

The woman startled and turned, her hand over her heart. "Heavens to Betsy! You scared the ever-loving daylights out of me."

"What the hell do y'all think you're doing in our barn?" Bonnie snarled.

In a tailored jacket, pencil skirt, cloche hat, and a low-hanging bag strapped across her chest, the woman moved toward Lena and smiled, her hand outstretched. She looked to be about Lena's age. "My name is Penelope Rodgers and I'm a student at Sweet Briar College, working with Professor Ivan McDougle and Arthur Estabrook of the Eugenics Records Office. Several of my fellow students and I have come up here in the hopes of discovering the origins of the lost tribe. Have you heard of the lost tribe?"

Lena ignored Penelope's question. And her hand.

"Ain't nobody lost here," Bonnie said. "So, you can get."

Disregarding Bonnie, Penelope chuckled casually, her attention still on Lena. "Well, of course you haven't. You see, the lost tribe is a mixed race produced by the intermarriage of Indians or Blacks with whites. And some of their mongrel descendants live in these mountains, which should concern you because they're often lazy and uneducated, not to mention promiscuous, unattractive, and unintelligent. Oftentimes they're quite mentally defective and feebleminded. A study was recently done proving that these people, through their faulty genes, produce hundreds of welfare recipients, criminals, and prostitutes, which cost the state of Virginia millions of dollars every year, so you can imagine how important our work is. It's critical for us to call attention to a very serious social inadequacy. Now, if you don't mind, I'd like to ask you a few questions."

Despite her inability to understand every word Penelope said, Lena recognized the word *feebleminded*. And that was enough. She pulled Ella closer and glanced nervously at Bonnie and Jack Henry. "I do not want to answer any questions."

"This is horseshit," Bonnie said, scowling at Penelope. "Y'all ain't got no right to be here. And you sure as hell ain't got no need to ask no questions. My daddy is on his way home so if I were you, I'd clear out."

With a condescending grin, Penelope looked down at her. "Well, I was headed toward the house when I saw this nice young man going into your barn." She nodded toward Jack Henry. "So I thought I'd talk to him first. Is he your brother?"

"You ain't got a need to know that either," Bonnie said. "Now shut your trap and get."

"My, my, you're a little spark plug, aren't you?" Penelope said. "Your brother didn't mind talking to me."

Bonnie gave Jack Henry the evil eye. "What did y'all say to her? You know Daddy don't want us talking to no strangers. You're gonna get a whoopin' when I tell."

"I ain't said nothing!" Jack Henry said. "I told her I wasn't gonna talk to her and she needed to get."

"That's true," Penelope said, still amused. "He wouldn't even tell me his name. But that's all right. According to my records, this is the Silas Wolfe household." Suddenly serious again, she removed a pen and clipboard from her bag. "Now if you don't mind, this will only take a few minutes."

"We ain't answering none of your dadblasted questions," Bonnie said. She waved Jack Henry toward her. "Come on, let's get her the hell out of here. Daddy ain't got no need to know she was even here."

Penelope regarded Lena, her pen poised over her clipboard. "Just so you know, it will be easier on everyone if you cooperate. Otherwise, the college will send Mr. Estabrook up here to talk to you, and he's not nearly as pleasant as I am. Now please, how many children live in this household? Is it just these three or are there more?"

Lena glanced at Bonnie and Jack Henry, trying to decide what to do. If they told Silas she'd talked to this woman, he would be furious again, maybe furious enough to throw her out this time. What had he said? She would be out of there faster than a pig ruts a 'tater? Then again, if the man from the college that Penelope mentioned showed up, that could be worse. Maybe the woman would leave if Lena did as she asked. "It is just these three children."

"And what can you tell me about your family's history?" Penelope continued. "Do you know if there are any non-white members in your lineage?"

"I . . . I do not know," Lena started.

"Y'all ain't gotta answer her," Bonnie said. "She's trespassing."

Penelope rolled her eyes and addressed Bonnie again. "Now listen here," she said. "There's no need to get yourself worked into a tizzy. I only want to ask a few more questions, then I'll be on my way." She turned to Lena again. "I also need to know about your health and the health of these children. And their father, of course."

Lena hesitated. Why did this woman need to know about their health? Then she said, "Everyone is healthy."

Bonnie stared up at her, fury twisting her pale features. "You best quit talking or I'll tell Daddy, and they ain't no telling what he'll do."

Penelope's brows shot up and she eyed Lena with concern. "Are you unsafe here?"

"No," Lena said. "I am fine. It is just—"

"It's just my Daddy's got a rifle and he ain't afraid to use it, especially on strangers," Jack Henry said. "And I ain't neither."

Penelope gave him a stern look. "I'm not speaking to you right now, young man," she said. "I'm speaking to your mother."

"Well, that's some trick, seeing how our mother is dead," Bonnie said, her eyes blazing.

Lena cringed inside. Now the woman would ask even more questions.

"Oh dear," Penelope said. "I'm so sorry. What happened to her?"

"Y'all got no need to know that," Bonnie said.

"Was she ill?" Penelope said.

"No," Lena said. "She died while giving birth."

"God damn it," Bonnie said. "What did y'all tell her that for?"

"So, you're the second wife?" Penelope said, ignoring Bonnie.

Lena gritted her teeth. Maybe she should have let Bonnie and Jack Henry chase this woman away. She took a step back. "I should not be talking to you."

"I promise it's perfectly fine," Penelope said. "I'm only here to help. You have my word that my intentions are good. Now, what can you tell me about the children's mother? Was she white?"

"What kind of idiotic question is that?" Bonnie said.

Reluctantly, Lena nodded.

Penelope wrote something down on her clipboard, then smiled sweetly at Ella, who watched warily, nestled in Lena's arms. "What a shame this pretty little girl never got to know her mother."

"Are y'all dumber than a coal bucket?" Bonnie said. "This here's her mother." She indicated Lena with a jerk of her thumb.

Lena shot Bonnie a wide-eyed look, hoping she'd keep quiet from now on, but Bonnie was too busy glowering at Penelope like she wanted to strangle her.

"Y'all need to shut up, Bonnie," Jack Henry said.

Disapproval lined Penelope's face. "I see," she said. Pinching her lips together, she scribbled something on her clipboard, then studied Lena with suspicious eyes. "I noticed you have an interesting accent. May I ask where you were born and how long you've been in the United States?"

Despite not wanting to answer, Lena needed Penelope to leave. And it seemed like the only way to get her to do that was to cooperate. "I was born in Italy but I grew up in Germany. I came to America this year."

Alarm flickered across Penelope's eyes. "Are you aware that some Italians are mixed with former Negro slaves? That means it's possible you could have a trace of Negro blood. And willful misrepresentation of race is a felony in this state, which means you broke the Racial Integrity Act by marrying a white man. Please give me the name of the clerk who issued your marriage license."

"I am not married," Lena said.

"But you're living on the premises?"

"I do not know what 'premises' means," Lena said.

"Are you and your daughter living on this property with these children and their father?" Irritation had snuck into Penelope's voice.

"*Ja,*" Lena said. "I mean, yes."

"So you admit to living in sin."

"Jesus, Mary, and Joseph," Bonnie said. "It ain't like that. She's family and she's helping out."

Penelope's eyes grew bigger, a look of horror sweeping over her face. "If you're family, then you're committing incest." She spat the words out like poison.

"I do not know what that word means either," Lena said. "But I have done nothing wrong."

"Listen," Penelope said. "We know there's intermarriage among family members up here. As a matter of fact, six families living in the Rock Creek Hollow are named Corbin or Nicholson. Their ancestors have been in these mountains since the end of the Revolution and their descendants have intermarried. They've had very little to do with the outside world since, and all the adults are cousins. So, if you're having sexual . . ." She glanced nervously at Bonnie and Jack Henry, then lowered her voice. "If you are having sexual relations with Mr. Wolfe, any child that is a product of your relationship will surely be physically deformed or mentally backward."

Lena gaped at the woman. How could she say such a thing? "We are not . . . I am not having relations with Mr. Wolfe."

Penelope studied Ella again, her sweet smile replaced by something that looked like disgust. "Then who is this child's father?"

Anger swelled in Lena's chest, along with a trembling fear. "That does not matter."

"I'm afraid you're wrong," Penelope said. "If your daughter was born out of wedlock or, even worse, as a result of incest, she likely has some, if not many, abnormalities. I will need to send someone up to get her so she can be evaluated. It's quite possible that you need to be evaluated too."

Lena drew in a sharp breath. "Her father is dead," she said. "And I am finished with your questions. Please leave."

"I'm sorry but I am not—" Penelope started.

Lena pointed at the door. "Go!" she shouted.

"Y'all heard her!" Bonnie yelled. "Now get!"

Jack Henry grabbed a pitchfork and held it up like a battering ram, the sharp points aimed at Penelope. "Get your skinny, stinking ass outta our barn!"

Penelope gasped and put her hand on her chest, then turned and hurried toward the side door, glancing wide-eyed over her shoulder to make sure they weren't chasing her. At the threshold, she tripped and nearly fell, then caught herself and disappeared around the corner. Lena, Bonnie, and Jack Henry followed her outside to make sure she left, Jack Henry still gripping the pitchfork. Halfway down the hill, Penelope dropped her clipboard, stopped to pick it up, and looked back at them, her hair disheveled, her face full of fear. She ran the rest of the way to her vehicle.

Lena turned to Jack Henry and Bonnie, tears stinging her eyes. "I am sorry," she said. "You were right. I should not have talked to her. I should have told her to leave."

"Saying sorry now is about as useless as tits on a boar hog," Bonnie spat. Then she stormed toward the house, her arms swinging.

"Don't fret too much," Jack Henry said. "She'll cool down after a spell."

Lena gave him a weak smile, thankful he was trying to make her feel better. But if Penelope sent someone up there to take Ella, Bonnie's wrath would be the least of her worries.

Chapter 13

With July in full swing, Wolfe Hollow seemed hotter than Lena's hometown ever had, and everything seemed to move more slowly, from the bees in the apple trees to the chickens pecking in the yard. The heat dragged on her like rocks sewn in the hem of her apron while she and Bonnie spent hours in the garden, watering and harvesting vegetables, pulling weeds and sowing fall crops. And like the children, she went barefoot most of the time now, her face and arms growing brown as a berry. Although Bonnie had withdrawn for a while after the incident with Penelope from Sweet Briar College, when she gave Lena a handkerchief embroidered with her initials, it was clear all was forgiven. The two of them, along with Jack Henry, had made a pact not to tell Silas about what happened in the barn; they'd never remember everything that was said anyway, and they didn't want Silas to be angry with Jack Henry for letting a stranger sneak up on him. But even though Lena wanted to protect Jack Henry, she sometimes wondered if not telling Silas was a mistake. Forewarned was forearmed, as her mother used to say. Then again, if Silas was at work when, and if, someone came for Ella or the man Penelope had warned them about showed up, knowing what happened would not help.

With regular meals of meat and vegetables, buckwheat pancakes, and homemade bread, Ella grew into a plump toddler who loved to help carry firewood and run after the chickens in the yard. Lena felt the change in her own body too, in her stronger arms and sturdier step, in her ability to work harder without getting tired. She also saw it in the cracked mirror above her dresser, in her receding ribs and longer, thicker hair, and the disappearing circles under her eyes.

Unfortunately, nearly two months after her arrival, there was still no word from Mutti and Enzo. Every Thursday, Lena watched for the mail wagon with her heart in her throat, praying the driver would bring her a letter, but he never did. Now, between worrying about her family and being on the constant lookout for the sheriff or another stranger to appear, a stranger who might take Ella, she was always on edge, dropping silverware or forgetting to add ingredients to a recipe, waking up a hundred times a night to check on Ella and look out the window.

On a particularly hot and hazy afternoon at the end of July, while Ella napped under the shade of an apple tree, Lena and Bonnie hung clothes on the line while Jack Henry carried buckets of water back and forth from the mountain stream to the barn, his face red and sweating. She and Bonnie still had to water the garden and clean the chicken coop before making supper, but Lena could hardly wait until they could take a break with tall glasses of lavender tea, which was cooling in the springhouse as they worked. As usual, despite the heat, Bonnie was singing.

After pinning the last sheet on the line, Lena picked up the empty laundry basket and looked over at Ella, who was curled up on a blanket with Poppy held to her chest, a slight, dreamy smile on her face. Lena had never dreamed her tiny girl could be so healthy and happy. Then she realized Bonnie had stopped singing. She stilled for a moment, listening. Maybe Bonnie was in between songs, trying to decide what to sing next. Suddenly, shrieks of laughter filled the air. Peeking between the wet aprons and shirts, Lena looked toward the springhouse. To her surprise, Bonnie and Jack Henry were knee-deep in the stream, dumping buckets of water over each other's heads. Lena smiled. She loved hearing the children having fun, especially when they were working. She put down the wicker basket and marched toward them with her hands on her hips, pretending to be angry. When Bonnie and Jack Henry saw her coming, they climbed out of the stream, their faces glum.

"What are you doing?" Lena said. "Do we not have enough clothes to wash and hang on the line?"

"Sorry," Jack Henry said. He wiped his face and picked up one of the buckets.

Bonnie pushed wet strands of hair off her cheeks. "We ain't done nothing wrong," she said. "We're just cooling off. It's hotter than blue blazes out here."

Lena frowned at Jack Henry. "Do all of the animals have water?"

Jack Henry nodded, water dripping from his nose.

"Then we need to do the garden," Lena said. "Fill that bucket and hand it to me. Bonnie, you fill the other one. We have much work to do before your father is home."

Jack Henry did as he was told and gave the bucket to Lena. When Bonnie straightened after filling the second bucket, Lena dumped the first bucket of water over her head. Bonnie yelped and hunched her shoulders, her mouth open in surprise. Then she laughed and threw water at Lena, who moved out of the way just in time. Lena climbed into the creek, refilled her bucket, and flung the water at Jack Henry. He and Bonnie jumped back in and splashed her, kicking up water with their hands and feet. The cold stream felt wonderful, even more refreshing than lavender tea. For the next few minutes, they hooted and hollered and poured water over each other's heads and Lena couldn't remember the last time she'd laughed so hard. It seemed like years. She stopped for a moment to catch her breath, happy to see Bonnie and Jack Henry having a good time.

"I will bring Ella over so she can cool off too," she said, climbing over the bank. "But do not dump water over her head."

"Aww, shucks, that ain't no fun," Jack Henry said, grinning. "Maybe she'll take a likin' to it."

Lena wagged a playful finger at him. "I do not think so."

While Bonnie and Jack Henry stayed in the stream, Lena wrung out her skirt and apron, then started toward the apple tree, the summer grass like a warm towel on her feet. After feeling sluggish and overheated all morning, she felt refreshed and ready to tackle the rest of the day. Maybe playing in the stream on hot sunny days should be part of their regular routine. Behind her, Jack Henry and Bonnie continued to get drenched, splashing and laughter filling the breathless afternoon.

What would Silas say if he saw his children in the stream, soaking wet and still wearing their clothes? What would he say if he saw her in the water too—the person who was supposed to keep them in line? Maybe it would do him good. Maybe after dinner she should tell them to get in the stream again, to remind him of the simple joys in life, and how little it took to make his children happy. She smiled at the idea, glancing over her shoulder to look back at them. Then she froze.

In the distance, a cloud of dust moved along the road, stirred up by an approaching vehicle.

"Someone is coming!" she shouted.

Bonnie and Jack Henry immediately dropped their buckets, clambered out of the water, and ran toward the low-roofed shed. For a second, Lena had no idea what to do. Should she grab Ella and go with the children? Go to the house and get a rifle?

Then Bonnie shouted, stirring her into action. "Come on!"

Lena raced toward the apple tree, scooped Ella up, blanket and all, and ran toward the shed. Jolted awake and frightened, Ella started to cry and tried squirming away from Lena's wet clothes.

"Shhhh," Lena said. "You're all right."

When Lena reached the shed, Bonnie and Jack Henry were already under the low roof, scurrying behind the old tractor. Before ducking inside the building, Lena looked toward the road. The approaching vehicle was still too far away to make out who or what it was, but the growl of an engine was getting closer. She hurried into the shed and went around the tractor, where Jack Henry had already moved the wheelbarrow and flipped the worn rug to one side. He grabbed the iron ring in the trapdoor and pulled it open. Bonnie hurried down the steep steps and disappeared into darkness. Lena froze at the edge of the murky hole, suddenly overcome by more memories of war—the blare of sirens; the pale, frightened faces of her neighbors; the fear that permeated the cellar like a living, breathing thing. Then a flickering glow filled the hole and Bonnie appeared at the bottom of the steps, an oil lamp in her hand.

"Hightail it down here," she said, her voice firm. She set down the lamp and reached up for Ella.

Lena started down the stairs, gripping the edge of the door frame with one hand, and handed Ella to Bonnie. Jack Henry followed, closed the door behind him, and, using a thick rope, tied the handle to the top step. When he got to the bottom step, he yanked on a second rope and the rug rustled back into place over the door. The hiding place was less than half the size of the 'tater hole and just as chilly, with earth walls and a bumpy, uneven dirt floor. A raw wood bench sat against the back wall, only wide enough for two people. Bonnie sat on the bench with Ella, who whimpered and looked around, bewildered. While the lantern cast flickering shadows on their faces, Bonnie whispered softly in Ella's ear and Jack Henry sat on the floor and leaned against the wall, breathing hard. Lena wrapped her arms around herself and sat next to Bonnie, water dripping off their dresses onto the floor.

Then Lena noticed drops of water on the steps, left on the wood by their wet clothes. What if they had left a trail on the shed floor too, making it easy for someone to find their hiding place? No. By the time anyone got around to looking in the shed, the water would be dried up. That's what she told herself anyway.

"How long must we hide down here?" she said in a quiet voice.

"Depends on how long whoever's out there plans on staying," Jack Henry whispered.

"How do we know when they are gone?" Lena said.

"I'll take a gander after a bit," Jack Henry said. "Unless we hear somebody banging around up there in the shed. But we reckon once they ain't seen nobody around the house or yard, they'll head out."

"How many times have you had to hide like this?" Lena said.

Jack Henry shrugged. "Four or five."

"Six," Bonnie said.

"Nah," Jack Henry said. "That ain't right."

"Is too," Bonnie said.

Ella fidgeted on Bonnie's lap, then reached up and, with gentle fingers, touched Bonnie's chin. "Sing, pwease," she said.

Bonnie tried to smile at her, but her lips trembled. Then she rocked her back and forth and quietly sang the lullaby Mutti used to sing, her voice barely above a whisper.

Glancing up at the trapdoor, looking at each other with worried eyes, and listening to Bonnie quietly sing, they sat that way for what felt like hours. Every once in a while, Jack Henry tilted his head toward the ceiling, listening for noises from above. Now that they were out of the sun, with wet hair and soaked clothes, they started to shiver. Thankfully, Ella had not played in the water too, but Lena wrapped her blanket tighter around her small body, just in case. Eventually, Ella climbed off Bonnie's lap to play in the dirt, blissfully unaware of the possible danger lurking above her head. While she dug into the small puddles formed by the water dripping from their clothes, staining her hands and knees, Lena took her blanket, wrapped it around her and Bonnie's shoulders, and the two of them huddled close.

"Looks like we got more warsh," Bonnie said, indicating Ella's yellow jumper.

"That is fine," Lena said. "It is keeping her quiet."

After a while, Lena sat on the ground and leaned against the wall. "Get under the blanket with Bonnie," she said to Jack Henry.

Jack Henry shook his head. "I ain't cold."

"Don't be a jackass," Bonnie said. "I ain't gonna bite."

"I ain't too sure about that," Jack Henry said.

"Suit yourself," Bonnie said. "But don't blame me when you get the crud."

Just then, footsteps plodded above, moving across the floor of the shed. Everyone froze, their eyes wide. A muffled bang sounded above the trapdoor. Then a metallic screech and another bang. Lena grabbed Ella and held her protectively against her chest, staring up at the trapdoor. Ella started to cry.

"Shhhh," Lena whispered. "I am sorry. Shhh."

"Play wif dirt!" Ella wailed, reaching for the mud.

Lena put gentle fingers over Ella's lips and shook her head. "In a little bit," she whispered.

Up above, the rug swished across the trapdoor and someone fumbled with the iron ring. Jack Henry leapt to his feet, scrambled up the steps, and grabbed the rope that held the door shut. The door shook and rattled and started to lift. Bonnie clasped a hand over her mouth and Lena bounced Ella up and down, whispering in her ear to stay quiet, her heart thumping hard against her ribs. The trapdoor started to open. A slice of sunlight pierced the dark hole. Jack Henry wrapped his arms around the rope and pulled down using all his body weight. The door slammed shut.

"Bonnie?" a male voice said above the door. "Jack Henry? You down there?"

"Daddy!" Bonnie said. She stood and rushed to the steps.

Lena opened her mouth to protest, to tell her to wait, to tell Jack Henry to hold onto the rope until they could be sure. But he had already let go, and the trapdoor flew open. Bonnie climbed out of the hole and wrapped her arms around Silas's waist.

Lena let out a sigh of relief, her shoulders dropping. She got to her feet and followed Jack Henry up the steps with Ella on her hip, both of them blinking against the bright sunlight.

Silas put a hand on Bonnie's hair. "Why in the Sam Hill are you all wet?"

She stepped back and looked up at him. "We were cooling off in the crick when Lena saw a vehicle coming up the road."

"Was it the sheriff again?" Silas said.

"We ain't sure," Jack Henry said. "We hid as soon as Lena saw it."

"Good," Silas said. "That's good." He glanced at Lena with something that looked like gratitude.

For the first time, she felt like he realized they were on the same side, and maybe he'd forgive her for what happened at the mill with the photographer, but she was too overwhelmed to do or say anything.

"What are you doing home so soon?" Bonnie said. "It ain't even close to suppertime."

"Virgil stopped by the sawmill," Silas said. "He said someone snatched the Widow Spinney off the bridge and hauled her away. I come home to make sure they warn't here."

* * *

The next day, Bonnie and Lena were pulling weeds in the garden when the mail wagon made its weekly appearance. Bonnie ran to meet it, then returned to the garden with a smile on her face and a letter in her hand. Lena's heart leapt to her throat. At long last, her mother had written. She grabbed the letter, then paused. Her name was on the envelope, but the handwriting was not Mutti's. She checked the return address.

Frau Carla Müller
Piesbacher Str. 7 // #2
66701 Beckingen
Germany

A powerful flood of unease washed over Lena. Frau Müller was a friend and neighbor whose eldest son had died in the war. Why in the world was she writing?

"Ain't that what you been waiting for?" Bonnie said.

Unable to speak, Lena gave her a weak nod. After checking to make sure Ella was still in the back corner of the garden, she went over to the shade of a nearby tree, inhaled deeply, and tore open the letter. Her fingers trembled as she unfolded the single sheet of airmail stationery and let the envelope fall to the ground.

Dear Magdalena,
It is with much sorrow that I write this letter to let you know that your beloved mother has passed away. According to Enzo, she was extremely ill on the return ship to Germany and she died on the fourth night of the voyage. The doctor said it was her heart. She will be buried next to your father tomorrow morning here in Beckingen. I know this is extremely difficult for you when you are so far away, but I hope you find comfort in the knowledge that she died peacefully in her

sleep. She was so happy and relieved when you and her beloved Ella were able to go to America with her, and even though it surely made her sad to leave you there, I'm certain the knowledge that the two of you have a better life will help her rest easy. I hope you can find peace in that too.

Unfortunately, I'm afraid I have further sad news. Your brother has been hospitalized with typhus, which we believe he caught on the ship. When he first arrived back in the city, I took him in and let him sleep in our dear late Hermann's room. But it soon became clear that he was very ill. God willing, he will survive. I will write again as soon as I have word. Again, I'm very sorry to deliver this dreadful news.

*Sincerely,
Carla Müller*

Lena stared at the letter, the words blurring in front of her eyes. For a moment she could not move. She could not think. She felt herself collapsing and falling, as if dropping off the edge of a steep cliff. Then she was on the ground, her hands over her face, her breath coming in short, shallow gasps. *Nein! This can't be true! It can't be! Not Mutti! And not Enzo!* One after the other, violent sobs tore from her throat, each gut-wrenching cry ripping like a dagger through her mind and body.

A gentle hand touched her shoulder. "Lena? Are you all right?"

Lena took her hands from her face. Bonnie stood over her with Ella on her hip, alarm darkening her young face. Driven by a sudden, desperate need to hold her daughter, Lena heaved herself onto her knees and pulled Ella into her trembling arms, crushing her to her chest.

"What the devil happened?" Bonnie said, her voice filled with concern. "Did y'all get bad news?"

Lena nodded and somehow the words came, even as her

heart shattered into a million pieces. "My mother died on the ship back to Germany. And my brother is very ill."

Bonnie's eyes went wide. "Damn. I'm mighty sorry. That's the worst kind of news."

Lena could only nod again, her face crumpling in on itself, her head pounding in time with her thrashing heart. She and her family never should have left Germany. Yes, they would have been hungry and poor, but at least they'd still be together now. Together and alive. It was too much to bear. She hugged Ella tighter, her shoulders convulsing, her hot tears dampening Ella's soft hair and cheeks. She was an orphan now. And Ella would never have a single clear memory of her Oma, who had loved her more than life itself. Even worse, poor Mutti would never hear Ella's first sentence or watch her grow up. She'd never celebrate her birthdays or Christmases. She'd never see her get married or become a mother.

Ella whimpered in Lena's arms and started to cry, each wail getting louder and more frightened. Lena drew away and looked at her, worried she'd squeezed her too hard. "What is it, *mein Liebchen?*" she said.

"I reckon y'all scared her by crying so loud," Bonnie said.

Lena kissed Ella's forehead and caressed her wet cheeks. "I am sorry," she said, forcing a smile. "Everything is all right. See?" She wiped away her tears. "I am fine. Please don't cry. Momma is here."

Ella curled her lower lip under, pouting and gazing at Lena with watery eyes. Lena kissed her again, grief and guilt like a boulder in her chest. Even though her heart was breaking, she had to be strong for her daughter, no matter what. To think she'd caused Ella even a second of fear or pain tore at her like a thousand knives.

"Do y'all want me to take her back to the garden so you can go lie down for a spell?" Bonnie said.

Lena shook her head. She needed Ella now more than ever.

She got to her feet, picked up the letter and envelope, and checked the postmark. July 5th, 1928. Over five weeks ago. Mutti was already in the ground. And Enzo's fate had likely been sealed. Either he'd survived, or he was already dead and buried. *Nein.* She refused to think like that. Enzo was young and healthy. If anyone could survive typhus, it was him. She had to stay hopeful until she knew one way or another. It was the only way she could be strong for her daughter.

She put the letter in her apron pocket and picked up Ella. Then she noticed Bonnie's face, tense with determination; the poor girl was trying not to cry. Lena's chest tightened further. Surely, her suffering had reminded Bonnie of her own losses. And Bonnie had lost her mother at a much younger age. Plus four siblings. How was she able to make it through every day without breaking down?

Lena's eyes grew wet again and she reached for Bonnie with her free hand. Tears welled on Bonnie's lids and she hesitated, unsure. Then she fell into Lena's embrace and wept quietly, one arm around Ella, the other around Lena's waist. Lena held Bonnie and Ella close, a vulnerable young girl in each arm, and cursed the cruel God who took mothers away from their children, and children away from their mothers.

Chapter 14

The long, horrible days following the devastating news of Mutti's death were overcast and humid, and the sky hung hazy and low. Despite her anguish, Lena did everything that needed to be done—cooking and gardening, cleaning and washing clothes, taking care of Ella and, when they'd let her, Bonnie and Jack Henry. Still, sometimes the truth hit her, nearly bringing her to her knees, and she had to sit down to keep from collapsing. At night, she woke up with a start every few hours, her forehead beaded with sweat, her heart hammering. And every time, she threw back the covers, jumped to her feet, and rushed over to Ella's crib to make sure she was still there. Then she'd fall back into bed, relieved no one had taken her child, trying to catch her breath, until realization sent a hollow draft of sorrow through her bones.

Mutti was dead.

And Enzo could be too.

Then the hot flush of panic would seize her all over again and she'd lie awake in bed, clammy and restless until morning.

Of course, she'd written back to Frau Müller right away, to

thank her for letting her know about Mutti and for taking Enzo in when he had nowhere to go. And even though Frau Müller said she'd write when she had news of Enzo, Lena begged her to reply as soon as possible, only because putting those words on paper made her feel a little less helpless. When the mail wagon came three days later, she ran down to meet it, praying for news that her brother had survived. But no letter arrived addressed to her. No letter arrived the next week either. Or the next. Then, finally, nearly four weeks after learning her mother had passed away, an envelope came bearing her brother's name and Frau Müller's address:

Enzo Conti
Piesbacher Str. 7 // #2
66701 Beckingen
Germany

Lena held the letter to her chest for a moment, praying Enzo had written it after he was sent to the hospital, not before. He had to be alive. He just had to be. Then she tore open the envelope with shaking hands.

Dear Lena,
I hope this finds you and my beautiful niece doing well in America. I'm certain the news of our mother's passing has been very hard on you, but I hope you do not let it stop you from fighting for a better life. I'm so sorry I could not do more to protect her. By the time I realized she was not sleeping and found a doctor on the ship, it was too late. She was already gone. Please don't be angry with me. I did the best I could. Every night she made me promise that if something happened to her before we found a way back to America, I would tell you how much she loves you and Ella, and that she wants you to stay strong and be happy no matter what. I hope you have been able to do that.

As for me, I have been released from the hospital and will be staying with Frau Müller until I'm fully recovered. She has written to her youngest son, who is a bricklayer in Berlin, to see if he might have work for me there. Hopefully he will say yes and I can save for a ticket to America. In the meantime, please send money if you are able. I would like to repay Frau Müller for her generosity. I miss you and Ella more than you can imagine and I hope to see you soon.

Love, your brother,
Enzo

Crying grateful tears, Lena hung her head and thanked God for saving her brother, then ran up the slope toward the house to tell Ella and Bonnie. Naturally, not being able to send him money weighed on her mind, but for the moment, relief and happiness overshadowed any guilt about not keeping her promise. Enzo was alive. And if he got a job in Berlin, maybe he could return to the United States sooner than she hoped. Maybe together they could find a place to live down the mountain, where life in America was more like she'd imagined. Maybe someday she would be like those fashionable women she'd seen in Hoboken, wearing pencil skirts and fancy heels to lunch and the theater with friends. Maybe she could get a real job with real pay, and Ella could go to a good school.

When she was halfway up the slope, the wind picked up, bringing with it the sweet aroma of honeysuckle and pine, flapping the letter in her hand. She stopped, folded the letter, and put it in her apron pocket. A strong, sudden gust rushed down the mountain, jingling the spoon chimes on the porch and whirling the laundry on the line. She looked up at the sky, half expecting a storm cloud to come rolling over the nearby peaks. Then, as suddenly as it had come, the wind stopped. The sunflowers in the garden stilled and a cardinal landed on the grass in front of her, singing a loud tune. A brown wren hopped along the split-rail fence and joined in, filling the unexpected silence with birdsong. Up at the house, Bonnie and Ella watched expectantly from the porch steps, Ella perched on Bonnie's knee. Bonnie lifted Ella's arm to make her wave.

"I hope y'all got good news this time!" Bonnie shouted.

Lena smiled and waved back. "My brother is alive!"

"Hooray!" Bonnie yelled, bouncing Ella up and down. Then she carried Ella down the steps, took both her hands in hers, and turned her in circles on the grass, singing a happy song. Ella giggled and beamed up at Bonnie, her eyes filled with adoration.

And then, as unexpectedly as the sudden wind that had washed the fragrant scent of trees and flowers over her face, Lena realized it was too late to leave. If Enzo came to America, he would have to work at the sawmill with Silas as originally planned until he was old enough to make his own decisions. Because her heart had already fallen in love with the mountains and Wolfe Hollow, and most of all, with the young girl and boy who lived there. Despite everything, or maybe because of everything, she and Ella needed Bonnie and Jack Henry as much as they needed them. And now, with even greater passion and purpose, she prayed Silas could stop the state from taking his land so they would be left in peace, and Bonnie, Jack Henry, and Ella could grow up happy and healthy in the Blue Ridge, where they belonged.

Chapter 15

After receiving Enzo's letter, Lena wrote back right away. She did her best to make sure he understood he held no blame for Mutti's death, and to let him know she and Ella were fine, with plenty to eat and a roof over their head. But it was too soon to admit she had no money to send. He needed to rest and heal, and she didn't want to worry him.

At breakfast three days later, Silas informed her and the children that, after the morning chores, they were going to a cornhusking at the McDaniels' farm. Lena had no idea what a cornhusking was, but Bonnie and Jack Henry seemed excited when they heard the news, so she figured it must be something good. And no matter how fleeting, it would be nice to have a distraction from the heavy ache of grief she carried, not to mention a day off from work. Enzo's letter had relieved her sorrow a tiny bit, but only briefly; the hole left by Mutti felt immeasurable and endless.

Now, she and Bonnie followed Silas and Jack Henry along a rocky dirt road leading higher up the mountain toward Chestnut Ridge and the McDaniels' farm. Beside Lena, Bonnie pushed

Ella in the wicker baby carriage, laughing and making silly faces at her. Ella giggled with delight and Lena laughed too, her spirit always raised by seeing Ella so happy. Even Jack Henry, who tried to imitate his father by taking long, manly strides, glanced over his shoulder and grinned. As usual, Silas was silent, looking straight ahead and walking with purpose.

When they turned up another steep road, the distant sounds of music drifted down through the narrow valley—a lively, fast tempo that seemed to bounce off the mountains and echo through the thick forests. It sounded like a polka, but without accordions or trumpets.

"What is that?" Lena asked Bonnie.

Bonnie gaped at her. "Y'all ain't never heard real music before?"

"I have heard music," Lena said. "But not like that."

"That there's mountain music," Bonnie said. "Momma loved it, and boy, could she sing." She grinned proudly. "Ain't that right, Daddy?"

Silas grunted.

"Wait until you hear Bushrod Conner and Hosey Ruf on the banjo and fiddle," Bonnie said. "Ain't nobody in these hills can play like them. When Bushrod starts sawing his fiddle, those boys will get to jumping as high as a table."

And then she started singing along with the music coming down the mountain, beaming at Ella and practically dancing behind the baby carriage.

> "I asked her if she loved me,
> She said she loved me some.
> I throwed my arms around her,
> Like a grapevine 'round a gum.
>
> Cindy in the summer,
> Cindy in the fall,

If I don't get Cindy,
I'll not marry at all."

Suddenly, Silas stopped and spun around. "Shut that bear trap you got for a mouth, girl!" he snarled.

Bonnie came to a halt, startled by his outburst. Lena stopped too.

"Yes, sir," Bonnie said, and hung her head.

"What'd I tell you about singing when I'm around?" Silas said.

Bonnie looked up at him with watery eyes. "I'm sorry, Daddy. But it was one of Momma's favorite songs and I thought Ella might take to it."

"I don't give a good goddamn what you thought," Silas said. "I don't wanna hear it coming out of your mouth."

"But Daddy," Jack Henry said. "That music is coming from the cornhusking. Ain't that where we're going?"

Silas glared at him. "Y'all think I don't know that? I can't tell them boys at the husking what to do, but I sure as hell can tell my own young'uns what to do!"

"Yes, sir," Jack Henry said, and started walking again.

With a hurt, miserable face, Bonnie waited for Silas to turn around and keep going. In the wicker baby carriage, Ella gazed up at her with a puzzled look, no doubt wondering why she'd stopped laughing and singing.

For the life of her, Lena could not understand how Silas was worried about someone taking his children one minute, and the next he was yelling at his daughter for singing. Yes, grief made people do and say awful things sometimes, but breaking his child's heart was beyond mean and unreasonable.

When Silas started moving again, Lena edged closer to Bonnie and whispered, "Maybe you can teach me that song later. Ella too."

Bonnie nodded but did not smile.

No one spoke the rest of the way.

At the McDaniels' farm, horse-drawn wagons and saddled horses lined the road, along with the occasional farm truck or random vehicle. Dozens of people filled the wide yard between the two-story cabin and the slat barn—women in gingham skirts and cotton dresses piled food on makeshift tables, barefoot children ran and played tag and jump rope, and men in overalls and work boots gathered around a massive pile of corn in the center of it all. Next to the barn, a woman and three men played music, two men with violins and a third picking the strings of what looked like a small guitar with a round body. The woman played a strange-looking instrument that rested across her lap, like a narrow guitar with no neck. In the dirt dooryard near the musicians, numerous women and children danced a fast jig while an old man in droopy overalls tried to keep up and others watched, tapping their feet.

"Where did all of these people come from?" Lena said to Bonnie.

"Y'all got any idea how many mountains and hollers is up here in the Blue Ridge?" Bonnie said. "I bet there's people up here *we* ain't even met yet." Normally, after saying something clever, she would have laughed, but sorrow creased her face.

While Silas and Jack Henry joined the men at the pile of corn, Lena and Bonnie took Ella up a slope at the back of the yard toward a row of ancient oak trees, where mothers sprawled on blankets with their toddlers and babies in the shade, and elderly men and women sat on rocking chairs, kitchen chairs, and wooden stools. Several people waved to Bonnie and she waved back. Some of the old men and women smoked corncob pipes, their nearly invisible lips turning inward toward toothless gums. In a clearing between the trees, a group of women sat around what looked like a tablecloth held open by a wooden frame. Lena thought they were eating at some kind of strange table, but no plates sat in front of them, no food or drinks.

"What are they doing over there?" she asked Bonnie, pointing at the group.

Bonnie glanced in their direction. "That's a quilting bee."

"I do not know what that is," Lena said. She took a blanket out of the carriage, spread it on the grass, and put Ella on it.

"They're stitching a quilt like the one on your bed," Bonnie said. "In a couple weeks, they're fixing to sell quilts and baskets down at the state fair."

"State fair?"

Bonnie rolled her eyes. "Y'all don't know what a state fair is either?"

Lena shook her head.

"It's like a carnival but bigger," Bonnie said. "With a Ferris wheel, merry-go-round, games of chance, popcorn, and candy apples. There's all sorts a contests too, like the best pig and cow, the biggest vegetables, and tastiest pies. Last year, Jack Henry won a prize at the dunking booth for soaking the clown three times in a row. Daddy usually lets me and him go with Teensy and Judd McDaniel on account of them being kin, but I reckon he ain't gonna this year."

"Why not?"

"'Cause last year Teensy was fixing to enter the Fitter Family Contest but they told her no mountain folk was allowed to enter on account of they warn't smart or fit enough to pass the tests. Then Judd got in a fight with the man in charge 'cause he said Teensy shouldn't be having no more children if she was too stupid to know they had to turn in a family history and have a doctor say if they was good enough in the first place. Punched the man so hard it pretty near knocked him into next week. Sheriff Dixon threw Judd in jail for two days. That was about the same time him and George Pollock started nosing around up here."

Lena shook her head. She could understand having a contest for the best pie or biggest potato, but judging people the same way seemed strange, not to mention wrong. And why did it seem like everyone in America was obsessed with whether or not people were smart?

Bonnie sat down cross-legged on the blanket next to Ella. Lena sat down too, Ella between them.

"Now that you got me to thinking about it," Bonnie said. "Remember that meddlesome woman who snuck up on Jack Henry saying she worked for a man from the... what was it called? The eu... eugenics office? I kept wondering where I heard that word before and I remember now. When they announced the Fitter Family winners, they always said it."

"What does it mean?"

Bonnie shook her head. "I ain't got a clue, but if it has anything to do with the same folk who run the Fitter Family contest, it ain't nothing good." She moved to the edge of the blanket, yanked out a handful of grass, and threw it hard, her face cross. Between Silas scolding her, talking about not being allowed to go to the fair, and remembering the woman in the barn, her mood had gone steadily downhill.

"I am sorry your father yelled at you," Lena said. "It was wrong for him to do that."

Bonnie shrugged one shoulder. "I reckon I'm used to it by now."

"He still loves you," Lena said. "Even when he is angry."

"Maybe," Bonnie said. "But I'm done talking about it."

Lena sighed. Bonnie had been so excited about the day and now it seemed ruined. Lena wanted to tell Silas he was ruining his relationship with his daughter over something as innocent as singing, but it would have to wait. "Why don't you have something to eat, then go play with the other children?"

"I ain't all that hungry yet. I'll sit with Ella while y'all get your vittles."

Lena knew better. Bonnie and Jack Henry had spent half the morning talking about the different foods that would be served today—spareribs and scrapple, boiled potatoes and sausage gravy, chicken and biscuits, apple butter and canned peaches, cakes and cookies and cobblers. They'd even talked about the coffee brewed on an outdoor fire. Maybe Bonnie wanted a few minutes alone to lick the wounds her father had inflicted.

"Are you certain?" Lena said.

Bonnie nodded.

"All right," Lena said. "I will get Ella's food too."

"Take your time," Bonnie said. "We ain't going nowhere." She picked a dandelion and showed it to Ella, twirling it between her fingers and forcing a smile.

Lena made her way down the slope toward the house, still amazed by the number of people who had gathered at this isolated mountain farm. Over by the road, Virgil climbed down from his wagon and walked toward the corn pile, his eyes on the musicians near the barn. When he stopped and did a little dance in the grass before continuing on, she smiled. So far, everyone she'd met seemed friendly—except Silas, of course—and hopefully it would continue that way. When she reached the long table filled with strange offerings, she took a white plate at the end of the line and tried to decide what Ella might eat. Like Bonnie and Jack Henry said, there were endless assortments of meats and vegetables and casseroles and breads and biscuits and desserts. But everything looked so different than what she was used to, sometimes it was hard to tell what was what.

"Hey there, Miss Lena!" a voice called out.

It was Betty Lee Blanchard, coming across the yard with a steaming platter of brown meat.

Lena gave her a small wave.

"It's real nice to see y'all here," Betty Lee said when she reached her. She put the platter on the table, then addressed a heavyset woman in a flowered dress who was setting a basket of cathead biscuits on another table. "Hey, Teensy, you met Miss Lena yet? She's come all the way from Germany to help Silas out with his house and children."

Teensy wiped her hands on her apron and came over. "Oh,

for heaven's sake," she said. "I sure haven't. It's grand to meet you, Miss Lena. I'm Teensy McDaniel, Silas's third cousin once removed. This here place belongs to me and my husband, Judd." She smiled proudly.

So this was the cousin Virgil had told her about. "It is nice to meet you too," Lena said.

"I reckon Silas ain't told you nothing about me," Teensy said.

Lena shook her head.

"Gosh darn that man," Teensy said, still grinning. "His grandpappy and my mother were brother and sister."

"My mother was a cousin to Silas too," Lena said. "But I am not sure how. She said his father was a good man."

"Well, I'll be!" Teensy said, practically squealing with delight. "That means we're family!" She hurried around the table, her generous bosom bouncing up and down, and hugged Lena so tight she could barely breathe. "Welcome to Old Rag Mountain. I wish Silas woulda told me you were coming, we would of throwed you a big ol' welcome shindig!"

Betty Lee came around the table too. "And Teensy knows how to throw one heck of a shindig," she said.

"Thank you," Lena said. When Teensy finally let go, Lena stepped out of line to let others go ahead.

"And your momma was right about Silas's daddy," Teensy said. "He was the hardest working man you ever could know. A real family man too. Always willing to help out a neighbor. And Silas's momma? Well, she's darn near a legend in these parts. She could saddle a horse in the morning, ride through the mountains to help a mother give birth, wait on the sick, shroud the dead, harness a mule, and plow the garden, all in the same day."

"That's right," Betty Lee said. "Silas's momma fed hundreds at funerals and picnics too. She always said she was glad to be born poor 'cause learning how to struggle taught you how to make do, and doing well for yourself and others was a big part of the joy in life."

Teensy nodded. "Anybody who tried to beat her in goodness and kindness, love and humor, mercy and order, well, they woulda found that a hard cat to shave. When she died, Silas was inconsolable for nearly a year. 'Course it didn't help none that he'd just lost his daddy in a mining accident and his brother got shot in the head a few years earlier when he was out riding 'cause his rifle was stuck upside down in his boot."

Good lord, Lena thought. *How many loved ones has Silas lost?*

A woman with a plateful of fried chicken edged over to join the conversation. "That Silas Wolfe is cursed, I swear," she said.

Lena cringed further. She had enough to worry about without wondering if Silas was cursed.

Teensy gave the woman a stern look. "That ain't at all true and you know it, Lucy. He's just had a spell of bad luck." She turned her attention back to Lena. "I offered to look after his young'uns awhile back, but he's too damn proud to accept a thing from anyone he knows. Used to be the first one at people's doorstep offering to help and glad to take aid in return, but he ain't the same man since his wife died. I'm happy to hear he's got you at least."

"She's pretty as a speckled pup, ain't she?" Betty Lee said.

"Sure is," Teensy said. She grinned at Lena like a prideful mother.

"I should introduce her to my boy, Watson," Lucy said.

Teensy chuckled, mischief shining in her eyes. "Lucy's always playing matchmaker for her boys, likely on account of having twelve of them and she wants them outta the house."

"Oh hush," Lucy said, waving a playful hand. "You'd be doing the same thing if you were in my shoes. Living with one man is bad enough, let alone a dozen."

Everyone laughed.

"Well, it ain't your place for matchmaking anyways," Betty Lee said. "And Lena lost her intended a couple years ago, so I reckon you should get her okay first."

"Oh dear," Lucy said. "I'm sorry. You poor thing."

"Sorry to hear that," Teensy said.

"Thank you," Lena said, hoping she sounded sincere.

"Where's your young'un at?" Betty Lee said. "Just wait till y'all see her, Teensy. She's cute as a button."

Lena pointed toward the line of ancient oaks. "Ella is over there with Bonnie."

"I can hardly wait to meet her," Teensy said. "But first I need to bring out the rest of the vittles, then I'll come see your little one." She regarded Lena with gentle, caring eyes. "If y'all need anything, don't be afraid to ask, you hear? And I mean anything at all. Blood sticks together in these hills, no matter what." Then she hugged Lena again, making her feel a little guilty for letting Teensy believe she had a dead fiancé.

"Thank you," Lena said again. "I will." For a second, she thought about asking Teensy if she knew anything about the state trying to take Silas's land or if she had children and worried about them being taken. But now wasn't the time, especially not in front of the other women.

Teensy pointed at a man in a straw hat near the pile of corn. "That there's my husband, Judd. And over there jumping rope is my two girls, Janie Sue and Bobby Joe. My youngest is in the house napping and my oldest, Charlene June, is in the kitchen helping with the dishes. If the good Lord's willing, we'll get a boy someday, but I'm right happy with the four we got. And they're already eating us outta house and home anyway."

Lucy elbowed Teensy. "I bet it ain't from lack a trying."

"Well, these days, Judd's more interested in trying than I am." Teensy chuckled.

"Ain't most men?" Betty Lee said.

"Speak for yourself," Lucy said, giving the women a mischievous wink.

"Ain't no wonder you got twelve boys," Betty Lee said.

The women laughed.

"How old is your little one?" Teensy said to Lena.

"Ella is two," Lena said.

Betty Lee's eyes went wide. "Two? When I saw her at the mill I could of swore she weren't no older than one. Why, she's no bigger than a tater bug. Y'all need to get you some of that health tonic from Granny Creed. That'll fix her right up. Wouldn't hurt you none to swallow some too. You're a mite thin yourself."

Heat crawled up Lena's face. She wanted these women to know she was a good mother, and Ella was healthier now. Not to mention Betty Lee had no right to say anything about them being thin while standing next to tables piled high with food. She had no clue how often she and Ella had gone hungry, or what Lena had given up to give her daughter a better life. She opened her mouth to respond, not entirely sure what would come out, but Teensy came to her rescue.

"The poor little darling," she said. "My Judd read in the paper how hard things was over there in Europe. It ain't no wonder y'all are a little thin." She grabbed a plate and led Lena back to the table. "Now, let me give you a hand fixing your young'un's supper. How about some of these mashed potatoes and sweet peas? I reckon she'd like a little chicken and gravy, and some stewed apples too."

"Don't forget to have her try my shoo-fly pie," Betty Lee called out. "It's the best she'll ever have."

Lena had no idea what shoo-fly pie was, but it sounded awful.

"Well, bless your heart, Betty Lee," Teensy said over her shoulder. "You know she's gonna be trying my strawberry pie first."

Betty Lee harrumphed and said, "Anyhow, it sure was nice seeing y'all again, Lena. I reckon my kin is wondering where I am, so I best get back to them. In the meantime, you can try whatever pie tickles your fancy." Then she smiled at Teensy and walked away. "Have a nice day!"

Lucy pushed her way into line beside Lena and added a spoonful of cabbage to her plate of fried chicken. "I need to skedaddle too. It was real nice meeting you though."

"Nice to meet you too," Lena said.

When the two women were out of earshot, Teensy leaned in and said under her breath, "Just so y'all know, I love Lucy and Betty Lee to death but Lucy ain't got the good sense God gave a rock. And Betty Lee's nosier than a pet coon. So just watch what y'all say when they're around."

Lena nodded. It felt good to have another adult on her side, and knowing Teensy was a relative made it even better, but Lena had no idea how to respond. When they finished filling plates for her and Ella, Lena thanked Teensy for her help and headed back up the slope.

Back beneath the oak trees, Bonnie was still on the blanket, chatting with a skeletal-looking woman in a rocking chair and two gray-haired men perched on tree stumps. The woman, in a long apron and an ankle-length dress the color of plums, and the man next to her, who had deep wrinkles and milky eyes, looked a hundred years old. The other man looked younger, but not by much. Ella stood in front of the rocking chair, playing with a pile of acorns in the woman's lap. The woman jerked her chin in Lena's direction.

"This her?" she said.

"Yep," Bonnie said. "This is Lena."

"Howdy," the woman said.

"Hello," Lena said.

Ella turned and held out an acorn to show her mother. "A con," she said, grinning. Then she put the acorn back in the old woman's apron. The old woman cupped her blue-veined hands around the acorns, lifted the pile, and let them fall clattering back to her lap. Ella laughed.

"This here's Arlene Hoy," Bonnie said. "That's her husband, Dice, and their son Clary. They been good friends of ours for as long as I can remember."

"That's right," Dice said. "I used to hunt with Silas's grandpappy while the womenfolk stayed home drinking moonshine."

Arlene gave him a playful slap on the arm. "That ain't true and you know it. More than likely we were catching fish over in Horsehead Creek in case you boys came home with nothing to show for your troubles."

"Don't listen to her," Dice said. "We always came back with something, even if it were just a scrawny squirrel or two." He leaned back and laughed, revealing toothless gums. Clary and Arlene laughed with him.

Bonnie got up from the blanket. "Well, it's sure been nice chatting with y'all," she said. "But I need to fetch some vittles."

"It was real nice catching up with you too," Arlene said. "Be sure and tell your daddy to come say hello."

"Sure thing," Bonnie said, and ran off toward the house.

Happy to see Bonnie's mood had improved, Lena got down on the blanket and called Ella over to eat. Ella looked back and forth between the acorns and the plate of food her mother was holding, then grabbed handfuls of acorns and started toward her.

"No," Lena said. "Put them back. They do not belong to you."

"Sure they do," Arlene said. "She and Bonnie had a grand time picking a mess of them off the ground."

"Oh," Lena said. "I did not know. Thank you." She offered Arlene a friendly smile and told Ella it was all right to bring the acorns over.

Ella toddled back to the blanket and sat down, happily clutching the acorns in her hands. When Lena held out a spoonful of food, as usual Ella opened her mouth like a little bird. But after her first taste of chicken and gravy, she dropped the acorns and grabbed the spoon to feed herself.

"Got a good appetite, don't she?" Arlene said, her eyes sparkling the way old people's did when they saw a young child.

Lena nodded. *And I'm beyond grateful that she finally has plenty to eat.*

When Bonnie returned with an overflowing plate, she sat down and balanced it on her knees. As always, Lena was astonished by how much someone so young could consume in one sitting. Then again, Bonnie worked as hard as an adult and needed the sustenance. While Bonnie and Ella enjoyed their suppers, Lena finished eating too, then rocked Ella to sleep and laid her on the blanket between them.

Bonnie leaned back on her arms and let out a satisfied groan. "I'm gonna hold off a bit on dessert," she said. "I'm so full I'm about to pop."

"I feel the same," Lena said.

In the center of the yard, the men continued working on the corn, yanking off the husks and silks, then throwing the shucked ears in another pile. Standing next to Silas, Jack Henry ripped off husks as fast as he could, trying to keep up with the older boys and men.

"Do you think your brother would like to eat now?" Lena said.

"I reckon he can't hardly wait to get to the vittles," Bonnie said. "But he ain't gonna stop until Daddy does."

Of course. Lena should have known better. Enzo used to be the same way at that age, trying to walk as fast as their father, or carry as much firewood. Sometimes, he even copied Vater by putting his head in his hands at the dinner table, as if he too worried about their many problems. *Enzo.* Had he gotten the job in Berlin? Was he recovered after being so sick? Lena could hardly wait to get another letter from him.

Over near the piles of corn, a man approached Silas, tapped him on the shoulder, and handed him what looked like a folded newspaper. After looking at the paper for a moment, Silas nodded his thanks to the man, then marched toward Lena and Bonnie, the newspaper clenched in one fist.

"Uh-oh," Arlene said. "He looks mad as a hornet."

Bonnie sat up and glanced nervously at Lena. When Silas reached them, he shoved the newspaper in Bonnie's face and jabbed a photograph with his finger.

"Y'all see this?" he said. Anger hardened his voice.

Bonnie peered at the photograph, then went pale.

"Read it," Silas demanded.

Bonnie sounded out the words, her voice trembling. "'M... most mountain hillbillies live in s... shacks no better than animal dens.'"

"I warned y'all, didn't I?" Silas snarled.

Bonnie nodded. "I'm sorry, Daddy."

"I don't give a good goddamn how sorry you are, just do as I say from here on out!" Silas said.

"Yes, sir," Bonnie said.

"What's got your bones rattled, Silas?" Dice said from his seat on the tree stump.

Ignoring him, Silas shot Lena a disgusted look. "That goes double for you." Then he threw the paper on the ground and stormed away.

"Howdy to y'all too!" Dice called after him. Silas glanced back but kept going. Dice shook his head in disappointment.

Lena picked up the newspaper. On the front page was a grainy photograph—Bonnie and the other children standing barefoot next to the ramshackle pigpen at Mr. Early's mill.

"*Ach, nein,*" Lena said. "I should not have let you in the pictures."

"It ain't your fault," Bonnie said, her eyes watering.

Arlene clucked her tongue. "You all right, Bonnie?"

Bonnie nodded, then got to her feet and picked up the dirty supper plates. "I reckon I'll go see what the other kids are up to."

Lena nodded. "Try to have fun and do not worry. Your father will not be mad forever."

"I ain't too sure about that," Bonnie said, then turned and headed down the slope.

Lena watched her go, wishing she thought Bonnie was wrong. Halfway to the house, Bonnie put both plates in one hand so she could wipe her face with the other.

"What's got Silas all riled up?" Clary said.

Lena got up and took the paper over to him. He and Arlene squinted at the photograph.

"Is that Bonnie with Betty Lee's and Sandy's young'uns?" Arlene said.

Lena nodded.

"Looks like a couple of Nellie McCauley's young'uns too," Clary said. "And Mr. Early's grandkids."

Just then, Teensy approached from the direction of the barn, waving at Arlene, Dice, and Clary. When she reached them, she put her hands on her hips and gazed down at Ella, who lay on the blanket with her head turned to the side, her breathing soft and slow.

"Would you look at that," Teensy said. "Betty Lee sure is right about one thing. Your young'un's a perfect little angel." Then she looked up at Lena and the others. "I saw Silas over here pitching a conniption. Everything all right?"

Clary handed Teensy the newspaper. "He's got a burr under his saddle about this here picture in the newspaper."

Teensy examined the photograph. "Oh lordy. How in the flipping hell did that get in there?"

"A photographer was taking pictures at the mill," Lena said. "He said he wanted to show people what life was like in the mountains."

Clary made a disgusted sound. "Well, I reckon y'all know why that went over like a turd in a punchbowl," he said. "Silas done warned us the state was trying to make us look ignorant and poor so they can steal our land."

"Judd heard they just want us out for a spell while they lay the road," Teensy said. "Then they're gonna let us come back."

"That's a load of horseshit," Dice said. "One of them slick-faced state men came right in my house. He done sat at my supper table and made a list of everything I owned. My old mule, my cracked saddle, butter churn, table and chairs, you get the idea. Now you tell me, why do they have a need to know all that if they're fixing to let us come back?"

"That's right," Clary said. "The one that come to my place was carrying slates to jot down his calculations. Head count, room count, livestock count. Ten children. Two milk cows. And so on. Just sizing everything up and saying nothing. Them bureaucrats don't give a fig for us mountain people any more than they do the local wildlife. They just want our land."

Worry transformed Teensy's face. "Ain't no one been here at the farm," she said.

"They just ain't made it over here yet," Clary said. "You and Judd better keep an eye out 'cause they're coming."

Teensy put a hand over her ample chest. "Lord have mercy. If the good Lord's willing, they'll pass us by."

"The good Lord ain't got nothing to do with it," Arlene said. "An awful lot of strange people been asking a lot of questions. And they weren't no preachers or missionaries. They didn't have no Bibles or pamphlets to save souls. And they weren't revenuers or lawmen neither. They didn't have no badges or guns to arrest people."

"Bosley Glick tried telling us not to worry 'cause the government is planning on buying people's homes and giving them farms down the mountain," Dice said. "But the government sure as hell ain't giving away free farms."

"That's crazy talk," Teensy said. "Even if they had a mind to, the government can't afford to give us all free farms."

"Well, if they ain't giving them resettlement houses away," Arlene said, "we won't be able to afford one of them neither. Especially when they're only offering pennies on the dollar for what our land's worth. The problem is, some folks around these parts don't know no better 'cause they ain't never felt the weight of a dollar bill in their hands."

"Hell," Dice said. "Most folks around these parts been walking cattywampus on these hills so long, their legs ain't gonna work right on flat land. And just how're they expecting us mountain folk to survive down in the lowlands anyway? They gonna make sure we got land to keep cows and gardens? And someplace to hunt possum and pick berries?"

"I heard the folks who already agreed to sell when the time comes have to ask permission to cut their brush, work their soil, even take wire off their own fence," Clary said. "And the dang government don't even own their land yet!"

"Them state scoundrels been itching for the park for years," Dice said. "Now the dad-blasted city folk think they can buy our land for nothing and give it to the nation as a gift. Who the hell do they think they are? They can't just run us outta here."

Teensy looked beside herself. "What's going to happen to the Carvers?" she said. "They're the most down-on-their-luck family in this holler, living on rocky land nobody wants, all seven of them in a one-room cabin not much bigger than a spring house. And the families selling baskets and quilts over at the Skyland Resort ain't got no other way a making a living."

Arlene shrugged. "I hate to think what's gonna happen to them poor folk, 'cause it sure enough ain't gonna be nothing good."

Lena started to ask if anyone was aware children were being taken when a sudden scream filled the air, a scream so shrill and loud the musicians stopped playing. Everyone froze. The woman screamed again. It was coming from the direction of the barn.

Two women bolted out of the open barn door with young children in tow, their eyes and mouths wide with horror. A teenage boy ran out behind them, then bent over and retched in the grass. The men husking corn dropped the ears in their hands and sprinted over to the barn. Most of them hurried inside, including Teensy's husband, Judd, while some waited outside the double doors, craning their necks to see. A flood of women followed from across the yard, abandoning their sewing, putting down plates of food, wiping their hands on dishcloths and aprons, carrying toddlers on their hips.

Frantic, Teensy hurried down the slope. Dice, Clary, and several other old people got up from their seats to see what all the commotion was about, while Arlene stayed in her rocking chair, wringing her blue-veined hands. Lena scanned the yard for Bonnie. Silas and Jack Henry were just outside the barn door with some of the men, but Bonnie was nowhere to be seen. Lena couldn't imagine what terrible thing had happened, or to whom, but the longer she searched for Bonnie, the more anxious she grew.

The women and children who'd been inside the barn when the screaming started were quickly surrounded by a crowd of people asking questions and trying to comfort them. Seconds later, some of the men who'd entered the barn came back out, shaking their heads, looking for their families. Then Judd rushed out, grabbed Silas by the arm, and dragged him back inside. Jack Henry tried to follow, but a man held him back. Lena's breath caught.

Bonnie.

For a second, she had no idea what to do. Wake Ella and take her down to the barn, or leave her on the blanket and ask Arlene to watch her? No. She refused to let her child out of her sight. She gathered Ella up, hugged her sleep-warm body to her chest, and hurried down the slope. Startled, Ella began to cry.

"You're all right," Lena said. "Momma has you."

Running across the yard, she dodged children and wagons and wayward chickens, until she finally reached the barn. Virgil caught sight of her and hurried over.

"Bonnie ain't with y'all?" he said.

Lena shook her head.

Virgil took her arm and pushed his way through the crowd. "Step aside, folks," he said, clearing a path. "We're in a need to get by."

As the men and women moved out of the way, some turned to glance at Lena with curious eyes while others looked at her with pity. Concern filled all of their faces.

When Lena saw Jack Henry, she shouted his name.

He spun around, his eyes filled with terror.

"What happened?" she said.

"It's Bonnie," Jack Henry cried. "But they ain't letting me inside."

Lena pulled him close. "Do not worry. Everything will be all right." She doubted her own words, but what else could she say?

Jack Henry buried his face in her blouse to hide his tears. With one arm around him, the other holding Ella tight, she stared at the barn door and waited, lightheaded and nauseous.

Suddenly the crowd inside the barn door parted and Silas came out carrying Bonnie. Her eyes were closed, her head lolled back on her neck, and her limbs hung limp. Blood streaked her dress and covered her face. Women gasped and everyone stepped back to give Silas room. Lena's stomach turned over.

Jack Henry trembled beside her. "Is she dead?" he said, his voice weak.

"I do not know," Lena said.

She wanted to run over to Bonnie and check for herself, to see what had happened and if she could help, but fear had suddenly struck her immobile. Before she could come to her senses, a petite, white-haired woman came out of the crowd and spread a patchwork quilt at Silas's feet.

"Lay her down carefully now," she said. She pushed her sleeves up her bronzed arms, coiled her long white braid into a bun at the back of her neck, and knelt at the edge of the quilt.

Silas knelt and gently laid Bonnie in front of the woman, his face knotted with anguish. Bonnie's eyes remained closed, her legs and arms still limp. A jagged gash ran along her cheek, mere inches below her left eye, and a thick stream of dark blood oozed out of it, running along her face and dripping on the quilt.

The white-haired woman turned Bonnie's head to one side, took off her apron, and pressed it hard against the wound. "What caused this?" she said.

Behind Silas, a boy stepped forward. "We was playing in the haymow," he said. "She fell out and landed on a bale hook." His face was pasty, his voice breathless.

"I need someone to fetch clean rags, suturing thread, and white mule," the white-haired woman shouted. "And what've we got for salve?"

"I got turpentine," Teensy said.

"That'll do," the white-haired woman said.

Teensy and Betty Lee turned and raced to the house as fast as they could, their long skirts gathered in their hands.

Silas bent over Bonnie, gently stroking her blood-spattered hair. "Can you hear me, darlin'?" he said. "I'm right here and you're gonna be just fine, I promise." He started to say more, but his voice broke and he kissed her forehead instead.

Emotion clogged Lena's throat, her vision starting to blur. Jack Henry covered his eyes and pressed his face into her side. Virgil put a hand on his shoulder.

"Don't you worry none," he said. "Your sister's gonna be right as rain before you know it. Just thank the Lord almighty that Granny Creed is here."

Lena prayed Virgil was right. If something happened to Bonnie, who knew what it would do to Silas and Jack Henry? They had already lost so many loved ones. Not to mention it would break Ella's heart. And Lena's too. She loved Bonnie like a daughter, and seeing her injured only intensified those feelings and protective instincts. Suddenly, Lucy's words echoed in her mind. *"Silas Wolfe is cursed, I swear."*

No. Curses did not exist. And Silas would not lose Bonnie too. He couldn't. *They* couldn't.

She knelt down in front of Jack Henry and looked him in the eye. "Can you hold Ella while I help with Bonnie?"

Jack Henry wiped his face and nodded. Lena gave Ella to him—thankfully she had calmed down—and went over to Silas and Granny Creed. "What can I do?"

Granny Creed looked up at her and Silas. "I reckon it'll take the two of you to hold her down while I clean the wound," she said.

Lena knelt on the edge of the quilt next to Granny Creed, near Bonnie's legs.

Suddenly, Bonnie's eyes flew open. She cried out and reached for her face, her arms and legs flailing. Silas grabbed her wrists and held her arms while Lena held her legs. Granny Creed pushed harder on her wounded cheek, the apron below her bony hand already saturated with blood.

Bonnie screamed, her voice hoarse. "Let me go!"

"Hold still now," Silas said. "Granny Creed is here to fix you up. You're gonna be all right."

"I know you are scared," Lena said. "But we need to help you."

Bonnie struggled for what seemed like forever, yelling and trying to reach for Granny Creed's hand, to pull it from her cheek. When she finally gave up, she went limp and gasped for air, her eyes wide with terror. Silas loosened his grip but kept hold of her arms.

"That's it," he said. "Y'all ain't gonna do yourself no favors if you're worn plumb out. And I have a need to know if someone pushed you out of that mow."

Bonnie tried to shake her head but Granny Creed was pressing too hard on her cheek.

Granny Creed gave Silas a scolding look. "Now ain't the time for that."

Lena reached up and gently took Bonnie's hand, one hand still on her legs, ready to hold them down again if need be. If only she could look Bonnie in the eye and reassure her. To her surprise, Bonnie squeezed her fingers.

"Hold on as hard as you need to," Lena said.

Just then, Teensy and Betty Lee returned with a jug of moonshine and the rest of the supplies. Betty Lee opened the jug and handed it to Granny Creed while Teensy eased black thread through the eye of a sewing needle.

Granny Creed addressed the person standing closest to Bonnie's head, a freckle-faced man in worn suspenders. "Take hold of her head," she said.

The freckle-faced man hesitated, looking doubtful, then knelt and did as he was asked.

Granny Creed bent close to Bonnie's ear. "Keep still as you can now," she said. "I'm fixing to stitch you up and it's gonna sting some."

Bonnie made a terrified noise in her throat, like an animal caught in a trap.

Silas gripped her arms, ready to hold her down again. With pleading eyes, Lena glanced up at Betty Lee, who immediately understood and dropped to the quilt to hold Bonnie's ankles. Still holding Bonnie's hand, Lena used her free arm to press down on her legs.

Working fast, Granny Creed lifted the blood-soaked apron and poured moonshine on the gash in Bonnie's cheek, soaking her face and neck and hair. Bonnie writhed and cried out in agony, trying to kick and sit up. Betty Lee and Lena held her legs while Silas held her arms, his face contorting as if he were the one in pain.

"I need a clean rag," Granny Creed said to Teensy, who quickly handed her one. After pouring more moonshine on the rag, Granny Creed placed it on Bonnie's cheek and instructed the freckle-faced man to straighten Bonnie's head. He did as she asked. Then she spoke to Bonnie again. "Open up. I need a look-see in your mouth."

Silas, Lena, and Betty Lee loosened their grip, but only a little. Trembling, Bonnie squeezed Lena's fingers again and slowly opened her mouth, tears of pain streaming down her blood-covered face.

"Wider," Granny Creed said. She held out her hands one at a time so Teensy could pour moonshine over them.

Bonnie moaned and opened wider.

Quick as a wink, Granny Creed hooked a moonshine-covered finger in Bonnie's mouth, pulled her cheek away from her jaw, and looked inside. "Looks like that hook was fixing to go clean through," she said. "Good thing you got your teeth." Then she reached in, yanked a broken, bloody molar out of Bonnie's gums, and dropped it on the quilt. Bonnie yelped and groaned in agony, her eyes practically rolling back in her head. Granny Creed pressed the clean rag to her cheek again and told her to sit up. "Now have a big ol' swig of white mule. It'll dull the pain."

Silas and Lena helped Bonnie sit up while Granny Creed held the jug of whiskey to her mouth and told her to drink. Bonnie took a swallow, her eyes squeezed shut, then started to cough. Blood and spit ran out of her mouth, spraying her skirt and Lena's arms.

"One more," Granny Creed said. "Come on. Have another good slug and swish that mule around in your mouth before you swallow."

When she stopped coughing, Bonnie took another drink and did her best to do as instructed, her face twisting in pain.

"Good girl," Granny Creed said. "Now lay back and we'll get this done."

Bonnie shook her head, her eyes flooded with fear. Gently but firmly, Silas and Granny Creed pushed her back down.

"Keep your head turned," Granny Creed said. Then to Teensy, "I need the suturing thread."

Teensy placed the needle and thread on Granny Creed's open palm, then poured moonshine over them. Growing more frantic by the second, Bonnie cried and begged Granny Creed to stop.

Lena looked at Silas. "Change places with me," she said.

He shook his head, frowning at her like she was out of her mind.

"Please trust me," she said. Then, before he could protest further, she hurried around to his side, knelt back down, and gave him a nudge with her shoulder. He scowled and moved.

With the needle and thread ready, Granny Creed looked at them, slightly perplexed by the sudden switch. But there was no time to explain. Lena lay on her side, face to face with Bonnie, and took her hands in hers. Wild-eyed, Bonnie blinked at her, blood dripping down her lips and nose.

"Teach me that song," Lena said.

Bonnie furrowed her brow, confused.

"The song about Cindy," Lena said. "The one your mother loved." She squeezed Bonnie's hands.

Granny Creed lifted the rag from her cheek and Bonnie shuddered.

"Please, Bonnie," Lena said. "Tell me the words to the song."

Out of the corner of her eye, she saw the needle moving toward Bonnie's cheek.

The freckle-faced man gripped Bonnie's head and held it still. Silas took hold of her shoulders and Betty Lee grabbed her ankles.

"I . . . I can't," Bonnie said.

"Yes, you can," Lena said. "Tell me the words and I will sing them." She glanced at Granny Creed, who finally seemed to understand what she was doing. Lena forced a smile, looking at Bonnie. "I am sure you will laugh at my terrible voice."

Tears fell from Bonnie's eyes and for a moment, Lena thought she was too distraught and in pain to try. But then, in a weak, shaky voice Bonnie said, "I asked her if she loved me."

Lena had forgotten the tune to the song but she sang the lyrics anyway. "I asked her if she loved me."

Granny Creed pushed the needle into Bonnie's cheek and Bonnie cried out.

Lena held her hands tighter. "Tell me more."

Bonnie grimaced, her eyes squeezed shut, and barely moving her lips, said, "She said she loved me some."

"She said she loved me some."

Granny Creed put the needle in again.

Bonnie sobbed and, in between gasping for air, said, "I throwed my arms around her, like a grapevine 'round a gum."

Singing badly on purpose, Lena sang the words.

Working fast, Granny Creed put in more stitches.

"Keep going, Bonnie," Lena said.

"Cindy in the summer," Bonnie mumbled, her lips quivering. "Cindy in the fall."

Lena repeated the lyrics.

Another suture.

Bonnie cried out again, then said, "If I don't get Cindy, I'll not marry at all."

"Almost there," Granny Creed said.

Lena finished the song in a high-pitched voice and pretended to laugh. "I told you I have a very bad voice."

Granny Creed tied off the last stitch. "I reckon that's it," she said.

Lena gave Bonnie's hands another hard squeeze. "It is over. I knew you could do it."

"Gimme the salve," Granny Creed said to Teensy.

Teensy held out a tin filled with a brown, sticky-looking substance. Granny Creed took a big swipe of it with her fingers, put it on Bonnie's cheek, then pressed another folded, clean rag over the wound. Exhausted, Bonnie went limp. Granny Creed looked at Silas.

"That tooth stopped the hook from busting all the way through," she said. "And her cheek is gonna mend, but it'll be a while. Keep it dressed for a few days, then let the air get to it. And give her lots of broth and sassafras tea. She ain't gonna be chewing for a spell."

Silas nodded.

"Y'all can sit up now," Granny Creed said to Bonnie, still holding the rag to her cheek. Silas and Lena helped Bonnie upright and stayed beside her, holding her up. Granny Creed regarded Teensy again. "We're gonna need something to keep the dressing on."

Teensy held out a handful of cloth strips. "I fetched some quilting material."

Granny Creed asked Lena to hold the dressing on Bonnie's cheek. Then she took the strips, tied them together, and wrapped them over and under, around and around, Bonnie's head and chin. After the cloth was tied off on top of Bonnie's head, Lena slipped her hand out of the makeshift bandage. Granny Creed sat back on her heels and looked at Bonnie. "How y'all doing? That white mule kick in yet?"

Bonnie nodded, her eyes less wild, her blood-spattered face squeezed like lumpy pudding inside the cloth strips.

Granny Creed lifted the whiskey jug again. "Have another good swallow. You'll be needing it."

Bonnie took another big drink, winced, swallowed, and held her shaking fingers to her lips.

"There you go," Granny Creed said. She cleaned her hands on an extra rag, then addressed Silas again. "Give her more of the mule when you get home. Change the dressing four days after tomorrow, and send for me if something ain't looking right. But young'uns heal real fast so she'll be good as new before you know it. The stitching can come out in two weeks. If you need me to come by and do it, tell me now."

"I reckon I can take care of it," Silas said. "I'm mighty obliged, Granny Creed."

"No need to be thanking me," Granny Creed said. "I'm just doing what God put me on this good earth to do." She put a hand on one knee and pushed herself up. "I reckon you better get a ride home though. She ain't in no condition to walk."

"I can carry her," Silas said. "It ain't far."

Virgil stepped out of the crowd, his hat in his hand. "I can give y'all a ride," he said. "Got my wagon right out front here."

"Might want to swallow your pride and let Virgil give you some of his white mule too," Granny Creed said. "Your girl will be needing it."

Silas offered Virgil a quick, grateful nod, then helped Bonnie up.

Lena stood and scanned the crowd for Jack Henry and Ella.

Teensy gave her a clean rag to wipe the blood off her hands, then patted her shoulder. "Y'all did real good," she said. "Bonnie and Jack Henry are lucky to have you here."

"Thank you," Lena said.

Jack Henry appeared with Ella in his arms, staring at his bloodied sister with worried eyes.

Lena took Ella and said, "Do not worry. Bonnie is strong. She is going to be all right."

Jack Henry nodded but he did not look convinced.

After Bonnie took a moment to steady herself, she gently touched the bandage on her cheek and gazed at the crowd. For a moment, Lena had no idea if she was going to cry, say something, or turn away in embarrassment. Then, to Lena's astonishment, Bonnie threw her arms around her and Ella, sobbing. Lena hugged her back, overcome by emotion. Even Ella reached over to pat the back of Bonnie's head.

"Oh my *Liebling*," Lena said. "You are going to be all right. Your father and I will make sure of it." Then she glanced at Silas. He was staring at them, his face strange. It was hard to tell if he was hurt or angry.

Chapter 16

After Bonnie was injured at the cornhusking, Lena slept with Ella on a tick mattress next to her bed, giving her swallows of Virgil's moonshine when she cried out in pain, wiping her forehead and arms with a wet cloth when she jolted awake, hot and sweaty, from nightmares. During the day, Bonnie was quiet, only answering with a nod or a shake of her head. Lena made sure she drank sassafras tea, ate plenty of soup, and took naps in the afternoon. Although she understood talking might be painful for a while and she told Bonnie it was all right not to speak, sometimes she worried Bonnie had been struck mute after being traumatized, like a neighbor girl back home who had lost a leg during an air raid. By the third day, Bonnie started feeling better and insisted on helping in the kitchen—using gestures and facial expressions—so Lena made her sit at the table to cut vegetables and stir the batter for biscuits and corn bread.

The next day, when a horse-drawn wagon came up the road just after suppertime, Lena grabbed Ella and shouted for everyone to run to the shed.

"We ain't gotta hide," Bonnie said, opening her mouth as little as possible. "Daddy's outside fixing a loose porch step." Her voice sounded like her cheeks were full of cotton.

Lena's shoulders drooped with relief. Not only did the breath-stealing panic of someone taking the children fall from her like a shroud, but she was beyond grateful to hear Bonnie speak. Not to mention she had no desire to hide in that grave-like hole beneath the shed again; the first time had given her nightmares for a week, along with the horrible ones she already had. She put Ella back down. "I forgot your father was home," she said.

Together, she and Bonnie went to the window to see who was coming. Silas had already left the porch to meet the wagon before it reached the drive.

"It's Teensy and Betty Lee," Bonnie said, and hurried toward the front door.

"Be careful," Lena said. "Do not fall."

She started toward Ella, intending to go down the hill with her and Bonnie, to say hello to the women. Then she stopped. Silas might not appreciate her acting as if it were her place to greet visitors, or to know why they were there. As it was, he'd hardly said two words to her since Bonnie's accident. Maybe he thought it was Lena's fault his daughter had sought comfort from her instead of him. Of course, she'd been surprised and touched by his compassion when Bonnie first got hurt, and was hopeful it would be a turning point for him. But instead, he had withdrawn and was moodier than ever, biting Jack Henry's head off for the smallest things, like dropping his fork or forgetting to put away a rake. Seeing the hurt on Jack Henry's face broke her heart.

She wanted to believe Bonnie's injury only added to his worries, and that it was a painful reminder of how easily he could lose his children. Or maybe he thought holding everything in would protect them, without realizing he was only making a sad situation worse. On the other hand, maybe she was too willing to give him the benefit of the doubt. Maybe he was just a mean, miserable man now, broken by what life had handed him. Maybe it was too late for him to change.

Whatever the reason, she did not want to intrude or anger him further. If Teensy and Betty Lee were not coming up to the house for a visit, when Bonnie came back inside, she would tell her why they were there. And as much as Lena might have liked to see the women again, especially Teensy, that would have to be enough.

As it turned out, they were dropping off a tin of cider, a pan of apple pandowdy, a dish of bread pudding, two loaves of fresh baked bread, and a jar of wild strawberry preserves, along with the rest of the mountain community's best wishes for Bonnie's speedy recovery. Of course, Bonnie had invited them up for coffee, but they wanted to get home before dark. And they said to tell Lena hello, which made her happy.

The next afternoon, while Ella napped and Silas took Jack Henry down the mountain to pick up supplies at the general store, Lena changed the dressing on Bonnie's cheek for the first time. When she removed the bandage and saw the circular pit of dark blood and jagged tissue pinched together by black thread, she almost gasped. The wound was more gruesome than she had imagined. Nevertheless, she did her best to act nonchalant as she gently smoothed turpentine salve over the stitches. Bonnie winced but didn't pull away.

"I reckon I look like Frankenstein now," she said.

"You do not look like Frankenstein," Lena said. "And Granny Creed said you will heal very fast, remember? Does it still hurt?"

"It ain't no picnic."

Despite the gravity of the situation, Lena grinned. Leave it to Bonnie to say something smart, even when she was in pain. "Did you know there is a castle in Germany called Frankenstein Castle?"

"Y'all are pulling my leg."

"No, I am not. It is true."

"You been to it?"

Lena shook her head. "I have only read about it."

"Why the Sam Hill would anyone name a castle after a monster?"

"It was not named after a monster. The castle was built in the early twelve hundreds. The Franks were a German tribe, and stein means stone or rock. And the castle sits on a very big rock. The Frankenstein in the book is the name of the doctor who made the monster, not the monster. But there is also a story about a man who used to do tests on dead bodies there."

Bonnie's eyes widened. "What kinda tests? Like experiments and stuff?"

Lena nodded. "It is said he feared death, so he tried to bring the dead back to life."

Bonnie made a disgusted face. "I reckon that'd be enough to make folks sick. That why somebody wrote a book about him?"

"Some people think so. I do not know if it is true."

"Well, I ain't the sharpest tool in the shed, but I reckon that doctor was the monster after all."

Lena laughed. "I think you are right. See how smart you are?" She covered Bonnie's wound with a clean rag, then retied the strip of cloth around her head. "Are you hungry? I made more chicken soup."

Bonnie groaned. "I've had my fill of soup. It's all I been eating for days. That and sassafras tea."

"I know, but Granny Creed said you must have soft food."

"How about mashed 'taters with extra milk and butter? That'll make them good and runny. There's a mess of fresh ones out in the garden."

Lena had to agree; a change from soup sounded good. And, along with mashed potatoes for Bonnie, she could make *Kartoffelpuffer*, potato pancakes, for Silas and Jack Henry. Then they could try the desserts Teensy and Betty Lee dropped off. Not that Silas deserved anything special made for him, but she had to feed everyone, and back home, Ella used to love *Kartoffelpuffers*—when they were lucky enough to have potatoes.

"You stay in here," Lena said. "I will dig the potatoes."

"But I ain't breathed fresh air in days," Bonnie said.

"Your father will be angry if he catches you digging in the dirt."

"He and Jack Henry ain't due back for another hour. Besides, we'll hear his truck coming."

Lena looked up toward the bedroom where Ella was napping, as if she could see through the ceiling. Surely, Ella would sleep for another half hour, long enough for them to run out and dig some potatoes. And the fresh air would do Bonnie good. "All right, but we must hurry."

Out in the garden on their hands and knees, they dug beneath three potato plants that looked ready for harvest, their fingers brown with dirt as they pulled the yellow spuds from the soil. Lena got up to retrieve a metal bin from one of the sheds while Bonnie gently brushed the rich earth from the potatoes. The entire job took little more than ten minutes, and they found more than enough for mashed potatoes and *Kartoffelpuffers*. Lena couldn't help thinking how much Mutti would have loved seeing so many potatoes at one time.

When Bonnie picked up the bin, Lena said, "I will carry it."

"I ain't no weakling," Bonnie said.

"I know, but you do not want your cheek to start bleeding, do you?"

Reluctantly, Bonnie put down the bin. "I reckon not."

"Go inside and check on Ella," Lena said. "I will be right behind you."

While Bonnie started along the path toward the back porch, Lena checked to make sure they hadn't left any potatoes hidden in the dirt. Hopefully, Jack Henry would like the *Kartof-*

felpuffers, and if there was a jar of applesauce in the 'tater hole, they'd have one of Mutti's favorite meals from when she was a girl. Bonnie could eat applesauce too, but the pancakes would be too crispy for her. Lena would have to make them again once her cheek healed.

She picked up the bin, glanced up the path, and frowned. Bonnie had stopped at the corner of the house. And she was staring, wide-eyed, toward the road.

When Lena looked in that direction to see what had caught her attention, her breath caught in her throat.

A man in a suit and tie was walking up the grassy slope, his black boots shining in the sun. But no motor vehicle sat in the drive. No horse-drawn wagon or farm truck.

"Get in the house!" Lena shouted at Bonnie. "Hurry!"

Bonnie gaped at her, unsure.

"Go!" Lena said.

Bonnie looked at the man again, then finally sprinted behind the house and up the back steps two at a time. Lena put down the potato bin, wiped her hands on her apron, and moved toward the stranger, her heart galloping in her chest. If the man was from Sweet Briar College, sent there by Penelope Rodgers, she had to get rid of him. She would not let him take Ella, or anyone else, to be evaluated. Trying to appear confident, she marched down the yard to meet him, arms swinging, forehead furrowed with determination.

He was short and stocky, with oiled hair and heavy facial features flushed pink from too much whiskey. He took off his hat and gave her a smile. "Mrs. Wolfe?"

She shook her head and crossed her arms.

"Then you must be Mr. Wolfe's daughter?"

She shook her head again. "Who are you and what do you want?"

He grinned wider, amused. "I'd like to know your name, for starters."

She fixed her eyes on his, certain he could see her shaking. "I asked for your name first."

Surprised by her boldness, he blinked, then chuckled under his breath. "You don't have a need to know my name just yet."

"Then you do not have a need to know my name either."

"Well, I happen to know this is the Silas Wolfe residence. And I know for certain he would not be happy to find someone trespassing on his property."

"I am not trespassing," she said.

"How do I know that?"

She stood up straighter, pushing back her fear. She could not let him get the best of her. "You are the one who is trespassing. Did Penelope Rodgers send you?"

He put his hat back on and scanned the horizon, his face no longer friendly. "I don't know any Penelope Rodgers. And I don't recall Mr. Wolfe or any member of his family having an accent, so clearly, you're the foreigner here, not me. Now let's stop playing games, and you go fetch him for me."

"I'm sorry, I will not."

He eyed her with scorn, his patience wearing thin. "And why is that?"

"Because Mr. Wolfe is busy and I was told not to bother him. Now if you do not mind, I have work to do." She started to turn away but he grabbed her arm and yanked her around to face him.

"Now hold on, missy," he said. "I'm not done speaking to you."

She yanked free of his grasp. "Well, I am done speaking to you!"

He smiled again, a shrewd, condescending smile that dared her to test him. "My, my, you are a spirited one." He glanced toward the house. "I happen to know Silas isn't here right now because I can see his vehicle is gone. But a little birdie told me there was someone new looking after his children and I wanted to stop by to say hello." He stepped closer, the sour odor of sweat and tobacco filling the air between them. "I'm sure Silas has been awfully lonely since his wife died. I can see why he wants a pretty little thing like you around." He reached out to touch her hair.

She took a step back, resisting the urge to slap his hand. "Please go away."

"Why don't we wait inside for Silas to return? You can make me a cup of coffee and tell me how you came to be here."

Anger welled up inside her, burning across her skin. If only she'd brought the metal bin with her instead of leaving it on the path. She could have dumped the potatoes and hit him over the head with it. Or, if she'd brought one of Silas's rifles outside, she could have used it to scare him away. Then she had an idea. "If I were you, I would leave now."

He chuckled again. "Any why is that?"

"Because someone is aiming a rifle at you right now and if I give the signal, they will shoot."

"Horseshit."

"Do you want to see if I am telling the truth?" She started to raise her hand.

He took a step back and glanced around nervously at the house and barn and sheds. "All right," he said. "I'll leave. But I'll be back. And you can count on me having a talk with Silas about you." Finally, he turned and headed toward the road.

She hurried back to the house as fast as she could without running, glancing over her shoulder to make sure he was still leaving, then climbed up the porch steps and went inside. Shaking and breathless, she rushed to the front window and pulled back the curtain. The man was on the road now, walking toward a horse tied to a tree, just over the ridge and out of sight. No wonder they hadn't heard him coming. She waited until he mounted the horse and started to ride away, then dropped the curtain, ran to the back hall, and pulled open the trapdoor.

"He is gone," she called into the darkness.

Bonnie appeared at the bottom of the steps with Ella in her arms. When Ella saw Lena, she reached up, her small hands unfolding like pale flowers. Bonnie carried her up the stairs and Lena closed the trapdoor behind them.

Still trembling, Lena took Ella and kissed her forehead, determined to act normal for her daughter. "Good afternoon, *mein kleine* mouse," she said. "Did you have a good nap?"

Ella blinked against the light, her dewy cheeks flushed.

Lena turned her attention to Bonnie. "Are you all right?"

Bonnie nodded, but her anxious eyes told a different story. "I had to wake her," she said. "And she warn't none too happy about getting in the 'tater hole."

Lena put an arm around Bonnie and pulled her close. "Thank you for keeping her safe." She looked down the hall toward the front window. "I wonder if that was the man Penelope said would come."

Bonnie shook her head. "No, I seen him here before. He was out front a few months ago, arguing with Daddy."

"What were they arguing about?"

"I ain't got a clue," Bonnie said.

"Is he the sheriff?" Lena said.

"No, Sheriff Dixon wears a uniform and drives a paddy wagon. Y'all can't miss him. Can't miss his deputy neither 'cause he's skinny as a gutted cat. I think that man who was just here mighta been that George Pollock everybody's been yammering about."

"He said someone told him I was here. Who would do that? And why would he want to talk to me?"

"I ain't got any idea," Bonnie said.

"What did you call the vehicle the sheriff is driving?"

"A paddy wagon. It's a truck with a box in the back for hauling people to jail."

Or taking children to be evaluated.

Briefly, Lena thought about telling Bonnie how she'd gotten the man to leave by saying there was a rifle aimed at him, but knowing her and Jack Henry, they'd think that was a good idea. And while she agreed with Silas that shooting someone would only cause more problems—plus, of course, she'd never want one of the children to shoot anyone, no matter how willing they might be—using a rifle to scare off strangers might be better than hiding in a hole in the ground, trapped and helpless in the event someone found them. Besides, if she was being honest, she was starting to believe she could fire a gun at someone to keep Ella safe, and to protect Bonnie and Jack Henry. A bullet to the leg or arm would work. But no sane person would let it get that far if she was pointing a rifle at their head. That was what she told herself, anyway. Of course, the sheriff and his deputy had guns too, and aiming a rifle at the police would be a good way to get killed.

"Come on," she said to Bonnie. "We need to peel the potatoes."

Chapter 17

As Granny Creed predicted, Bonnie's cheek healed fairly quickly. By the time Silas took the stitches out two weeks after the accident, the wound no longer looked angry or swollen, and fresh, new skin had started to appear. True to form, Bonnie sat like a statue on the kitchen table as Silas cut and pulled out the thread. Her eyes watered and she squeezed Lena's hand in a viselike grip, but she never flinched. When Silas put down the scissors, she loosened her hold on Lena's hand, but only a little.

"That's the last of it," Silas said.

Bonnie touched her cheek with gentle fingers and looked up at him. "Thank you, Daddy."

"It don't do no good to thank me," Silas said. "Just be more careful from here on out."

"Yes, sir," Bonnie said.

"Does it still hurt?" Lena said.

Bonnie opened her mouth and moved her jaw back and forth, testing her muscles and skin. "Some parts feel funny, and other parts is numb."

"I reckon it'll leave a nasty scar," Silas said.

Lena wanted to kick him. "No, it will be very hard to see."

Bonnie shrugged and dropped her gaze.

Lena shot Silas a harsh look, then tapped Bonnie on the arm. "Do not worry," she said. "Do you see the mark above my eye?" She touched the skin above her right eyebrow.

Bonnie squinted at Lena's forehead, then shook her head.

"I had a scar there when I was eight years old," Lena said. "After I fell on a rock, blood was all over my face, but you cannot even see the cut now. That is because children heal better than adults. And you will too. Now, tell me about the new recipe you wanted to show me. I do not remember what it was called."

A weak smile played around Bonnie's lips. "Ham bone broth and dumplings?"

"*Ja*, that was it," Lena said. "Do you want to make it for supper?"

"And molasses stack cake?"

Lena nodded. "We can make a summer squash casserole too."

In the kitchen an hour later, Lena was happy to see Bonnie acting like her old self again, stirring the dumpling dough with vigor, skillfully adding seasonings to the kettle, and checking on the stack cake, which filled the house with the sweet smell of warm molasses. She had no idea if the scar on Bonnie's cheek would disappear completely, and maybe it was wrong to tell her it would, but Bonnie had enough to worry about at her young age. Lena did not want her to waste her childhood being upset over something she was helpless to change. And besides, even if she had a scar on her face, it was becoming more and more obvious that Bonnie would grow up to be a beautiful young woman.

Then, at the supper table that evening, Bonnie grew quiet again.

"I ain't going back to school like this," she said.

"Me neither," Jack Henry said.

Bonnie scowled at him. "What the devil are y'all talking about? You ain't got no hole in your stupid face. The other kids ain't gonna pick on you."

"The scar does not look bad," Lena said. "I think it looks like a little daisy."

"No, it don't," Jack Henry said. "It looks like a bullet hole."

"See?" Bonnie cried. "My own kin is making fun of me!" She crossed her arms and threw herself back in her chair.

Hunched over his plate, Silas stopped eating and glared at Jack Henry. "Say you're sorry," he said.

"Sorry," Jack Henry said, shooting Bonnie a sheepish look.

"Y'all ain't going back to school right now anyway," Silas said. He shoved half of a gravy-covered biscuit into his mouth and started chewing, his face hard. "Not till we put an end to this damn feud over our land."

"But Daddy," Bonnie said, "I still wanna go back after my face heals. I miss learning."

"I don't," Jack Henry said.

Silas fixed stern eyes on his daughter. "It's too damn far for two young'uns to be wandering alone right now."

"Lena can take us," Bonnie said. "We can saddle up Ole Sal and she can follow on Buttercup. Then she can fetch us when we're done."

"Lena's got work here," Silas said. He sawed a biscuit in half with more force than necessary and stabbed it with his fork. "And a young'un to look after." He eyed Bonnie again. "You ain't going. That's my final word."

Bonnie opened her mouth to say more, but three insistent knocks on the front door silenced her protest. Silas turned toward the sound, alarm creasing his brow.

"Open up, Wolfe!" a man's muffled voice demanded.

With that, Silas shot to his feet, raced over to the fireplace, and grabbed a rifle from above the mantel. "Get the hell off my property, Pollock!" he shouted. "I ain't got nothing to say to you!"

"I wouldn't be too sure about that," Pollock said. "You might change your mind after you hear what *I* got to say."

A chill ran up Lena's back. She recognized the voice. It belonged to the man who had snuck up on her and Bonnie the other day. Bonnie had been right: It was George Pollock.

Silas cocked the rifle and went to the door. "If it's about my land, you can piss off."

"Well, that ain't no way to treat a man wanting to offer you a deal," Pollock said. "But if you're not interested in keeping your home, I can leave you in peace."

Silas swore under his breath. "What're you getting at? What kinda deal?"

"Come on out so we can talk man to man," Pollock said.

Silas let his head drop, clearly frustrated, trying to decide what to do. Then he looked back at the children and Lena, sitting at the kitchen table. "Y'all stay put," he said. "I'll be right back." Before anyone could object, he opened the door and slipped outside.

Bonnie and Jack Henry sat silent and motionless, their anxious eyes locked on the front door. The men's muffled voices came in from outside, loud, quick, angry. No one could make out the words.

Lena had to admit she was relieved to see Silas grab a rifle to defend his family; not only because it made her feel safer, but because it'd make it easier for her to scare someone off with one if the need arose again. Although, that might make it easier for Jack Henry too, which was not a good thing.

"That is the man who came when we were digging potatoes," Lena whispered.

Bonnie nodded.

"Y'all talked to Pollock?" Jack Henry said, his eyes wide.

"I did, yes," Lena said.

"Not 'cause she wanted to," Bonnie said. "We were in the garden and didn't hear him coming."

"Did you tell Daddy he was here?" Jack Henry said.

"No, you jackass," Bonnie hissed. "We didn't tell him he was here, just like we didn't tell him when that woman snuck up on you in the barn!"

"Shhh," Lena said. "Please do not fight. Just eat your supper before it gets cold."

Bonnie and Jack Henry picked up their forks and pushed their food around on their plates. After cutting more tiny pieces of ham for Ella, Lena gave her a spoonful of summer squash, then turned to her own plate, only to realize her appetite had disappeared too.

Just then, Silas came back inside, rifle in hand, and looked directly at her. "Y'all need to come outside," he said.

Lena sat up straighter, her heartbeat picking up speed. "Me?"

Silas nodded.

Lena gaped at Jack Henry and Bonnie as if, somehow, they might know why their father wanted her out on the porch. But they looked as surprised and scared as she felt. She gave Bonnie Ella's spoon. "Will you help her eat, please?"

Bonnie took the spoon, scooted closer to Ella's high chair, and gave her more squash. Lena got up, knees quaking, and went out the door with Silas. When she saw George Pollack on the porch, she took a step back.

He tipped his hat at her. "Ma'am."

She clasped her hands together to keep them from shaking and waited, trying to imagine why Silas wanted her out there.

Silas studied her for a moment before he spoke, his eyes full of suspicion. "Pollock here says he paid y'all a visit not too long ago," he said.

She swallowed. "We . . . I was in the garden. I did not see him coming."

"His account of things is that you were mighty welcoming," Silas said. "Even invited him into my house."

Lena frantically shook her head. "*Nein.* I mean, no. That is not true. I told him to leave. He asked to come inside for coffee but I told him no."

Pollock smiled, a sly, greasy smile. "Oh, let's not be telling fairy tales, young lady," he said. "You know that's not the way it was. I turned you down on account of Mr. Wolfe not being home. It would have been improper of me to accept your invitation, no matter how tempting you made it sound."

Lena's throat grew thick and hot. What was he trying to do? Why was he making up lies? She looked at Silas, praying he'd believe her. "That is not what happened. He asked to come into the house. I did not even tell him my name."

"Horsefeathers," Pollock said. "Your name is Lena." Then he leaned toward her and lowered his voice conspiratorially. "Now listen, we're all grown-ups here. And I understand it might be a little embarrassing to admit you took a liking to me. We just met, after all. But there's no shame in it. We all know what it's like to be lonely." He winked at her, then regarded Silas, feigning concern. "She told me about losing her child's father before he could make an honest woman out of her. And how she came here to help out with your house and children."

"That is a lie," she said. "You have talked to someone else about me!"

"Oh, come now," Pollock said. "We both know which one of us is telling the truth here. And I don't know about you, but I rest easy at night with the knowledge that I'm an honest man. Either way, meeting you the other day is why I came up here to talk to Mr. Wolfe." He turned his attention to Silas again. "I'm not sure if you're aware of it, but the state is allowing a few mountain folk to keep lifetime use of their homes after the park goes through, particularly folks whose families have been here for generations. Of course, most got papers to prove they own their land legally and the state plans on paying them for it, but seeing's how you're a squatter who don't own the acreage your dwelling sits on, the state can't pay you a nickel. The thing I'm here to tell you is, I've got connections with the men in charge and I believe I've devised a way to see to it that you and your children can keep living in your home."

"Ain't nobody taking my land *or* my house," Silas snarled. "So you're wasting your time coming up here knocking on my door."

"Oh, I can guarantee you the government is indeed taking your land," Pollock said. "They'll claim eminent domain, condemn your property, and use it as they see fit. It's too late to change that, so you might as well get used to the idea."

"They're gonna have to kill me first," Silas said, fuming. "And I'm done talking. You need to get."

"Now listen here," Pollock said. "I can make certain you're allowed to stay in your home, with certain conditions, of course. Or, if you insist on being stubborn, the government can burn your house, take your land, and you can go down the mountain to one of the resettlement homes they're talking about building, if you qualify for a mortgage, that is."

Silas's face knotted with fury. He lifted his rifle and aimed it at Pollock. "No, *you* listen, you no-account sumbitch, my great-granddaddy built this house! Ain't nobody burning it down or taking my land."

Pollock took a step back, his hands raised. "Easy now. I'm not the one holding the matches. I'm just here to tell you the truth about what's going to happen, whether you like it or not, and offer you a chance to save your home."

Silas tightened his grip on the rifle, his eyes darting back and forth between Pollock and Lena. She edged backward toward the door, her mind racing. How and why was she involved in any of this? She turned and grabbed the door handle, hoping to escape inside.

"Now hold up, young lady," Pollock said. "I haven't gotten to the part that concerns you yet."

Lena let go of the handle and turned to face him again, her back against the door.

"Say what you have to say," Silas growled. "Then get the hell off my mountain."

"Lower your rifle first," Pollock said. "I refuse to talk with that thing pointing at me."

Silas let out a hard, exasperated sigh, then lowered the rifle, but not all the way.

Pollock put down his hands, relief lowering his shoulders. "That's better. Acting like an uncivilized hillbilly won't get you anywhere." He straightened his jacket and cleared his throat, settling his nerves. "Now, as I was saying, if you agree to this little deal I've come up with, I can offer you and your family lifetime use of your house after the park goes through. I might even be able to talk the state into letting you keep an acre or two, enough for a garden and a few chickens." Despite his friendly words, a threatening undercurrent ran through his voice.

"Keep talking," Silas said.

"What I'm proposing is a trade. Your family home for your house servant here." He gestured toward Lena. "My wife has been having health problems as of late and we could use the extra help."

Lena went rigid. He couldn't be serious. He just couldn't be. Had he lost his mind? She gaped at Silas, her breath coming shallow and fast. He wouldn't agree. He couldn't. She'd take Ella and run away before she went anywhere with Pollock.

"Of course, everyone knows womenfolk who engage in sexual relations outside of marriage are more likely to be feebleminded and degenerate," Pollock continued. "So, we'd commit her to the Colony first. A quick phone call to the doctors there will make certain she has no more illegitimate children."

Terror blackened Lena's heart. She had no idea what "the Colony" was, but she knew the meaning of *feebleminded* now. And doctor. And *no more children.* She leaned against the doorframe to anchor herself, certain she was about to faint. "I will not go," she said. "I am not feebleminded. And I do not need a doctor."

Silas shot her an angry look. "Shut your trap," he hissed.

"Sterilization is a perfectly safe and legal procedure," Pollock said. "As a matter of fact, several acquaintances employ women who have been sterilized. Makes it easier to avoid a scandal too, if you know what I mean." He winked at Silas.

Lena started to tremble. Everything she understood and expected had flipped upside down and inside out, twisting into something she could not comprehend. She'd come to America to escape hunger and helplessness, and now she was more trapped than ever. If Silas agreed to this, she would run away for sure. Then she had another thought and her blood turned to ice. What if he let Pollock take her now, before she had a chance to leave on her own? And what would happen to Ella?

"No," she said. "You cannot do this. You cannot."

"I said hush," Silas spat. He turned his attention to Pollock again. "And just what do you reckon I do for help if she's at your place?"

"I heard your kids have been taking care of things since your wife died," Pollock said. "Seems to me like you got all the help you need." He gave the front of the house a disapproving once-over. "Not that it takes a whole lot of work."

Silas lifted the rifle again, aiming the barrel at Pollock. "Why, you lily-livered piece a shit, I listened to what you came here to say, but I ain't putting up with your insults. Now get off my porch."

Pollock raised his hands and took another step back. "Now listen here. I'm making you a generous offer."

"Is that right?" Silas said. "How the hell do you reckon I

trust a man who's hell-bent on helping the state take land from people who ain't done him no wrong?"

"Whether you trust me or not is up to you," Pollock said. "But without me, you're on your own."

Silas glared at him for what seemed like forever, as if trying to make up his mind whether to believe him or shoot him. Lena thought she'd scream before he said something.

"I reckon you know she's got a young'un," Silas said.

The porch seemed to drop out from beneath Lena's feet. He was thinking about turning her over to Pollock. And Ella too. "I will not go with him," she said. "You cannot make me."

Silas scowled at her. "I been feeding and housing you and your young'un for a good while now. I have to think of my family."

"Is the child old enough to work?" Pollock said.

Frantic, Lena shook her head. "No," she said. "She is only a baby. And she is not well. She cries and fusses and she does not sleep."

Silas glared at her. "How many times do I gotta tell you to shut up?"

"A little one won't be a problem," Pollock said. "My Addie always did want a baby to look after. The child would be properly taken care of."

Bile rose in Lena's throat. *This can't be happening. It just can't be.* She wanted to grab Silas by the neck and shake him. Was he really that heartless?

Pollock watched Silas for a moment, impatiently waiting for an answer. "I tell you what," he said. "Take some time to think it over, and I'll come back in a day or two. I'm already late for supper." Then he addressed Lena. "You'll thank me later, darling, just wait and see, especially when you're living in a real house instead of this shack."

With that, Silas stepped toward him, his gun still raised. "I thought you were leaving," he said between clenched teeth.

Pollock tipped his hat. "It's been a pleasure, as usual," he said, then turned and went down the steps.

Silas waited until Pollock mounted his horse and headed toward the road before he lowered his rifle and turned toward the house. Lena stood with her back against the door, lightheaded and sick. How was she still standing upright? She looked at Silas with pleading eyes. "You cannot let him take us."

Silas grunted and reached for the door handle. She blocked his way. "Please. You cannot."

He pushed her out of the way with one hand and yanked open the door. She stumbled and nearly fell. Then she got her feet under her and followed him inside, the roar of her blood growing louder and louder in her ears. He leaned the rifle against the wall, sat down at the table, and got back to his supper. Bonnie watched Lena walk toward them, worry lining her face.

"What did Pollock want?" Jack Henry said.

"It ain't nothing y'all need to worry about," Silas said. "Just finish your supper."

Quaking with fear and fury, Lena took Ella out of the high chair and started toward the stairs. The house seemed to shrink as her panic grew.

"Where y'all going?" Bonnie called after her.

"I said finish your supper," Silas said.

"But Lena's crying," Bonnie said. "What happened out there?"

"Don't you never mind," Silas said. "It don't concern you."

Halfway across the room, Lena wheeled around to face them, unable to hold back. "*I* will tell you what happened," she said. "Your daddy wants to send us to live with Pollock. But we are not going. We are leaving before he comes back."

Jack Henry's mouth fell open and Bonnie's eyes went wide.

"What?" Bonnie said, her voice loud with shock. "Why would you do that, Daddy?"

"I got my reasons," Silas said.

"No," Bonnie cried. "You can't." She jumped up and ran over to Lena. "You ain't gonna make them leave." She wrapped her arms around Lena and Ella, her lips quivering.

"This is *my* house," Silas said. "And I'll do whatever the hell I want. Now get back here and sit down." He glared at Lena. "All of you."

"I no longer need to do as you say," Lena said.

"Is that right?" Silas said. "Well, you ain't going nowhere, not even up them steps, unless I say so."

Tears started down Bonnie's cheeks. "If you're fixing to make Lena and Ella leave, I'm going with them."

"I said get over here and sit down!" Silas shouted.

Bonnie shook her head. Lena put an arm around her shoulders. She was shaking.

"Don't make me get the switch, girl," Silas said.

"Go on and get it," Bonnie said. "I don't care."

Silas jumped to his feet, his chair falling to the floor with a bang. "Now listen here, God damn it! It's either them or this house! And we'll be in a heap a shit if we get kicked off our land and put out of our house with no money to show for it!"

"I said I don't care!" Bonnie shouted. "I ain't losing one more member of this family, let alone two. I lost enough already!"

With a sad face, Jack Henry got up from his chair and looked at his father. "I don't want Lena and Ella to go either, Daddy," he said. "I like having them here. And you said Pollock was a no-account son of a bitch. Why would you send Lena and Ella to live with him if he ain't no good? I thought we was supposed to protect the people we care about."

"Please, Daddy," Bonnie said. "Don't make them go."

Lena kept her eyes fixed on Silas, her breath coming fast and hard. Was he going to say something else? Pick up his chair and sit back down? Grab his rifle, force her into his truck, and take her to Pollock? Lock her in the 'tater hole until Pollock came to get her? But he just stood there, seething and staring at them. Then he suddenly left the table and picked up his rifle again. Lena tightened her grip on Ella, ready to flee down the back hall and outside. If she ran fast enough, maybe she could make it to the woods, where they could hide for a little while at least. Then, to her surprise, Silas put on his hat and went out the front door, slamming it behind him. His footsteps tromped across the porch and hurried down the steps.

Bonnie gaped up at Lena with frightened eyes. "What do y'all reckon he's up to?"

Lena shrugged and put a protective hand on Ella's back, still shaking. Should she pack their things and run before Silas returned, or stay and pray he'd listen to his children? Would he let Bonnie and Jack Henry lose the only home they'd ever known, or a woman and child they'd just met? The answer to that seemed clear.

Bonnie went to the front window and looked out. "Think he's fixing to go after Pollock?" she said. "If he gets thrown in jail, we'll be up shit crick."

Jack Henry shook his head. "Daddy said after the war he ain't ever killing nobody again. And shooting somebody don't bring nothing but more trouble."

"Daddy said a lotta things he don't stick to no more," Bonnie said.

Hopefully, Jack Henry was right, but Lena tended to believe Bonnie had a clearer view of things, especially since there was no telling what Silas would do to protect his home. Of course, it'd be a relief not to worry about Pollock anymore, but if Silas went to jail and the state took his land and house, what would happen to her and the children?

Ella started to fuss in Lena's arms, reaching for the food on the kitchen table. "Hungee," she said.

Lena put her back in the high chair so she could finish her supper. A half-eaten dumpling sat on the tray, along with pieces of ham and a cup of sweet milk. Ella picked up the dumpling with her chubby little hands, took a bite, and smiled innocently up at her mother, chewing. Despair scoured Lena's insides. If she packed their things and left, how would she feed Ella? Was she willing to let her child go hungry again to avoid living with a man who clearly wanted more than help around the house? Was she willing to let a strange woman bring up her baby while she was at the mercy of Pollock? But first, of course, Pollock planned on separating them and sending Lena to a place for the feebleminded, where doctors would make sure she was no longer able to have children.

She could not let any of those things happen.

Chapter 18

At midnight on the day of Pollock's unwelcome visit, Lena sat on the front porch, restless and waiting for Silas to return, a pine-scented breeze pushing her hair back from her face. The north star hung above the silhouette of the big spruce near the end of the drive, and a billion pinpricks of light dotted the darkness above the mountains. Now she understood why Bonnie said the hollow at night got as black as the inside of a wolf's mouth.

Earlier, even after a hundred promises not to leave without telling them, and to wake them as soon as their father got home, it'd been difficult getting Bonnie and Jack Henry to bed. They said they couldn't sleep until they knew he was not in jail for shooting Pollock, and knew for certain he wouldn't send Lena and Ella away. She begged them to lie down at least and, despite being plagued by the same fears, reassured them that their father just needed time to think. Whatever he did would be best for his family. Of course, what was best for his family might be horrible for her and Ella, but there was no point in telling them that. They already knew. By the time she got them calmed down, it was too dark to leave anyway.

So now she waited. Because if Silas had any intention of making her go, she needed to know as soon as possible, not tomorrow or the next day or next week. Her nerves wouldn't allow much more of a delay. She prayed Virgil and Teensy were right about him being an honest man with a good heart who was burdened by tragedy, and that the war hero who had saved lives would realize turning her over to Pollock was wrong. If not, if he came home and said she had to leave, she would sneak out after he went to bed, despite it being dark. Despite her promises to Bonnie and Jack Henry about saying goodbye. And if Silas failed to return tonight, she had no idea what she'd do. Pollock said he'd give him a couple of days to make a decision, but what if it was a trick? What if he came back sooner than he'd said he would? Obviously, she'd feel terrible leaving Bonnie and Jack Henry without telling them, but if she waited too long, it could be too late. Of course, if Silas killed Pollock, that would create an entirely different set of problems.

She gathered her sweater beneath her chin and peered into the night, listening for the sound of Silas's truck coming up the road. An owl hooted in the distance, and what sounded like a wolf let out a chilling, lonely howl. Amid the near silence and the fragrance of evergreens, if she closed her eyes, she could almost imagine being back home in Germany, hiking in the hills that surrounded her hometown. Homesickness made it easy to understand why Silas refused to leave such a beautiful place, and why he'd do almost anything to stay here with his children. He was rooted to this land—he belonged to these mountains and they belonged to him, as much as the rolling streams belonged, and the bears in the hills.

With that thought, panic and fear swelled inside her again. Silas belonged here. So did his children. And he would do anything to stay. Even if it meant sending her and Ella away. Maybe she should leave now while she had the chance. Maybe she should go upstairs and pack while Silas was gone and the children were in their rooms. But where would she go? Down the mountain? What if she got lost in the dark? To Mr. Early's mill? To Teensy's farm? She had no idea if she could remember the way. And what if their loyalty stood with Silas? What if they told him she was there?

Maybe she could tell Teensy that Enzo had come to America and was waiting to be picked up at the train station. That Silas was delivering lumber and she needed a ride. That she had to hurry before her brother got conned into taking unsafe shelter from a criminal. And after they gave her a ride down the mountain, she could enter the train station and disappear. She could go back to Ellis Island and find the nun who told her to come to her church. Surely, a nun would be willing to help, at least until Lena could figure out what to do next.

She jumped to her feet and went inside. It was now or never. She would not let someone else decide her fate. If she took a light and stayed on the roads, they would be fine. After grabbing a lantern and going upstairs to her bedroom, where Ella slept peacefully in the crib, she took off Silas's late wife's aprons, put on a sweater, then wrote a note to Bonnie and Jack Henry, telling them she was sorry and she would come back to visit someday. Then she packed her and Ella's things in her worn satchel, tied her shawl round her shoulders and waist, and gently lifted Ella from the crib. Ella squirmed for a moment, but thankfully fell back asleep as soon as Lena tucked her, warm and snug, inside the shawl. Then Lena left the room.

Every sound was amplified in the quiet house—the squeak of the hinges and the click of the latch as she shut the door, the creak of the floorboards as she snuck back down the hall. When she passed Bonnie's and Jack Henry's bedrooms, her eyes filled. She hated deserting them, especially after they had stood up to Silas by making it clear they wanted her to stay. Not to mention the fact that she loved them and was starting to realize they loved her too. The last thing she wanted was to add to their mountain of sorrow. But she had to leave before she changed her mind, or risk being separated from her child. She tiptoed down the stairs, Ella nestled against her chest.

At the front door, she paused. She needed to take food, if not for herself then at least for Ella. The thought of stealing made her stomach churn, and she didn't want Silas to accuse her of theft, but letting her daughter go hungry was out of the question. And surely, Silas wouldn't want her and Ella to starve, would he? She went to the kitchen, set the lantern on the table, took a loaf of bread and two apples from the counter, and put them beside the lantern. From the pantry, she grabbed a jar of strawberry preserves, a jar of corn relish, and a slab of hard cheese wrapped in a clean cloth, then put them on the table with the bread. She looked around the kitchen for something to carry everything in, like a flour sack or an old bucket. She needed to grab a tin of milk from the springhouse too.

And then she heard it.

Tires crunching up the drive.

She froze, trying not to panic. She could run out the back door, but not without the food. Or she could wait out there until Silas went to bed, then come back inside to get it. But if Ella woke up crying, he might hear her. Maybe she should go back to her room and try again later. She held her breath. Silas's truck came to a stop in front of the house. She picked up the bread and apples, started to return them to the counter, then changed her mind and left them on the table. She grabbed the lantern and ran to the stairs. Halfway to the top, Ella woke up and started to cry.

Behind her, the front door opened and closed.

"What are y'all up to so late?" Silas said.

She stopped on the steps and turned to face him, struggling to breathe normally. "Ella was crying and I did not want her to wake Bonnie and Jack Henry. I think her belly hurt." As if on cue, Ella let out another wail. Lena patted her back, shushing her. Ella's eyes fluttered and she leaned against her mother's chest, then fell fitfully back to sleep.

Silas frowned and set his rifle against the wall. "Looks to me like y'all are fixing to go somewhere."

She shook her head, certain he could hear her heart pounding. "Now that she is settled down, we are going back to bed."

"Y'all running?"

Lena tried to keep her eyes locked on his, but within seconds, she lowered her gaze. If only she were a better liar. Of course, the satchel on her back and Ella being strapped to her chest gave her away, not to mention the fact that she was wearing a dress and shoes instead of a nightgown.

"Best put that idea out of your head," Silas said. "Y'all get lost in these hills. The only way we'll find you is when the buzzards start circling."

She looked up at him then, determined. "I will not go with Pollock. I refuse to let you send me to live with him."

He took off his hat and hung it on a hook next to the door, his face that of a man tormented. "Well, y'all got no need to worry about that anymore."

She swallowed. "Why? Did you . . . Did you kill him?"

He scoffed. "Thought about it. That low-down, good-for-nothing piece of trash deserves a load of buckshot in him or worse, but no, I ain't shot him. Yet."

A strange mixture of relief and confusion washed over her. "I do not understand. Why do I no longer need to worry about him?"

"'Cause I ain't never trusted the bastard. He's crookeder than a dog's hind leg. Even if I agreed to him taking you, there ain't no way the government's gonna let us stay in this house. Pollock ain't got that kind of power, don't matter none how much he thinks he does. And even if he *warn't* lying, those state scoundrels would find some other reason to throw us out."

Overcome, her legs nearly gave out. She grabbed the railing

and sat down on the steps, hard enough to make her teeth rattle. Thank God, Silas had come to his senses. Thank God, she and Ella could stay. At the same time, it was heartbreaking to hear Silas so certain about losing his house. But now that her panic had eased, she noticed his eyes were bloodshot, his words slightly slurred, like he'd been drinking. And she'd made the mistake of being too trusting before. "How do I know you are telling the truth?"

"'Cause if I make you and your young'un leave, those two wouldn't never forgive me for doing it." He pointed at the top of the stairs.

Lena turned to look up the steps. On the dim landing, Bonnie and Jack Henry stared down at them, like skittish ghosts in their white nightshirts.

"At least if the government takes everything we got," Silas continued, "the blame for y'all being gone won't be on me. I got enough regrets in this life."

"Thank you, Daddy!" Bonnie said.

She hurried down the steps and Jack Henry followed. Lena thought they were going to hug Silas, but they sat on either side of her and wrapped their arms around her and Ella. She hugged them back and started to cry.

Chapter 19

By late September, Lena dared to hope the imminent dangers that had worried her since her arrival in America had lessened. Or maybe by some miracle, they'd even passed. It was probably wishful thinking, but George Pollock had not returned to the house, Penelope Rodgers had not sent anyone up from Sweet Briar College, and Sheriff Dixon had not come to Wolfe Hollow Farm. More importantly, Silas no longer talked about the state taking his land. Not to her anyway. At the same time, anger and frustration continued to seep from him like an invisible haze, and his silence made her wonder if there was a storm growing in the distance, a quiet gathering of dark clouds that would crack open overhead when it was too late to seek shelter.

Still, despite signs that they might be safe, she decided not to take any chances. After asking Jack Henry to teach her how to load, aim, and shoot one of Silas's rifles, she hid it under the back steps whenever Silas was gone and she and the children were outside. Understandably, it took a while to convince Bonnie and Jack Henry that even though they had more experience with guns, she was the only one who could scare someone off with it. And after explaining how she'd seen people shot during the war and it was something she could never do, she promised she had no intention whatsoever of shooting anyone, and she never wanted them to do it either. The rifle would only be there for protection in case they were caught off guard again. She worried one of them would grab it if Pollock or the sheriff showed up, but nevertheless, it was a risk she had to take.

On the last day of the month, the mail truck brought a letter from Enzo that said he was working as a bricklayer five days a week while living with Frau Müller's son and his wife in Berlin. And although he said he missed Lena and Ella terribly, he sounded content and proud to have a good-paying job. He also mentioned Frau Müller's granddaughter, who had shown him around the city and was teaching him more English. Lena was happy to hear he'd found a friend and seemed to be doing well, which made it easier to admit in her reply that she had no money to send to him. She also explained that, because the people in the Blue Ridge Mountains knew how to live off the land, money was not as important as she had thought it would be. Silas Wolfe and his children had more food and domestic comforts than many people she'd known back in Beckingen. She told him she was keeping her promise to Mutti by staying strong and being happy—even though it was only partially true—and she hoped he was doing the same. Of course she told him about Ella too, how healthy she was now and how much she'd grown.

A week later, on a bright autumn day, Lena held a narrow ladder against an apple tree so Bonnie could scurry up the rungs to reach the tallest branches. High in another tree, Jack Henry added more apples to the already bulging bag hung over his shoulder.

"I picked a mess more apples than you!" he shouted.

"I don't give a fig!" Bonnie shouted back.

"Please be careful," Lena said. "I do not need you to fall and break your necks."

On a blanket nearby, Ella held up an apple and squealed with delight. "Apple, Mama," she said. "My haz apple."

Lena smiled. Her baby girl was learning more words every day. "Yes, *Kleine.* You have an apple."

"I'm fixing to make fritters and applesauce when we're done," Bonnie said.

"What about apple butter?" Jack Henry said.

"We'll make apple butter tomorrow," Bonnie said. "Daddy likes fritters best."

Jack Henry slipped on a branch and caught himself before he fell. "Whoa," he said. "I purt' near bought the farm that time."

"Please wait and use the ladder," Lena said. "We are almost finished with it."

"Ladders are for sissies," Jack Henry said.

"Who y'all calling a sissy?" Bonnie said. Not to be outdone, she stepped off the ladder and climbed sideways into the tree.

"Bonnie, please," Lena said. "Get back on the ladder."

Ignoring her, Bonnie reached for a high apple.

"*Ach, Gott,*" Lena said. "You two are going to make me give a fit."

Bonnie laughed. "It's *pitch* a fit, not give a fit." She put a few apples in her bag and got back on the ladder, while Jack Henry continued picking from his dangerous perch.

Just then, an engine growled in the distance. Bonnie looked over her shoulder toward the road. "I wonder why Daddy's home early again."

"Maybe the sheriff's been nosing around some more," Jack Henry said.

Lena glanced in that direction. From where she stood, she could not see over the trees. "Are you certain it is your father?"

"Yup," Bonnie said. "It's his truck."

Lena swore under her breath. How would she put the rifle back before Silas got to the house? Maybe she could ask him to hold the ladder while she took some apples into the kitchen. Then she could grab it before she went inside. "Your father might be angry if he sees you up so high, Jack Henry," she said.

"Dang it," Jack Henry said. "I was close to reaching the top." He climbed halfway down, then jumped out of the tree, his knees hitting the ground as he tumbled forward. Apples spilled from his bag and rolled across the grass in all directions. He hurried to pick them up, then he froze, staring at the road. Lena turned to see what he was looking at.

A dust-covered truck and a Model T turned off the lane and rumbled up the drive. The truck looked identical to Silas's, but it was not his. Another truck with a black box on the back followed close behind. Lena's heart skipped a beat. It was the *polizei.*

"Come down from the tree, Bonnie!" she shouted. She looked back and forth between the house and the shed. The house was closer. "Leave the apples and take Ella in the house!"

Bonnie glanced over her shoulder. "Shit," she said. "It's Sheriff Dixon."

"Ain't we going to the shed?" Jack Henry said.

"We will not make it in time," Lena said.

Bonnie scurried down the ladder, shrugged the bag of apples off her shoulder, grabbed Ella, and started toward the house. Jack Henry dropped his bag and followed. Halfway there, Bonnie stopped to see if Lena was coming. Jack Henry ran past her and kept going.

For a split second, Lena stood motionless, panicked, and unsure. She'd played the scenario over and over in her mind: grabbing the rifle from beneath the back steps, cocking and raising it, aiming the barrel with her finger just below the trigger. But multiple people showing up at the same time had not been part of the plot, let alone the black wagon used for taking people to jail. She started toward the house. It was too late to change plans now. "Keep going!" she shouted at Bonnie.

The vehicles sped over the grass, drove up the yard, and came to a hard stop between Lena and the house. Doors opened. Pollock got out of the dust-covered truck. A man in a suit jacket climbed out of the Model T, along with the teacher who had brought the photographer to the mill, Miriam Sizer. Sheriff Dixon and his deputy got out of the paddy wagon and hurried toward Bonnie and Jack Henry.

And then, to Lena's horror, Jack Henry grabbed the rifle from under the back steps and started running toward the men. Bonnie followed a few yards behind, crying and screaming at him to stop.

Lena raced around the trucks toward the children. "No!" she shouted. "Go back!"

Jack Henry stopped and cocked the rifle.

Lena's stomach clenched. "Jack Henry, no!"

Before Jack Henry could lift the rifle to aim, the deputy seized it and grabbed him by the arm. Jack Henry kicked and yelled and struggled to get loose, but it was no use. The deputy held on tight, the weapon held out of Jack Henry's reach.

When Bonnie caught up, she put Ella down and clawed at the deputy. "Leave my brother alone!" she shouted. "Don't you touch him!"

Sheriff Dixon grabbed her by the shoulders and yanked her back. She tried to shrug out of his grasp, but he was too strong. Terrified, Ella started to wail. When Lena reached them, she picked Ella up with trembling arms and pleaded with the sheriff.

"What are you doing?" she cried. "Please! Let them go!"

"Sorry, but they're coming with us," Sheriff Dixon said.

"The state has deemed Silas Wolfe incompetent as a father and provider. He is an unfit parent without the proper means to provide for his family."

"That is not true," Lena cried. "His children have everything they need!"

"Get the hell away from me, you son of a bitch!" Bonnie cried. She kicked the sheriff in the shin with her heel, then turned her head and chomped down on his fingers.

"God damn it!" the sheriff said, yanking his hand from her mouth.

She almost got away but he grabbed her again, then wrenched her arm behind her back.

"Stop it!" Lena said. "You're hurting her!"

"Get your dirty rotten hands off my sister!" Jack Henry yelled. He fell to his knees, trying to break free, but the deputy pulled him up and pushed him toward the paddy wagon. The sheriff followed with Bonnie.

"Help!" Bonnie screamed. "Somebody help!"

Lena ran after them, Ella shrieking in her arms. "No!" she cried. "You cannot take them!"

Bonnie twisted and turned like a wild animal, desperately trying to get away. "You wait until my daddy hears about this," she shouted. "When he's done with y'all, you're gonna feel like you been ate by a wolf and shit over a cliff!"

"We'll see about that," Sheriff Dixon said. He opened the back of the paddy wagon and shoved her inside.

When the deputy started forcing Jack Henry in beside Bonnie, Lena fought her way between him and the sheriff, reached into the wagon with her free hand, and grabbed at Bonnie and Jack Henry's arms and clothes, anything to pull them back out. The deputy pushed her away, then closed and locked the doors.

"Stop," Lena sobbed. "Please. You cannot do this! It is not

right! They have done nothing wrong. Silas has done nothing wrong!" Ella bawled harder and harder.

Inside the paddy wagon, Bonnie and Jack Henry pounded on the walls and cried to be let out, their frightened voices echoing through the barred windows.

"I am sorry," Lena sobbed. "I am sorry I could not stop them." She pushed past the deputy and rattled the door handles. They didn't budge. She tried to look through the barred window but it was too high up. "Do not worry, your father and I will find you."

"Tell Daddy I'm sorry," Jack Henry said.

"Me too," Bonnie whimpered.

"No," Lena said. "It is my fault." She turned to Sheriff Dixon, angry tears running down her face. She wanted to grab the gun from his holster, hold it to his forehead, and make him let Bonnie and Jack Henry go. But the deputy might shoot her or throw her in the paddy wagon too. She tried to think of something, anything to stop them from taking the children. Or at least slow them down.

"They do not have their shoes. Please. Let me get their shoes." Maybe, if she took long enough, Silas would come home and put a stop to this.

Sheriff Dixon shook his head. "Where they're headed, they'll be getting shoes without holes."

The deputy went to the front of the truck, put Silas's rifle inside, then came back to where they stood.

"What about food?" Lena said. "Can I please pack them some milk and corn bread?"

"They'll be getting plenty to eat too," the sheriff said.

She put a hand over her heart, certain it was breaking. "Then please . . . please. Tell me where you are taking them."

The sheriff hooked his thumbs over his belt. "Can't say."

"Lena Conti?" someone said behind her.

She spun around.

George Pollock, Miriam Sizer, and the man in the suit stood looking at her, their faces solemn. Then Pollock smiled.

Lena took a step toward him, fighting the urge to slap the self-satisfied grin off his face. Luckily for him, she was still holding Ella. "What did you do? What lies did you tell the sheriff about Silas?"

"Now listen here," Pollock said. "I don't have a thing to do with this. I'm only tagging along because Sheriff Dixon and Miss Sizer asked me to, in the event things got out of control."

"You are a liar," she hissed.

"I suggest you calm down, young lady," Miriam Sizer said. "Otherwise, it won't bode well for you. Not to mention, you're frightening your child."

"*You* are scaring her," Lena said. "Not me."

"But we're not the ones causing a scene," Miriam said. "We've come here on official business. I'm not sure if you're aware of it, but an investigation has been done by several social workers into the condition of the mountain people. I believe you talked to Miss Penelope Rodgers not too long ago?"

"We told her to leave," Lena said. "Now let Bonnie and Jack Henry go!"

"Yes," Miriam said. "Miss Rodgers said she was chased away with a pitchfork." She *tsked* her disapproval. "Such uncivilized behavior. But that is neither here nor there. What matters is that we have information about Silas Wolfe, pertaining to the fact that he is living in sin with a young woman who is his kin. I assume that's you."

Lena struggled to control her fury. "That is not true. I am only working for Mr. Wolfe." She glared at Pollock. "He is telling this lie so I will work for him."

"Believe what you will," Pollock said. "But my offer was an act of kindness."

"Is it kind to lock a woman away and make sure she cannot have more children?" Lena said. Her voice was filled with hatred.

"If the situation warrants it, yes," Pollock said.

Miriam shook her head, suddenly flustered. "Please let me finish speaking. What happened between the two of you is irrelevant. Our information comes from Miss Rodgers. And as I was trying to say, we're here because it's important to stop ignorant, immoral hollow folk from inbreeding." She pointed a fat finger at Ella. "Miss Rodgers has informed us that this child is a result of your relations with Silas Wolfe."

A hot rush of panic burned up Lena's neck. "That is another lie!" she said. "Ella's father is dead."

Miriam waved a dismissive hand in the air. "Miss Rodgers warned me you would say that, along with other things you'd try to hide." Then she addressed the man in the suit. "We'll take her now."

The man in the suit grabbed Lena's arm.

"What are you doing?" Lena shouted. "Let me go! I am telling the truth!"

Miriam reached for Ella. "Give me the girl."

Lena yanked Ella out of her reach. "No!" she cried. "You cannot take her!" Her breath came in short, shallow gasps, her stomach twisting in on itself. She wrenched her arm from the man's grasp and tried to run. He and Pollock caught her before she could get away.

"Give me the child before you drop her," Miriam said.

"Get away from me!" Lena screamed. "I will not let you have her!"

Bonnie and Jack Henry cried and yelled from inside the paddy wagon. "Leave them alone!"

Miriam reached for Ella again, her rough hands prying her from Lena's grasp. Lena tried to shove Miriam away, but the men held her arms. Ella screamed harder, her face crumpled and red. Miriam tried to take her again. Lena turned sideways and kicked Pollock's legs. He grunted and strengthened his grip, his fingers pushing into her muscles. The man in the suit did the same. Miriam forced her hands around Ella, her knuckles digging into Lena's breasts. Lena thrashed and writhed, trying to break free, but the men were too strong.

"No!" she screamed. "You cannot take my baby!"

"We can and we will," Miriam said, her face cruel with determination. She ripped Ella from Lena's grasp.

With every ounce of strength she had left, Lena pulled her arm free and dug her fingernails into Miriam's cheek. Miriam staggered backward, then touched her face and stared at the blood on her fingers. Pollock wrenched Lena's arms behind her back and moved her away from Miriam.

"This is for the best," Miriam said. "Someday you might understand that." And then, with a smug smile, she started to walk away with Ella.

"Mama!" Ella screamed, reaching back for Lena. "Mamaaaaaa!"

"No!" Lena sobbed. "Do not take her! Please! I will do anything." She pleaded with Pollock. "I will do what you want, I promise. Please. Just give me my baby back."

"I told you," Pollock said. "I had nothing to do with this."

Lena screamed and fought with everything she had as Pollock and the man in the suit started steering her toward the Model T.

Miriam handed Ella to the deputy, then went to the Model T and waited. The deputy climbed into the front seat of the paddy wagon and shut the door, muffling Ella's cries. Her small head was in the window, her blond hair sticking up in all directions. Sheriff Dixon got in and started the engine.

"Nooooo!" Lena screamed. "Please don't take her!"

When the paddy wagon started to reverse down the yard,

she screamed again until she tasted blood, then sagged to her knees, every muscle and bone aching with agony and grief. Pollock and the man in the suit yanked her back up, but the world started to close in on all sides, like a curtain being drawn. The last thing she saw was the ground coming toward her, then her cheek hit the dirt with a bone-jarring thud and everything went black.

Chapter 20

Lena regained consciousness little by little, her aching head thumping against something hard as she bounced like a ragdoll inside a carriage. For a moment, she thought she was still on the ship on her way to America, but ocean storms did not jostle the steerage beds up and down. They rocked them back and forth. Then she remembered; she and Ella had already disembarked on Ellis Island. They had already traveled to the Blue Ridge Mountains to move in with Silas and Bonnie and Jack Henry. Was she in Silas's truck? Had she fallen asleep? If so, where were they going?

Dazed and disoriented, she opened her eyes and sat up, certain Bonnie would be sitting beside her with Ella on her lap. But to her shock and horror, Miriam Sizer was on the other side of the bench seat, her face pinched, her plump hands gripping a leather satchel on her lap. And Pollock and the man in the suit were in the front, with Pollock at the wheel.

A jolt of terror shot through her. "Where are you taking me?" she cried. "Where is Ella? And Bonnie and Jack Henry?"

Miriam kept her eyes straight ahead. "We're on our way to

the Virginia State Colony for Epileptics and Feebleminded," she said, her voice calm and matter-of-fact, as if sharing the weather forecast.

Lena's stomach turned over. Pollock had threatened to send her to a place called "the Colony," where the doctors would make certain she could no longer have children. *No. This can't be real. It can't be!* She pushed her fingernails into her palms, hoping pain would force her awake. But this was no nightmare. Somehow, the things she feared most were happening. Ella had been taken, along with Bonnie and Jack Henry. And she was being sent to a hospital for the feebleminded. "You do not need to take me there," she said. "There is nothing wrong with me."

"We shall see," Miriam said. "After your evaluation."

Nearly hyperventilating, Lena leaned back in the seat to keep from fainting. "What about the children? Are they being taken there too?"

Miriam opened her mouth to answer, but paused, as if rethinking her reply. And then, with certainty, she said, "Yes, they are."

Lena stared at her, dizzy and lightheaded, trying to figure out if she was telling the truth. But Miriam's face was calm, her eyes unreadable. Lena looked out the windows to see where they were and if the sheriff was coming too. They were nearing the foothills of the mountains. But no other vehicle drove along the road ahead or behind them. No paddy wagon with terrified children inside.

"You cannot do this," she said.

"I assure you, I can," Miriam said. "And if you want to see your daughter again, you'll cooperate."

Lena wanted to smash her fists into Miriam's smug face or wrap her hands around Pollock's neck and choke him until he stopped the vehicle. But that would accomplish nothing. Even if it were possible to undermine Miriam or Pollock, the man in the suit would not help her find Ella. He would not take her home to wait for Silas so they could find the children together. Feeling helpless and trapped, she leaned against the door and closed her flooding eyes, her heart like a boulder in her chest. Between the powdery smell of old perfume and the rancid odor of sweat wafting off Miriam Sizer, she thought she might be sick. She put a hand over her mouth, hoping the feeling would pass, but anguish thickened her throat. Ella's scent was still on the skin of her palm; the familiar, sweet bouquet of baby breath, warm milk, and homemade lavender soap. She could even smell the juicy apple Ella had been holding earlier. Struggling to compose herself, she sat up straight. If she wanted to see her daughter and Bonnie and Jack Henry again, she needed to keep her wits about her. She needed to prove she was not feeble-minded, and she was a strong and capable mother.

After several hours of riding in near silence, they came to a sprawling city nestled in a wide valley, the streets lined with gabled houses and tall trees. Near what looked like the center of town, they passed a row of stores, a park, and a stone church, then coasted down a slight hill toward a main thoroughfare and turned left toward a complex of brick and stone buildings. Behind the stone buildings, wooden barns and storage shops dotted the landscape, along with horses in a fenced pasture, and people working in a field.

As the brick buildings drew closer, each structure seemed bigger and more sinister than the one before, like a fortress with no escape. When Pollock pulled up to what looked like the main building, a massive two-story with white columns and extensive wings on either side, a surge of fear and grief surged through Lena, so strong she nearly cried out. She looked at Miriam with desperate eyes.

"Is my Ella in there?" she said, her voice breaking.

Ignoring the question, Miriam straightened her glasses and wiped nonexistent fuzz off the front of her dress. Lena wanted to grab her by the collar, to make her tell her what they'd done with her baby girl. But that would only make matters worse.

Behind the white columns of the main building, a dark blue door opened and a nurse in a ghostly white uniform stepped out onto the stone entryway. Pollock turned off the engine and got out. The man in the suit exited the vehicle, opened the back door for Miriam, then went around to the other side and opened the door for Lena. Miriam appeared beside him.

"Come along," she said. "It's time to go inside."

After taking a moment to gather her courage, Lena stepped out of the car on unsteady legs and stood on the cracked drive. She looked up at the massive structure, at the low black roof and rows of dark windows, like black teeth ready to swallow her whole. Her mouth went dry. The man in the suit took her arm and led her up the walk while Pollock stayed with the vehicle. Miriam followed, her hard shoes clacking along the sidewalk. The nurse, stern and rigid, met them at the top of the steps, eyeing Lena up and down. Lena tried to imagine how she looked to her—a young woman in a worn dress, her hair wild, her bare feet and work apron smudged with garden dirt—living proof of the poverty-stricken mountain people in Arthur Rothstein's photographs.

The nurse addressed Miriam. "Another one so soon?"

"I'm afraid this is just the start of it," Miriam said. "Her name is Magdalena Conti. Uneducated, promiscuous, ill-tempered, and unmarried with an illegitimate child. Possible imbecile, like the rest."

"I see," the nurse said. Then she gave Lena a smile, a fake, sympathetic smile that proved she had no need or desire to understand Lena at all. She simply believed what Miriam told her. "I'm Nurse Irene. Welcome to the Colony." She spoke slower and louder than necessary, as if Lena were hard of hearing or unable to understand English.

Lena fixed her eyes on the nurse, trying to look confident

and intelligent, all while shaking inside. "Where is Ella? Did the sheriff bring her here?"

"Who?" the nurse said.

"Ella. My daughter."

"I'm sorry," Nurse Irene said, still speaking loudly. "But I have no idea who you're talking about. Now, let's go inside, shall we?"

"I will not go anywhere until I see my daughter," Lena said. She turned to Miriam. "You said she would be here. I need to see her, and Bonnie and Jack Henry."

"I understand," Miriam said. "But I believe you must talk to Dr. Bell first. Isn't that right, Nurse Irene?"

"Yes," Nurse Irene said. "We must follow protocol."

"I do not need a doctor," Lena said. "I am not feebleminded or an imbecile. I am a mother who needs her child."

Nurse Irene let out a frustrated sigh. "If you won't come inside peacefully," she said. "I have someone who will take you where you need to go. So, what is it going to be, Miss Conti? Are you going to cooperate or not?"

Lena swallowed the sour taste of dread in the back of her throat, beads of sweat building up on her forehead. The Ellis Island inspector's words rang in her ears: *If your brother is put in there, he'll never get out. People like him can't be helped.*

Maybe she should run. Surely, she could outrun Miriam, and maybe the nurse too, but the man in the suit looked young and strong, and he was blocking her way. Even if she could get past him, Pollock was by the car and he might be able to catch her. More importantly, what if Ella was really inside?

As if reading her mind, Nurse Irene said, "I'm sure Dr. Bell knows where the children are."

Lena felt herself nearly swoon, a million thoughts and fears clashing and tangling inside her head. How could she trust these women? Especially Miriam, who'd lied about why she brought a photographer into the mountains and had ripped Ella from her arms?

Nurse Irene stepped back and put her hand on the door, smiling that friendly, yet disparaging, smile. "Are you ready, Miss Conti?"

Lena stared at her, more desperate than she'd ever felt in her life. She had no choice. If Ella was in the Colony, she had to go inside. She braced herself and, trying not to collapse, followed Nurse Irene through the door.

Miriam followed, turning on the other side of the threshold. "Thank you for your help," she said to the man in the suit. "Please tell Mr. Pollock I'll be out shortly." Then she closed the door in his face.

Inside the dim foyer, another nurse looked up briefly from behind a desk, her pale features lost in shadows cast by gilded gasoliers, then returned to the papers in front of her. The rest of the room was empty except for a velvet settee with missing buttons sitting against the opposite wall, its ornately carved legs scraped and worn. The air smelled of mold, dust, and cobwebs, along with the sour, visceral odor of bleach. Long lengths of timber covered the high ceilings, the wood so dark it looked black and greasy, and flowered wallpaper clung tight to the walls, bunched together here and there like the veins of an old woman's hand.

Following Nurse Irene across the foyer, Lena tightened her jaw, a growing ache throbbing inside her skull. With every step farther into the maw of the Colony, her instincts screamed louder and louder, telling her to run. But where would she go? And how could she leave without Ella? An excruciating image flashed in her mind: her little girl alone somewhere in this vast building, crying and afraid, wondering why she'd been taken from her mother and left in this scary, unfamiliar place. It was almost more than she could bear. Lena prayed that, at the very least, Bonnie and Jack Henry were with her.

When Nurse Irene stopped briefly to speak to the desk nurse, her voice quick and hushed, Lena strained to hear but could not make out the words. The desk nurse glanced at Lena, then nodded, got up from the desk, and disappeared through an archway into what looked like a tiled corridor. Nurse Irene continued on, taking them into a short hallway lined with empty shelves and cupboards. At the end of the hall, she unlocked a set of double doors leading to another wing, let Lena and Miriam through, then locked the doors again behind them. Cracked floor tiles, dingy wallpaper, and closed doors seemed to stretch on forever in the next corridor, and the sharp tang of urine and human waste filled the air. Muffled cries and shouts filtered through the walls as if coming from underwater. Lena put a hand to her nose, nearly gagging. What was this horrible place? And how could anyone think sending people to a filthy, decrepit building would help them get well? When they finally reached the end of the hallway, the nurse turned right, unlocked another door, and took them into a narrow lobby lined with wooden chairs. She knocked lightly on a door with a brass nameplate that read: DR. JOHN BELL, SUPERINTENDENT.

"Enter," a male voice called from inside.

Nurse Irene pushed the door open, waited for Lena and Miriam to go through first, then followed them into a paneled office. Framed medical degrees hung on the back wall above a row of filing cabinets, along with black-and-white portraits of men in top hats and women in long bustled dresses gathered in front of the main building. Two more pictures hung below the others, one of a stern-faced woman in a ruffled bonnet, the other of a gaunt man with porkchop sideburns. Two cane-back chairs faced a paper-strewn desk, where a man with a prominent nose and thick eyebrows sat smiling politely at Miriam.

"Good afternoon, Miss Sizer," he said. "Who do we have here?" He looked Lena up and down, pausing briefly on her bare feet.

"Good day, Dr. Bell," Miriam said. "Thank you for seeing us on such short notice." She pulled a large envelope from her satchel. "I intended to mail this to you here at the Colony, but the situation escalated more quickly than expected. This is Magdalena Conti." She took a paper from the envelope and handed it to him. "And this is the information we have on her. She is unmarried, unemployed, living with a male relative, and has an illegitimate child." Then she stepped back and waited, clearly proud of herself.

Lena scowled at her. "You know nothing about me."

Miriam kept her focus on Dr. Bell, studying him while he scanned the paper. Lena had no idea what lies he was reading about her, but she thought she'd scream before he finished. Finally, he looked up. "You're in luck, Miss Sizer," he said. "I have some free time to do a quick evaluation before my next meeting." Then he addressed Lena, speaking even more loudly than Nurse Irene. "Please, have a seat, Miss Conti."

Lena shook her head. "I want to see my daughter."

"All right," Dr. Bell said. "But I need you to sit down first." He graciously indicated the cane-back chairs in front of his desk, as if he were offering her tea or about to tell her good news.

She thought for a moment, then reluctantly sat down, back straight, hands folded in her lap, like a reasonable, civilized person. Inside, she felt like a wild animal, ready to do anything to protect her young.

"That's much better," Dr. Bell said. "Thank you. Now we can have a nice, friendly talk."

"You do not need to speak so loud," Lena said. "I am not hard of hearing."

He lifted his eyebrows, slightly amused. "All right," he said. "That's good to know. Thank you for telling me. So, how are you feeling today, Miss Conti?"

It was a ridiculous question. "How do you think I'm feeling?" she said. "My daughter has been stolen from me, along with the two children I have been asked to protect. I was brought to this place against my will, and this woman is telling you lies about me." She tried to stay calm, but her voice shook and her chin quivered.

Dr. Bell smiled again. It was the same artificial smile Nurse Irene had given her earlier, but more condescending. "I understand," he said. "It's perfectly normal to find all of this very confusing."

Her stomach clenched. He was no longer talking too loudly. Instead, he was talking to her as if she were feebleminded. She could hear it in his voice, in the arrogant tone and fake sympathy. Still, she pushed her fury away and concentrated on sounding intelligent and calm, not senseless and scared to death. "But I do not understand why I am here. I am not dim-witted or an idiot."

"Perhaps," Dr. Bell said, folding his hands on his desk. "But I will try to explain things to you. You have been brought here on the recommendation of a social worker from Sweet Briar College and several others, including Miss Sizer, George Pollock, and Sheriff Dixon."

"That is . . ." Her voice was high and tight, near hysterics. She paused and cleared her throat. She needed to do better, sound smarter, calmer. "I have not spoken with those people. They know nothing about me."

Dr. Bell held up the paper. "This document says otherwise. It clearly states that you were interviewed by Miss Penelope Rodgers. And obviously, you've spoken to Miss Sizer." He sneered at her, as if he'd caught her in a lie. "This also states you have a daughter born out of wedlock and you're living with a man who is your cousin."

She shook her head. "I work for Silas Wolfe, taking care of his house and children. That is why I live in his home. And my daughter's father is dead. He passed before we were to be married."

Dr. Bell gave her another disdainful smile. Then he spoke slowly, as if she were the imbecile Miriam said she was. "His passing does not change the fact that you had sexual relations with him *before* you were legally man and wife."

"I know this," she said. Her words were hard and forced. She could barely control her anger. "I made a mistake. Have you not made any mistakes?"

"Of course," Dr. Bell said. "We all make mistakes. What worries me is that, like most mountain people I've evaluated, you don't seem to grasp the difference between right and wrong. And you don't care to live by the rules of civilized society. Miss Sizer and the others feel the same way. Among other things, they believe you're an unfit mother."

Lena recoiled as if slapped. "That is not true! I told you they know nothing about me! I am a good mother. Ella is happy and healthy and I would do anything for . . ." Her voice caught and her eyes flooded. She swallowed the burning lump in her throat, fighting the urge to sob out loud. "I would do *anything* for my daughter. That is why I came to this country, to give her a better life. That is why I allowed Miss Sizer to bring me in here to talk to you, even though I know you will try to lock me up. She said my daughter and the Wolfe children are here. She said you can tell me where they are."

Just then, someone knocked on the office door. When Nurse Irene opened it, the desk nurse entered with a syringe on a metal tray.

Lena gaped at Nurse Irene. "What is that? Is it for me?"

"Only if you decide not to behave," Nurse Irene said.

Lena looked at Dr. Bell, shaking her head. "You do not need to give me that. I will do as you ask."

"It's just a precaution," Dr. Bell said. "Nothing more. But whether or not we need it is up to you."

The desk nurse walked behind the desk, set the tray on a filing cabinet, then turned to leave.

"Thank you, Nurse Mabel," Nurse Irene said, closing the door behind her.

After the desk nurse was gone, Dr. Bell regarded Miriam with a furrowed brow. "Is it true you led Miss Conti to believe that I could tell her where the children are?"

"I'm sorry, Doctor," Miss Sizer said. "But it was the easiest way to get her to cooperate, which only proves her mental deficiency. Ella is not here. She and the other children are being redistributed as part of a eugenic effort at raising them in the more appropriate home of an elite family."

Panic plowed through Lena's chest, stealing the air from her lungs. Had she heard Miriam correctly? Ella was *not there*? She turned in the chair, looking frantically back and forth between Miriam and Dr. Bell. "I do not understand what you are saying. Where is my daughter?"

Irritation pinched Miriam's brow; she had neither the time nor patience for someone so feebleminded. "I don't know how I can make it more plain. The children will be moved to a different location and placed with a mother and father who have the means and intelligence to raise them properly."

Lena's heart went black. "No!" she cried. "I am Ella's mother!" She shot to her feet and stepped toward Miriam, ready to strangle her. "You have to give her back to me!"

"The wheels of progress have already been set in motion," Miriam said. "There is nothing you can do about it. If anything, you should thank your lucky stars that your daughter will not end up like you."

Horror and fury writhed in Lena's stomach. She covered her face with her hands, her mouth twisting in agony. *Ella can't be given to someone else! She can't be! She is my little girl!* Unable to hold back any longer, she screamed and lunged at Miriam, arms outstretched, hands like claws. She would force the truth from her, no matter what. Miriam backed away, her face filled with fear, her satchel held up like a shield. Nurse Irene stepped between them and grasped Lena's arms. Dr. Bell hurried around the desk and grabbed Lena from behind.

"If you don't calm down," he yelled in her ear, "we'll give you something to calm you down. It's up to you if you want to move forward or end this now!"

"I want my daughter!" Lena cried.

"You might as well give in," Nurse Irene said, unfazed by her struggle. "You're not getting away from us."

Lena thrashed and writhed for a few more seconds, then let Dr. Bell and Nurse Irene wrestle her back into the chair, anger burning like fire inside her heaving chest. She should have known Miriam and the nurse were lying about the children being there. And now she was trapped. Fighting to get free would get her nowhere. Devastated, she went slack, shoulders convulsing.

Finally, Nurse Irene and Dr. Bell slowly loosened their grip. While Miriam cowered in the corner and Dr. Bell waited to make sure Lena stayed put, Nurse Irene retrieved the syringe from the filing cabinet and set it on the desk, ready to use it if need be. Then Dr. Bell went back to his chair, straightening his tie and pushing back his disheveled hair.

Lena turned to him, her eyes burning and swollen. "Please," she said. "You must listen to me. The sheriff took Bonnie and Jack Henry because the state wants Silas Wolfe's land. And George Pollock wanted me to work for him, but I would not. He said he would send me here to make sure I could not have babies. Miriam took my Ella and brought me here. She and the woman from the college must be—"

"I only did what needed to be done," Miriam said.

"I understand you're very upset," Dr. Bell said to Lena. "But you need to compose yourself or this will not end well for you."

Trying not to scream or throw up, Lena closed her eyes. She felt like she was losing her mind. Then she looked at Miriam.

"Please tell me Ella is with Bonnie and Jack Henry. I do not want her to be alone."

At first, Miriam said nothing, clearly afraid Lena would come after her again. Then she sighed and said, "For now, yes. But finding a family willing to take all three will be difficult, so it's very likely that, eventually, they will be separated."

Lena groaned and slumped forward, her head in her hands, the agony of grief seizing her heart. The idea of Ella without someone familiar to comfort her, someone she loved to kiss her cheeks and tell her everything would be all right, was more than she could bear.

Nurse Irene yanked her upright. "You need to sit up," she said. "Dr. Bell is not finished with you."

"I'm sorry, Miss Conti," Dr. Bell said. "But Nurse Irene is right. We must move forward with this evaluation so I can decide what the next step will be for you."

Lena wiped her face. "I do not need to be evaluated," she said. "There is nothing wrong with me."

"This is nothing to worry about," Dr. Bell said. "It's just part of the process. Now please pull yourself together so we can get on with it." He retrieved a pen and clipboard from his desk, wrote Lena's name on a folder, and put the document from Miriam inside. "Miss Sizer, you're free to go. I'll let you know what I decide."

"Thank you, Dr. Bell," Miriam said. "I'm sure you'll do what's best for everyone involved."

Lena wanted to get up and slap her across the face. She wanted to spit at her feet. Yank out her hair. Break the teeth from her mouth. How could she think taking children from their parents was best for anyone? But no matter how badly Lena wanted to punish Miriam Sizer, she had to stay in the chair. If she was going to convince Dr. Bell to let her go home, she needed to act educated and civilized.

After Miriam left, Dr. Bell said, "I know this can be frightening but try to remember, we only want to help you." He poised his pen over the clipboard. "Now, let's begin, shall we? Please state your full name, age, and place of birth."

Struggling to breathe normally, Lena tried to think straight. She had no choice. She had to answer his questions. "Magdalena Sofia Conti. Nineteen years old. Born in Italy."

Dr. Bell wrote her information at the top of the paper on the clipboard. "When did you immigrate to the United States?"

"In May."

"Did you come here alone?"

"No. I came here with my daughter, my mother, and my brother. But my mother and brother were sent back."

He raised his eyebrows. "What was the reason given for their deportation?"

Lena swore under her breath. She should have lied. If Dr. Bell found out Enzo was deported because he was deemed feebleminded, he might assume the same thing was wrong with her. But she could hardly string two thoughts together, let alone be one step ahead of him. "They gave no good reason," she said. "My mother and brother were healthy. But my mother had been seasick and my brother did not want to answer questions. He is only fourteen."

Dr. Bell scribbled on the paper, a smile playing across his lips. Lena wanted to ask why her family being deported amused him, but she bit her tongue.

"And how old is your daughter?" he said.

Her throat grew tight again. She swallowed several times and then, somehow, she said her baby girl's name. "Ella is two."

"And her father's name?"

"Jonathan Dankworth." After not mentioning him in years, his name tasted like poison in her mouth. If he hadn't lied to her, she wouldn't be in America. She wouldn't be in this hospital for the feebleminded, trying not to get locked up. And Ella would be safe in her arms.

"Last name spelled *D-A-N-K-W-O-R-T-H*?" Dr. Bell said. She nodded and he wrote it down.

"Have you had intercourse outside of marriage?"

"You know the answer to that question," Lena said.

"Answer the doctor," Nurse Irene insisted.

"Yes," Lena said.

"And what is your relationship with Silas Wolfe?" Dr. Bell said.

"I work for him. I help with the house, the cooking, and the children."

"And you are living in his home?"

"Yes."

"Does he pay you?"

She hesitated. If she said no, he might believe the claim that they were in a relationship. "I thought he was going to, but my daughter and I pay nothing to stay in his house and eat his food. He said there is no need to give me money too."

"Are you related to Mr. Wolfe in any way?"

Lena could feel Nurse Irene's disapproval, burning a hole in the back of her head. She thought about lying, but Penelope Rodgers had already told them the truth. "He is a distant cousin to me," she said.

"Are you having sexual relations with Mr. Wolfe?" Dr. Bell said. "And please be honest with your answer. We know the fear of inbreeding means little to the mountain people."

"No. Ella and I sleep in our own room."

Dr. Bell looked doubtful. "Sexual intercourse is not always performed in sleeping quarters. Are you certain you're being frank with me? Your answers are being put in your records."

She nodded so hard her head hurt. How many times did she have to tell them? "Yes. I am certain. I am not having sexual relations with Silas Wolfe."

"Has anyone in your family shown signs of feeblemindedness? Perhaps a parent or sibling?"

She started to say she had no family in America, then stopped. She had Ella, and Bonnie and Jack Henry. Then another hollow wave of grief hit her. She no longer had them either. "No."

He wrote down her answer.

"Have you ever been convicted of a crime?"

She shook her head.

"Do you have syphilis?"

She had no idea what syphilis was but it sounded bad. "No."

"Have you had any venereal diseases?"

"I do not understand what venereal means."

"Venereal diseases are spread through sexual intercourse."

"No."

"What about any other diseases or sickness?"

"No. I am healthy and strong."

He turned to the next page. "Can you tell whether or not there is salt in bread?"

She scowled. It was another ridiculous question. "Of course."

"Do you know how to tie your shoes?"

She lowered her gaze and stared at the desk, trying not to let her anger take over again. "Yes."

"Is the picture directly behind me a dog or a lady?" He pointed over his shoulder at the portrait of the stern woman in the ruffled bonnet.

"Your questions are *töricht*."

He frowned, confused. "Excuse me?"

"I said your questions are *töricht*," she said. "It means foolish. Do you know anything but English? I am able to speak two languages."

Dr. Bell set down his pen, folded his hands on the desk, and regarded her with a serious look. Clearly, he understood her point. "Just answer the question please. Is it a dog or a lady?"

"A lady."

He picked up the pen and wrote down her answer. "Are

there any alcoholics in your family? Anyone who drinks too much whiskey or wine?"

"No."

"Criminals?"

"No."

"Sex offenders?"

"I do not know what that is."

"Someone who hurts another person through unwanted sexual acts."

"No."

"Liars?"

"No."

"Did you attend school?"

"Yes, until I turned thirteen."

"Did you receive good marks?"

She nodded. "I did very well."

"Did you stop attending because you couldn't handle the coursework? Did the lessons become too difficult for you?"

"No. That is not why. My mother had no money to send me any longer." She paused, and then, before he could ask another question, she said, "I know what you are trying to do. You are trying to make me sound senseless and ignorant. You are trying to . . ." She hesitated and looked down at her hands. She needed to be careful. He might twist her words or misunderstand.

"Is something wrong?" he said.

She shook her head. "You cannot keep me here," she said. "I did nothing wrong. And I am not slow, dim-witted, feeble-minded, a moron, an imbecile or any other name you want to call me. Please. You have to let me go. My daughter needs me."

He shifted in his chair and sat up straighter. "I'm sorry, Miss Conti, but I'm afraid you're not qualified to measure your intellectual well-being, whereas I, on the other hand, am. I can assure you that Miss Sizer and the social worker from Sweet Briar College will make sure your daughter is raised by a well-to-do family who can give her everything she needs. A reasonable person would want that for their child, especially someone in your position. Don't you want what's best for her?"

"Yes. Of course I do. But I am what is best for her. I am her mother!"

"You might be her mother, but you have no home or place of employment. How do you expect to provide for her or any children you may have in the future?"

"We have everything we need at the home of Silas Wolfe. We have our own bedroom, clean clothes, and more food than I have ever seen in my life. Silas will soon allow my brother to come here and there is plenty for him too. Please, I have to go back." She tried blinking away her tears but they spilled down her cheeks. "I am begging you, help me find the children and let us go home to Wolfe Hollow."

Dr. Bell was unmoved. "I'm sure it was an ideal situation for you," he said. "But according to the local sheriff, Mr. Wolfe has been deemed unfit as a father and his home is going to be condemned. So, you see, even if we agreed to your release, you have no place to go."

"That is not true. Silas does not want to leave. He is fighting to keep his land."

"I have no doubt he is. But when you, Miss Conti, were allowed into this country, it was on the condition that you wouldn't become a burden to society. And Silas Wolfe has been providing you and your child with food and housing since you arrived. You have done nothing to support yourself."

Lena threw up her hands, on the verge of laughing and screaming at the same time. "What am I to do? I came to America believing I would be paid for my work, that I would have money like everyone else. But Silas Wolfe does not want to pay me. That is not my doing."

"Regardless, the fact remains that you are unable or unwilling to change your situation. Now we must deal with the way things are, not with what you thought they would be." Suddenly distracted, he put down his pen and retrieved a pocket watch from his vest to check the time. "And I'm afraid our time is up. I have an important meeting to attend in another building." He dropped the watch back in his vest pocket, attached her folder to the clipboard, and stood. "We'll finish the rest of the evaluation tomorrow. In the meantime, Nurse Irene will take you to your ward. After I share my findings with the review board next week, I'll let you know what they decide."

A sick, sudden sweat broke out on her forehead. *Next week?* She couldn't stay that long, wondering where Ella was the whole time. She would lose her mind.

"No!" Lena cried. "You cannot do this. I need to find Ella!"

"Your daughter is not lost, Miss Conti," he said. "It will serve you well to remember that."

Furious, Lena jumped up and slammed her hands on his desk. "You are right! My daughter is not lost! She was *stolen* and Miriam Sizer knows where she is!"

Dr. Bell started around the desk, giving Nurse Irene a quick nod. In that moment, Lena realized her mistake. She stepped back, but there was nowhere to run. Then, to her surprise, Dr. Bell put his hands on her shoulders and looked at her with sympathetic eyes. For a brief moment, she thought he was going to say he empathized with her situation and he would help her find the children. Then the compassion in his eyes changed to pity and resolve.

The sting in her arm was sharp and immediate. She turned toward Nurse Irene, who was plunging the syringe into her skin. Dr. Bell tightened his grip on Lena's shoulders, pushed her back down in the chair, and held her there. "Try to remember this is for your own good," he said.

Lena struggled to get back up, but he pinned her arms to her sides while Nurse Irene pressed down on her shoulders.

"No," Lena said. "Please. Do not do this." She begged them

to listen but suddenly felt woozy and weak, her thoughts and words mixed together in her mind, all soft and squished together like mud. She squeezed her eyes shut and blinked twice, fighting against the sinking sensation that seemed to pull her body toward the floor. Then the room grew fuzzy and dim, and Dr. Bell started to melt, his features swirling together in a white-and-gray mass.

"Just relax," Nurse Irene said, her voice low and slow.

Lena struggled to keep talking, to tell them to let her go, but her arms and legs went limp. Then the room disappeared.

Chapter 21

Lena's neck was stiff, her head tilted at an odd, uncomfortable angle, and her legs were folded awkwardly beneath her. She felt like she'd been in a fight, every muscle aching and sore. And her ears were ringing. Had she fallen down the stairs? Carried too many bags of apples into the house? No, this heavy, sluggish feeling was not the result of hard work. It was more like recovering from a serious illness or severe accident. She opened her eyes and turned her head, blinking to clear her vision.

The yellow light of early morning filtered in through a far window, painting bars on a white-tiled floor. At first, she thought she was in her bedroom back in Wolfe Hollow. But no toys lay scattered on a braided rug. No crib sat along the far wall. She glanced down at herself. She was still in her housedress. Still barefoot. Suddenly, the ringing in her ears stopped, replaced by whimpering, crying, coughing, humming, and mumbling. Then she noticed the rancid stench of human sweat, urine, and feces. Was she back in steerage? Deep in the bowels of a ship on her way to Germany? Struggling to sit up, she looked around.

Women of all ages filled the cold, gray-walled room, some wandering aimlessly, others sleeping or sitting on metal beds with grimy pillows and sheets. Most wore shabby clothes or nightgowns, while a few were in various stages of undress. One woman wore a strange white jacket with leather straps tying her arms around her waist. Another paced the floor singing a lullaby, a limbless doll cradled in her arms. All were pale and thin, with haunted expressions and hollowed out eyes.

Terror clawed at Lena's mind, closing her throat, choking her. She was in the Colony. And the sheriff had taken Ella. She swung her feet off the bed and stood on weak, watery legs. She had to get out of there. Had to find Ella. And Bonnie and Jack Henry. Dizzy and lightheaded, she staggered through the crowd, skirting around a young woman sitting cross-legged on the floor, hurrying past a wild-haired lady staring up at the ceiling with her arms outstretched, dodging a wrinkled old woman who danced and twirled, memories of happier days shining in her eyes. Several of the other women turned toward her with knowing expressions, watching her make a frantic dash toward escape. One of them jumped off a bed, reaching for her and laughing. Lena hunched her shoulders and bolted beyond her grasp. Finally at the door, sweating and out of breath, she tried the handle. It was locked.

"I wouldn't be fixing to do that if I was y'all," a voice said behind her.

Lena spun around to see who had spoken.

A heavyset woman sat on the edge of a dirty mattress, watching her with sad eyes. She looked to be around seventy years old, with swollen legs and sagging jowls. "Y'all try and run, they'll put you in the blind room. But first they'll give you douches to clean you out in case you been with a man. Then they'll keep you locked up two, three weeks, with nothing to eat but stale bread and dirty water."

"I do not belong here!" Lena said.

The woman pointed at the next bed, where a young woman

lay motionless on the mattress, her wrists tied to the iron headboard, a bed sheet knotted in her mouth. "Ain't none of us belong here, darling."

Lena turned and pounded on the door. "Someone please let me out! I need to find my baby!"

"I'm telling y'all," the woman said. "That there's a bad idea."

Just then, keys jangled in the lock. Lena stepped back, ready to fight or run. The handle turned and the door opened. Nurse Irene entered. Lena tried to push past her, but the nurse shoved her backward, yanked the keys from the lock, and closed the door behind her. She was stronger and faster than she looked.

"Please let me go," Lena cried. "There is nothing wrong with me."

Nurse Irene gave her a surly look. "Dr. Bell will determine that," she said. "Now, are you going to come with me willingly for the rest of your evaluation or do I need to call for help?"

Lena pressed her hands into fists, fighting the urge to scream. Trying to reason with the nurse was pointless. Somehow, some way, she had to prove to Dr. Bell that she was intelligent, strong, and capable. "I will go with you."

"That's better," Nurse Irene said. She unlocked the door, led her out of the room, slipped the keys into her uniform pocket, and took her down a dim hallway. Cries and moans filtered through rows of closed doors, along with the occasional sharp shout or pain-filled scream. Lena took deep, deliberate breaths, fighting against the claws of panic. Dr. Bell could not keep her in this wretched place. He just *couldn't*.

Halfway down the corridor, a door opened and a gray-haired woman holding a swaddled baby flew out of a room, her face contorted with terror. Two nurses rushed out behind her. One grabbed her by the waist while the other ripped the baby from her arms and threw it on the floor. Lena gasped and raced toward the infant, certain it would be injured or worse. Nurse Irene caught her by the arm and shook her.

"What do you think you're doing?" she said.

"Helping the baby!" Lena cried.

"What baby?"

Lena looked again. A tangled blanket lay on the hall floor, but no baby lay inside. No crying infant or wailing newborn. She looked at the gray-haired woman again, at her bone-white face and black eyes. Her long, tangled hair had been chopped off, but there was no denying it was the Widow Spinney, the poor woman who had paced back and forth on the bridge near Wolfe Hollow. When the nurses dragged the woman back through the door into the room, she grabbed the doorframe with both hands, fighting to break free. Then she was yanked out of sight and the door slammed shut. Lena's heart thundered in her chest. Was everyone from the mountains locked up in the Colony?

No, not everyone. Ella was not here. And neither were Bonnie and Jack Henry.

And then she heard it. The Widow Spinney shrieking behind the door, her long, low cries like the howls of a tortured animal. Unlike the first time Lena heard the widow, this time she felt the poor woman's sorrow deep in her soul, like a horrible, aching echo of her own grief and pain. Now she understood why the Widow Spinney cried out in agony. Now she understood why she walked the bridge, weeping for her lost child.

Nurse Irene yanked on Lena's arm. "Keep moving," she hissed.

Lena staggered down the hall, trying to imagine what the nurses were doing to the widow, wondering if the same grief-driven madness would befall her too. No. She would find her daughter. She had to. Surely, Silas was already looking for her and the children. Surely, he would find her at the Colony and, if he had not already found Bonnie and Jack Henry and Ella, they would search for them together. Unless he blamed her for his children being taken. Unless he had been taken somewhere too.

At the end of the corridor, Nurse Irene unlocked a set of double doors leading to another wing, relocking it after they went through. After several more twists and turns through the massive building, they entered a white-walled room with an examination table, a counter with drawers, and a glass-doored cabinets full of sharp-looking instruments. Lena started to shiver, a deep-seated tremble that shook her insides.

"Step up on the scales," Nurse Irene said.

Lena did as she was told. Nurse Irene wrote her height and weight down on her chart, then had her sit in a chair to take her temperature and blood pressure. When Dr. Bell entered the room, she placed a step stool on one end of the examination table.

"Good morning, Miss Conti," Dr. Bell said. "I hope you got some rest." He picked up her chart from the counter, scanned it briefly, then set it down again. "Please remove your dress and get on the table."

Nurse Irene pulled a hospital gown out of a drawer and handed it to Lena.

Lena looked around the room for a dressing screen or a door to another room.

"You can change right here," Doctor Bell said. "It's perfectly fine."

"But I—"

"Let's get on with it," Nurse Irene said. "We don't have all day."

And just like that, Lena was back inside the delousing plant on Hoffman Island, undressing in front of strangers, shaking and trying to cover herself with Ella's small, naked body held tight to her chest. Except this time, Ella was not in her arms. *Ella.* Where was her sweet Ella? Would she ever hold her again? With tears flooding her eyes, she turned away from Dr. Bell and Nurse Irene, her face burning, and pulled off her dress. After removing her undergarments and brassiere, she slipped into the thin gown and turned to face them again. Nurse Irene placed her clothes on a chair in the corner of the room. Lena climbed onto the paper-covered examination table and crossed her arms over her breasts.

Dr. Bell removed a stethoscope from a wall hook, put the earpieces in his ears, and asked her to put down her arms. She did as he said. He had her take several deep breaths while he listened to her heart, his brows knitted, then picked up her chart and wrote something down.

"I do not understand why you are doing this," Lena said. "I am not epileptic or feebleminded or sick." She had trouble pronouncing epileptic, but surely, they knew what she meant.

"Uh-huh," Dr. Bell said.

Lena clenched her jaw in frustration. He was not listening.

He checked her reflexes with a rubber hammer, looked in her ears and throat, and ran his fingers along her spine. "Do you have pain anywhere?" he said.

"No," Lena said.

He felt under her arms and beneath her jaw, pressed his fingers along the shape of her skull, and measured her head. While he recorded his findings, Nurse Irene pulled two metal footrests out of the end of the examination table, then went over to one of the cabinets, pulled a small bottle and a syringe out of a drawer, and placed them on a metal tray.

Dread fell like a rock in Lena's stomach. She knew why Dr. Bell needed the footrests.

"Lie back on the table, please," Dr. Bell said. "And put your feet up in the stirrups."

Nurse Irene pushed a rolling stool over to the end of the examination table for him, then stood beside Lena, ready to do whatever was needed to keep her in line.

"There is no need for this," Lena said. "I am not pregnant."

"Hopefully not," Dr. Bell said. "But I'm also checking for venereal and pelvic diseases. And evidence of an immoral lifestyle."

"But I have already told you," Lena said. "I do not have any diseases."

Nurse Irene let out an irritated sigh. "If you don't cooperate," she said, "we have ways of making sure you do." She lifted a leather strap on the side of the examination table, held it up so Lena could see, then nodded at the syringe on the metal tray.

Lena shook her head. "You do not need that."

"Then do as the doctor says."

"Try to remember that we're not doing any of these things to hurt you, Miss Conti," Dr. Bell said. "We just need to make sure you're healthy. And if you're not, we want to help you get better."

For what felt like the hundredth time, Lena started to say she was healthy. She was fine and strong and civilized. But there was no point. They did not listen. Swallowing the gorge in her throat, she lay back on the table and lifted her feet into the stirrups. When Dr. Bell's cold hands touched the soft, vulnerable place between her legs, she turned her head, closed her eyes, and prayed for it to be over.

Chapter 22

The days following Dr. Bell's physical evaluation were the longest of Lena's life. Nearly every night, rain pelted the barred windows of the ward, thunder shook the building, and lightning flashed in the black sky. It felt like the end of the world. Every second of every hour of every day, all she thought about was Ella, how scared and confused she must be, wondering where her mother was and why she hadn't saved her yet. Was she cold? Hungry? Tired? Crying? Were Bonnie and Jack Henry with her, or had they already been separated? And were Bonnie and Jack Henry all right? The unanswered questions nearly drove her mad. But she had to believe they were still together, had to imagine the three of them in a warm, cheerful room, Bonnie singing to Ella, Jack Henry making them laugh. It was the only thing that kept her sane.

Like the other patients in the Colony, she was locked in the grimy room for what seemed like endless hours, wearing the same clothes, breathing in the same rancid air, wondering what the next minute would bring, the next day, the next week. Unless someone got in a fight, injured themselves or someone else, had a violent breakdown, or caused a commotion of some kind, the only change in their routine came twice daily, when they were allowed to go to the dining hall for runny oatmeal or thin soup and stale bread. Lena could hardly think about eating—her stomach churned with nerves and grief—but she forced herself to swallow the tasteless food. She needed to keep up her strength so when she was released, she could search for Ella. Every day, she asked the nurses and attendants when Dr. Bell would see her again, but they either ignored her or told her they didn't know.

The rest of the time she sat at the head of her bed hoping she'd be left alone, eyes down, arms wrapped around her knees, and tried to picture Ella's pink cheeks and sparkling eyes, or remember the words to Bonnie's favorite songs, anything to pull her attention from the chaos and tragedy surrounding her. She did not want to look at the women tied to their beds or crawling on the floor. She did not want to see the adolescent girls crying in a corner with their heads hanging, or wandering the ward as if lost. Maybe it was foolish or cruel, but talking to the other patients would mean she was one of them. And she would never be one of them. She refused to let that happen. Somehow, some way, she would get out and find her daughter.

Four days after her arrival, when the heavyset woman with the swollen legs who warned her about the blind room got up and waddled over to her bed, Lena stretched out on the mattress and turned away. She didn't want to hear anyone else's stories, didn't want to know about the heartbreak that brought them here. Because what if their stories were similar? What if she learned that, no matter what she did, she'd end up the same way?

"Mind if I sit a spell?" the heavyset woman said. "These old legs ain't so good at holding me up no more."

Lena wanted to tell her to go away, but the woman had tried

to help, and she seemed normal enough. Reluctantly, Lena sat up, pulling back her feet to make room.

"Thank you kindly," the woman said. She sat down hard at the foot of the bed, the metal frame creaking in protest, and scooted backward on the mattress until her feet were off the floor. "Whoo-wee," she said. "Getting old ain't for sissies, that's for ding-dang sure. I'm Ethel Buck. Nice to make your acquaintance."

Lena hugged her knees to her chest. "Lena."

"I reckoned you might need a friend," Ethel said. "And if you got a need to know something, I been here a good while. Suppose it's about five years now."

Lena cringed inside. *Five years?*

Ethel must have seen the shock on her face. "Yep, it's a long time. But I ain't the only one who's been here too damn long." She pointed at an old woman shuffling along the wall with her back stooped and her head down. "That there's Sylvia. Been here twenty-three years, she has." Then she jerked her chin at a girl who looked to be around Lena's age. "Jerilyn's lived here since she was thirteen."

A cold eddy of fear opened up inside Lena, threatening to swallow her whole. The inspector at Ellis Island had said if Enzo was locked up, he'd never get out. But she had no idea Colony patients could be forced to stay *that* long. What if Dr. Bell thought she should be imprisoned forever too? And how did the women stay sane in such a horrible place? If they *were* sane.

"Sylvia don't talk much no more," Ethel continued. "But some years ago, she said the cops took her and her four daughters away while her husband was off working. They gave the two younger daughters to another family and stuck the other two in here with her. Said they was accused of running a house of ill repute or some other such nonsense. But it was a boardinghouse, as sure as the sky is blue."

Lena glanced around the ward. "Her daughters are in the Colony too?"

"Well, one is and one ain't. Turned out the oldest was so good at taking care of young'uns they kept her on to help out. Sylvia tried for years to find out what ward she was in, but never did. 'Course, that was afore her mind started slipping. Her other girl got released and sent to work for some high-falutin family to see if she'd behave under what the doctors call *the care of proper persons*. As for Jerilyn, some good-for-nothing bastard forced himself on the poor girl, then left town when he found out she was with child. After her baby boy was born, the Red Cross workers took him away and put Jerilyn in here, accusing her of not being in control of her carnal urges."

Terror and anger writhed in Lena's stomach. In some ways, Sylvia's and Jerilyn's stories were similar to hers. What if she was locked up for the same reasons? She swallowed, trying to find her voice. "Did Sylvia ever find out what happened to the daughters who were given to another family?"

Ethel shook her head, her mouth downturned. "She asked after her girls for years, but nobody weren't ever gonna tell her anything. I tried to make her feel better by saying maybe my Carrie adopted them. Thinking that way made me happy too, 'cause my Carrie always wanted young'uns. But she was in the Colony for a spell too, till they made sure she couldn't have no more babies and let her go."

Lena had no idea what to say except "I'm sorry." And she *was* sorry, and disgusted and furious too. At the same time, it helped to know someone had actually been released.

"No need to say sorry," Ethel said. "Not to me, anyways. It's my own damn fault for not getting off the booze and drugs and giving Carrie a proper home. They took her away from me and gave her to another family, just like they did with Sylvia's girls. Problem is, the family who took Carrie only wanted free help. Then their nephew got her with child. He denied it, of course, but the Dobbses, that's the family my Carrie worked for, sent her to the Colony to save face. And they kept the baby." She paused briefly, looking off in the distance as if imagining the grandchild she'd never seen, then continued. "I ain't for sure, but I heard Carrie's girl was real smart, even got good grades in school. But I reckon she was doomed from the start, just like me and her momma. She was only eight years old when she got sick and died."

Lena shook her head, her eyes flooding. She never should have let Ethel sit on her bed. Never should have talked to her. She did not want to hear any more heartbreaking stories. Did not want to hear about daughters being taken from their mothers, about little girls dying. It was too much to bear.

"What about you, sugar?" Ethel said. "How'd you end up in this here snake pit?"

"I am sorry, but I do not feel well," Lena said. "I need to rest for a while." She released her knees and started to stretch her legs along the mattress.

"Sure thing, darlin'," Ethel said. "I reckon this place is already starting to wear you down." She scooted forward off the mattress, swollen feet reaching for the floor. "You just let me know if you need an ear, all right?" And then, with great effort, she got her legs beneath her and pushed herself into a standing position.

Certain she could not speak without breaking down, Lena turned away and lay on her side, struggling to control the black mass of dread growing inside her.

Ethel patted her leg with a warm hand and, without another word, left her alone.

Six days after Lena's examination, Nurse Irene finally took her to see Dr. Bell. When she knocked on his office door, Lena held her breath. After talking to Ethel, she had barely slept, certain she would be locked up forever like Sylvia and Jerilyn. If she never saw her daughter again, she would die. And what if Ella, Bonnie, and Jack Henry were brought up by families who treated them like slaves? What if they were physically or sexually abused? No. That was not how their story was going to end. Either Silas would find them, or she would be released to begin the search. Maybe, by some miracle, Dr. Bell was going to apologize and say they'd made a terrible mistake. Maybe he was going to tell her where she could find the children. Then she heard muffled voices on the other side of the door and hope flickered inside her chest. Maybe Ella, Bonnie, and Jack Henry were waiting in the office now. Or maybe it was Silas, come to rescue her. Then Nurse Irene opened the door and Lena froze.

Penelope Rodgers from Sweet Briar College, her jacket spotless, her shirt white and crisp, sat beside Dr. Bell on the other side of his desk, along with two men in dark suits, their faces devoid of emotion. One man had coal-black hair and pasty skin; the other wore a sparse, red beard that did little to hide his gaunt face. Dr. Bell, who was writing in a folder, looked up and smiled.

"Ah, there you are," he said. "Everyone, this is Colony patient number 1969, Magdalena Sofia Conti." He gestured toward the chairs in front of his desk. "Have a seat, Miss Conti."

Lena stood rooted to the floor, glaring at Penelope.

Nurse Irene gave her a nudge. "I'd do as I was told if I were you," she said.

Reluctantly, Lena went to the chairs and sat down, her chest on fire.

"I assume you remember Miss Penelope Rodgers from Sweet Briar College?" Dr. Bell said, as if she and Lena were old friends.

"Yes," Lena said. "I remember her. She snuck up on Jack Henry in Silas Wolfe's barn and frightened the children."

"Are you talking about the children who chased me away with a pitchfork?" Penelope said with sarcasm.

"We asked you to leave," Lena said. "You would not go and you said terrible things."

"That's not how I remember it," Penelope said.

"Let's move on, shall we?" Dr. Bell said. He turned to the other men. "Before we get started, Miss Rodgers has asked to address this board."

"Thank you, Dr. Bell," Penelope said. She stood and went to the end of the desk, faced the men and read from a paper in her hand. "Over the past year, I've had the opportunity to visit a mountainous section of our beloved Virginia, where I found one family numbering sixteen children, twelve of whom with a mentality I was able to grade, at a glance, as imbecile. The family was living in the direst of poverty without any of the decencies or comforts of life. I have also visited fifty other families living in the same county in the same environment with the same degree of mentality. This means that Virginia is allowing to accumulate within her borders hordes of these clans who have no right to be born, who are challenging the intelligence of her citizenry, who are filling her courts with crime and criminals, and who are placing on our treasury an incalculable burden. If even one of these families is allowed to propagate, their future generations will add millions of dollars in relief work and an endless trial of social sores wherever they settle. That is why my colleagues and I refuse to sit back and let things like that happen. And also why I'm honored to, once again, assist the Colony review board with their evaluation."

"Thank you for your commitment to the cause," Dr. Bell said. "I'll be sure Professor Ivan McDougle and Arthur Estabrook over at the Eugenics Records Office are made aware of your dedication."

The other men nodded to acknowledge their gratitude. Penelope beamed and returned to her seat.

"Is it true that the mountain people live in mud-plastered log cabins and have no community government, no organized religion, little social organization wider than that of the family and clan, and only traces of organized industry?" one of the men asked her.

Penelope nodded. "They are not of the twentieth century." After she put the paper back in her bag and got settled, Dr. Bell regarded Lena.

"As promised, I took my findings of your evaluation to the review board, which, along with myself, includes Dr. Fischer"—he gestured toward the man with the coal-black hair—"and Dr. Crampton." He gestured toward the bearded man. "Both of these fine men are respected members of the American Eugenics Society. They also do work for the state of Virginia."

With her heart thudding so hard it felt like it would explode, Lena forced herself to nod at the men, to acknowledge their presence and the fact that she understood what Dr. Bell said. Otherwise, they'd believe she was feebleminded, or worse.

"Now that we have the introductions out of the way," Dr. Bell said, "Miss Conti, I've called you into my office today to share the review board's results with you."

Lena's head swam, dark and heavy, nearly toppling her. She locked her hands and elbows on the armrests to keep upright. The doctors had to let her go. They just had to.

"We have reviewed Dr. Bell's findings," Dr. Crampton said, "and we will now read our professional opinions and recommendations."

"Magdalena Sofia Conti," Dr. Fischer said, "the review board of the Virginia State Colony has deemed you feebleminded, and by the laws of heredity you are the probable potential parent of socially inadequate offspring who will be likewise afflicted. As such, you may be sexually sterilized. The practice of surgical sterilization of persons believed to be incompetent because of feeblemindedness, insanity, alcoholism, epilepsy, or other traits regarded as defects and assumed to be hereditary in origin and therefore preventable by sterilization is legal in the state of Virginia."

Lena drew in a sharp breath, struggling to comprehend what he was saying. Deep in her heart she knew the horrible truth, but it couldn't be real. It just couldn't be. She opened her mouth to speak but her tongue felt like stone.

"Do you have any questions?" Dr. Bell said.

"Are . . . are you saying you want to do an operation on me?" Lena said. "To stop me from having more children?"

"That's correct," Dr. Fischer said. "It has been proven that sterilized women are more proficient and productive workers. Other women sterilized here at the Colony have gone out into the world to earn their own good living and are behaving themselves well. In your case, that will depend on you, of course."

"But I am not feebleminded or any of the other things you said!" she said. "I am normal and healthy!"

"We recognize that this may be upsetting news," Dr. Crampton said. "But your welfare and that of society will be promoted by your sterilization. You come from a class of shiftless, ignorant, anti-social whites. And as evidenced by your mental defectiveness, you have a chronological age of nineteen with a mental age of nine years, according to the Stanford Revision of the Binet-Simon Scale. You are of social and economic inadequacy. You have never been self-sustaining and have one child, now twenty-nine months old, who is likely to be a mental defective as well."

Lena shook her head furiously. "There is nothing wrong with Ella!"

"To the untrained eye it can be hard to distinguish whether or not a person is feebleminded," Dr. Bell said. "Some people, children even, have none of the stigmata of the lower-grade mental deficient and are not easily recognized. That is why it's important for professionals like ourselves to be vigilant in protecting others from invisible contamination."

"According to my observations," Penelope Rodgers said, "the child showed signs of slow mental development. There was a look about her that was not quite normal, but just what it was, I couldn't tell."

Lena jumped to her feet. "That is a lie!" she cried. "You do not know her. You did not even speak to her! My daughter is very intelligent. She is learning English before three years old. My brother is smart too, but this country wanted to lock him up if he did not leave. What is wrong with all of you? Why do you think you have the right to do these things?"

"Calm down, Miss Conti," Dr. Bell said. "Or we will have to restrain you."

Nurse Irene grabbed her, pushed her back down in the chair, and held her there. Lena's mind screamed to get up and leave, to push Nurse Irene away and run out of the building. But she had no keys to the locked doors. No idea which way to go or where to hide. They'd catch her before she made it to the end of the hall. And then they'd drug her again, or worse. Trying not to hyperventilate or throw up, she searched for something to say to make them understand that she was fine, that her only offense was an imperfect understanding of the English language during questioning and her refusal to move in with George Pollock. That she was being punished for trying to protect herself and her child.

"I understand you're distraught," Dr. Bell said. "But it's for the best."

"Why are we wasting our time trying to explain this to a coarse, unintelligent woman?" Dr. Fischer said. "It's impossible to convince her of the value of the operation for sterilization either for her own protection or for that of society. She is retarded, possessing an IQ lower than eighty. It is our job to protect others from the menace of the feebleminded, who are permanently and expensively antisocial."

"Because it's procedure," Dr. Bell said.

"If nothing else," Dr. Crampton said, "we can confine her for not being able to control her nerves."

"Do you agree to the surgery, Miss Conti?" Dr. Bell said.

She shook her head so hard it hurt. "No, I do not agree. You cannot do this to me. It is not right!"

"If you refuse," Dr. Bell said, "we will have no choice but to commit you to the Virginia State Colony for the remainder of your life."

Lena felt her bowels turn to water. After everything she'd been through—the war, the hunger, the poverty, losing her father and mother, losing *her child*—this was what it came down to: the possibility of being locked up in this horrible place until the end of her days. The room started to spin and the walls closed in around her, shock and agony and grief pulling her down. It took all of her strength not to fall out of the chair and collapse in a heap on the floor. She closed her eyes for a moment to regain her equilibrium. When she opened them again, Penelope and the doctors were staring at her, calmly waiting for an answer. An answer that, in the long run, would mean nothing to any of them.

"What is your decision, Miss Conti?" Dr. Bell said. "I can perform the operation as soon as tomorrow."

Lena put her hands over her mouth, certain she was going to be sick. There was no other choice. Being released from the Colony was the only way she'd ever find Ella. And if she could hold her baby girl in her arms again, nothing else would matter. Not an operation. Not being forced to give up any hope of ever having more children. She lowered her hands, looked at the doctors, and nodded, tears blurring her vision. "I agree to the operation," she said. Her voice was high and tight, and for a moment she wondered if she was losing her mind.

Lena woke up, dozed, then woke again. Over and over and over. It was impossible to tell the difference between her nightmares and reality. Her body felt bruised and beaten, her limbs immobile and heavy. She was lying on a stiff mattress, with a thin pillow under her head. But she had no idea where she was. Hazy images blinked through her mind—sharp, silver instruments; people standing over her; someone wiping her brow with a cool cloth. She blinked and forced her eyes open, squinting against the light. She turned her head. A water pitcher and a drinking glass sat on a small table beside her. Mumbled words and low moans filled the air. Somewhere, a woman was crying. A dark silhouette hovered nearby, blurry and unfocused.

"Bonnie?" she said.

No one answered.

And then she remembered.

She was in the Colony.

She had been sterilized.

And she had no idea where Ella was.

She struggled to sit up, winced in pain, and lay back down. It felt like a knife was stuck in her lower abdomen.

"Lie still," a male voice said. "You need to rest."

Little by little, the dark figure solidified and became clear. It was Dr. Bell in a white lab coat, his hands behind his back, looking down at her.

"The procedure went as planned," he said. "One inch of each of your fallopian tubes was removed, then each tube was ligated and the ends cauterized by carbolic acid, followed by alcohol. Providing you do as you're told, your recovery should be uneventful."

She tried to speak. "And then . . . " she said, her voice raspy and weak. "Then you will let me go?"

"Let's just get through the next few days and we'll see how you're doing," he said. "All right?"

Lena started to ask how long she'd been sleeping—every day that passed meant Ella was getting farther and farther away—but he turned and left the room.

CHAPTER 23

Shafts of sunlight filtered in through the long, caged windows, cutting through the dim light of the green-tiled room, illuminating the mold-darkened floor. A group of women stood in a cluster near one wall, naked and crying, moaning and swaying, waiting for their turn in one of four claw-foot tubs. Three women struggled and screamed in the tubs while nurses scrubbed their hair and bodies and other patients held them down. No steam rose from the bathwater. No warm, moist humidity filled the air. The water, the room, the floor—were all ice-cold. Lena stood next to one of the tubs, shivering and trying to pay attention to what Nurse Irene was telling her.

"Every patient is bathed once a month," she said.

Lena nodded to let her know she understood.

Earlier, when Nurse Irene had retrieved her from the ward, Lena thought she was finally being released. But instead of heading toward Dr. Bell's office, they went in the opposite direction, toward another part of the building.

"Where are you taking me?" Lena said. "It has been ten days since I had the operation. Dr. Bell said he would let me leave."

"I'm taking you to get cleaned up," Nurse Irene said.

A flicker of hope quickened Lena's step. Surely, they'd want her to wash before she went home. She could hardly wait to scrub the filth and grime from her skin. "Then I will be released?"

"No, I'm still waiting for word from Dr. Bell. In the meantime, we need help bathing the low-grade patients."

Lena's stomach dropped. "But if I am to leave soon, why are you giving me a job?"

Nurse Irene stopped and glared at her. "If you need time to think about whether or not you'll do as you're asked, I can take you to the blind room instead."

Lena shook head. "No, I do not need time to think about it. I will help."

Now, in the next bathtub, a nurse used a stained scrub brush to scour the chest and arms of a patient while a stocky woman in a nightgown held her down. Coughing and trying to breathe, the woman in the water was old and skeletal thin, her blue-veined hands like claws on the side of the tub as she struggled to stay upright. One side of her face sagged and drooped, and her eyes rolled wild inside her head. She looked terrified.

"Are you listening to me?" Nurse Irene said.

Lena pulled her eyes away from the old woman and nodded.

"Every patient is bathed once a month," Nurse Irene repeated. "When we don't have soap, we make do. And we never have enough time to do a proper job, so it's imperative to get them in and out as fast as we can." She started toward the other side of the room. "Stay here, I'll be right back."

After retrieving a naked woman from the group of patients, she dragged her over to where Lena stood. Another nurse, muscular and mean-looking, picked the woman up and put her in the bathtub. The woman shrieked and tried to get out, her hands slipping on the wet porcelain. She went under, then came back up, choking on a mouthful of water.

"Hold her down!" Nurse Irene yelled at Lena.

Lena did as she was told, pushing on the woman's slippery, wet shoulders and grabbing at her arms, ignoring the pull and sting of the still-tender scar on her abdomen.

"I'm sorry," Lena said to the woman as she held her down. "I'm sorry."

The muscular nurse scrubbed the woman's face and hair with lye soap, working fast. Then she washed her neck and chest, roughly shoving aside the woman's ample breasts, and under her arms.

"Hold her legs open!" the muscular nurse yelled at Lena.

Lena grabbed the woman's knees and pushed them apart. The muscular nurse reached into the water and scrubbed between her legs. When she was finished, she dumped buckets of icy water over the woman's head and yanked her upright. Soaked, Lena wiped her face and took the woman's arm to help her out.

"I'm sorry," she said again. "Are you all right?"

Shaking violently and nearly hyperventilating, her head trembling on her thin neck, the woman looked at Lena and said in a quaking, raspy voice, "No one has ever asked me that before. I'll be fine. Thank you."

Before Lena could reply, a nurse whisked the woman away, giving her a once-over with a damp towel and pushing her clothes into her shaking hands. Nurse Irene brought another patient over and the muscular nurse lifted her into the tub.

"Hold her down," the muscular nurse yelled at Lena.

Lena did as she was told.

After what felt like a hundred cold baths later, the final patient was dressed and the nurse took all of them back to their ward. Drenched and shivering, her hair dripping down her face and neck, Lena leaned against the wall to catch her breath. Nurse Irene crossed her arms and looked at her.

"Your turn," she said, jerking her chin toward the tubs of cold, filthy water.

More than anything, Lena wanted to wash up, but she could

not bring herself to get in the bathtub after so many others, some of whom had been covered with human waste and vomit. "Will I be helping again tomorrow?" she said. "Or will Dr. Bell be releasing me?"

"You will be here again tomorrow," Nurse Irene said.

"Then I will get in before the others," she said, then walked to the door and waited to be let out.

Chapter 24

Outside the barred window of the third-floor ward inside the Virginia State Colony for Epileptics and Feebleminded, everything looked cold and wet—the trees and sidewalks, the grass and street. Leaves littered the lawn and gray clouds hung low and ominous in the early morning sky, hiding the distant mountains. If Lena's estimates were right, she'd been imprisoned in the Colony for over two months, watching warm September days give way to the gray days of late October and early November. Wolfe Hollow seemed a million miles away, along with everything and everyone associated with it—Silas, Bonnie, Jack Henry.

Ella.

Dear, sweet Ella.

She'd never forget the last few seconds of holding Ella in her arms, the fear and panic in her little girl's eyes, her terrified crying when Miriam took her away. How could Lena survive without her? After losing her father, being separated from her family, and learning Mutti had died, Lena thought she knew grief. But nothing could have prepared her for the insurmountable torture of losing her child. Yes, Ella was alive, but the hope of ever seeing her again diminished with every passing day. A thousand times an hour she whispered Ella's name and pictured her sweet face, the black manacle of grief tightening around her chest so hard it felt like her heart would shatter. The bleakness of her future seemed clear. She was destined to lose everyone she cared about; destined to be separated from everyone she loved most. And, if and when she got out of this place, destined to spend the rest of her days searching for her daughter.

She tried to hide it, but her crying spells came three to four times a day; the sense of being trapped inside a nightmare continued on and on and on. She walked, she talked, she did the work assigned to her—but the entire time she felt detached, as if everything was going on at a distance. She only put one foot in front of the other to stay alive in case she ever saw her daughter again.

Every day she asked to see Dr. Bell. Every day the nurses said no. She was starting to wonder if he'd tricked her into getting the operation. But what would be the point in that if they never planned on letting her go? And if she *was* released, what would she find back in Wolfe Hollow? Would Bonnie and Jack Henry be there, miraculously rescued by Silas? Would he have found Ella too? Or would Silas also be gone, the house and barn empty? And if Silas was gone, did that mean everyone was gone? Teensy and Judd and their girls? Betty Lee Blanchard and Sandy Craig and Nellie McCauley? And if they had all been driven from their homes and land, where would she go? How would she ever find Ella if she had nowhere to live and no one to help?

Now, sitting on the edge of her dirty mattress, she shivered and wrapped her arms around herself. As usual, the radiator sat silent and still, a cold iron block beneath the crumbling sill. According to Nurse Irene, it was too early to turn on the heat, even though the high-ceilinged room grew frigid at night and some of the women and girls had taken to sharing beds, their arms and legs wrapped around each other to get warm. Despite the fall weather, today looked warmer outside than it felt inside. She got up and went to the barred window, longing to push it open and let in some fresh air. She wanted, *needed*, the aroma of rich earth and damp grass to fill her lungs, to evict the rank odors of mold and disinfectant, urine and sweat, infection and disease. Putting her hands on the cold glass, she closed her eyes and tried to remember the warmth of the sun. When she heard the ward door open, she opened her eyes and turned.

Nurse Irene entered the ward and locked the door behind her. A patient hurried over and said something to her, gesturing wildly. Nurse Irene shook her head and shooed the woman away, then moved farther into the room. Another woman rushed to her side, pulled up her sleeve, and pointed at a mark on her arm.

"It's just a scrape," Nurse Irene said. "You'll be fine." Then she headed toward Lena.

Apprehension inched like ice along Lena's skin. Unwilling and unable to wait and see what the nurse was going to say, she left the window and met her halfway.

"It's time," Nurse Irene said.

"Time for what?" Lena said.

"For you to be discharged."

Lena's breath quickened. Dr. Bell was finally letting her leave.

"You're being released on parole," Nurse Irene said.

A flicker of panic surged through Lena. "What does that mean? I thought you were letting me go?"

"We are, Miss Conti. But we will be checking up on you. George Pollock inquired about you working for him but—"

"No!" Lena said. "You cannot send me to work for him. I will not go there!"

Nurse Irene frowned. "Let me finish, Miss Conti."

Lena shook her head. "I will not work for George Pollock!"

Irritated, Nurse Irene sighed long and loud. "Do I need to give you something to calm you down or will you allow me to speak?"

Lena tried to find the words she needed. She could barely string two thoughts together. "I am . . . I am listening."

"As I was trying to say," Nurse Irene said, "Dr. Bell believes Mr. Pollock has plenty of help, what with his Skyland Resort and all, so you're not being sent to work for him. For now, you're being allowed to return to the Silas Wolfe residence."

Overcome with relief, Lena's knees nearly buckled beneath her. She grabbed the headboard of a nearby bed to keep from collapsing. She was being sent back to Wolfe Hollow, where surely Silas had gone looking for his children, if he hadn't already found them. And surely, he'd help her find Ella too. She had to believe it was true.

"But first, you must agree to all conditions of your release," Nurse Irene continued. "If we discover that you're being promiscuous or getting into trouble of any kind, we will readmit you to the Colony, very likely for the rest of your life. And you are not allowed to try and locate your daughter in any way, either through the police or by other means. Do you understand?"

Lena tightened her jaw. They had no right to control what she did after she was released because they'd had no right to admit her in the first place. And they certainly had no right to stop her from searching for her child. But saying so would not help. Too overwhelmed to speak, she only nodded. If it meant she'd be set free, she'd agree to anything.

"Good," Nurse Irene said. "After you sign the necessary paperwork, we'll call a taxi to take you there."

Chapter 25

In the back seat of the sputtering taxi, the stench of the Colony wafted from Lena's clothes and hair, filling the vehicle. Earlier, she'd opened a window to let in some fresh air, but the wind was cold and the driver yelled at her to shut it. Now, she sat up straight to look out the windshield at Silas's house, praying she would see Jack Henry bringing in the cows or Bonnie hanging laundry on the line. Silas's truck was parked in the drive, but no thin, blond girl worked in the garden or yard. No tall, lanky boy herded a trio of brown cows into the barn. Not one chicken scratched for bugs in the grass or pecked the ground under the apple trees. The place looked deserted.

Trying to control her panic, Lena told herself everyone was in the house, eating supper or doing household chores. But she knew she was fooling herself. The sheriff had taken Bonnie and Jack Henry away the same horrible day he took Ella. And they were being "redistributed" to more "appropriate" families.

Then she had another thought and a sudden rush of fear came over her, so strong it stole her breath. Silas might blame her for what happened. He might refuse to let her inside. He might tell the taxi driver to take her back to the Colony. *No.* She wouldn't let that happen. She would make him listen and understand. And he had no idea where she'd been anyway. At least, she hoped not. Because what if he'd found out she was at the Colony and left her there to punish her for letting the sheriff take his children?

The taxi pulled up beside Silas's truck and stopped. Lena swallowed the sour taste in the back of her throat, slid across the seat, and got out. She closed the door and started up the frost-bitten grass toward the house, her heart knocking hard against her ribs. When the taxi driver gunned the engine and pulled away, Silas stepped out of the front door in filthy overalls and bare feet, carrying his rifle. His hair and beard were scraggly and unwashed, his eyes wild and bloodshot. He looked like he hadn't bathed in weeks. He staggered to the edge of the porch, lifted the rifle, and pointed it at Lena.

"Who's there?" he bellowed.

She came to a halt. "It me, Lena!" she shouted.

"Who?"

"Lena Conti. I worked for you, remember?"

"Where's my young'uns?" he said, slurring his words.

Her stomach turned over. He had not found Bonnie and Jack Henry. And clearly he'd been drinking. "I . . . I do not know where they are. I hoped maybe they were here with you."

"What do you want?" he growled.

"I do not want anything," she said. "They said I could come back to work for you."

"Who's they?"

"The doctors at the Virginia Colony. That is where I have been. They would not let me go."

Silas lowered the rifle, a spark of anxious hope in his usually stern eyes. "Is that where they took my Bonnie and Jack Henry?"

She shook her head. "No. I do not know where they took them."

Silas's face went dark again, and he swayed back and forth as if struck. For a second, she thought he was going to drop the gun or fall down.

"I been looking for 'em," he said, near tears. "But I can't find them. They said I warn't a good father. But I took care of my young'uns as best I could."

Her eyes welled. Seeing him so broken made her heart constrict further. If he had given up hope, how could she hold on to hers? "I do not know where Ella is either," she said. She considered telling him about Miriam Sizer and Penelope Rodgers, how they were giving the children away, but decided to wait until he was sober. Wiping her cheeks, she approached the porch stairs. "Please forgive me, Silas. I tried to stop Pollock and the sheriff from taking the children, but there was nothing I could do."

He stumbled down the steps and grabbed her arm. "Where'd those bastards take Bonnie and Jack Henry? Did they tell you what they did with them?" The sour tang of whiskey and old sweat washed over her.

She shook her head, her face crumpling in on itself. "No, they would not tell me anything."

He let go of her arm and sat down hard on the steps, defeated. "I went over to that highfalutin resort of Pollock's. Put him against a wall and tried to force him to tell me what he did with my young'uns. Got myself thrown in jail for three weeks. Come home to dead livestock and an empty henhouse. Virgil and Judd came by and saved one of the cows and Ole Sal, but it was too late for the rest."

Oh God. Not the animals too. "I am sorry," she said. "It is my fault."

"I reckon it don't matter now. I ain't got no more mouths to feed anyways." He stood, swayed, then found his balance and staggered back up the steps. "Ain't got no work for you neither," he said over his shoulder.

"But I have nowhere else to go," she called after him.

At the top of the steps, he turned to look back at her. "Well, I reckon it don't matter if you stay or go. They're fixing to take it all anyway."

"But we still need to look for the children."

He scoffed and turned back toward the door. "Ain't nobody found their young'uns yet."

His words sent a chill up her spine. She took a deep breath and closed her eyes for a moment, desperately clinging to what little optimism she had left. She wanted to scream and yell at him, to tell him they could not give up so easily, no matter what had happened to anyone else. Ella and Bonnie and Jack Henry were out there somewhere, waiting to come home. But he was drunk. Reprimanding him wouldn't do any good.

At the same time, a small, nauseated part of her knew he was right. They had no one on their side. And she had been told not to look for her daughter or she would be put back in the Colony. But she was not going to allow herself to give up. Especially since she had just returned to Wolfe Hollow. Determined not to let Silas defeat her, she went up the steps and followed him inside. At least she'd have a familiar roof over her head and plenty of food while she figured out what to do next. Right now, she needed a hot bath, a healthy meal, and a good night's rest. Maybe, when he was no longer drunk, Silas would listen to her and together they could come up with a plan. Then she stepped through the door and came to a halt, shocked by what she saw.

Dirty plates, stained cups, and used silverware filled the sink and table. Soup-crusted kettles and greasy cast-iron pans crowded the stove. Empty canning jars littered the counter and floor, and ashes spilled out of the fireplace. Tears burned her eyes again. Silas had given up completely. And she understood why. But the children could not live in this mess. The house needed to be ready for their return. While she stood stunned in the doorway, he fell into the sofa with his rifle across his lap, picked up a jug of moonshine, and took a long swig.

Suddenly her body seemed to weigh a thousand pounds. She craved sleep like a person lost in a desert craved water. Now that she was safe, she longed for the escape of unconsciousness, at least long enough to give her battered heart and mind a short respite. Even the thought of heating bath water seemed insurmountable. And she would deal with the house later.

She started toward the stairs, desperate for a soft, warm bed, certain she was moving in slow motion. Then a flash of yellow under the kitchen table caught her eye and she stopped. It was Poppy, the yarn-haired rag doll Bonnie had given Ella. A vicious assault of grief overwhelmed her. How could she go on without her baby girl?

Moving into the kitchen on legs that felt like stone, she got down on her knees and pulled the rag doll out from under the table. A line of dirt smudged Poppy's forehead, and her yellow hair was tangled. Lena brushed the dirt from the doll's face and raked her hair back into place, then struggled to her feet, the doll pressed to her chest, and went upstairs. When she opened her bedroom door and saw Ella's empty crib, she grabbed the doorframe to keep from falling. After a moment, once she could trust her legs again, she put Poppy in the crib, staring at the soft-edged blanket Ella used to hold against her cheek while she fell asleep. It was all too much. She covered her face with clawed hands, her mouth twisting in agony. *Ella can't be gone. She just can't be! Not my baby girl!* She fell to her knees and crumpled in a heap on the floor, howling.

She should have taken a rifle out to the barn when Penelope Rodgers showed up. She should have listened to Bonnie and Jack Henry and chased her away without answering any of her questions. She should have left Wolfe Hollow after Pollock showed up, asking her to work for him. Or maybe she should have agreed to move in with him. Maybe she should have packed Ella up and gone with him right there and then. Even if he was lying about needing a housekeeper, at least she'd still have Ella. At least they'd still be together. Anything, even letting Pollock into her bed, would have been better than losing her child. Nothing he could have done to her would have been more painful than living without her baby girl, even if he'd sent her to the Colony to be sterilized first. It was her fault. Her fault Ella had been taken. Her fault she might never see her again. Her fault Bonnie and Jack Henry had been taken too.

After a few minutes of anguished sobbing, she pushed herself up, took off her filthy clothes, and dropped them on the floor. Whatever source of strength had carried her through the last few months at the Colony had left her body an empty shell. How was her heart still beating? Her lungs still drawing air? She curled up on the bed, praying her mind would shut down and release her into sleep. She would figure out what to do tomorrow.

Chapter 26

After a restless night filled with nightmares and cold sweats, Lena wrapped a blanket around herself, went downstairs, and started a fire in the woodstove. Silas was nowhere to be seen and his truck was gone, which meant she had time to burn her filthy clothes in the woodstove and heat up kettles of bathwater. While waiting for the water to boil, she went back upstairs to put on a worn-out house dress, then dragged the wooden bathtub into the kitchen, stacked the dirty dishes on the kitchen counter, gathered the empty canning jars, and threw away the rotting food.

When the water was ready, she scrubbed her hair and body until her skin was nearly raw, then put on a clean dress. After washing a frying pan and mixing bowl, she made buckwheat pancakes and ate them outside on the porch. Not that she felt like eating—how could she enjoy food when her little girl was gone?—but she needed to regain her strength if she ever hoped to find her. When she finished the pancakes and a cup of strong coffee, she relished the fresh air for a few minutes and then, despite being more tired than she'd ever been in her life, she got to work: cleaning up the kitchen, washing the dishes, sweeping the floors, straightening the pantry, and scrubbing the table and counters. She opened the windows, washed a pile of Silas's clothes and hung them out to dry, cooked some apples that were about to spoil, and made a kettle of potato soup. Grateful for the mindless work, she did her best to ignore the weakness in her body and the dark detours of her mind. Still, sometimes her dark thoughts nearly brought her to her knees, her grief so overwhelming she wondered how she'd survive.

Later that afternoon, Silas staggered into the house and collapsed on the sofa, drunk again. She got him to eat a bowl of soup, but he refused to talk. Over the next few days, they repeated the same patterns—Silas disappearing for hours and coming home reeking of moonshine and hopelessness; Lena crying herself to sleep at night and working from sunup to sundown.

Along with trying to figure out how they should begin their search and getting the house put back together, she took an inventory of the pantry and springhouse: ten pounds of flour, two pounds of cornmeal, half a pound of bacon, a jar of lard, two dozen eggs, plenty of milk and butter; and in the 'tater hole under the house, the many jars of provisions she and Bonnie had put up earlier in the year. In the garden, the winter squash looked like it would be ready for harvest soon, and the last of the potatoes were still in the earth. Along with a clean home, she had to make sure there was plenty of food for the children. Otherwise, what was the point of going on?

Every night she persuaded Silas to eat more food and, while he was sleeping, she replaced some of his moonshine with water and wild cherry bitters. Once, she even convinced him to take a bath. When the time was right, she would tell him her plan—how, together, they would drive out of the mountains to the nearest city and tell the authorities that their children had been stolen. If no one would help, they would move on to the next city, and the next, until they found someone who would. But first, she had to get Silas to stop drinking so much. And if he refused to take her, she'd figure out how to drive his truck and go alone.

A week after her release from the Colony, while she was carrying a basket of newly harvested squash through the back hallway to be stored in the 'tater hole, the roar of an approaching engine came from the front of the house. At first, she thought it was Silas, coming home early for once—maybe he'd finally listened to her pleas and was ready to look for the children—then she realized the engine was too loud to be his truck. And it sounded like there was more than one. She put down the squash, raced to the front window, and pushed aside the curtain to look out. A massive flatbed truck came up the drive, followed by four more trucks and Sheriff Dixon's paddy wagon. She dropped the curtain and pressed herself against the wall, her heart racing. A rifle still hung above the fireplace, but if she drew a weapon on the sheriff, she'd end up back in the Colony.

Outside, the trucks came to a stop, gears grinding. Heavy doors opened and closed. Footsteps sounded on the porch steps. Someone pounded on the front door.

"Mr. Wolfe," a man shouted, "my name is Mr. Doug Clancy. We're here to move you out."

Lena put a hand over her mouth, swallowing a whimper. Silas had said this day would come. But they couldn't leave. If and when they found Ella, Bonnie, and Jack Henry, they had to bring them back here, where they'd have everything they needed. And if the children were let free or ran away from their new families, how would they find her and Silas? She looked around the cabin, panicked and trying to figure out what to do. Should she run out the back door and hide, or tell the man Silas was not home?

"Mr. Wolfe?" Mr. Clancy shouted again. "Open up!" The door handle rattled. "I'm afraid there's nothing you can do to stop this from happening. The government owns this property now and I'm allowed to break down your door if need be. We really don't want this to get ugly."

Lena edged toward the door on trembling legs. If they were going to break it down, she might as well let them in. She opened the door partway and peered out. "Mr. Wolfe is not here," she said.

In a suit jacket and black fedora, Mr. Clancy studied her, one hand on his hip. "And you are?" he said. Behind him, a dozen men stood next to the vehicles, including Sheriff Dixon and George Pollock.

Lena swore under her breath. She should have run out the back door. She should have hidden in the 'tater hole—anything to avoid George Pollock. "I . . . I am Lena Conti. I work here. And I live here."

"I'm sorry, miss," Mr. Clancy said. "But I'm afraid you don't live here any longer. Please, gather your belongings and come out of the house."

She stepped through the door onto the porch and closed the door behind her. "Please wait until Mr. Wolfe returns. He should be back soon."

Mr. Clancy shook his head. "I'm afraid we need to get started. If indeed Mr. Wolfe is due back soon, we'll still be here. Now please, gather anything that's important to you while you've got the chance."

To her horror, a group of men, two carrying kerosene cans, hurried over to the barn and went inside. Three more made their way over to the sheds.

She shook her head, a hot lump growing in her throat. "You cannot do this," she said. "It is not right. This is Silas's home. It is his children's home. It has been in his family for years. You cannot just take it."

Over at the barn, the main door opened and the men pushed out a horse-drawn wagon. They carried out bridles and harnesses, pitchforks and buckets, and threw them in the wagon bed. One of them led the remaining cow and Ole Sal away from the barn and tied them to a tree.

"What are they doing?" Lena cried. "They cannot take everything!"

Before Mr. Clancy could answer, Silas's truck raced up the drive, dirt and gravel spewing from his back tires. He came to a hard stop next to the flatbed truck and stumbled out of the driver's door, his eyes bloodshot, his hair disheveled. He reached back in the truck, pulled out his rifle, and staggered toward Pollock. Sheriff Dixon drew his revolver, pointed it at Silas, and headed toward him.

"Silas, no!" Lena shouted.

A red flash caught her eye and she looked toward the barn. Fire crawled up one side of the main door and lapped out a window, the dry logs bursting into flames. The men ran out into the dooryard and began pushing the wagon toward the trucks. Silas raised his rifle and pointed it at the men closest to him.

"Get the hell off my land or I'll shoot every last one of y'all!" he yelled. His words were slurred.

"No, you won't, Silas!" Sheriff Dixon shouted back. "You're three sheets to the wind. Now put down the weapon before you do something you'll regret!"

Silas aimed his rifle at the sheriff. "Y'all think you can take my young'uns *and* my house? I'll kill you 'fore I let that happen!"

Lena raced down the steps and hurried toward them, stopping a safe distance away. "Silas, stop!" she shouted. "Remember what you told Jack Henry about guns?"

He ignored her.

The barn fire crackled and popped, filling the air with the smell of burning wood and torched hay. Over by the sheds, men were carrying out tools and shovels and bins and machinery, loading everything in the back of the smaller trucks.

"Put my shit back, you good-for-nothing thieves!" Silas bellowed.

"We're not here to steal your things, Mr. Wolfe," Mr. Clancy replied. "The state sent us to help move out you *and* your belongings. We don't want any trouble."

Silas laughed manically. "If y'all don't want no trouble, you came to the wrong place!"

Frantic, Lena looked back and forth between Sheriff Dixon and Silas. Should she put herself between them? Try to take Silas's rifle?

Just then, a loud crack filled the air and the barn roof caved in on one end. Then, in what seemed like slow motion, the entire building collapsed section by section, sparks and flames flying into the sky, bits and pieces of burning wood breaking away and falling to the ground like fiery leaves. Luckily, Ole Sal and the cow were far enough away to be safe, but Ole Sal brayed and danced, pulling on the rope that held him to the tree, terrified and trying to get free. The cow threw her head up and yanked against her rope, her eyes bulging with fear.

"Y'all sons-a-bitches!" Silas yelled. "Who the hell do you think you are?"

"There's temporary housing down the mountain until the resettlement homes get built," Mr. Clancy said. "We're here to take your belongings there, free of charge."

"I ain't going nowhere," Silas bellowed. "Y'all have to shoot me first."

Over at the paddy wagon, the deputy took a rifle out of the front seat, crouched beside another truck, and came around behind Silas. Lena thought about calling out a warning, but if Silas turned and shot the deputy, he'd be killed or thrown in jail for the rest of his life. And maybe she'd be arrested too. Or sent back to the Colony. All she could do was watch and pray.

"I'm giving you one last warning, Silas," Sheriff Dixon said. "Put down your weapon. This is happening whether you like it or not. The government says you have to vacate your house and there's not a damn thing you can do about it. We don't need anybody getting shot."

Mr. Clancy motioned the men toward the house. "Start loading up." The men hurried up the porch steps and went inside.

"Get the hell out of my house or I'll shoot!" Silas said. He cocked the rifle, still aiming at the sheriff, his face twisting with fury.

"Silas, please!" Lena shouted. "Do as they say!"

"You don't want to do this, Silas," the sheriff said. "Now calm down or you'll end up in jail or worse."

"It'll be worth it to see you and that worthless piece of shit die," Silas said, waving the rifle in Pollock's direction. Pollock ran to the paddy wagon and hid behind it. When two men came out of the house carrying the kitchen table, Silas aimed his gun at them. "Put that back!"

Two more men came out carrying chairs, and Silas fired a shot in the air. Everyone ducked. The deputy ran out from behind a truck and pressed the barrel of his rifle into Silas's back. The sheriff moved forward, his pistol aimed at Silas's head.

"Drop your gun!" Sheriff Dixon shouted.

Silas straightened and lowered his rifle, glaring at the sheriff with rage. The deputy tore the weapon out of Silas's hand, threw it to one side, and grabbed him by the arm. Moving fast, Sheriff Dixon holstered his gun and grabbed Silas's other arm. Together, they tried to yank Silas's arms behind his back, grimacing with the effort. Silas writhed and turned, his face contorted with fury.

"Get off me!" he shouted.

"You're under arrest!" Sheriff Dixon yelled back.

He and the deputy tried to push Silas to the ground, but it was like trying to crush a mountain. Two of the moving men leapt off the porch and ran over to help. The four of them wrestled Silas to his knees but Silas pushed back and tried to straighten, his face dripping with sweat.

"Leave him alone!" Lena cried. "He did as you said! He put down his gun!"

"You stay out of this," Sheriff Dixon said. "Or I'll take you back to the Colony."

Lena stepped back, a jolt of horror hitting her. Now that Silas was being arrested and evicted from his home, she had no place to go, which meant the sheriff could easily have her committed again. No matter how difficult it was to do nothing, she could not interfere.

A third moving man came over to help with Silas and together the five men shoved him into the dirt, scaling his back and clambering on top of him. Silas thrashed and bucked and grunted beneath them, but they managed to hold him down. After Sheriff Dixon and the deputy shackled Silas's wrists with handcuffs, Pollock came out from his hiding place to watch. The deputy ran over to the paddy wagon, opened the back door, and pulled out a coil of rope. The other men yanked Silas to his feet, red-faced and grunting with determination, and dragged him over to the big pine tree. Nauseated and desperate, Lena followed, praying she could talk Silas into cooperating. The men sat him against the tree and tied him to the trunk, wrapping the rope around his heaving chest several times and knotting it securely. When Silas was finally restrained, they fell back, panting and wiping their faces.

Pollock drew closer to Silas, a smirk on his face. "Maybe you should have taken me up on my offer," he said.

Silas thrashed and turned against the rope, glaring at him with murderous, bloodshot eyes. "I'm going to kill you, you bastard!" he roared.

"That'll be mighty hard to do considering where you're going," Sheriff Dixon said. He and Pollock turned and went back to the house to talk to Mr. Clancy, occasionally glancing over their shoulders to make sure Silas stayed tied up. The other men followed.

Lena knelt beside Silas. "I am sorry," she said. "But please do as they say so they will not put you in jail."

"I'm gonna kill every last one of 'em," Silas snarled.

"Then you will never see Bonnie and Jack Henry again," she said.

He gave her a tortured look, darkened by the hardness of scorn and pity. "It don't matter what I do. We ain't never seeing our young'uns again."

She shook her head. "Do not say that. I cannot give up. We will find someone to help us. But I cannot do it alone." She looked toward the house, hiding frustrated tears. She would not let him take away what little hope she had left. At the same time, a cold block of fear settled in her chest. Deep down she knew he was probably right, but hearing him say the words made her feel like throwing up.

While the barn continued to burn and black smoke filled the sky, what seemed like an army of men traipsed in and out of the Wolfes' home, carrying out the sofa and the kitchen hutch, the dressers and the beds, the chairs and the end tables, the sewing and washing machines, then loading it all on the flatbed and trucks. Silas watched in agony, howling and struggling to get loose. Stunned and helpless, Lena wanted to scream at the men, to demand they put everything back and leave the house alone. She wanted to tell them that she and Silas needed to stay in case the children returned. But it would do no good. They were only following orders. When two men carried Ella's crib down the porch steps, she ran over and stopped them long enough to grab Poppy and the soft-edged blanket, then held them to her chest and followed the men to the truck.

"Please, do not take it," she cried. "My daughter needs her bed."

Ignoring her, the men lifted the crib into the truck, balancing it precariously over the arms of a rocking chair, then headed back toward the house. Halfway there, one of them stopped and came back to her.

"Excuse me, ma'am," he said. "I know you're mighty upset, but if you want anything else out of the house, you better get it now. We're almost finished emptying the furniture."

Lena stared at him, her mind suddenly blank. Everything was happening too fast.

"Ma'am?" the man said. "Did you hear me? We ain't loading up the pictures and jugs and things, so if you want those items you need to get them now. Might be a good idea to get the pots and pans too."

Lena blinked as if coming out of a trance, then nodded.

"I figure you might be needing those belongings at your new place," the man said.

"We do not have a new place," she said.

"Sorry to hear that, ma'am. But if you don't mind me asking, where we taking all this furniture?"

"I do not know," she said, her eyes growing moist.

She followed him toward the house. She might not have anyplace to go, but she refused to let every last trace of the Wolfe family be erased. And wherever they ended up—if they ended up anywhere at all—they would need whatever she could save. Dodging two men carrying a chest of drawers, she ran up the porch steps and went inside. Starting upstairs, she took the extra blankets from a closet, packed her and Ella's clothes that hadn't already been carried out in a dresser into her old satchel, and snatched the framed photographs off the wall. Then she grabbed everyone else's clothes, jackets, and winter hats, pulled the thin curtains from the windows and picked up the throw rugs from the floor, piled it all downstairs, and made multiple trips carrying everything outside to Silas's truck.

Panting and out of breath, she went over to Silas. He had stopped fighting against the rope and just leaned back against the tree, broken and tied up like a dog, staring at the house. "I cannot do this alone," she said. "If I get them to untie you, will you help me?"

No response.

"Silas, please. I need help getting everything out of the house."

Still nothing.

"If we find Bonnie and Jack Henry and Ella," she said, "how are we going to take care of them if everything is gone?"

"Everything is already gone," he mumbled.

She pointed at the trucks. "Everything is not gone. Where do you want them to take the furniture?"

"It don't matter."

Fighting the urge to slap him back to his senses, she tried to keep her voice steady. "You cannot just give up," she said. "You must think of your children. You are their father."

He closed his eyes and hung his head, refusing to answer.

She huffed and ran back to the house. In the kitchen, she piled the kettles, frying pans, and other kitchen utensils in the wooden washtub and asked one of the men to take it out to Silas's truck. Down in the 'tater hole, she packed as many jars of food as possible into four wooden crates, carried them up the steps one by one, and took them outside, glass clinking against glass with each hurried step. After emptying as much of the pantry as possible into three wicker baskets, she wrapped the flower-covered dishes from the Sears and Roebuck catalog between washrags and packed them carefully inside a sturdy crate. Then she retrieved the milk, butter, and other items out of the springhouse and put them in the front seat of Silas's truck. When she thought she finally had everything, she collapsed on the ground near Silas, sweating and out of breath.

Meanwhile, Sheriff Dixon and the deputy stood talking to Pollock and Mr. Clancy, every now and then glancing over at Silas. After a few minutes, they went to the trucks. Lena got to her feet and started toward them. If Silas refused to tell them where to take the furniture and other belongings, she would do it for him. The only place she could think of was Teensy and Judd's farm. Unless Mr. Clancy insisted on taking everything off the mountain. Then she had no idea what to say.

Halfway to the trucks, she froze. The moving men were carrying cans of kerosene over to the house, pouring it on the porch, splashing it up on the walls and windowsills. She ran toward them. "No!" she cried. "Please! Do not do that!"

The deputy ran after her, grabbed her by the arms, and held her back. Furious, she yanked out of his grasp and looked back at Silas. Tears were streaming down his dirt-covered face. For a second, she thought about untying him, setting him free to do his will. But Sheriff Dixon would shoot him. Maybe he'd shoot her too. Breathing hard, she looked back at the house. The men threw torches on the porch and the kerosene-soaked wood caught fire in a flash, the red-hot flames cracking and spitting and growing like a living, breathing thing.

Lena cried out and fell to her knees, stunned and helpless and sick. In less than a minute, the entire house was on fire. Thick, black smoke filled the air, windows shattered, and curtains went up in flames. In the blasts of heat, the spoon wind chime rocked and twisted, then fell to the ground, followed immediately by the burning front porch. Then the entire house started to collapse, the wood and metal and glass screaming like a tortured beast.

Chapter 27

Drawn by the billowing smoke, Teensy and Judd came up the drive in their mule-drawn wagon, followed a few minutes later by the Blanchards and the McCauleys, all of them gawking at the burning house and the smoking remnants of the barn, their eyes wide with shock, their faces drawn by misery and the knowledge that their homes could be next. Steering clear of the men and the trucks, they parked their wagons, climbed down, and hurried over to Silas and Lena. Silas showed no signs of acknowledgment, his grief-hollowed eyes staring off in the distance. Lena had seen that blank, lost look before, when peoples' homes and businesses had been bombed out during the war. It was like their minds had been damaged too. And unfortunately, sometimes they did not heal. Teensy, Betty Lee, and Nellie gathered around her.

"You're back," Betty Lee said.

"Silas ain't looking right," Teensy said.

"I reckon he's had quite a shock," Betty Lee said.

"Where's Ella?" Nellie asked.

Lena closed her eyes, her chin trembling, and tried to find

her voice. Then she took a deep breath and said, "I do not know where Ella is. They took her the same day they took Bonnie and Jack Henry."

The women gasped.

"Oh God in heaven," Teensy said. "We was hoping the two of y'all were safe somewhere." She pulled Lena into her arms, hugging her tight. "You poor thing. I'm awful sorry."

Suddenly overcome and weak, Lena leaned into Teensy, worried she might collapse on the ground. Teensy held her up and Betty Lee and Nellie put comforting hands on her back.

"I'm mighty sorry too," Nellie said. "That's just awful."

"I swear," Betty Lee said. "I don't know what in tarnation this world is coming to."

After a few moments, Teensy pulled away and wiped the tears from Lena's cheeks. "Where you been all this time?" she said. "Looking for your girl?"

Lena shook her head. "Miriam Sizer took me to the Virginia State Colony for Epileptics and Feebleminded."

Nellie gaped at the other women. "Ain't that where they sent Jeanie Lambert a few years back? But she never got out."

Betty Lee nodded. "That's the place, all right."

"How'd y'all get out?" Teensy said.

Lena shook her head again, her vision blurred by tears. How could she tell them what she'd been forced to do for freedom? "It does not matter anymore."

Teensy looked at the burning house. "I suppose it don't," she said. "Y'all got other problems now."

With tortured groans, the house's blackened beams and warped hunks of wood buckled in and around the stone foundation, shooting sparks and ashes into the sky. The women took a step back, flickering flames reflected in their eyes.

Teensy turned to Lena. "Did Silas tell y'all everything he did trying to find Bonnie and Jack Henry's whereabouts?"

"No," Lena said. "He has given up."

"Well, sadly it ain't for lack of trying," Teensy said. "That man's been running all over hell's half acre looking for his young'uns. He went to the orphanage down in Staunton, one over in Charlottesville, and every other place he could think of. They just kept telling him to stop looking 'cause he weren't ever getting them back. Sheriff Dixon said he'd never find them and if he didn't quit harassing everyone, they'd throw him in the nuthouse. So Silas went to the governor, even talked to the federal authorities. But no one gave a hoot. They finally told him Bonnie and Jack Henry were adopted by a 'more suitable family,' which don't make a lick a sense to me."

Lena could hardly believe what she was hearing. All this time, Silas had known the children had been given to other people. All this time, he had searched for Bonnie and Jack Henry without any luck. Why hadn't he told her? Was he trying to spare her more pain? And now that she knew the truth, now that she knew he had tried everything but had gotten nowhere, how would she go on? Her legs started to give out. She grabbed Teensy's arm and lowered herself to the ground before she fell.

Teensy knelt beside her. "You all right, darling?"

Lena could only shake her head.

"I reckon she's had a shock too," Betty Lee said. "I'll fetch our jug of white mule." She started toward her wagon.

"No," Lena called after her. "I will be all right."

Betty Lee stopped and turned. "You sure? A couple good swigs will settle you down."

"I am sure," Lena said. If only she could drink enough to erase her misery. But there was no escaping this wretched grief, this horrible, heavy ache in her chest. And keeping her wits about her was already hard enough without moonshine clouding her brain.

Betty Lee returned to where the women stood. "Well, there ain't no shame in it if you change your mind."

"Where you and Silas gonna go now?" Nellie said.

Lena shrugged and glanced over at Silas. He was slumped over completely now, held up by the tight coils of rope around his torso. Judd and the other men were trying to get him to talk, but he looked lifeless. "He has been drinking every day. And I think he needs a doctor."

"I'll fetch Granny Creed," Betty Lee said. She started toward her wagon again, shouting to her husband. "I'm fixing to fetch Granny Creed up from Slaughter Pen Branch and bring her back here."

Her husband raised a hand to let her know he heard.

"Don't be worrying yourself sick now," Teensy said. "I don't know how much longer we got before they take our place too, but we can make room for you and Silas for as long as you got the need."

Lena took Teensy's hand and thanked her, nearly wilting with relief. At least they'd have somewhere to stay until they could figure out what to do next. And if someone from the Colony found her, Teensy could say she was working for her family until Silas got out of jail. Or maybe when they saw the ruins of Silas's house, they'd think Lena was dead. She could only hope.

Teensy stood and helped Lena to her feet, pushing stray strands of hair back from her tear-covered face and wiping the dirt from her dress.

Nellie turned worried eyes on Teensy. "You and Judd got a place down the mountain yet?"

"Judd don't wanna talk about it," Teensy said. "But seeing this ought to change his mind."

Sheriff Dixon started toward them. "Y'all need to clear on out of here," he shouted. "There's nothing more to see."

"There some law against being here supporting our neighbor?" Judd McDaniel called back.

"Why don't y'all untie Silas?" Mr. Blanchard said. "He done suffered enough!"

"Mr. Wolfe is under arrest for interfering with a state order and for aiming a weapon at an officer of the law," the sheriff said. "And unless you all head on home, I'll arrest you too."

The men shook their heads in dismay and anger. Judd gave Silas's shoulder another shake, trying to get him to wake up, but got no response. Gesturing for Teensy to come with him, he started toward their wagon.

"Wet your apron in the stream and meet me over by Silas," Teensy instructed Nellie.

Nellie did as she was asked while Teensy and Lena went over to Silas. Teensy put a hand under his chin and lifted his face. His eyes were open but unfocused. When Nellie brought over the wet apron, Teensy wiped the sweat and ashes from Silas's face.

"I know it don't seem like it now," Teensy said. "But everything's gonna come out in the warsh. Soon as that no-account sheriff sets you free, you can stay with me and Judd, and together we'll figure out what's next."

Silas said nothing.

"Y'all listening?" Teensy said. She patted his cheek. "Come on, Silas. I know you're in there."

No response.

Worry creased Teensy's brow. "I reckon Granny Creed's the only one who can help him now," she said. She turned to Lena. "I'll have Judd tell these men to bring the furniture over to our place and then we'll head on home. I got a warshtub ready for hot water and a kettle of vittles on the stove. There ain't nothing more you can do here."

Lena shook her head. "I cannot leave now."

"You sure?" Teensy said. "Judd can go down to the jailhouse and check on Silas in the morning. There's no need for you to stay here and watch any longer than you already done. Ain't that right, Nellie?"

Nellie nodded.

Lena was far from sure. She wanted to leave with Teensy, longed to run from this horrible, tragic scene. But she had to stay with Silas until Granny Creed came or Sheriff Dixon took him away. Because it was the right thing to do. And it was what Bonnie and Jack Henry would have wanted. "Thank you," she said. "But I will wait and see what will happen to Silas."

"Suit yourself," Teensy said. "Just know it'll be a bit before Granny Creed gets here. Slaughter Pen Branch is up yonder a ways."

"It is fine," Lena said.

"I reckon Betty Lee can drop you off at our place on her way taking Granny Creed back home."

Lena nodded, grateful to Teensy for not forcing the issue.

And then, one by one, the McDaniels and McCauleys, along with Betty Lee's husband, climbed up on their wagons, turned their mules and horses toward home, and left Wolfe Hollow Farm for the last time. The bulk of the house was gone now, collapsed into a black pile of burning beams and smoldering timbers, both sad and happy memories made by the Wolfe family within its walls reduced to nothing but rubble. The only thing left standing was the massive fireplace and chimney, where flames scorched the gray stones and devoured the rest of the mantel.

Satisfied that the McDaniels and McCauleys were leaving, Sheriff Dixon went over to the smoking remains of the barn, where the deputy and Pollock watched as the men who had emptied the house worked with shovels and picks to break up the bigger pieces. Lena got a bucket from Silas's truck, filled it with cool water from the stream, and carried it over to Silas, who was still sagging forward with his head down, his eyes closed. She soaked the edge of her apron, pushed his head back, wiped his face again, then tried to get him to drink from her cupped hand. The water ran out of his mouth, down his beard and shirt, useless. He looked dead. Maybe his broken heart had given out.

"Silas," she said. "You need to wake up." She patted his cheeks, lightly at first, then a little harder.

Footsteps approached. It was Sheriff Dixon and his deputy, with Pollock following a few feet behind. Lena gently let Silas's head back down, taking her hand from his forehead.

"He awake?" Sheriff Dixon said.

She shook her head.

The sheriff kicked Silas's foot. It flopped to one side. He grabbed Silas's hair with a rough hand and lifted his head. Silas's mouth fell open, his eyes still closed, his features unresponsive. Sheriff Dixon let go of his hair and let his head drop.

"We're gonna untie you now, Silas," Sheriff Dixon said. He drew his pistol and pointed it at him. "So don't try anything stupid."

Silas was still as a stone.

The deputy started to untie the rope.

"He is not well," Lena said. "He needs help."

"He'll come around," the sheriff said.

"Granny Creed is on her way," she said. "She will be here soon."

"There's no time for your witch doctor," the sheriff said. "He's going to jail."

"But why?" she cried. "He was only protecting his home. Would you not do the same?"

"If you'd like a ride to the Colony," Sheriff Dixon said, "there's room in the paddy wagon for you too."

Lena bristled, her temples pulsing in and out, but said nothing.

"That's what I thought," the sheriff said.

With every loop of rope the deputy uncoiled, Silas slumped further forward. Once he was completely untied, he fell over, his head hitting the ground with a hard thud.

"He dead?" Pollock said.

The deputy put his hands on his hips and looked down at Silas, the rope dangling from one hand. "Darned if I know," he said.

Lena knelt beside Silas and shook his shoulder. "Silas? Wake up!" His shoulder flopped back and forth, rocking his limp body. With great effort, she pushed him over onto his back and put her ear to his chest. He was still breathing.

Still pointing his pistol at Silas, Sheriff Dixon drew closer. He kicked Silas in the ribs. Silas's body jerked to one side, but he did not wake. The sheriff lowered his weapon. "Looks like you boys'll have to carry him to the truck," he said. "Might need a few men to help."

When Sheriff Dixon started to holster his pistol, Silas suddenly opened his eyes and jumped to his feet, shoving Lena out of his way. He grabbed the sheriff's gun and aimed it at him, gripping it with both hands. The sheriff and deputy backed away, their faces pale, their arms out as if ready to fend off a wild animal. Pollock turned and ran.

"You don't want to do this, Silas," the sheriff said.

"The hell I don't," Silas snarled.

"Silas, please," Lena said. "Do not shoot anyone."

"We can work this out," the sheriff said. "Help you find a new place to live and—"

"I ain't looking for a new place to live!" Silas shouted. Spittle flew from his lips. "I want my land back! I want my young'uns back!" He waved the gun back and forth between Sheriff Dixon and the deputy, hot tears streaming down his furious face.

"Let me see what I can find out about your children," Sheriff Dixon said. "I'll find out where they are."

"Y'all are lying!" Silas screamed. "I tried everything! Talked to everyone! They ain't telling me nothing! They just keep saying my young'uns is better off someplace else. They just keep saying they're gone!"

"I know, but maybe I can—" the sheriff started.

"You can't do a damn thing," Silas said. He took a step toward Sheriff Dixon, the pistol aimed at his head.

The sheriff raised his hands. "Yes . . . yes, I can," he said. "I'll make some calls and—"

"Liar!" Silas said. "I hope you bastards rot in hell."

Then Silas put the gun under his own chin and pulled the trigger.

The gunshot ricocheted off the hills and sent a flock of birds from a nearby tree into the sky. It bounced around inside Lena's head, making it impossible to hear anything else. In what seemed like slow motion, a bright blossom of red spurted from Silas's head, a spray of blood and brains as he jerked back and collapsed on the ground. Lena shrieked and fell to her knees, her hands over her face, her sobs stealing the air from her lungs.

Chapter 28

Richmond, Virginia
October 1948

After bagging five pounds of potatoes and half a dozen onions for her last customer of the day, Lena hung her apron on a hook in the back of the vegetable stall at the Sixth Street Market, smoothed the front of her dress, and made her way around the front counter. Normally, she would have spent part of the day making deliveries—her routine had been unchanged for the past few years—but with the first annual Tobacco Festival in town for the weekend, an event that included a parade, a talent show, a beauty contest, and numerous street performances, the market had been packed all day and the deliveries had been moved to Monday morning.

"See you tomorrow, Teensy," she said.

Teensy closed the cash register and frowned at her. "Tomorrow? You ain't going to the Grand Ball tonight?"

Avoiding Teensy's stare, Lena pretended to straighten a counter display. "I don't think so," she said.

"What do y'all mean you don't think so?" Teensy said. "Of

course you're going. The Tobacco Festival is the biggest thing to happen to this place in a coon's age and everybody's going to the ball. Don't you want to see Frank Sinatra crown the new Tobacco Queen?"

Lena sighed. After all these years, she still hated disappointing Teensy. Judd too, for that matter. When she had no place to go after the state burned down Wolfe Hollow Farm and Silas shot himself, they had taken her in without question, despite losing their own home a few weeks later too, along with the hundreds of other mountain families evicted from their land to make room for the Shenandoah National Park. Starting over had been one heartbreaking challenge after another, including the resettlement houses not being built on time, Judd and Teensy not qualifying for a mortgage, and no one being able to find work due to the insidious belief that mountain folk were ignorant and backward.

Nevertheless, through it all, Teensy and Judd had continued to treat Lena like part of the family, insisting she stay with them and their four girls—at the time, their daughters were six, eight, nine, and ten—in a one-bedroom apartment near Lynchburg. The first few years had been rough, to say the least, and only got worse after the stock market crash, but eventually Judd found work at a cereal factory. Teensy, Lena, and the girls mended clothes for money, and somehow, they'd made it through. Things turned around during the war when they moved to Richmond, where Teensy took a job as a switchboard operator, Judd went to work welding bomb heads, and Lena found work as a cast-maker in a foundry. And when she was finally able to stand on her own two feet, Lena rented a room in Mrs. Tucker's Boarding House, which was around the corner from her job.

One by one, the McDaniel girls went off and got married, and after scrimping and saving for a few years, Teensy and Judd bought a farm on the outskirts of the city, where they returned to their roots by making a living off the land. Then, when the war was over and Lena lost her job at the foundry, Teensy and Judd came to her rescue again by offering her work at their vegetable stand, McDaniels' Fruit & Vegetables, which quickly became one of the busiest spots in the Sixth Street Market.

For Lena, selling produce in an open-air market was certainly better than working with trowels and shovels in the hot and dirty foundry, where her back hurt, her arms ached, and her mouth tasted like metal. Not to mention, at the market, she was forced to be friendly and talk to the customers, which gave her less time to think. The only downfall was that sometimes she thought she'd lose her mind studying every unfamiliar young woman who walked past the stand or stopped to buy something. For the most part, not giving up hope that she would see Ella again felt right and good, but at other times, it felt like an unhealthy obsession. If only she could silence the desperate need to know where her daughter was, and if she was happy and healthy. But it was impossible. All too often she found herself staring at a fair-haired young woman with blue eyes, certain she was Ella, only to have that certainty fade to doubt, and then utter misery. She thought she saw Miriam Sizer once too, on the sidewalk outside the market, marching along with her purse swinging like a pendulum from her arm. She ran after her and grabbed her by the shoulder, only to find a stout, wide-eyed stranger, startled and befuddled by Lena's sudden intrusion.

For years, she tried to live some sort of life without Ella, always hoping against hope that she would find her somehow, some way, someday. But her lost daughter haunted her life, flickering into her memory and clouding her thoughts with a grief so deep she sometimes teetered on the edge of madness.

Every clue to Ella's whereabouts had led to a dead end. Along with writing a string of unanswered letters to orphanages and institutions, explaining her situation, praying someone would know something or be sympathetic to her plight, she and Teensy had talked to other displaced mountain folk whose children had been taken to see if they'd had any luck. No one had. Some had lost older family members around the same time but had never been able to track them down either. Thinking about all the women and girls she'd seen at the Colony, Lena couldn't help wondering how many others, not just from the Blue Ridge but across all Virginia, were looking for vanished family members too. Eventually she learned that boys and men were also held at the Colony, which made her wonder if the institution was even bigger than she thought. Her greatest fear was that Ella, Bonnie, and Jack Henry had been sent to another state, or even across the country.

Over the years, she'd kept in touch with Enzo, writing to let him know her new address every time she moved, explaining—without going into too much detail—what had befallen her and Ella while also making sure he understood she was doing everything in her power to find her. Even after he married Frau Müller's granddaughter, Suzanne, she hoped he would still make it to America someday. She sent a few dollars when his two children were born, a sympathy card when Frau Müller died, and they exchanged greeting cards on birthdays and Christmas, but her memories of her brother—and Germany—felt like a dream, or another lifetime ago. Of course she'd worried endlessly about Enzo during the war, especially after his wife wrote saying he'd been drafted as a foot soldier into the Wehrmacht. Suzanne wrote again when Enzo came home on leave, emaciated, filthy, and exhausted, but after that, Lena received nothing, not a card, or a note, or a letter. Eventually, she grew convinced that they'd all been killed and she went through a period of mourning. But then, to her great relief, at the end of 1945, Enzo wrote saying he'd been captured by the English and held in a POW camp until a few months after the war. His children and wife had escaped Berlin; he had finally found them living in a farmhouse with Suzanne's relatives. After that, he wrote several times a year to let her know they were raising pigs and growing vegetables and doing as well as could be expected.

In the meantime, everywhere Lena went, the open-air markets and trolleys, the alleyways and crowded streets, she looked for Ella. Everything made her think of her—a rag doll, a fresh pear, a ladybug, the chickens on Teensy and Judd's farm. But like Bonnie and Jack Henry, it seemed Ella had disappeared from the face of the earth. Every day Lena was left wanting and sad. Even now, she could still picture her daughter sleeping in her arms, her little legs pulled up to her belly, her soft-skinned face, her long eyelashes like feathers on her cheeks. She could almost feel her small hand inside hers, the warmth of her palm, her soft, satiny skin. If she'd known back then what she knew now, she never would have left Germany. The guilt of losing Ella, and her failure to find out what had happened to her, felt like a bleeding hole inside her heart, a raw wound constantly ripped open by the slightest reminder of all she had been through and all she had lost.

And today had been one of those days.

Earlier that morning at the fruit and vegetable stand, when a young mother carrying a blond-haired, blue-eyed toddler stopped to admire the display of shiny apples, Lena faltered and dropped a customer's change. The little girl could have been Ella's twin, and the young mother looked like an older version of them both. Lena had to hold the counter to steady herself before she could retrieve the coins, falling helplessly back to the day Miriam Sizer had ripped her baby girl from her arms. Still staring at the woman and her toddler, she absently handed the customer her change.

"Excuse me," the customer said. "May I have my beets too?"

Lena blinked, confused.

"You didn't give me my beets," the woman said, pointing at the cash register behind Lena.

Lena turned to look. The bag of beets still sat on the counter. She grabbed them and handed them to the customer, praying the young woman was still looking at the apples. "I'm sorry," she said, forcing a smile.

The customer took the beets and hurried into the crowd. The young woman started to walk away too.

"Wait," Lena called out, louder than intended.

The young woman stopped and turned, frowning. "Me?"

Lena nodded. "Yes," she said. Breathless and more than a little overwhelmed, she swallowed the tightness in her throat. "I'm sorry, I didn't mean to startle you." She picked up an apple and held it out to her. "I was wondering if your little girl would like to try an apple. They're fresh-picked this morning."

To Lena's relief, the woman smiled and returned to the stand. "They're beautiful," she said. "Are you sure it's all right?"

Lena nodded. "Of course," she said, trying to keep her voice steady. "My treat." The young woman—who looked to be about twenty, the age Ella would be now—was a perfect mix of Lena and Enzo. Lena racked her brain, trying to come up with a question that sounded casual, some way of discovering who she was without prying.

"How kind of you," the young woman said. "Thank you." She gave the apple to the toddler, who wrapped her chubby fingers around it and grinned at Lena. Then the young woman started to leave again.

Fighting the urge to rush around the counter and grab her by the arm before she disappeared, Lena called after her. "Excuse me," she said. "I don't mean to be rude, but you remind me of someone I used to know. Is your name Ella, by any chance?"

The woman shook her head. "I'm sorry, no. It's Camille."

"Please forgive me," Lena managed. "But I had to ask."

"It's fine," Camille said. "No harm done."

Lena's mind raced. She couldn't let them go. Someone could have changed Ella's name. "You have a beautiful little girl," she said.

"Thank you, but she's not mine. This is my sister, Olivia."

"Well, the two of you certainly resemble each other."

"That's what everyone says," Camille said. "But she really looks more like our mother."

Lena forced herself to keep smiling. The chances of Ella's adoptive mother looking just like her were small to nonexistent. But she was not ready to rule it out completely. "How nice. Is your mother here at the market with you?"

"No, she's back at the hotel, but she's meeting us here soon. We're just taking a stroll to give her a few minutes of peace and quiet."

"I take it you're in town for the festival?"

"Yes," Camille said. "And as much as I'd love to buy some of your wonderful produce, I'm afraid we're not returning home for another week, so I wouldn't want it to spoil. But thank you again for the apple."

"You're welcome," Lena said. "If you don't mind me asking, where is home? There have been so many people from out of town this weekend. It's interesting to learn where everyone comes from for the festival."

"South Boston," Camille said. "Did you know that's where the Tobacco Festival originated?"

Lena shook her head. "I didn't know that," she said. "You came all the way from Massachusetts for the festival?" *Maybe they did send the children out of state.*

Camille laughed. "Oh goodness, no. South Boston, Virginia. It's only a half a day's drive from here."

Heat rose in Lena's cheeks, partly from embarrassment and partly from renewed hope. South Boston was even closer to Lynchburg—where the Colony was—than Richmond. "Oh yes," she said. "How silly of me. I wasn't thinking clearly. I'll bet they don't grow tobacco in Boston, Massachusetts."

Camille laughed again. "I'm sure they don't."

"Do you have a lot of family in South Boston?"

"Yes," Camille said. "My parents were both born there, along with about a hundred aunts and uncles and cousins."

"Were you born there too?"

As soon as the words left her mouth, Lena realized her question sounded odd.

A strange look crossed Camille's face. Before she could reply, an older woman came out of the crowd and took her arm.

"There you are," the woman said. "I've been looking everywhere for you two."

"I'm sorry," Camille said. "I stopped to admire these beautiful apples and this lovely woman . . ." She looked at Lena. "I'm sorry, I don't know your name."

"Magdalena Conti. Everyone calls me Lena."

"Lena gave Olivia an apple to try," Camille said.

"That's very nice," the woman said. "But we have to get going. You need to get back to the hotel and get ready for tonight." She took the toddler from Camille. "Come to Mommy, sweetie pie."

Camille was right; Olivia looked just like her mother. And seeing the three of them together, Lena could see the differences between the mother and Camille. There was still a chance she could be Ella.

Camille smiled at her. "Thank you again," she said. And then she was gone.

After she left, Lena sat down hard on the stool behind the counter, her knees quivering and her heart pounding. Hundreds of young women visited the vegetable stand every week, some who certainly could have passed for her daughter, but none had ever reminded her so much of Ella. And Lena had let her get away. But what else could she have done? There'd been no way to make her stay any longer. And how could she have learned the truth anyway, especially if Ella had no idea who she really was?

For the rest of the day, Lena had thought nonstop about Camille, her heart breaking over and over again. And now, Teensy wanted her to go to the Grand Ball, but it was the last thing she wanted to do.

"I don't have anything to wear," Lena said.

"Hogwarsh," Teensy said. "Y'all can borrow that green cocktail dress from our youngest, Janie Sue. It fits you perfectly and I guarantee Howard Branscum will take a shine to it." She gave Lena a wink.

Lena rolled her eyes. "I have no interest in Mr. Howard Branscum, and you know it."

"Yeah, I know it," Teensy said. "But that don't mean I understand it. He's got a real steady job over at the school and he's got a nice place over on Simmons Street. And Judd said he was asking about you just the other day."

Lena scoffed. The last thing she needed was the obligation to explain herself to a man. There had been other interested suitors over the years, but she had turned them all down, for a number of reasons. For one thing, she still had little trust in men after Ella's father had sweet-talked her into his bed by promising marriage, then deserted her without so much as a goodbye. Back then, when she first learned she was pregnant, she had been thrilled about becoming a mother until she realized she'd been abandoned and would be struggling, with little to no resources, to raise a baby on her own. She did not want to be hurt again when a prospective spouse left because she could *not* give him children, even if it meant spending the rest of her life alone. Teensy and Judd were her family now and, when they came to visit, their daughters and grandchildren felt like her own. And once every couple of years she and Teensy made the trip back to Lynchburg to visit Betty Lee, Nellie, and the other women who had been removed from Old Rag.

"Well, even if y'all ain't interested in Howard Branscum," Teensy said, "there'll be a mess of other fellas there looking for a dance. And you could use a little fun in your life."

"I have not danced since I was a little girl and I'm not about to start again now. Besides, I don't know any of the latest steps."

"Come on," Teensy whined. "Everybody and their brother's gonna be there. People are coming from miles around and y'all are gonna just sit home alone?"

Lena opened her mouth to make another excuse, then suddenly remembered Camille and Olivia's mother saying they needed to "get ready for tonight." Maybe Camille was going to the Grand Ball too. Maybe Lena could talk to her again.

"All right," Lena said. "I'll go, but I'm not dancing with anyone."

Chapter 29

Standing alone near the back wall of the music arena while Teensy and Judd danced to "Texarkana Baby," Lena chewed her lip and scanned the crowd for what seemed like the thousandth time, searching for Camille. Walking around the packed arena and moving among the partygoers would have covered more ground, but she'd already run into Howard Branscum twice. And refusing his invitation to join him on the dance floor a third time was something she'd rather not do.

Up on stage, the musicians, Eddy Arnold and His Tennessee Plowboys, had the crowd in the palm of their hands. When the song ended, Teensy and Judd came back to where she stood, laughing and breathless.

Judd wiped his brow and looked at Lena. "I'm fixing to fetch us a couple more beers. Want another one?"

"No, thanks," Lena said.

"Hurry it up, Judd," Teensy said. "I'm about worn slap out and dying of thirst." She raked her fingers through her hair and laughed. "Oh my Lord! I ain't hoofed it like that since I don't know when! Now, why ain't y'all out there enjoying yourself a little? I saw Howard asking you to dance."

"I told you I'm not dancing, especially with him."

"Oh, horsefeathers," Teensy said. "A little amusement would do you good. And just dancing with a fella don't mean you gotta marry him."

Lena gave her a weak smile. She hadn't admitted that the real reason she had come to the ball was to look for Ella—there had been too many disappointments over the years, and she was reluctant to ruin Teensy's good time—but she'd been there for over two hours and there was no trace of Camille. Maybe she was wasting her time. The odds of finding a woman she'd only briefly spoken to in this enormous crowd were small, let alone the odds of that woman—Camille—being Ella. Between the long day at the stand and getting her hopes up only to have them shattered again, she was exhausted and wanted to go back to her room at Mrs. Tucker's. "I think I'm going home," she said.

Teensy pouted. "Just stay a little longer," she begged. "They're gonna name the new queen soon."

On stage, Eddy Arnold finished a guitar solo and stepped up to the microphone. "Ladies and gentlemen," he said, "thank you so much for your wonderful hospitality tonight. We have a couple more songs this evening and then Mr. Frank Sinatra is going to crown your new Tobacco Queen. But first, let's have another look at the beautiful contestants, shall we?" He looked off to his right and extended his arm, welcoming the young women onto the stage. Smiling and waving, the contestants strolled out, all of them covered with tobacco leaves made to look like evening gowns. Everyone broke out in applause.

"Aren't they lovely?" Eddy Arnold said. "And now, let's give a big round of applause to last year's reigning Tobacco Queen—from South Boston, Miss Camille Baker!"

Goose bumps rose on Lena's skin. No wonder she had not found Camille out on the dance floor—she'd been backstage getting ready. Lena stood on her tiptoes, looking over heads and shoulders toward the stage. Camille walked out in a tiara and chiffon ball gown, looking like a princess in a fairy tale.

Lena started toward her, pushing her way through the clapping, whistling crowd. She had no idea what she would do or say once she got to the stage; she only knew she had to talk to Camille again.

Teensy called after her. "Where in the devil are y'all going, Lena?"

Lena ignored her and kept moving, zigzagging through the excited throng. The beauty pageant contestants were already starting to exit stage left, followed by Camille. Lena craned her neck to see where they were going, praying she could find a way to get to her.

"Like I said," Eddy Arnold said into the microphone, "it won't be too much longer before we find out which of these beauties is your new Tobacco Queen. In the meantime, I'd like you to give a warm welcome to a young lady who opened for us at the Virginia State Fair last summer. She's a new voice on the country music scene, and me and my Plowboys are going to accompany her tonight as she sings a couple of her favorite songs. Please give a big round of applause for Bobbi Jo Gately!"

Apologizing as she pushed past the tightly-packed audience, Lena made her way toward the left side of the stage, hoping to see where the contestants were going. A stern-faced man stood in front of a floor-level door several yards away, his arms crossed, watchful eyes on the crowd. When he saw Lena coming, he blocked her way.

Winded, she forced herself to smile at him, trying to look harmless. "Does this door lead backstage?" She had to shout to be heard above the clapping.

"You're not allowed through there," he shouted back.

"Please," she said. "I need to speak to Camille Baker. She's a friend of mine."

He shook his head. "Sorry."

"But it's an emergency. I have to talk to her!"

Behind her, the crowd stopped clapping and grew quiet. A female voice spoke into the microphone.

"Thanks so much, everybody," the voice said. "I want y'all to know I owe my love of music to my late momma, and I'd like to begin with a real old song that used to be her favorite. I changed it up a little bit, but I hope you still enjoy it."

Then the singer's voice came out through the speakers and filled the hall, and Lena froze.

> "I asked her if she loved me,
> She said she loved me some.
> I throwed my arms around her,
> Like a grapevine 'round a gum."

In what felt like slow motion, Lena turned to look at the singer, certain her ears or the acoustics of the arena were playing tricks on her. The melody of the song was slightly slower and the accompaniments had been modernized, but the refrain was unmistakable. And so was the voice, sweet and pure, with a distinctive touch of Blue Ridge Mountain twang.

> "Cindy in the summer,
> Cindy in the fall,
> If I don't get Cindy,
> I'll not marry at all."

Overcome by the memory of a hot summer day in the mountains, Lena stood stunned and staring, the woman's voice echoing through her heart and mind, giving her chills. Clear as a bell, she could picture Bonnie happily singing to Ella, and then her face falling when Silas yelled at her to stop.

A hand on her arm snapped her out of her trance.

"Are you all right, miss?" the man guarding the door said.

Lena took a step back, unsure for a moment where she was

or how she had gotten there. She nodded and stared up at the singer again, certain her desperate mind was playing tricks on her. Then she moved toward the center of the stage, shouldering past happy couples smiling up at the band. Stopping directly in front of the singer, she prayed the person she thought she was seeing was really there. An orchestra railing separated the dance floor from the edge of the stage by several yards, but Lena was close enough now to get a better look.

The flaxen pigtails and girlish features were gone, replaced by golden curls, a long, elegant neck, and cheekbones angled by maturity. But Lena knew that face. And when the singer turned to look out at one side of the audience, Lena was certain. No one else would have noticed the faint outline of a daisy-shaped scar below a hint of pink blush on the singer's cheek, but she did.

It was Bonnie.

Shaking uncontrollably, Lena tried to understand the reality of what was happening. Along with searching for Ella all these long years, keeping an eye out for Bonnie and Jack Henry was second nature. But she never expected to find one of them like this—up on a stage in front of hundreds of people. Maybe she was dreaming.

Thank God she had seen Camille at the stand.

Thank God she had come to the ball to look for her.

Except . . .

What if Bonnie had forgotten her? What if she had no memory of her real identity? What if she was a mirage, manifested by wishful thinking? For a moment the floor seemed to shift beneath Lena's feet, the walls starting to pitch and sway. She grabbed the orchestra railing with both hands, anchoring herself in place.

When the song came to an end, the audience clapped and Bonnie smiled and bowed, saying "thank you" into the microphone. Her smile was unmistakable. It had to be her. It just had to be. Bonnie held up a hand to quiet the crowd, then spoke into the microphone again.

"My next number is an original," she said. "I hope y'all like it."

Lena lifted a hand to get her attention. "Bonnie!" she shouted. "Over here! It's me, Lena!"

But the band had started playing and Bonnie closed her eyes, waiting for the introduction to end. Lena kept her hand in the air, every ounce of her attention locked on Bonnie, as if she could communicate with her using her mind. When Bonnie started to sing, she opened her eyes again, but it was as if she were somewhere else, lost in the words to the song.

> "Though memories call my name,
> The future beckons me on
> While my heart aches for the familiar,
> And the place I once belonged.
>
> For there's something about the comfort
> Of the place where you are raised,
> And the people who knew you best,
> Even in your darkest days.
>
> How I miss our mountain home,
> Where the air was fresh and clear,
> Where the rivers and streams ran free,
> How I wish I could go back there.
>
> But it is not to be,
> Because all that remains,
> Are the faces and names
> Of the betrayed and lost children of Shenandoah."

The heartbreak in Bonnie's voice made Lena's eyes flood. Clearly, she remembered who she was and where she came from. But what else did she remember? Did she remember her and Ella? After all, they'd only spent a few months together. And who knew what she'd gone through since? Starting over with a new family at ten years old had to be beyond difficult, to say the least. Who knew how she'd been treated, or if she'd ever seen her brother again?

When Bonnie reached the chorus a second time, Lena thought about waving again, hoping Bonnie would notice her, but she needed to let her finish the song without any distractions. Bonnie deserved every second of this moment, every second of the audience standing in stunned silence, awed by the raw emotion in her voice. Finally, at the end of the last lyric, Bonnie looked right at Lena as if drawn by an invisible force.

Lena searched her face for recognition, for a sign that she knew who Lena was, but there was none.

Suddenly, Lena's head filled with the drumming of her panicked heart. She had to talk to her. But how? And what if Bonnie left the arena before Lena could get to her? She glanced at the security man blocking the doorway to the left of the stage. Even if she could distract him, the entryway was probably locked. Another man guarded the stage to the right of the orchestra pit.

When Bonnie finished singing, the crowd erupted in applause, whistling and hollering. Bonnie thanked them, waved, and started to leave the stage. Eddy Arnold came forward and stepped up to the microphone again.

Lena took a deep breath.

It was now or never.

She crawled over the railing and jumped into the orchestra pit, knocking over a chair and nearly tumbling forward when she landed. Seeing what she'd done, one of the men guarding the doors climbed over the railing and grabbed her before she could reach the stage. She struggled to break free of his grip but he held on tight.

"Bonnie!" she shouted.

Eddy Arnold noticed the commotion and laughed nervously into the microphone. "Say now, Bobbi Jo," he said. "It looks like you got yourself an overly eager fan."

Bonnie slowed and glanced over her shoulder, still smiling. At first, she seemed amused, but then she turned, concern lining her face.

"Bonnie Wolfe!" Lena shouted. "It's me, Lena!"

The security man yanked on her shoulder, trying to drag her away.

Bonnie stopped for a minute, unsure, then hurried over to the edge of the stage with a strange look of curiosity and confusion.

Eddy Arnold pushed the microphone aside to address her. "What are you doing?" he said under his breath. "Let the hired men take care of her."

Ignoring him, Bonnie knelt down and spoke to the security man. "It's all right. Y'all can let her go."

"Are you sure, Miss Gately?" the man said.

"Yes," Bonnie said. "There ain't no need to manhandle her."

Eddy Arnold laughed into the microphone again. "Well, it looks like we've got a little holdup on our hands. But that's why we all love Bobbi Jo. She's a true country sweetheart. Ain't that right, folks?"

The audience laughed and clapped and whistled.

Reluctantly, the man let go of Lena's arm.

Bonnie looked at her with troubled eyes. "You all right, sugar? I appreciate your excitement and all, but y'all can't be out here causing trouble like this. How about I give you an autograph after the show?"

Lena's heart dropped. Even eye to eye, Bonnie had no idea who she was. Then again, it shouldn't have been a surprise. Twenty years of grief and worry had given Lena an early start on gray hair and wrinkles. Sometimes she barely recognized herself. "Bonnie," she said, her voice tight with emotion, "don't you remember me?"

Bonnie frowned and edged closer, studying Lena's face for what felt like forever. "Y'all look familiar," she said. "But I'll be darned if I can place where I've seen you before." Before Lena could reply, Bonnie turned toward the security man. "Bring her to my dressing room."

Chapter 30

Backstage, Bonnie led Lena down a narrow hallway, past clothes racks and music stands, stagehands and tittering beauty pageant contestants in tobacco leaf gowns. Near the end of the hall, she took her into a dressing room and closed the door behind them. When she turned to face Lena, her cheeks were flushed, her eyes eager.

"Now I reckon I should know y'all from somewhere," she said. "But I'm having trouble remembering who you are. How in the heck do you know my real name? Did you know my father?"

Lena nodded, a hard knot forming in her throat. "I took care of you and Jack Henry for a while when you were children."

Bonnie furrowed her brow. "Up in Wolfe Holler?"

Lena nodded again, fighting the impulse to bombard her with a million questions, at the same time terrified she'd have no answers. If Bonnie couldn't remember who Lena was, how could she remember Ella? "I was there when you fell out of the haymow at the McDaniels' farm. That's how you got that scar on your face. Do you remember that?"

Bonnie thought for a moment. Then her brows shot up and she grabbed Lena's hands. "Oh my God! *Lena?*"

Lena nearly wilted with relief. "Yes," she said. "I'm so happy you remember me."

"Of course I remember y'all. Sorry it took me a bit, but it's been a few years. I'll never forget how y'all sang my momma's favorite song to me while Granny Creed stitched me up."

"And now you're a famous singer," Lena said. "I always said you had a beautiful voice."

"Y'all did?"

Lena nodded, smiling a weak but real smile. "All the time. And you always said your momma taught you how to sing. I hope you know how proud she'd be seeing you up on that stage."

Bonnie's eyes grew glassy. "I think she would be too."

Lena reached out to touch Bonnie's face with gentle fingers. "After you got hurt, I changed your bandage and put salve on your cheek for weeks. The scar is hardly noticeable now, but that's how I knew for sure it was you."

"I thought Granny Creed did that," Bonnie said.

"No, it was me," Lena said. Then she dropped her gaze, suddenly overcome with guilt and shame. "I'm sorry for not doing a better job of protecting you."

Bonnie laughed. "There ain't nothing for y'all to be sorry for. It was my own dang fault for not watching my step in that mow."

Lena looked up at her, tears stinging her eyes. "That's not what I mean," she said. "I'm sorry for not being able to stop the sheriff and his men from taking you."

With that, Bonnie's face fell, as if she'd suddenly realized she had no idea who Lena was after all. "Taking me? What in tarnation are y'all talking about?"

"You don't remember? They took you and Jack Henry. And that horrible Miriam Sizer gave them my Ella too."

Bonnie frowned, shaking her head. "I remember fighting to get away from the sheriff 'cause we didn't want to go, but we weren't *taken*. Daddy was a drunk. He got rid of us so he could sell the house and land."

Lena grabbed Bonnie's hands. "That's not true! They called your father unfit and said he didn't have the means to raise you right. They said you needed to be brought up by a 'more suitable family.' But they only did that so the state could steal your family's land to put in the park. Don't you remember your father telling you to hide when the sheriff came?"

"I remember him telling us to hide, but that's because he was making moonshine and he owed people money."

"Who told you that?"

"Everybody," Bonnie said. "The sheriff. The people at the orphanage. The people who took me in."

Anger welled up in Lena's throat. "That is a lie. Your father wanted you to hide from the sheriff because he knew someone might take you. He would have done anything to keep you safe!"

Bonnie's eyes filled, her chin trembling. "How . . . how do y'all know?"

"Because *I was there*," Lena said. "Don't you remember? I saw and heard everything. I was there when they took you and Jack Henry and . . . and Ella."

"I remember y'all tried to stop them, but there was nothing you could do because Daddy was the one who told them to take us. And they took Ella by mistake 'cause they thought she was our sister."

Lena shook her head furiously back and forth. "More lies. They took her because they said I was feebleminded and living in sin with your father. And because I wouldn't work for the man who helped take your father's land."

Confusion and pain muddied Bonnie's eyes. "Are y'all sure you didn't confuse what they were saying?"

"Of course I'm sure," Lena said. "I know exactly what they said. I know exactly what happened and what they did. They stole other children too, not just you. They took the Corbin boys. And they put Arlene and Dice Hoy in the state asylum. They did it so they could take their land."

Bonnie went over to a chair and sat down hard. "Oh my God," she said. "All this time . . . we reckoned Daddy stopped loving us." She hung her head, wiping at her cheeks. "I'm sorry but I need a minute."

Lena pulled a stool over in front of her and sat down. "Your father never stopped loving you, I promise," she said. "And he did everything he could to try and find you. He loved you so much he didn't want to live without you."

Sniffing, Bonnie gazed up at her. "What are y'all saying?"

"Did anyone tell you what happened to him?"

"They said the moonshine killed him."

"That is not true. I never saw him drink when I was living in Wolfe Hollow. But he was heartbroken without you. Between losing your mother and you and Jack Henry, then seeing your home burned to the ground, he couldn't take any more heartbreak. He lost all hope."

"So that's when he took to drinking? After us kids were taken?"

"Yes, but drinking isn't what killed him. And there's no other way to tell you this. He shot himself, Bonnie. I saw him do it."

Bonnie clamped a hand over her mouth, her eyes wide with shock and grief.

Lena wrapped her arms around her. "I'm so sorry," she said, holding her while she wept. "For everything. You deserved so much better. I've wondered every day since then if I could have done something different."

After a few moments, Bonnie drew away, wiping her face. "It ain't your fault. Them bastards had no right to take us."

"No, they didn't. Are you going to be all right?"

Bonnie nodded. "I reckon I will be eventually, but... I hated Daddy for such a long time. I thought he was the reason we got sent to that awful orphanage down in Lynchburg."

Lena's chest tightened. Every second since realizing who Bonnie was, she'd wanted to ask about Ella, but at the same time she was terrified to utter the words. Because if Bonnie had no idea what happened to Ella or where she was, Lena might just drop dead right then and there. She couldn't bear losing her all over again, not when she was this close to finally finding her. "You and Jack Henry were taken to an orphanage in Lynchburg?"

Bonnie nodded. "I tried getting out, but they punished me by making me push a broom weighed down by a twenty-pound block of wood to sweep the hallways."

Searching for the courage to ask the question that had been burning a hole in her throat, Lena pressed her nails into her palms. "Do you have any idea what happened to Ella?" Her voice came out raspy and weak.

Bonnie nodded again. "She was in the orphanage too. At least that's what they told me."

Fiery panic crawled up Lena's neck. Bonnie had no idea where Ella was. "What do you mean, that's what they told you? You didn't see her while you were there?"

"No. The nurses at the Colony told me Jack Henry was in the boys' ward and Ella was in the baby ward."

Lena recoiled. "The Colony? I thought you were in an orphanage."

"It was an orphanage."

Lena closed her eyes, trying not to choke on the gorge rising in her throat. The Virginia Colony consisted of more than one building—she had seen that when she'd arrived and when she was released—but she had assumed they were filled with other people who were considered feebleminded or epileptic. She never dreamed one of the buildings might house orphans. Or babies. Her heart cramped in her chest. Had she been in the same institution as her daughter the entire time? Had her baby girl been only a few feet or yards or buildings away? Thinking of Ella in that dreadful place was almost more than she could take. She shook her reeling head. No. It couldn't be true. She would have known. She would have sensed her daughter was nearby. Someone must have lied to Bonnie about Jack Henry's and Ella's whereabouts. But why? She inhaled deeply and struggled to compose herself.

"Were there only girls on your ward?"

Bonnie nodded. "Some younger than me, some older."

"How long were you there?"

"Three months and nine days. Until I was sent to live with my adoptive parents."

Lena tried to process this new information. If Bonnie was adopted while in the Colony, there must have been an orphanage there after all. "And Jack Henry and Ella? Do you know how long they were there?"

"They were only there a couple of weeks," Bonnie said. "I had to stay longer on account of me not taking to the surgery too well. They said I was out of my head for a spell."

Ice filled Lena's veins. *No.* Bonnie was only a child when they took her. They couldn't have sterilized her. "What surgery?"

"They cut out my appendix," Bonnie said.

"Why? Were you sick?"

Bonnie shrugged. "No, I felt right as rain. Other than missing home, of course. But Dr. Bell said my appendix was gonna bust open if he left it in me. A good number of the girls in the ward had the same problem. We thought it was on account of the nasty food they fed us."

Nausea curdled Lena's stomach. It couldn't be true. It just couldn't be. How could they sterilize a ten-year-old girl? Seething with anger and disgust, she tried to stay calm. A dozen memories flashed in her mind. Bonnie playing with Ella in the grass, lovingly placing a crown of daisies on her small head. Bonnie carrying Ella on her hip, lifting her up so she could touch the apple blossoms. Bonnie singing to Ella in the garden and on the way to the mill, smiling and laughing as if Ella were her baby sister. Lena had never seen such a young girl filled with such a strong maternal instinct. But Bonnie was a grown woman now and deserved to know the truth.

Except how did you tell someone, especially someone who loved children as much as Bonnie did, that she would never have babies of her own? Lena had been lucky enough to have Ella, to know the joy of giving birth, that powerful, immediate love a new mother felt for her newborn, but she also knew the pain and emptiness of losing a child, and the knowledge that there would be no more. It would break her heart to inflict that pain on anyone, especially Bonnie.

"What is it?" Bonnie said, pulling Lena from her thoughts. "What's wrong?"

"Nothing," Lena said.

"Are y'all sure? You look like you're staring down ten miles of bad road."

Lena chewed on the inside of her cheek, thinking. If there was a possibility that Bonnie had been sterilized, she had a right to know. But Lena had no proof. And before she could say a word about that possibility, she needed to be more certain of her suspicions. "Can I ask you something?" she said. "Why did Eddy Arnold introduce you as Bobbi Jo Gately?"

"Bobbi Jo is my stage name."

"And Gately?"

"That was my married name. Been meaning to change it back but ain't gotten around to it yet."

"Change it back?"

"Me and Dale been divorced nearly five years now. He

wanted a family and I couldn't give him one, so he found someone who could."

Lena's heart dropped. "So you tried to have children?"

Bonnie sighed. "Yup. For years. And he proved it was my fault by knocking up our neighbor's eighteen-year-old daughter. Now they got three kids—two girls and a boy."

"I'm sorry."

Bonnie let out a sarcastic laugh. "It's all right. He didn't cotton to the idea of me singing neither, so it worked out."

"So, you're happy?"

"I am," Bonnie said. "And I got me a new fella anyway. One who cares about my dreams."

"Does he want children?" As soon as the words left Lena's mouth, she regretted them. She was pushing too hard.

Bonnie drew back, frowning. "Why are you asking so many questions about young'uns?"

"I'm sorry," Lena said. "I don't mean to pry. It's just . . . I need to tell you something. They put me in the Virginia State Colony too. I was there at the same time as you."

Bonnie gaped at her. "What? Why? I don't understand."

"Maybe you already know this, but it's called the Virginia State Colony for Epileptics and Feebleminded. That's why I was surprised when you said there was an orphanage there. Dr. Bell and the other doctors claimed I was feebleminded and shouldn't have any more babies because they didn't want me to bring more 'mentally defective' children into the world, even though there was not a thing wrong with me or Ella. So they gave me a choice. I could agree to be sterilized or get locked up for the rest of my life."

Bonnie's mouth fell open. "That's horrible," she said, her voice barely a whisper. "How could they do something so downright cruel?"

"I truly don't know," Lena said. "They said it was legal, but I think they should all be behind bars. And I hate to tell you this, but I think they lied to you about your appendix. I think they sterilized you."

Bonnie stiffened, shocked into silence. The only sound was the muffled music coming through the walls from the stage down the hall. Then she leapt up and paced the room, one hand on her forehead. "Jesus H. Christ," she said. "Jesus H. Christ! Those fucking bastards! How dare they. How *dare* they!"

Lena gave her an apologetic look. "I didn't want to tell you but—"

"All this time," Bonnie said. "All this time I reckoned there was something wrong with me. I thought I was being punished or some other bullshit." She paced back and forth a few more times, then suddenly stopped and stared at Lena, nearly hyperventilating. Then she put her hands over her face and started to sob.

Lena went to her. "I'm so sorry," she said, putting a gentle hand on Bonnie's arm. "I know this is devastating news. I mean, there is a slight chance I'm wrong, but honestly, I don't think I am."

Bonnie leaned into her, hands still over her face, and wept. Lena wrapped her arms around her again, still struggling to hold herself together as well.

"After all the awful things I just told you," Lena said, "you're probably wishing you'd never seen me again."

Bonnie pulled away and shook her head. "No. This ain't your fault. None of it. I want to know the truth. About everything." She gave Lena another hug and sat back down again, scraping the tears off her red cheeks. "I'm sorry for getting all tore up about this. It ain't like me."

"I know it's not like you. You've always been one of the strongest girls I've ever known. But that was a lot to hear all at once."

"Well, it sure as heck changes some of the things I thought

about my life," Bonnie said, laughing quietly through her tears. "Including the way I feel about the people who raised me."

"Were you close?"

Bonnie shrugged. "They gave me what I needed, a roof over my head, plenty of food, clean clothes, and good schooling, but they weren't exactly the loving type. They handed out more rules than hugs. And now, knowing they lied about my daddy and who knows what else, I ain't sure what to think."

"I can only imagine. It makes me angry too. But part of me wonders if they were just repeating what they were told by the people at the Colony."

"Maybe. And I hope y'all are right, but it ain't like I can ask them."

"Why not?"

"Because they were in an awful car wreck over on the interstate going on three years ago. Coroner said they were killed instantly."

"Oh God. How terrible."

"Yeah, I been working on making my peace with it, but now . . . well. Now I want answers I ain't ever going to get. To a lot of things."

"I understand. And I know you have a lot to think about, but if it's all right, I need to ask you a few more questions."

Bonnie nodded. "Sure."

"You said you were adopted," Lena said. "But what about Jack Henry and Ella? Do you know what happened to them?"

Bonnie nodded again, her eyes filling. Lena thought she would scream before she answered.

"The doctors at the Colony said Jack Henry was dimwitted, so they sent him away to work on a peanut farm. They said he was a social misfit and threw him away like a piece of trash. We wrote back and forth for years, even got together a few times on account of me pitching a right fit until my parents agreed to find out where he was, but then he was drafted and sent off to war. Guess he was smart enough for that."

"Oh no," Lena said.

"Yep. He was so darn worthless, he somehow managed to win the Bronze Star and a Purple Heart." Bonnie ran a hand beneath her nose. "Guess we should be happy they thought he was worth something after all. 'Cept it was too late by then, of course. There wasn't even anything left of him to bury."

Hot tears welled up in Lena's eyes, the familiar vise of grief squeezing her chest. "I'm so sorry," she said, for what felt like the thousandth time. "You've suffered far too many losses for someone your age."

Bonnie let out a soft, shaky laugh. "Well, they say what don't kill y'all makes you stronger, right? And I got a bushel of good memories of Jack Henry to look back on, but poor Ella. We were both mighty upset when they sent him away, but she took it pretty hard, even though she was so young she hardly knew him. I reckon she ain't as tough as me."

Lena's heart suddenly thrashed inside her rib cage, pounding so hard she thought she might pass out. After all this time, was it possible her luck had finally changed? "Are . . . are you talking about my Ella?"

Bonnie nodded. "Yup. Us girls were adopted by the same couple, Georgia and Matthew Ryan."

Lena could hardly breathe. "Do you know where she is now?"

"Of course I do," Bonnie said, grinning through her tears.

Chapter 31

The morning after the Grand Ball, Lena stood beside Bonnie on the sidewalk in front of a three-story brick building in a small town outside of Richmond, her knees vibrating, her pulse thundering inside her head. A hand-painted sign above the building's mint green door read in cursive script: CHARLIE'S FLOWERS. And on either side of the door, pink carnations, yellow freesia, white lilies, orange daisies, and red roses filled the shop windows. Window boxes overflowed with red petunias and green ivy on the second and third stories, and a white cat sat like an Egyptian statue between lace curtains, looking down on them with sleepy eyes. After a long hesitation, Lena straightened her shoulders and looked at Bonnie.

"All right," she said. "I'm ready."

"Y'all sure?"

Lena nodded. She was not at all sure. But there was no going back now.

Bonnie started toward the door.

"Wait," Lena said. "What if she doesn't want to see me?"

"She does, I promise."

"How do you know?"

"Because, when she got old enough, I told her we had different mothers but we'd always be sisters. After that, every now and then she talked about what it'd be like to find y'all. I told her what I remembered about the time you stayed with us, but it wasn't much, only a few snippets here and there."

"She doesn't remember anything about me?"

With a sorrowful expression, Bonnie shook her head.

Then Lena had another thought and her breath hitched in her chest. If Bonnie had been told Silas had gotten rid of her and Jack Henry, Ella might have been told the same thing. "She doesn't think I gave her up willingly, does she?"

Bonnie put a comforting hand on her arm. "It'll be fine, just you wait and see." Before Lena could say anything else, Bonnie pushed the door open and went inside. Lena followed, her heart in her throat.

A bell jingled to announce their arrival. The fragrant perfume of flowers and greenery scented the cool shop air, a welcome relief from the unusually warm day outside. Decorative vases and ceramic pots filled wooden shelves above tables bursting with lilies and chrysanthemums, daisies and snapdragons, gladiolas and baby's breath. Here and there, garden gnomes, bells, birdhouses, and white iron flower stands were tastefully displayed, transforming the shop into an oasis, like a secret garden. Behind the counter, a dark-haired man arranging yellow roses in a glass vase looked up when Bonnie and Lena walked in.

"Good morning, Bonnie," he said, smiling while continuing his work. "What brings you in for a visit so bright and early?" He picked up a rose, trimmed the leaves, and added it to the vase.

"Morning, Charlie," Bonnie said. "I've got someone here who'd like to see Ella."

"Is that right?" Charlie said. He gave Lena a cursory glance but kept working. "She'll be down any minute."

"Do y'all reckon it'd be all right if we went up?" Bonnie said.

"Of course," Charlie said. "Tell her to take her time and enjoy your visit. I've got everything under control down here."

"All right," Bonnie said. "Thank you kindly." She started around the counter toward a door at the back of the room, gesturing for Lena to follow.

"Hey," Charlie said. "I want to say again how sorry we are that we couldn't make it last night. We just aren't quite ready to paint the town yet."

Bonnie stopped and turned to face him. "Oh, don't worry about that," she said, waving a dismissive hand in the air. "I understand."

"How did it go?" Charlie said.

"It went great," Bonnie said. "As a matter of fact, Eddy Arnold wants me to open for him and the Plowboys at the state fair in Maryland next month."

"That's wonderful," Charlie said. "Congratulations!"

Just then, the door at the back of the room opened and a young woman in a white tea gown with a high collar and ruffled shoulders entered the shop from upstairs. After propping the door open partway with a cast-iron cat statue, she turned toward the counter, smiling at Charlie. With her blond hair piled loosely on the top of her head and skin as pale as porcelain, she looked ethereal, like an angel on a Victorian postcard.

Lena felt herself sway, just slightly enough that no one would notice, but hard enough to send a wave of alarm through her. She couldn't faint. Not here. Not now. She looked around for something to hold on to, but there was no doorframe or chair to cling to, nothing to keep her from falling over. Silence like a pressure filled her ears. She put her hand over her heart to make sure it was still beating.

She would have known the young woman anywhere.

Ella.

"Y'all holding it together?" Bonnie said quietly. Her voice sounded muffled, as if coming up from inside a box.

Somehow, Lena managed to nod.

As soon as Ella saw Bonnie, she hurried over and threw her arms around her. "There's my famous big sister!" she said.

Bonnie laughed. "I reckon it takes more than singing at state fairs and tobacco festivals to get famous."

"Oh rubbish," Ella said, releasing Bonnie. "Before you know it, you'll be recording your own album. And you're a hell of a lot more famous than I'll ever be." She laughed with Bonnie, and Lena swore she heard echoes of her little-girl giggle.

"I ain't so sure about that," Bonnie said. "From what I hear, you and Charlie got the best-selling flowers in town."

Ella smiled and glanced over her shoulder at Charlie, her blue eyes soft. "We do make a pretty darn good team." Then she greeted Lena, her smile suddenly shy and uncertain. "Do I know y'all from somewhere?" she said. "I feel like I've seen you before."

Struggling against the lump in her throat, Lena nodded, certain if she tried to speak, she'd burst into sobs. More than anything, she wanted to grab her daughter and hug and kiss her and never let her go. She ached to tell her how sorry she was too, but she had to take it slow or Ella would think she'd lost her mind.

"Can we go upstairs and talk for a bit?" Bonnie said.

Ella looked back and forth between Bonnie and Lena, concern furrowing her brow. "Of course," she said. "But is everything all right?"

"Everything's peachy keen," Bonnie said.

"Go ahead, sweetheart," Charlie said. "I'm not expecting a big rush anytime soon."

Ella glanced at him, somewhat puzzled, as if he knew what was going on. Then she turned her attention back to Bonnie and Lena. "All right," she said. "Would either of you like a cup of coffee or tea?"

"I have a hankering for some tea if it ain't too much trouble," Bonnie said.

"It's not any trouble at all," Ella said. "Come on up." She turned and started toward the door at the back of the room. Before heading up the stairs, she stopped and said in a soft voice, "But we need to be quiet until we get to the kitchen." Then she tiptoed up the steps.

On legs that felt like water, Lena followed Bonnie and Ella up the staircase, her trembling hand gripping the banister to keep from tumbling backward. Now that she was aware of all the lies Bonnie had been told, the fear that Ella might think she'd abandoned her made it hard to breathe. Was that why Bonnie wanted to go upstairs to talk? Because she knew Ella would be upset?

At the top of the stairs, a painted railing and several doors lined the plank-floored hallway. Ella walked quietly across the landing, stopped at a door, and turned to look back along the hall, craning her neck to see around Bonnie and Lena. Then she smiled at them and put a finger to her lips. When Lena glanced back to see what she was looking at, her breath caught.

Two matching cradles sat pushed up against the wall, lengthwise between two doors. Inside each one, a downy-haired baby slept peacefully on snow-white sheets, head turned to one side, arms up, fingers and hands in tiny fists.

Lena gaped at Bonnie, who smiled knowingly and gently took Lena's hand to lead her forward, following Ella through the door. A dizzying lightheadedness came over Lena and for a second, the floor seemed to tip. Then it was over and all she could hear was her blood pounding inside her head. She wanted to rush over to the cradles to get a closer look. She wanted to pick the babies up and snuggle them to her chest, to kiss their sweet little heads.

When they entered the cozy kitchen, Ella closed the door softly behind them, then offered them a seat at the table. Her mouth was moving but no sound came out. Then Lena's hearing returned and she caught Ella's last words.

"... just got them back to sleep," she said in a quiet voice. "We put them in the hall while we're working so we can hear them crying from the shop." She pulled out a chair and offered it to Lena, who took it without hesitation. "Now which was it, tea or coffee?"

"Tea, please," Bonnie said. "With a little honey, if you have it."

"Of course," Ella said. She looked at Lena. "Can I get the same for you?"

For a second, Lena couldn't speak. Her gaze was locked on Ella's familiar blue eyes. "Are they yours?" she finally managed. "The babies?"

Ella smiled proudly. "Yes. They're twins. Rory and Rosie."

Lena felt like her heart might burst. Her little girl was a mother. *A mother.* She had escaped the horrors of the Colony and Dr. Bell and gone on to have two beautiful babies. Twins, no less. "How wonderful," Lena said, trying to keep her voice steady. "Congratulations."

"Thank you," Ella said. "Charlie and I are very lucky. Now, did y'all say you'd like tea or coffee?"

Lena was too anxious to care about tea or coffee or anything besides Ella and the babies, but she said yes to tea anyway.

While Ella busied herself putting the kettle on the stove, reaching into the cupboards for the cups and saucers, setting the honey and milk on the table, Lena couldn't take her eyes off her.

"Y'all doing all right?" Bonnie whispered.

Lena nodded, struggling to hold back her tears.

"I wish the twins would wake up so I could hold them," Bonnie said. "I reckon they've changed a lot since I saw them two weeks ago."

"They sure have," Ella said. "Rory is smiling now and little Rosie is really starting to fill out." She pulled out a chair across from Bonnie and sat down, her pale, delicate hands clasped together on the table. "So, what's this all about? I feel like y'all want to tell me something."

Bonnie hesitated. Then she said, "Well, for one thing, I just found out me and Jack Henry was told a pack of lies when we were kids."

Ella raised her eyebrows. "A pack of lies? About what?"

"About my daddy. He never got rid of us. They took us."

"Who took you?"

"The sheriff and his deputy. They said Daddy weren't fit to take care of us anymore so they stole us while he was gone. Then the state took his land and burned down our house."

Ella's eyes went wide.

"I reckon y'all remember how the nurses at the orphanage thought you were our sister."

"You told me that later on, yes."

"That was a lie too. I mean, they knew y'all weren't, but that didn't matter to them. Somebody made up lies about your momma so they could take you too. They said she wasn't fit to raise you right either, called her feebleminded and locked her up."

A pained expression crossed Ella's face. "Why would they do that? And how do y'all know all this?"

Bonnie smiled and touched her cheek. "Y'all know how I got this scar, right?"

"Of course I do," Ella said. "When I was little you drove me crazy, always telling me to watch my step when I climbed a tree or swung too high on the playground. But what has that got to do with anything?"

"Y'all remember me telling you who sang to me so I wouldn't be scared?"

And with that, something flashed in Ella's eyes, a sudden, profound flicker of understanding, a swift realization of what Bonnie was about to say. Her watery gaze drifted to Lena. "Y'all are . . . y'all are my mother, aren't you?"

Lena pressed her lips together to keep from crying out, the

room a sudden blur behind her flooding eyes. "Yes," she said, her voice barely a whisper. "I am. And I've been searching for you since the day they stole you from my arms."

Ella clamped her hands over her mouth, her face falling in on itself. Then she stood and reached for Lena, arms outstretched. Lena jumped to her feet and they wrapped their arms around each other, laughing and sobbing at the same time.

"I knew you were my Ella the second I saw you," Lena said.

"My heart told me y'all were someone special too," Ella said. "But I tried not to get my hopes up."

After a long moment, Ella drew back and wiped her cheeks. "I have a hundred questions," she said. "But would y'all like to meet your grandchildren first?"

Lena nodded, her chin quivering. How it was possible that her heart could be filled with immeasurable joy after so many years of sorrow? "I would love it more than anything in this world," she said, smiling through her tears.

Chapter 32

It was a beautiful sunny day and the mountains were vibrant with the colors of fall, the leaves on the trees covering the ridges and valleys like red and orange carpets. Judd gunned the engine and steered the Ford sedan across a gravel riverbed, then drove up a narrow dirt road toward a sloping field across from high cliffs. Beside him in the passenger seat, Teensy stared out the windshield in silence, no doubt overwhelmed by a flood of sad and happy memories of her previous life on Old Rag. In the back seat, Lena glanced occasionally at Bonnie, wondering how much she remembered about her childhood home. Ella, who was sitting between Lena and Bonnie, looked quietly out the windows. The twins were home with Charlie and, although Lena knew making this trip was important, she could hardly wait to get back home to the flower shop to cuddle them.

Home.

It had been forever since she'd felt truly at home anywhere. Sure, Teensy and Judd were like family now, and she was beyond grateful for everything they'd done for her. And yes, she'd had her own room in the boarding house after moving to the city. But those houses and rooms had only been places to live, not a home in the real sense of the word. Now, she finally had a real home with Ella, her husband, and their children. *Her grandchildren.* She slept in a spare room in their apartment above the flower shop and had dinner with them every night when she came home from work. She helped take care of the twins as often as needed, and best of all, she sometimes had those precious babies all to herself, when Ella and Charles went out on the town. And she cherished every sweet second of it.

Now, as Judd drove the car next to steep, rocky drop-offs, along craggy roads, and through woods set so close the light within looked green, she wondered if he and Teensy had ever felt at home since they were forced down the mountain all those years ago. She hoped they had. She also hoped they knew how grateful she was to them for agreeing to take Bonnie up to Wolfe Hollow Farm. Hopefully, this trip would not be too difficult for them.

Every few miles or so, they passed the overgrown remains of burned-out barns and sheds, and stone walls that marked farmyards or separated fields. Higher up the mountain, they passed twin rock chimneys and a crumbling foundation.

"That's the old Cray place," Judd said. "Seven generations lived in that house since they bought over a thousand acres up here back in the seventeen hundreds. Their land took up most of the western crest, all the way through the forests of the area we called the Wilderness. 'Course, back then there weren't nothing but a horse trail up the valley to the slope of Big Cat Knob. The Crays owned nine hundred acres of grazing land next to the Conway tract over on the next mountain, and more than a thousand acres in Dark Hollow. Silas's great-grandparents met members of the Cray family in the German community of Heborn. That's how your kin ended up in these mountains, Bonnie."

"Where did the Cray family go after they were evicted?" Lena said.

"Old man Cray dropped dead a year after taking his last walk on the trail he'd been hiking for seventy years," Teensy said. "I heard his wife died around 1934, I think it was. Penniless. The state didn't pay them hardly nothing for their land. I ain't heard what happened to the rest."

For the next half hour, no one spoke, each lost in their own thoughts. Finally, they turned onto an overgrown dirt road between rows of spruce trees. The trees fell away on one side, revealing a panoramic view of mountain ridges stretching for miles in all directions. In the hills and valleys below, where rooftops and stone chimneys once dotted the landscape, huddled here and there between trees and winding footpaths, cars now drove along a paved road and tourists stopped to take pictures.

When they reached the former site of Wolfe Hollow Farm, the driveway and yard were thick with brambles, brush, and saplings. Judd parked the car as close as he could and everyone got out. Where the house used to sit on the slope, the rock fireplace and chimney stood on one end of the collapsed foundation, which was overrun with Virginia creeper, moss, and prickly bushes. The mountain stream still ran down the hill, but the only remnants of the springhouse were two crooked rows of moss-covered stones. The mountain laurel, white birch, pine, and walnut trees that once edged the back of the property had invaded the yard from all sides, and the apple trees stooped and twisted like ancient creatures hiding beneath the overgrowth. It was impossible to tell where the chicken coop and sheds used to stand, and all that remained of the barn were flat rocks and decayed black timbers.

Despite the destruction, Lena could still picture the chickens in the yard, pecking at bugs, roaming beneath the grape arbor. She could still picture Jack Henry bringing the cows down from the mountain, bells ringing around their necks. She could still picture Bonnie in the garden and on the porch, singing and working and playing with Ella.

Now, standing between Bonnie and Ella, all of them staring up at the ruins of the house, she put an arm around Bonnie.

"Do you remember anything?" she said.

Bonnie nodded, her eyes growing wet. "I remember everything."

"If this is too hard for y'all," Teensy said, "we can go back down the mountain. Just say the word."

"No," Bonnie said. "I want to stay." Then she started up the slope, tramping over tall grass, stepping around prickly bushes and brambles.

Not surprised by Bonnie's reply, Lena went after her. Everyone followed.

When they reached the ruins of the house, Bonnie knelt where the steps to the porch once stood. At first, Lena couldn't figure out what she was looking at, but then she noticed the yellow petals peeking out from between the weeds.

Bonnie looked up at her. "My mother's black-eyed Susans are still blooming." She pulled some of the weeds out of the way and picked a small bouquet of the bright flowers. Then she straightened, stepped over the moss-covered rocks of the destroyed foundation, and made her way over to the still-standing fireplace.

"Be careful," Teensy said.

Bonnie ran her hands along the stones of the fireplace, then turned and gazed at the charred skeleton of what used to be her childhood home. "I can't believe they did this," she said. "How could they burn down our house? And destroy our family?"

Teensy shook her head and wiped a tear from her cheek. Judd put a comforting arm around her.

Ella started to step across the foundation, then stopped and looked at the ground. She reached down, pulled something out of a clump of vines, and held it up. "I think I remember this," she said, her face full of wonder.

The homemade wind chime was green and tarnished, with

black dirt edging the silver spoons, but it still tinkled softly when moved. Bonnie made her way over to Ella and ran her fingers through it, smiling.

"My mother made this," Bonnie said. "You used to love it." Then she turned to Lena, Teensy, and Judd. "Thank you for bringing me here. I've always wondered where our home was in these mountains."

"Do you want to see your father's final resting place?" Teensy said.

"Do you know the way?" Bonnie said.

"'Course I do," Teensy said, pointing toward the back of the property. "It's up yonder in the woods."

After Bonnie put the wind chime and bouquet of flowers in the car, Judd led everyone up the hill and into the woods on what looked like an animal trail, winding around ancient trees and gangly saplings. While he pushed back branches and broke around scrub and brush, Teensy stayed close behind him, telling him which way to go, followed by Bonnie, Ella, and Lena. High-skirted evergreens rustled softly overhead, and patches of sunlight broke through to the musty forest floor. Lena remembered walking behind Silas's casket along this same path, before it was swallowed by the forest, wishing—as she had wished more times than she wanted to admit—that she were dead too. Now, she thanked God the universe had not listened.

Near what looked like the end of the trail, Judd pushed aside the branches of a tall oak and held them back, waiting for everyone to go through. On the other side of the tree, hawthorn and juniper bushes encircled a ragged clearing full of tussocky grass, dry leaves, and moldering logs. In the center of the clearing, a crude stone fence surrounded a group of lichen-covered gravestones, some leaning sideways and backward, as if pulled toward the earth by an underground force. Judd kicked aside leaves and broken branches, then led the way through an opening in the fence.

The chiseled inscription on a headstone in the first row read:

SILAS ALEXANDER WOLFE
1888-1928
BELOVED HUSBAND OF CELIA,
DEVOTED FATHER

Next to Silas's gravestone stood four smaller stones: three engraved with his dead children's names and one unmarked. And at the end of the row, another large headstone read:

CELIA IRIS WOLFE
1891-1926
BELOVED WIFE, LOVING MOTHER

Blinking back the moisture in her eyes, Bonnie moved closer to Silas's stone and knelt beside it.

"Your daddy woulda gladly given up every square inch of land he owned to be with you and Jack Henry again," Teensy said. "But the government lied and took everything he had, including his family. And that's what killed him."

Chapter 33

Christmas Day, 1950

Wearing her favorite red dress and high heels, Lena looked out the dining room window of Teensy and Judd's farmhouse to check the road. It had been snowing hard all day and she couldn't help worrying about Ella, Charlie, and the twins, who had nearly an hour's drive from Charlie's parents to the McDaniels' farm. Supper would be ready soon and it wasn't like them to be late. Behind her, sitting at two tables placed end to end, Bonnie and her new husband, Miles, who were in between music tours, along with Teensy and Judd's family—the four girls, their husbands, and ten grandchildren—filled the room with laughter and conversation.

"A watched pot don't never boil," Teensy called out to Lena. "Come sit down. It's slow going out there today with the storm and all. I reckon they'll be here any minute."

Lena dropped the curtain and turned toward the dining room. She'd been working in the kitchen all day with Teensy and Bonnie, peeling potatoes, boiling squash, making pies, rolls, and stuffing, laughing and happily awaiting Ella and her family's arrival. Now, it was difficult to hide her concern. She went over to the table and took her place beside Bonnie, trying to ignore the empty seats and high chairs beside her. Teensy and Judd placed two perfectly browned turkeys on each end of the extra-long table, setting them between the mismatched place settings that included Bonnie's mother's cherished dishes from Sears and Roebuck. While Judd and his oldest son-in-law got to work carving the meat, Lena forced a smile and tried to enjoy the moment. Teensy was probably right. Ella and her family would be there soon and, for the third year in a row, they'd have another perfect Christmas together.

Since taking Bonnie up to Wolfe Hollow and her father's grave, Teensy, Judd, Lena, and Bonnie had returned once or twice a year to clear the path and clean up the graveyard, which included Silas's parents, grandparents, great-grandparents, and members of Teensy's family. They added a plaque to the stone wall that read WOLFE FAMILY CEMETERY and a headstone for Jack Henry, which sadly reminded Lena that she'd never see her mother's grave. But having Ella in her life again, not to mention her treasured grandchildren, helped soothe and protect that tender wound. And of course, the entire McDaniel family helped fill her heart too.

After Judd finished slicing the turkey and Teensy brought out an extra basket of warm rolls, Judd took a seat at one end of the table and Teensy sat at the other. Their daughters and sons-in-law told the grandchildren to be still, and little by little the room grew quiet as everyone prepared for the yearly tradition of Judd's Christmas speech, during which he told everyone how thankful he was for their good fortune. Lena scanned the shining, happy faces in the room, her heart overflowing with love and gratitude for each and every one of them. But until Ella and her family were sitting at the table beside her, the most important people in her world would be missing from this precious gathering.

Just as Judd stood and clinked his knife on his glass, a knock sounded on the front door. Lena jumped out of her chair and rushed down the hall, Teensy on her heels. When Lena yanked open the door, a blast of cold air and snow filled the foyer. And to her great relief, Ella and Charlie stood on the stoop with Rory and Rosie in their arms, snowflakes covering their coats and hats. At two years old, Rosie had a headful of blond curls while Rory had straight auburn hair like his father. They both had chubby cheeks, roly-poly legs, wet smiles full of baby teeth, and they were the most beautiful children Lena had ever seen.

"I'm sorry we're late," Ella said, winded and trying to catch her breath. "The roads were awful."

"It's all right," Lena said. "We're just glad you're here safe and sound." She took Rosie from Ella and stepped back to let them inside.

Teensy took Rory from Charlie. "Come on in and get yourselves warmed up," she said. "Y'all are just in time for supper."

"I need to get the presents out of the car," Charlie said. "I'll be right back." Then he turned and headed down the steps, disappearing into a curtain of snow.

Ella closed the door behind him, then stomped her boots on the rug and unbuttoned her coat. "The twins slept all the way here, thank goodness."

Lena kissed Rosie's pink cheeks. "How are Gramma's little sweethearts? Are you hungry?" She set Rosie down and removed her coat and boots.

Teensy did the same for Rory, then took his hand and started toward the dining room. "Everybody's going to be so happy to see y'all," she said.

Ella and Lena followed, Rosie holding tight to Lena's hand as she toddled down the hall. When they entered the living room, everyone waved and smiled and said hello. Lena and Teensy lifted the twins into the high chairs, and Ella sat between Rosie and Lena, sighing in relief. But instead of relaxing, she pushed her damp hair back from her cold-reddened face and fidgeted with the silverware.

"Are you all right?" Lena said.

"Yes, of course," Ella said. "The ride here was a little nerve-wracking, that's all."

Lena put a gentle hand on her back. "Are you sure?"

Ella smiled. "Yes, I'm fine. I promise."

Satisfied, Lena gave her a quick squeeze, then turned back toward the table.

"Good thing we got plenty of vittles," Judd said, laughing. "'Cause I reckon this storm is gonna keep y'all here tonight."

"Yay!" the older grandkids shouted.

The adults laughed too and started talking all at once, calling out what rooms they wanted to sleep in, asking Teensy if she had enough blankets and Judd if he had extra moonshine.

Lena turned to Ella again. "Did you have a good time with Charlie's parents?"

Ella nodded. "Yes, it was lovely. But you know being here with all of you will always be my favorite part of Christmas."

Lena smiled, her heart swelling. "It will always be my favorite part too."

A sudden draft of icy air flowed into the dining room and, after what felt like forever, the front door slammed shut. Out in the foyer, Charlie stomped his boots on the rug. One of the sons-in-law got up and called down the hall. "Need help with anything?"

"Nope," Charlie said. "I'll be right there!"

Teensy picked up a bowl of mashed potatoes and handed them to one of her daughters. "How about we pass the vittles before they get cold."

"What about my speech?" Judd said.

Teensy rolled her eyes good-naturedly. "We can listen and fix our plates at the same time." But Judd decided to wait until Charlie had joined them.

While the room filled with the sounds of silverware, passing bowls, and the small talk of filling plates with food, Charlie came into the dining room, blowing into his hands to get warm.

"Sorry about that," he said.

"Ain't no problem at all," Judd said. "Come on in and sit down. The vittles are still hot." Then he stood and looked at Teensy. "Can I get started now?"

"Wait," Ella said in a loud voice. "I have something to say first."

Surprised, Lena started to ask her what was going on, but Ella got up, went around the table, and stood next to Judd, who, looking amused, stepped aside. The adults grew quiet and hushed the children.

Lena stared at Ella, wondering what in the world she was about to say. Then she remembered what she'd said about Christmas, how being there with them *would always be* her favorite part. Alarm bells went off in her head. What if she and Charlie were moving away? What if they were taking the twins closer to his parents, or leaving the state of Virginia altogether? Was that why she seemed nervous? Then Lena had another thought and her shoulders relaxed. Wherever they went, she would go with them. If they let her.

At the head of the table, Ella looked out over the faces gazing up at her. "I could hardly wait for today, not just because I love spending Christmas with all of you, but because it's been really hard keeping this secret from my mother. And I'm so glad you're all here to see her reaction." She gave Lena a soft, loving look.

Lena held her breath. What secret? What was Ella talking about? She glanced at Bonnie, who was wearing a mischievous smile. Whatever was happening, Bonnie was in on it.

Then Ella gave Charlie a nod, as if telling him to get started. He got up from his chair and went out into the hall. Everyone looked at each other with curious expressions and whispered questions, wondering what was going on. When Charlie came back into the dining room, he stepped aside to let someone through the door.

Looking shy and uncertain, a dark-haired man slowly entered the room, followed by two children and a pretty woman. The man was tall and broad-shouldered, with the bristled shadow of a beard, while the woman was petite, with wavy blonde hair and delicate features. The children looked to be close in age, around eleven or twelve years old, with matching light hair and blue eyes. When the man saw Lena, a broad grin broke out across his face and he struggled against a sudden rush of tears.

"Surprise!" Ella shouted.

Lena squeezed her eyes shut, then opened them again, unable to believe what she was seeing. He had sent a few photographs over the years of himself and his young bride, and the children when they were babies, but they were all older now, and had changed. She never dreamed she'd see any of them in person. With flooding eyes, she got up from the table and made her way across the room, reaching out with trembling hands.

Enzo closed the distance between them and they threw their arms around each other, laughing and crying at the same time. Behind them, everyone at the table gasped and started to clap.

"What are you doing here?" Lena cried, her German returning easily. "How is this possible? How did you get here?"

"Ella asked us to come," Enzo said. "And Bonnie paid our way."

Overwhelmed and nearly out of breath, Lena drew back. "Are you staying for good?"

Enzo shook his head. "No," he said. "Only for a visit."

Lena hugged her brother again, her head spinning, then felt his shoulders and arms to make sure he was real. His resemblance to Vater was uncanny. "You're really here! It's really you!"

Enzo laughed. "Yes, it's really me."

"I never thought I'd see you again!" Lena said.

"I felt the same," Enzo said. "So I was very excited to say yes to Ella's invitation."

"How long can you stay?"

"Two weeks. Then I must get back to the farm." He reached for his family, proudly bringing them forward. "This is my wife, Suzanne, and my children, Gisele and Otto."

Gushing, Lena gave Suzanne and the children hugs and introduced herself to Gisele and Otto as their aunt Lena. "I'm so delighted to finally meet you."

"We are happy to meet you too," Suzanne said in broken English.

Lena gazed lovingly at Ella and Bonnie. "I can't believe you did this."

They grinned at her with watery eyes. "Merry Christmas," they said at the same time.

Lena motioned Ella over. "Come meet your uncle and his family."

With a shy expression, Ella joined them, offering her hand.

Enzo shook her hand, then pulled her in for a quick hug. "You are as beautiful as I remember," he said in English. "And I am very happy to see you again."

Ella laughed. "I'm happy to see y'all too."

"To say goodbye to you and your mother was very difficult," Enzo said.

Lena put an arm around Ella's waist. "Yes, it was. Especially for your Oma. She loved you more than anything in the world."

"That is right," Enzo said. "Maybe she even loved you more than me and your mother." He grinned, clearly making a joke. Lena and Ella laughed.

After introducing Ella to her aunt and cousins, Lena waved Bonnie over, made introductions, then led Enzo and his wife and children over to the table. "Everyone, I'd like you to meet my brother, Enzo, and his beautiful family."

Everyone got up to shake Enzo's hand or pat him on the

back, and to welcome his wife and children. Enzo and Suzanne smiled and nodded, saying hello and answering questions about their trip while Gisele and Otto looked wide-eyed at the room full of noisy, grinning strangers.

Lena could hardly take her eyes off her brother, marveling at the adult he had become. No longer the eager, gangly teenager she remembered, now he was a handsome man with the mature eyes of a husband and father, and a soldier who had seen the worst of war. Best of all, he seemed happy and content, as if he'd found his place in the world, which gave Lena another measure of peace.

Ella and Bonnie came over to her.

"Are y'all all right?" Bonnie said.

Lena nodded, hugging them both. "How can I ever thank you for this?"

"Ain't no need to thank us," Bonnie said. "Seeing the smile on your face is enough."

"How on earth did you get them here?" Lena said to Ella. "Is that why you were late?"

Laughing, Ella shook her head. "No, the storm really did slow us down. Enzo and his family arrived the day before yesterday, but Charlie's parents were kind enough to let them stay in their home until we could surprise you. At first, I was afraid we'd be stuck there because of the storm, then I was afraid y'all would see the taxi in the driveway when we got here, so I was almost grateful for the snow!"

Bonnie agreed. "I was nervous as a long-tailed cat in a room full of rocking chairs. I didn't think y'all would ever get here! And your mother kept looking out the window!"

Just then, Teensy began making her way around the room, cheerfully shooing everyone back to the table. "All right, all right," she said. "Y'all know I ain't one to break up a happy reunion, but let's get back to the vittles before they turn ice cold. I reckon you boys better get another table and more chairs."

In no time at all, the men set up more seating and Teensy and Lena made sure Enzo and his family were filling their plates. Lena grabbed her plate and took a seat beside her brother. While everyone chatted and enjoyed the delicious food, Lena and Enzo talked about his life in Germany, his farm in the country, and a million other things.

"Mutti would be so proud of you and your family," Lena said.

"I know," Enzo said, his eyes glassy. "I wish she could have met my children."

"She sees them," Lena said. "I know she does. And I've never told anyone this, but somehow, some way, I think she led me back to Ella." She glanced at Ella and the twins. "I thank her every day for that. Otherwise . . ." She paused, her throat tightening around her words.

Enzo put his hand on hers. "I can only imagine what you've been through."

She blinked back another round of tears, trying not to cry again. Today was a day for celebrating, not stirring up the past. They would have time to talk later. "By the way, your English is very good," she said, trying to lighten the mood.

"Well, I promised you I'd learn more English. I'm just sorry I could not visit you and Ella sooner."

Lena put a gentle hand on his shoulder. "It's all right. I wish I could have visited you too. But some things can't be helped. What matters is that we're all together now. And we're going to enjoy every second of it."

"Yes, of course, you're right," Enzo said.

When everyone had finished eating, Teensy's daughters cleared the dishes while the older children got up to play and Teensy passed out slices of mincemeat and pumpkin pie. Still exhausted from their trip, Otto started to fall asleep at the table. While Teensy offered Enzo and Suzanne a nearby sofa for their son to lie down, Ella brought her pie over and sat beside Lena.

"How is it going?" she said.

"It's like we were never apart," Lena said. "Thank you again for bringing him here. Next to finding you and the twins, this is the happiest day of my life."

"Y'all are welcome," Ella said. "But I have one more surprise for you."

Lena gaped at her. "What do you mean? You've done enough already, more than I could have ever dreamed. I don't need anything else."

"Okay," Ella said, teasing her. "I won't tell y'all then." Smirking, she turned her attention back to her pumpkin pie.

"Tell me what?" Lena said.

"That's all right," Ella said. "It can wait." She put a forkful of pie in her mouth.

"Well, now you've *got* to tell me."

Grinning like a cat who ate a canary, Ella put a hand over her lips until she swallowed. Then she said, "All right. If y'all insist." She reached into her skirt pocket and set a pair of white knitted baby booties on the table.

Lena stared at the booties, confused. Then she gasped and practically jumped out of her chair. "Oh my God! Really?"

Ella nodded, beaming. "In about five months the twins are going to have a little brother or sister."

Lena picked up the booties and pressed them to her heart. "I'm still in shock that Enzo is here, and now you're telling me you're having another baby? I don't even know what to say except I'm happy as a . . . a . . ." She called across the table to Bonnie. "What do you say when you're really happy?"

"Happy as a possum eating a sweet tater!" Bonnie said.

"Happy as a hog in a wallow!" Teensy called out.

"Happy as a dog with two tails!" Judd said.

"Yes!" Lena said, "I'm all of those!"

Everyone laughed.

Lena turned to Ella again and said in a low voice, "Who else knows?"

"Well, everyone does now," Ella said, smiling and looking around the table.

Only then did Lena realize that they'd all noticed the booties and were staring at her, amused. "I'm going to be a gramma again!" she shouted.

"Congratulations!" everyone yelled, then got up to hug Ella and Charlie.

With her heart on the verge of bursting, Lena gazed at the beloved people around her, at Ella and Charlie and the twins, at Enzo and his family, at Bonnie and Miles, at Teensy and Judd and all the members of their close-knit clan. After so many years thinking she'd never see her younger brother again, he was sitting right next to her, a grown man with perfect children of his own. Even more unbelievably, after so much time thinking she'd never hold another baby in her arms, the privilege and joy of loving so many felt like a miracle. Now there would be a new one to love. And no matter what some people believed about their worth, or how hard they tried to stop them from living a normal life, the love and legacy of her family would continue on.

Author's Note

The American eugenics campaign—a racist pseudoscience determined to wipe out all human beings deemed "unfit" and preserve only those who conformed to a Nordic stereotype—is a truly shocking, tangled web that I could only touch upon in this novel. I still wonder what made me think I had the chops to tackle it, but if nothing else, I hope this story will encourage others to do more research on the subject.

I first began learning about eugenics while writing my debut novel, *The Plum Tree*, when I discovered that the United States was the first country in the world to undertake forced sterilization programs, and that the Nazi party in Germany took many of its policies, procedures, and theories from American eugenicists. (For more information, check out the discussion questions following this Author's Note.) I also learned that the U.S. was the leader in the eugenics movement and, after WWI, held international conventions to spread the word to other countries. In the mid-1920s, many foreign eugenicists traveled to America for training and to attend meetings and conferences.

While researching two of my other novels, *What She Left Behind* and *The Lost Girls of Willowbrook*, I continued to find connections to eugenics due to the fact that those stories are about asylums and institutions built to isolate, and in many cases sterilize, anyone considered a burden to society or a threat to the American gene pool. And while researching *The Lies They Told*, I was surprised to discover that eugenics theories played numerous and significant roles in the history and culture of the United States, including stricter immigration laws, marriage laws, anti-miscegenation laws, and segregation.

I was also astonished to learn that one commonly suggested method of getting rid of "inferior" populations in America was euthanasia using "lethal chambers" or public, locally-operated gas chambers. Some eugenicists did not see euthanasia as a "merciful killing" of those in pain, but rather a "painless killing" of people deemed unworthy of life. However, many in the eugenics movement did not believe Americans were ready to implement a large-scale euthanasia program, so some doctors found clever ways of subtly implementing euthanasia in various medical institutions. For example, a mental asylum in Lincoln, Illinois, fed its incoming patients milk infected with tuberculosis, reasoning that genetically fit individuals would be resistant; this practice resulted in 30–40% annual death rates. Other doctors practiced eugenicide through various forms of lethal neglect.

And while this book primarily tells the story of how one young woman's dream of a better life in America is shattered by eugenics, I included the inspection process at Ellis Island and the displacement of the Blue Ridge Mountain people because those endeavors were two of many instances when eugenics was used against both immigrants and American citizens. In the case of the Blue Ridge people, eugenics theories were used in part to take away their land and, in some cases, their children and the ability to continue their families by reproducing. Once efforts to form the national park were underway, in the government's effort to evict them from their land, the Blue Ridge Mountain people were labeled lazy, illiterate, incestuous, ignorant, undernourished, feebleminded, promiscuous, ill-tempered, and unattractive. And as hard as it may be to believe, law enforcement officials were allowed to seize children from their homes and take them to institutions, like the Western State Lunatic Asylum and the Virginia State Colony for Epileptics and Feebleminded in Virginia. In these institutions, teenagers and elementary-school-aged boys and girls were told they were undergoing an appendectomy or other unspecified procedure before being given vasectomies and tubal ligations. As they got older, many wondered why they were unable to conceive children. Some never escaped those institutions. Others were redistributed as a eugenic effort at "raising the children in a more appropriate home of an elite family." Some were torn forever from illegitimate babies they bore as teenagers. It is important to note that similar raids happened all over the country to families who were considered socially inadequate, along with those at mental institutions and orphanages.

Carrie Buck, who is mentioned in *The Lies They Told*, was the plaintiff in the Supreme Court case *Buck v. Bell*. Carrie was raped and impregnated by her foster parents' nephew, after which she was ordered—by those same foster parents—to undergo compulsory sterilization, for allegedly being feebleminded. The surgery, carried out while Carrie was an inmate of the Virginia State Colony, took place under the authority of the Sterilization Act of 1924, part of the Commonwealth of Virginia's eugenics program. I mention this because it's important to remember her story, and because I changed her mother's name from Emma to Ethel in this novel (to avoid any confusion with the name Ella).

It's also important to note that when Lena is released from the Colony, it's very unlikely that she would have been allowed to return to Wolfe Hollow; female victims of Virginia's eugenics movement were usually handed over to prominent families as cheap labor. (This was very likely the practice in other states as well.) Sterilized women were especially desired as workers, because not only did they work for free, but they could not get pregnant and cause a scandal.

Author's Note

As always, while writing this book, I've taken some liberties with the timing of certain historical events for the purpose of plot. While working for the Resettlement Administration, photographer Arthur Rothstein went into the mountains a few years later than presented in this story. Likewise, George Pollock, who said, "I knew that without actually visiting these people in their homes one could never conceive of their poverty and wretchedness," paraded potential park supporters through the hollows in the early 1930s. Pollock also hired schoolteacher and social worker Miriam Sizer, encouraging her to join up with his Washington connections to perform the study of the mountain people, which was carefully timed to coincide with the debate over their removal.

While this is a dark time in history to look back on, thirty-one states in the U.S., as well as Washington, D.C., *still* have laws that allow forced sterilization for the disabled, the incarcerated, and immigrants. In 2020, forced sterilizations at a U.S. Immigration and Customs Enforcement (ICE) detention center in Ocilla, Georgia, attracted national attention.

During the writing of *The Lies They Told*, I relied on the following books: *War Against the Weak: Eugenics and America's Campaign to Create a Master Race* by Edwin Black; *Pure America: Eugenics and the Making of Modern Virginia* by Elizabeth Catte; *A Century of Eugenics in America* edited by Paul A. Lombardo; *Forgotten Ellis Island* by Lorie Conway; *Island of Hope, Island of Tears* by David M. Brownstone, Irene M. Franck, and Douglass L. Brownstone; *Shenandoah: A Story of Conservation and Betrayal* by Sue Eisenfeld; *The Undying Past of Shenandoah National Park* by Darwin Lambert; and *Memories of a Lewis Mountain Man* by John W. Stoneberger.

LEARN MORE:

https://www.historynewsnetwork.org/article/the-horrifying-american-roots-of-nazi-eugenics

https://www.nps.gov/articles/the-displaced.htm

https://www.npr.org/transcripts/695574984?fbclid=IwAR3jXwH4QoMJ7wcfPasew8pEbAzB-hJKuMQwkgHs9UjM4RCW9BbpolN_AmE

https://www.smithsonianmag.com/history/puzzle-given-ellis-island-immigrants-test-intelligence-180962779/

https://time.com/3779502/rothsteins-first-assignment/

https://www.youtube.com/watch?v=m7WWWWc2ey0

A READING GROUP GUIDE

THE LIES THEY TOLD

ABOUT THIS GUIDE

The suggested questions are included to enhance your group's reading of Ellen Marie Wiseman's *The Lies They Told.*

1. As early as the 1880s, "feebleminded" children in Pennsylvania were being sterilized. In 1907, Indiana was the first state with a compulsory sterilization law, which became the benchmark for the rest of the nation. Eventually, thirty-two states enacted similar laws, and in the 1930s and '40s, California became the country's most prolific eugenics practitioner. The victims of American eugenics were poor urban and rural dwellers from New England to California, immigrants from across Europe, Jews, Blacks, Mexicans, Native Americans, epileptics, alcoholics, petty criminals, the physically and mentally disabled, orphans, sexually active single young women, the infirm, and anyone else who didn't fit the blond-and-blue-eyed Nordic ideal the movement valued. What was your awareness of eugenics in America before reading *The Lies They Told*? Why do you think so many people today are unfamiliar with it?

2. Lena and her family sell everything they own for a chance at a better life in America, despite the knowledge that if they're deported, they will return home to nothing. They have no idea Mutti and Enzo will be sent back to Germany. Many poor immigrants experienced similar circumstances, and sometimes families were separated. Do you know the circumstances of your ancestors' immigration to America?

3. In 1910 the Carnegie Institution established the Eugenics Record Office, or ERO, a research laboratory at Cold Spring Harbor on Long Island that stockpiled millions of index cards on ordinary Americans and carefully plotted the removal of families, bloodlines, and whole peoples. The laboratory also produced propaganda posters and pamphlets, had their own newspaper, and studied

children from institutions for the feebleminded. The ERO's reports, articles, charts, and pedigrees were considered scientific facts in their day, but have since been discredited. The research on the American families, which was collected by field workers going door-to-door with questionnaires about temperament and characteristics, provided much of the information which facilitated the passing of several laws during the 1920s. Do you think people today would willingly fill out a questionnaire about their families handed out by a research laboratory? Why or why not?

4. After being put through numerous physical examinations and IQ tests on Ellis Island, Lena and her daughter are sent to Hoffman Island to be deloused, where they are instructed to strip naked and sprayed with chemicals. Had you ever heard of Hoffman Island and the process that was used there to get rid of lice? Did the description of the shower chambers remind you of anything?

5. When Lena's brother, Enzo, is labeled "feebleminded," one of the immigration inspectors threatens to send him to the Psychopathic Pavilion for the rest of his life. Were you aware that Ellis Island had a psychiatric ward, a maternity hospital, an isolation ward, and a contagious disease hospital? Were you aware that thousands of immigrants were detained and died on Ellis Island?

6. With support from the American Eugenics Society's Committee, the first Fitter Family Contest was held at the Kansas State Free Fair in 1920. The contest was founded by the pioneers of the Baby Health Examination movement, which sprang from a "Better Baby" contest at the 1911 Iowa State Fair and quickly spread

to forty states. To compete for the title of a "Fitter Family," a "healthy" family had to provide a condensed record of family traits and history before being administered a medical exam, syphilis test, and psychiatric evaluation. While waiting for their examination, contestants could learn about heredity in Mendel's Theatre or watch a display of flashing light bulbs that supposedly illustrated the alarming social cost of the high birth rate of the unfit. At the time, it was believed that certain behavioral qualities were passed down from parents to children. This led to the addition of several judging categories, including generosity, self-sacrificing, and quality of familial bonds. Additionally, there were negative features that were judged: selfishness, jealousy, suspiciousness, high temperedness, cruelty, feeblemindedness, alcoholism, and paralysis.

Each family member was given an overall letter grade of eugenic health, and the family with the highest grade average was awarded a silver trophy. All contestants with a B+ or better received bronze medals bearing the inscription, "Yea, I have a goodly heritage." As expected, the Fitter Families Contest mirrored the eugenics movement itself; winners were invariably white with western and northern European heritage. Had you ever heard of these contests? What about the Better Baby contests, which in some states were only open to white babies?

7. In 1928, Virginia passed the Public Park Condemnation Act, which took 200,000 acres from landowners and farmers and donated it to the federal government to establish the Shenandoah National Park. Soon afterward, strangers appeared in the mountains: surveyors, commissioners, social workers, and doctors, all talking about evictions, condemnation proceedings, proof of owner-

ship, and resettlement. Not only were five hundred families forced off the land, but most did not qualify for compensation. More than half, nearly three hundred of them, did not legally own the land they had farmed and lived on for generations. And with the Great Depression in full swing, real estate values had plummeted across the nation, making it a buyer's market in the Blue Ridge. Of the 197 owners who received money, only thirty-four were paid more than $2,000. Fertile pastures were valued at $10 to $25 an acre, mountain parcels at $1 to $5. Some left willingly, while others did everything they could to stay. Some wrote letters or threatened violence. Others waited until the last minute, departing only when the sheriff and a Civilian Conservation Corps crew came to put them out. Ultimately 2,800 people were forced from their homes. To discourage people from returning, every vacated homesite was destroyed by burning, bulldozing, or disassembling. All signs of schools, churches, stores, and mills were largely removed from the park, considered historically insignificant. Of 2,000 homesites marking nearly three centuries of habitation, only a single structure remains intact in Shenandoah National Park: Corbin Cabin in Nicholson Hollow.

Did you realize mountain families were displaced to form Shenandoah National Park? Do you know anyone who was affected by the formation of the park? How do you think it made them feel? How would you feel if someone took your home from you? Do you think it was right for the government to evict 2,800 people for the park? Do you think it could have been handled differently?